The fiery brilliance of the Zebra Hologram Heart which you see on the cover is created by "laser holography." This is the revolutionary process in which a powerful laser beam records light waves in diamond-like facets so tiny that 9,000,000 fit in a square inch. No print or photograph can match the vibrant colors and radiant glow of a hologram.

So look for the Zebra Hologram Heart whenever you buy a historical romance. It is a shimmering reflection of our guarantee that you'll find consistent quality between the covers!

SHE CAPTURED HIS SOUL . . .

"You haunt me, woman," Tshingee whispered.

"I do?" Deborah couldn't take her eyes off the handsome Indian. It was as if she were in a trance. She knew she should turn and run, but she couldn't. She was drawn to him like flint to steel. "But I can't be here with you," she breathed.

"That's all right," he answered. "Because I cannot be here with you."

Deborah knew he was going to kiss her, but instead of pulling back, she leaned into him. Shamelessly she raised her arms to rest her hands on his back. Her fingers spanned the breadth of his bare back as his lips touched hers ever so gently.

Tshingee was awed by the fire that danced between them. *This cannot be!* his inner self warned, and yet he was powerless to stop it.

Deborah's head spun. No man had ever kissed her like this before. No man had ever ignited a heat so deep within her. She would never be the same again . . .

EXHILARATING ROMANCE
From Zebra Books

GOLDEN PARADISE (2007, $3.95)
by Constance O'Banyon

Desperate for money, the beautiful and innocent Valentina Barrett finds work as a veiled dancer, "Jordanna," at San Francisco's notorious Crystal Palace. There she falls in love with handsome, wealthy Marquis Vincente—a man she knew she could never trust as Valentina — but who Jordanna can't resist making her lover and reveling in love's GOLDEN PARADISE.

SAVAGE SPLENDOR (1855, $3.95)
by Constance O'Banyon

By day Mara questioned her decision to remain in her husband's world. But by night, when Tajarez crushed her in his strong, muscular arms, taking her to the peaks of rapture, she knew she could never live without him.

TEXAS TRIUMPH (2009, $3.95)
by Victoria Thompson

Nothing is more important to the determined Rachel McKinsey than the Circle M — and if it meant marrying her foreman to scare off rustlers, she would do it. Yet the gorgeous rancher feels a secret thrill that the towering Cole Elliot is to be her man — and despite her plan that they be business partners, all she truly desires is a glorious consummation of their vows.

KIMBERLY'S KISS (2184, $3.95)
by Kathleen Drymon

As a girl, Kimberly Davonwoods had spent her days racing her horse, perfecting her fencing, and roaming London's byways disguised as a boy. Then at nineteen the raven-haired beauty was forced to marry a complete stranger. Though the hot-tempered adventuress vowed to escape her new husband, she never dreamed that he would use the sweet chains of ecstasy to keep her from ever wanting to leave his side!

FOREVER FANCY (2185, $3.95)
by Jean Haught

After she killed a man in self-defense, alluring Fancy Broussard had no choice but to flee Clarence, Missouri. She sneaked aboard a private railcar, plotting to distract its owner with her womanly charms. Then the dashing Rafe Taggart strode into his compartment . . . and the frightened girl was swept up in a whirlwind of passion that flared into an undeniable, unstoppable prelude to ecstasy!

Available wherever paperbacks are sold, or order direct from the Publisher. Send cover price plus 50¢ per copy for mailing and handling to Zebra Books, Dept. 2759, 475 Park Avenue South, New York, N.Y. 10016. Residents of New York, New Jersey and Pennsylvania must include sales tax. DO NOT SEND CASH.

PASSION'S SAVAGE MOON

Colleen Faulkner

ZEBRA BOOKS
KENSINGTON PUBLISHING CORP.

For our third son, Devon Forrest

"Wither thou goest, I will go; and where thou lodgest, I will lodge; thy people shall be my people . . ."

The Book of Ruth

Chapter One

Maryland Colony 1698

Deborah Montague leaned forward in the sidesaddle, pressing her left knee into the bay gelding's side as she laid her crop lightly on his neck. The huge steed gave a snort and broke stride, lowering his head as he picked up speed.

The smell of the saddle's soft leather mingled with sweaty horseflesh, filling Deborah's nostrils with the heady, familiar scent of a good ride. Riding at breakneck speed like this, balanced precariously on the saddle, made her feel exuberant . . . alive. Her own heart beat wildly beneath her breast, seeming to match that of her destrier's.

"Lady Deborah!" a male voice called from behind. "Deborah! Slow down! You'll break your sweet neck, you damnable fool!"

Deborah laughed, ducking a low-hanging branch. Her feathered cocked hat flew off her head and her dark, thick hair fell from its neat chignon to whip wildly in the breeze.

"Deborah! Slow down this minute!" Thomas Hogarth dodged branches wildly from astride his horse, trying to catch up.

Laughing so hard that she nearly tumbled from her horse, Deborah pulled up on the reins, slowing him to a walk. She leaned forward to pat the gelding's foamy neck. "Good boy, Joshua. Whoa . . . good boy."

"Have you lost your head?" Thomas rode up behind her, swinging down onto the ground. He helped her dismount. "Are you all right? Did he get away from you?"

Deborah wiped her damp brow with the sleeve of her scarlet waistcoat. "God's teeth, Tom, you sound like my brother's nursemaid!" She pulled off her matching dyed gloves and threw them over the saddle.

Thomas caught her around the waist. "Everyone else veered to the left back near the bent oak. Didn't you see them?" The distant sound of barking hounds and a tin horn carried on the breeze.

"Of course I saw them!" She fingered the ruffles of Thomas's stiff white stock. "But they ride so slow! My old grandmother could keep up at that pace!" She pushed out her lower lip in a seductive pout.

"Oh God, Deborah," he groaned, lowering his head to brush his lips gently against hers.

She sighed, knowing the routine well, and lifted her hands to rest them on his shoulders. Thomas's lips were warm and wet against hers; she allowed him to linger just a moment before she pulled away. "Thomas, please!"

He took a step back, extracting a lace handkerchief from inside his coat to wipe his mouth. "You can't expect me to just stand there with you looking so pretty."

"Thomas, you took advantage of me," she chastised, feigning injury. "What would my father say?"

He returned the handkerchief to it's place. "I suspect he'd say it was high time I asked for your hand."

Deborah's face hardened. "I told you I wasn't interested in marrying you."

"What, you prefer Charles MacCloud?" His blue eyes narrowed. "Or is it John Logan? Is that why you refused to attend Roger and Mary's betrothal supper with me last week?"

She sighed, taking her horses reins. "I like you well enough, I just don't want to marry you."

He followed in her footsteps, offering his hands to boost her into her saddle. "And what of this?" He spread his arms. "It isn't the first time it's happened. I'm not certain how much longer I can control myself. A man has needs, you know."

Deborah laughed, taking her reins from his hand. "Tom . . . I never said I didn't like kissing you." She urged her bay forward in a trot. "But I'd not bed you for all the silks in China!" she shouted over her shoulder as she disappeared around a bend in the path.

Still chuckling, Deborah followed the path back to the bent oak and turned to catch up with the rest of the hunt. Behind her she could hear the hoofbeats of Thomas's horse.

Heading in the direction of the sound of voices and barking hounds, Deborah entered a clearing. Just ahead she spotted the rest of the hunting party. The men had dismounted and were standing, pointing at a broken fence. The ladies, still astride, giggled among themselves as their horses trampled a small vegetable garden.

"What's happened here?" Deborah rode through the break in the fence. "Charles, what's going on?"

Charles MacCloud, a red-faced man with a mop of orange-colored hair, lifted a hand. "We came right through the fence." He laughed. "Nearly unseated John."

Deborah surveyed the garden and glanced over at the crude wooden cabin and barn that stood a hundred yards away. "Is anyone home? You've ruined the garden."

Charles shrugged, mounting his horse. "What difference? Belongs to some stinking half-breed."

Deborah watched as the other men mounted. "You're not going to do anything? That man's probably got a family to feed." She lifted the reins to keep her horse from nibbling at a row of half-uprooted turnips.

Thomas came riding up behind her. "Have they lost the fox? I told Father the hunting would never be any good in these bloody Colonies. The forest is too dense." He glanced at the disturbed garden with disinterest. "I can still hear the hounds. How far could the fox have gotten?"

Deborah slipped her hands into her gloves. "They broke the fence." She watched a cow wander into the garden and begin to munch a squash vine.

Thomas adjusted his cocked hat as he looked up at the sun. "That they did, but no matter. This is the land Father's in the process of acquiring. Mr. John Wolf won't be needing his fence much longer." He looked at the other men. "Shall we go, gentlemen? Ladies? Tea is promptly at three."

The group started off, passing the small cabin as

they reentered the woods. Deborah trailed behind. Three-quarters of a mile down the narrow wooded path, she swung around and headed back toward the cabin. In the commotion of catching up with the dogs, no one noticed her departure.

When Deborah entered the clearing near the cabin, she pulled up on her horse's reins, coming to a complete stop. Across the yard stood a man surveying the ruined garden, a red man . . .

Taking a deep breath, Deborah gave a toss of her head, pushing her dark hair off her shoulders. Tapping Joshua lightly with her heel, she moved her mount forward.

Tshingee stood in the center of his brother's garden, assessing the extensive damage. At the sound of an approaching rider, he looked up, then lowered his gaze.

"Afternoon . . ." Deborah stared at the Indian brave. She'd seen red men before, crossing the street in Annapolis, or standing back from her father's house at Host's Wealth, but she'd never seen one up close like this before. She was fascinated.

The man turned, glancing up at her, his mouth twisted in a scowl. He was the most glorious man she had ever laid eyes on. His skin was the color of red clay, his nearly nude body so finely sculptured that it was godlike. His nose was long and straight, his cheekbones high and slanted, his eyes as dark as the depths of hell. His sleek raven hair fell about his shoulders in a curtain of mystery.

"I said, good afternoon," Deborah repeated, her tongue darting out to moisten her dry lips.

"And I said nothing," replied the red man. Their gazes locked and for a moment Deborah felt as if the man had reached out and embraced her very soul.

Her rosy lips trembled. She couldn't take her eyes from the man, his broad, muscular chest . . . his long sinewy legs. Her eyes lingered on the leather breechcloth at his groin for just a instant. She looked up to see him laughing. Laughing at her!

Angrily, Deborah swung down out of the saddle. "I came back to apologize"—she opened her arms — "for this."

Tshingee dropped his hands to his narrow hips, looking away. The spark of magic that had just leaped between him and this white girl was undeniable. Tshingee ground his bare foot into the soft garden soil. "You did this?"

Deborah nearly smiled. His voice was beautiful, soft and flowing yet deeply masculine. His enunciation was impeccable, his words rising rhythmically on the late summer breeze like some ancient song. "Yes, well no, not me actually, but my friends." She faced the man. He was exactly her height; their gazes met again. "They should have been more careful."

Tshingee shrugged his broad, sunbaked shoulders. "What is the difference? A few stalks of corn, a basket or two of squash . . ." A bitterness rose in his voice. "A life or two lost to starvation in midwinter. What is a life to you if it's not your own?"

"I said I didn't do it," she repeated, her anger rising. She dropped the reins and lifted the heavy skirting of her petticoats to move closer.

"If you didn't feel responsible, you wouldn't have come back." Tshingee studied her oval face. Her eyes were a deep golden brown. Her hair was a rich sable, falling straight over her shoulders and down her back. But it was her mouth that intrigued him. Her lips were

12

full and rosy with a small brown mark above the left corner. It was the most sensuous mouth he had ever laid eyes on.

Deborah's eyes narrowed. What right did this man have to speak to her in this manner? What right did he have to blame her for the ills of the world? "I only came back because I was worried that you might have a family." She fumbled with the waistband of her skirt, withdrawing a small leather pouch.

Tshingee watched the white woman with interest. She had a backbone, this girl, to speak to him like this. Most of the aristocratic English women he had encountered were too frightened of him to speak.

"I don't know what the vegetables were worth, but here . . ." She offered her hand. Lying in her palm were several coins, the silver glimmering in the afternoon sun.

Tshingee struck Deborah's hand hard with his own, sending the coins flying into the dust.

Deborah looked up at him, her mouth hung open in surprise. "What's wrong with you? I want to pay for the damage caused to your garden. I don't want you to go hungry."

"You think your silly coins can replace my brother's toil?" Tshingee scoffed. "You think you can buy the love that went into harvesting those precious seeds, planting them, watering them, watching them grow?"

"It's your brother's garden? With the money he could buy vegetables." Deborah retrieved the coins.

"You're all alike, you know." He shook a bronze finger at her accusingly. "You come to our land, you drive us from our homes, you buy and sell our mother earth. Don't you see that this land can no more be bought than you or I can? It's a living, breathing, thing!"

At a loss as to how to remount without assistance, Deborah spotted a tree stump near the edge of the garden. Relieved, she tugged on Joshua's reins, leading him across the grass. "What are you talking about, you lunatic? All I wanted to do was pay for the damage. It isn't even your garden!" She lifted her red petticoats and climbed awkwardly onto the stump, trying to guide her horse close enough to mount him.

Tshingee laughed aloud, mocking her as he watched her try to maneuver herself and her cumbersome white woman's clothes.

Finally seated on the saddle, Deborah hurried out of the yard, the red man's laughter ringing in her ears as she galloped down the path.

Impatiently, Deborah yanked a silver-handled hairbrush through her tangled tresses. Dropping the brush on the bed, she went to her mirror. Taking a long scarlet ribbon from a box on the table, she tied her hair in a thick mane down her back. In the three days that had passed since she'd encountered the angry red man, she often found herself looking into her mirror. It was odd, but she kept wondering how she had appeared to him.

A knock came at the door and it swung open. Deborah's younger sister, nearly sixteen, stepped into the bedchamber. "If you don't hurry, Deborah, you're going to be late for supper again and you know how angry that makes the Earl."

Deborah glanced up at her sister's reflection in the

14

gilded oval mirror. "More likely than not, he'll be angry with me anyway. He always is . . . or at least when he has the time."

"That's not true, it's just that he has his mind on other things. You don't realize how much work there is to running this place, and now that he's been appointed a squire, his duties are tenfold."

"Excuses!" Deborah rubbed a spot on her bodice. There was an unmistakable stain of blueberry over her left breast. "You're always making excuses for him, all of you. I don't know why you do it. He could care less about us. You're lucky he knows your name, you simple goose."

Elizabeth lowered her head. "Deborah, you mustn't speak that way of our father."

Deborah turned. Poor Elizabeth was so plain with her sullen face and nondescript hair. "I thought you were going to wear the blue brocade I gave you." She shook her head. In that dark brown gown with beige trim her sister looked like an emaciated wren.

"I . . . I tried it on but Lady Celia said . . ."

"Lady Celia! Who gives a fat rat's ass what she thinks!"

"Deborah!" Elizabeth's hands flew up to cover her ears, her eyes round in horror. "You sound like a field hand! You know what the Earl said about your cursing. He'll have you whipped, he will!"

"No he won't." She shook her head. "It would take too much of his precious time. Time better spent with our little brother James."

"It's not Christian to be so jealous of him, Deborah. He's the Earl's only son."

Deborah dropped onto her four-poster bed and lifted her petticoats to slip on a pair of heeled shoes.

"Pity he's so useless. Celia's spoiled him so badly; he'll never be much of a man."

"He'll be the Earl of Manchester someday."

"And what? Inherit a few acres of tobacco and a house in Essex fallen in ruin. What if he doesn't want to plant tobacco?"

"What . . . what else would he do?"

Deborah dropped her skirts and stood up, ready to go. The blueberry stains on her bodice would have to stay; there wasn't time to redress. "I don't know, be a surgeon." She made a sweeping gesture. "A barrister . . . an Indian . . ."

Elizabeth covered her mouth, giggling. "An Indian? Now who's being simple?" She lifted her skirt gracefully. "You'd best hurry. Thomas . . . Thomas and the Viscount have already arrived."

Deborah couldn't help noticing her sister's faint blush. "Why do you give a fig about Tom?"

"I . . . I don't."

"Liar!" Deborah grinned, leaning until her face was only inches from her sister's. "Think he's handsome?"

Elizabeth shook her head, intimidated, mortally embarrassed. "Deborah, I would never. . . he—he's your . . ."

"My what?" She knitted her eyebrows.

The younger girl took a step back. "Your intended, of course."

"Says who?"

"There . . . there's been talk. I . . . saw him kiss you at the Christmas ball last winter at the Fetterman's. I thought you were in love with him," she finished breathlessly.

Deborah laughed, dropping her hands on her sis-

16

ter's quivering shoulders. "You're the second person this week who's thought I've got to marry over a stupid kiss!"

"I would never kiss someone I wasn't going to marry. It—it wouldn't be . . ."

"I know, Christian." Deborah opened her bed-chamber door. "So, are we going down to see this paragon, or not?"

Twenty minutes later, Deborah sat at one of the small square supper tables in the parlor, spreading a biscuit thick with blueberry jam. Across from her sat Elizabeth, her face nearly obscured by her linen napkin. On Deborah's right sat Thomas, on her left, her sister Martha's rotund husband, Lord Danforth.

Lord Danforth droned on about the evils of drink as Deborah licked the blade of her knife. Under the table, she rested her right hand on Thomas's knee. She was quite amused to find that Thomas was having a difficult time following Danforth's conversation. It was a game she often played to entertain herself at the supper table.

"Yes, yes, I quite agree, Lord Danforth," Thomas stumbled. He slid his hand beneath the table to rest it over Deborah's as she moved it higher to his thigh.

Elizabeth stared in confusion at her sister across the table, wondering what ailed Thomas. Accidentally dropping her napkin, she leaned to pick it up. When her head reappeared above the edge of the table, her face was crimson.

Deborah winked at her sister and Elizabeth tipped her glass, taking a swallow of her table wine. It was all just a diversion! Her sister was toying with poor

Thomas's emotions!

Directly behind Thomas, Deborah's father stood up, taking his glass with him. "Ladies and gentlemen . . ." He cleared his throat. "As I said before the meal, I have an announcement to make and that time has now come."

Deborah leaned across the table to whisper to her sister, but the girls' stepmother rapped her fan sharply on the table, catching their attention. Deborah sat back.

"Lord Hogarth and I have just sealed a fine arrangement." He lifted his glass to the tall, reed-thin Viscount across the table. "It gives me great pleasure to tell you, my children, my neighbors"— he looked to Thomas — "my friends, that a betrothal agreement has been signed. My fourth daughter, Lady Deborah, will marry the honorable Thomas Hogarth come Palm Sunday."

Everyone in the parlor stood in salutation toasting the happy couple. Deborah sat stunned. She couldn't marry Thomas! She glanced across the room at her eldest sister, Martha, struggling to get to her feet, heavy with child. *If I marry Thomas,* she thought in panic, *I'll end up just like Martha . . . miserable.* Martha had given birth to seven children in the last six years and it was killing her. She worked harder than any slave or free man on her husband's plantation by day and bore her lord's brutality and drunkenness by night.

Deborah pushed away from the table, her face ashen. He linen napkin fell to the floor. The candlelit room was stifling.

"What is it, dear? Are you all right?" Thomas reached for her hand, but she pulled away, getting up

18

from the table.

If I don't get some fresh air, she thought, *I'll be sick.* Running from the room, she raced through the hall and out onto the front step. A wall of cool night air hit her sharply in the face and she took a deep breath.

"Lady Deborah? Deborah?" Thomas called, coming through the door. "Where are you going? You can't just run out like that! Not in front of my father!"

She swung around, her face red with anger. "Why didn't you tell me the other day at the hunt?"

"I didn't know," he replied defensively.

"Hah!" she scoffed. "I detest liars!"

Thomas caught her by the wrist. "How dare you! It was just as your father said. An arrangement was made between your father and mine only last night. I knew it was to be you or Anne Greenbee but the girl always smells of bad mutton."

"Oh!" Deborah laughed, unamused. "So I won out over Anne because I smell better!" She jerked her wrist from his grasp.

"I've always been fond of you," he told her none-too-kindly.

"I told you I wouldn't marry you. I haven't changed my mind."

"It looks like you haven't been given a choice. Your father has agreed to acquire that parcel of land my father needs to build a second dock on the river. They're going to split it in half. One half is to be your dowry."

"What parcel?" She stared at Thomas. Moonlight filtered down from the heavens to cast shadows across his face. As always, his thinning hair was neater than her own. "You know . . . where we passed the other day."

"The red man's land? He sold it to my father?" An image of her Indian brave flashed through her head. It was funny how she'd come to think of him as *her* Indian.

"No." Thomas gave her a lopsided grin. "But he will . . ."

Chapter Two

Deborah stood in the shadows of an ancient leaning pine tree, her horse's reins clutched tightly in her gloved hand. Just through the clearing she could see the crude cabin with its door hanging ajar. An Indian man diligently swung an axe in the side yard; but he was not her Indian. This had to be the brother, the man who owned the garden her friends had trampled.

Though it had been more than a week since the incident, Deborah couldn't push it from her mind. It was not so much the garden and the uprooted vegetables she thought of, as it was the man. Instead of concentrating on figuring out a way to escape her impending marriage to Tom, she found herself thinking of the sharp-tongued red man and the argument they'd had. She'd told herself when she'd left Host's Wealth this afternoon that she was coming to attempt to make amends with the owner of the garden. But she knew she came to get another glimpse of *him*.

Inhaling the warm September air, Deborah stepped out of the shadows of the woods line and walked toward the man chopping wood. He looked much like her Indian, only he was shorter with a broader nose. His thick midnight hair was cut at shoulder's length with a battered leather hat perched on his head. Instead of the shocking loincloth her Indian had worn, the man was clothed in a pair of dark breeches and a threadbare white shirt.

The Indian brother looked up from his arduous task, squinted, then laid down his axe and came toward her. There was a hesitant but welcoming smile on his lips. "Good afternoon." He swept off his hat. "I am John Wolf. Are you lost?" His English was clear and plain, but lacked the rhythm of his brother's.

"Hullo." Deborah shaded her eyes with her hand. She wasn't even sure what she intended to say. "No, no, I'm not lost. I came because of the garden." She pointed in its direction. Some of the vegetables had been replanted, but most of the uprooted plants lay in the dirt, brown and wilted beyond saving.

John glanced at the ruined plot. "Much of my crop was lost." He looked up at her with dark, complacent eyes. "Our Lord has always provided for my family. Somehow he will replace the loss."

"That's why I came. To pay for the damages."

"You did this?"

Deborah blinked. "No, I didn't. Didn't he tell you?"

John smiled. "My brother? He said a red bird had flown through."

"A red bird?"

"You are the woman who was here wearing a coat of red?"

"Yes, yes, that was me. Then he told you I offered to pay for the damages and he refused."

"If you did not commit the sin, there is no need for absolution."

22

Deborah moved her reins from one hand to the other. "I'm not asking for absolution." She pulled a small bag from the waistband of her riding gown. "But will you accept my offering anyway?"

John looked up at the sun directly overhead. "It is warm for September. Will you come into my home and quench your thirst?" He motioned toward the cabin.

"Won't you just take the coin?" She eyed the cabin, wondering if her Indian might be inside.

"Come and we will speak of it. Let no man say a guest comes to my door and I do not offer comfort." He took the reins from her hand and led her horse to a tree where he attached the leather ties securely. "Please," he urged.

Curious, Deborah nodded. "Come to think of it, I am thirsty."

John led the way to the cabin. "I have only water to offer, but it is cold and good." He smiled, showing a set of crooked white teeth. "My well is deep."

Deborah followed him into the dimly lit one-room cabin. To her surprise she saw a white woman with a heavy mane of brilliant red hair standing in the corner. The woman spun around to face them.

"Bridget, bring a drink to share with our guest." John turned to Deborah. "I'm sorry, but I do not know your name.

"Lady . . ." she hesitated. "I'm Deborah Montague of Host's Wealth."

A crease of concern etched John's forehead. "Your father is Lord Manchester?"

She nodded. "He is."

Bridget wiped her hands on her apron. Her bright red cheeks were dewy with perspiration. "John, I've nothing but water. She glanced at Deborah in obvious embarrassment. "Don't you think the lady—"

"Water will be fine, wife," John interrupted softly. "You can send Mary for it if you wish. Mary . . ."

To Deborah's astonishment a little girl appeared from behind Bridget's worn but clean skirts. "Yes, Papa?" she called softly. The child's skin was a deep copper-brown like her father's but down her back hung a thick braid of red hair.

"Bring up a bucket of water." He patted the child on the head as she slipped by. "Hurry, *daanus.*"

Bridget watched her husband offer Deborah a hand-hewn chair at their tiny table in the center of the room.

"Haven't I seen you before?" Deborah asked the young woman hiding in the shadows.

The woman shook her head. "Must be someone else you've mistaken me for."

"No? Didn't you once work at the Friendship plantation down the river?"

John sat across the table from Deborah. "Yes, that was my Bridget. She was once indentured there but now she is free."

Deborah surveyed the cramped cabin with interest. Though the room was dim, it was obviously well kept with swept floors and sweet-smelling herbs sprinkled across the wood floor. Bark baskets, animal hides, and strings of dried vegetables hung from the ceiling and lined the walls. It wasn't what she'd expected at all. "Could we discuss the payment now, Mr. Wolf?"

"Just John . . ."

"John, then."

Little Mary came in the door carrying a bark bucket. Water sloshed over the sides, spilling onto her knee-length woolen gown. "Here 'tis, Papa." She set the bucket at his feet, staring at Deborah, her eyes round with curiosity.

Deborah smiled. "Your name is Mary?"

She nodded.

"What a pretty name," Deborah went on. "I have a sister named Mary who lives across the Chesapeake."

John got up and returned to the table with two dented pewter tankards. He dipped one into the water bucket and offered it graciously to Deborah before filling his own.

Deborah sipped the icy water from the cup, realizing how thirsty she'd been. Mary continued to watch her father's guest, her dark eyes fastened on a silver broach pinned to Deborah's lace stock.

Deborah set down her tankard. "Do you like it, Mary?" She fingered the shiny metal.

The little girl nodded.

"Then you may have it." Deborah removed the oval pin at her neck and placed in Mary's tiny bronze-colored hand.

Mary looked to her father, and when he nodded his approval, her lips turned into a heavenly smile. "Thank you."

"You're welcome." Deborah thought Mary was the most beautiful child she'd ever seen.

John leaned to whisper in his daughter's ear and the child nodded, running to a platform bed along the wall. A moment later she returned with a doll cradled in her arm. Without a word, she laid it in Deborah's lap.

Deborah lifted the doll high in the air, smiling. "What a pretty doll," she marveled. The doll was shaped of a soft cloth with hair made from black wool. It was dressed in a soft animal hide tunic with an intricate pattern of quilling and beadwork across the front. Smoothing the doll's braided hair, Deborah held it out to return it.

Mary's smile faded. She shook her head. "A gift for a gift," she said softly. She spoke just like Deborah's Indian with the same singsong melody in her voice.

Deborah glanced at John in confusion.

"You must accept it," he told her. "To not accept would . . . would cast dishonor across your face and hers. My daughter is right, a gift for a gift."

Touched, Deborah lowered the doll to her lap. It had to be the child's greatest possession, and yet she had offered it gladly. It was the sincerest gift Deborah had ever been given. "Thank you, Mary," she offered.

The child beamed.

"Has she a name?"

"Olekee."

"O-le-kee," Deborah repeated. "What does it mean?"

"Olekee Suuklan, Yesterday's Rain in the tongue of my mother's people," John answered.

"Well, I will treasure Olekee always, Mary." Deborah turned to John. "I have to go now, but I want you to accept this"—She slid the pouch of coins across the table—"as my gift."

John hesitated.

"You said the Lord always provides; well, he's providing. Take it."

"I'm not a man in need of charity."

She frowned. "It's not charity. My friends ruined your crop and I'm repaying you. Someone has to be responsible for their actions even if they aren't."

John nodded thoughtfully. "This is true. A man must be responsible for his friends."

She smiled.

John laid his hand on the soft leather bag. "Thank you, Deborah."

Footsteps coming in the door made Deborah turn. She was so startled to see her Indian that she gave a small gasp. Today he wore a pair of buckskin breeches, but his chest was still bare. On his feet he wore a pair of knee-high moccasins. He carried a string of trout in his hand.

"Brother . . ." John rose. "You've met Deborah."

"What's she doing here?" he demanded crossly.

"Have better manners," John chastised. "In my home no one is unwelcome. The Lord our Jesus turned away no one."

Tshingee handed his string of fish to Bridget and she made a hasty exit from the cabin. Mary trailed behind her mother, engrossed in studying her shiny new gift.

"She shouldn't be here." Tshingee's face was stony with rage. "She destroyed your property."

"She didn't do it."

Tshingee turned his dark gaze on Deborah, who rose out of her chair beneath his scrutiny. "Why did you come? I told you we didn't want your coin," he told her hotly.

"It wasn't *your* loss," Deborah answered with equal intensity.

"And what would you know of losses, my little red bird?" The whipcord muscles of Tshingee's shoulders tensed.

"Tshingee!" John raised his voice. "This is my

home. I will not have my guests spoken to in this manner."

"It's all right." Deborah lifted her hand. "I'm going."

"No. Stay," John urged. "Share our meal. There's fresh trout and corn cakes."

"Thank you, but I must get home. I appreciate your kindness and your welcoming me into your home." Her smile slipped from her face as she turned to stare at his brother. "But you!" she accused. "I've never met anyone any ruder." Picking up momentum she stepped forward, poking his bare chest with a finger. "Where were you when your mother was teaching your brother manners, hm?"

Startled, Tshingee stared at the woman. How dare she speak to him in such a tone! But the faster she spoke, the more amused he became.

"What have I done to you, tell me that. I have apologized for what I had nothing to do with. I brought money to buy more food for the winter for your brother's family . . ." Deborah paused, her dark eyes widened indignantly. "What, pray tell, is so damned funny?"

John stood stock-still, watching the exchange between his brother and the woman he called his "Red Bird." It was obvious Tshingee was attracted to the sharp-tongued white girl. It seemed the Wildcat of the Wolf Clan had met his match.

Tshingee made no response but to broaden his grin.

Miffed, Deborah walked past him and out into the sunshine. Tshingee followed a footstep behind. "My brother accepted your coin?"

"He's got more sense than you have," she answered

over her shoulder. She untied the reins of her horse and moved to mount. "Well?"

Tshingee arched his left eyebrow. "Well?" he mocked her.

"Are you going to give me a hand or not?"

He chuckled, lifting a hand to smooth her steed's mane. "You want my hand?"

Deborah was certain he was taunting her. He knew *exactly* what she meant. "Yes, to help me into my saddle," she snapped.

Tshingee studied the leather sidesaddle, his mouth twisting in concentration. "I always wondered how one got into one of those things."

She lifted her dark eyelashes. Her cheeks were bright red, her lips pursed. Tshingee had never met a more attractive woman . . . nor one as irritating.

"A gentleman aids a lady into the saddle," she told him.

Tshingee took a step back, crossing his arms over his bare chest. "If you cannot get onto the horse on your own, you should not ride. Mary did not ride until she was old enough to mount herself."

In a huff of exasperation, Deborah brushed passed Tshingee, leading her horse. Climbing up on the stump she'd used before, she struggled to get up on the saddle. The hem of her gown caught on the horn and she nearly fell to the ground.

Deborah glanced over to see Tshingee standing in exactly the same place. He was still chuckling, his bronze face spread in a wide grin.

"Blasted skirts," she muttered, lifting them above her knees. Grasping the leather horn, she swung unceremoniously into the saddle, righting herself before she fell over the other side. Catching her balance, she arranged her skirts presentably and lifted her reins to go. "You see, I'm perfectly able to mount myself," she told Tshingee.

"It would be much easier if you rode astride."

Deborah raised her chin aloofly, straightening her befeathered cocked hat. "Ladies do not ride astride, sir."

He smiled lazily. "You would be surprised at the things a lady such as yourself might do . . . given a chance."

The tension in the air was so sharp that Deborah could taste it on the tip of her tongue. A pleasant shiver trickled down her spine; she was entranced. It was obvious this man was attracted to her. But what was shocking to her was that the feeling was mutual.

"Good day to you, sir," she said, tearing her gaze from his.

"Tell me your name again, my Red Bird," he urged gently. His voice carried on the wind, bathing her in a strange warmth.

"Deborah," she answered.

He nodded, then turned and walked away.

"You wanted me, sir?" Deborah stood in the doorway of her father's paneled office. It was a dark, ominous room with heavy, faded drapes pulled across the windows. Deborah had always hated this room — it was a place where decisions were made and deals were struck. No doubt the Earl had bargained for her betrothal in this very room.

"Yes, Deborah. Come in and sit down," her father answered from behind his desk. The Earl of Manchester was a rotund man with a red face and sagging jowls.

Deborah eyed her half-brother, James, standing near the fireplace. He had a smug grin on his face. He was barely fourteen, without a hair on his chin, yet in their household he was given all of the rights of a full grown man. *Silly child,* Deborah thought. *Poor, silly child.*

Closing the door gently behind her, she leaned against it. "What do you wish to speak to me about?"

The Earl waved a chubby hand. "No. Sit down. Lady Celia will be with us in a moment."

Deborah seated herself in a stiff, high-backed chair. Catching James's attention, she lifted her eyebrows questioningly. It was obvious he knew why she'd been summoned. More than likely, he had something to do with it. But the young blond-haired boy responded only with a smirk, moving to stand behind his father.

The office door swung open and Lady Manchester hurried in with a flurry of silk skirts and rustling undergarments. "My apologies, sir." She closed the door behind her. "The entire kitchen was in an uproar. I fear supper will be late."

The Earl indicated a seat. "Please sit, my lady."

Celia glanced disapprovingly at her stepdaughter as she passed her, taking the chair nearest the Earl's desk.

Lord Manchester cleared his throat. "I've two matters to take up with you, daughter."

"Oh?" Deborah folded her hands neatly in her lap, hoping her stepmother wouldn't notice the tear along the bottom of her white stomacher. She'd ripped it rescuing her little half-sister Anne's kitten from a tree

31

in the orchard.

"James tells me that you told him you'll not be marrying Thomas Hogarth."

Deborah glared at James. His pinched little face was still screwed up in a smug grin. *You're as ugly as your mother,* she thought to herself. Her eyes met her father's.

"Well, Deborah. Did you or did you not tell James that you have no intentions of marrying your betrothed?"

"You didn't ask me if I wanted to marry him."

"That was not my question."

"Deborah," Lady Celia interrupted with a squeak. "Answer your father's question. He has no time for your mummery."

Deborah stared at the portrait of her grandfather Montague that hung over the cold fireplace. "Yes. I told James I wasn't marrying him."

"Why?" her father demanded.

She glanced at him. "Because I'm not. I don't love him."

Celia gave another squeak and James giggled.

"I fail to see what has that to do with anything." The Earl pushed up from behind his desk. His burgundy waistcoat was unbuttoned at his middle to reveal a bulging stomach.

Moisture formed in the corners of Deborah's dark eyes. She looked away, refusing to allow them to see her weakness. "I'm not a piece of livestock to be auctioned off."

"A young lady doesn't choose whom she's to marry!" Celia declared. "Only a father knows what is best for his daughters."

Deborah blinked away her tears. Her father could

32

care less about her and she knew it. They all knew it. She was a female and, therefore, unimportant. At her age, she was becoming a burden.

The Earl was silent for a moment and then he spoke again. "I want to hear nothing else of this, do you understand me? You will marry Thomas Hogarth come spring. The papers have already been signed. Is that clear?"

Deborah nodded, her determination growing stronger. She wouldn't marry him. That was final. But for right now all she wanted to do was escape from this cloying room. "May I be excused?" She rose up in her chair.

"No. Sit down. I told you, there were two things." Lord Manchester folded his arms over his protruding stomach. "James says you've been across the north woods. He says you spoke with the half-breed that lives on that plot of land I'm acquiring."

Deborah looked up at James. "An enemy spy, are you?"

Celia glared at Deborah. "Don't speak to your brother in that manner. It's not becoming of you."

Her father poured himself a draught of sherry. "Did you or did you not speak with John Wolf?"

"On the hunt last week we went through his garden, ruined it all. I went to apologize." She didn't tell him about the coins she took from his box beneath the loose panel near the hearth. "You always said you wanted James to be responsible for what he did."

"Young ladies do not traipse about the woods unescorted at your age." Celia leaned forward in her chair. "You know the dangers. Your virtue could be at stake."

Deborah laughed. "It seems my virtue has already

been sold."

"Deborah! Apologize to your mother!"

"I'm sorry, Lady Celia. That was uncalled for," Deborah responded by rote.

"I do not wish to hear about you being near that man or his family again," he ordered. "Is that understood?"

"What if he doesn't want to sell you his land? He has a wife, a child," Deborah stood up. "He has as much right to this land as we do."

"Lord Hogarth is in need of that water access and so are we. You know the price of tobacco these days, girl. With the price she's bringing in England, we can't afford not to put up that new prize house."

"You're talking about expanding your business, I'm talking about the man's livelihood!"

"He's a half-breed," James scoffed, repeating what he'd heard his father say only yesterday.

"And what has that to do with anything?" Deborah demanded, enraged.

James sauntered forward. "This is men's business. You can't be expected to understand."

"You little worm!" Deborah slammed her fist into her brother's chest, nearly knocking him over backward.

"Deborah!" Lord Manchester bellowed. "How dare you!"

Celia leaped to her son's rescue. "I told you she was getting out of hand! It high time she was married and out of this house! She's nothing but a disruption!"

The Earl pushed aside his wife in an effort to get to Deborah. "You ever lay a hand on my son again and I'll take a switch to your back, young lady!"

Deborah's lower lip quivered, but she held her ground.

"You are dismissed!" her father shouted. "Go to your chamber! You will have supper in your room and see me in the morning! There'll be no riding for you for a week."

Deborah left the study, her head lowered, but the moment she was in the hall, she broke into a grin. The punishment would be well worth it. She'd been wanting to smack that whining little brat for ages . . .

Chapter Three

Deborah rode her horse at an easy trot beside Thomas's, saying nothing. James trailed behind, complaining of the heat.

It had been a week since she'd hit her brother and today was the first day the Earl had allowed her to leave the confines of the house. Every day she'd been assigned tasks by her stepmother to complete. First she had done an inventory of the kitchen larder, then the linen closets. When every morsel of food and every bed sheet had been accounted for, she had been set to work mending servants' clothing. It was a wonder she hadn't died of boredom.

When her father had finally released her, it was only to ride with Thomas, with James as an escort. Deborah turned her head to see her brother well behind them.

"Keep up James or you'll be lost." She chuckled as he hurried to catch up. He'd been born and raised on this land, he'd been riding since he was four, and he still got lost on the five-thousand-acre property.

Thomas glanced over at Deborah. Her hair was piled high beneath her silver fringed hat. Her cheeks were rosy from the sun. She was such a picture of loveliness in her azure camlet coat and lace petticoats that it made his chest swell with pride. She was a good choice for a wife. She'd bear him a dozen sons and bring a certain grace to his home, Deliverance. He just wished she were more pleased about the match.

Tom cleared his throat. "Did you hear Mary Ross is with child?" he asked, making conversation. "They say old Charlie MacCloud will have to wed her."

Deborah glanced at Thomas. He thought it was always necessary to be talking. He couldn't just ride along, enjoying the scent of the musty woodland plants and the breeze off the Chesapeake. Silence made him uncomfortable. "Every six months someone is saying Mary Ross is with child. If half the rumors were true, she'd have a brood by now!"

"Well, you know what they say. She's slept with half the eligible men in the county . . . and a good third of the ineligible!"

Deborah looked at him, smiling. "I understand they say the same of Deborah Montague."

Thomas's face turned crimson.

"Of course, you would know best of all the lack of validity in that rumor, wouldn't you?"

"You shouldn't speak like that, Deborah." He brushed a fleck of dust from his breeches. "I'm to be your husband. A man doesn't wish to know of rumors of his bride-to-be."

"That's just it, Tom. They're rumors. We've nothing better to do with ourselves but fabricate stories about one another."

"Well, I'll grant you you'll be busy come summertime." He laid his hand casually on her knee as their horses continued to walk side by side. "You'll be my wife by then."

Deborah sighed, pushing his hand away. She wasn't in the mood for games today. "Tom, I think you're making a mistake. I told you, I don't want to marry you." She ducked as their mounts passed beneath a low-hanging branch along the trail.

"Nonsense. You're just nervous," he soothed. "Every young woman is. It's to be expected."

She turned on him. "Don't use that tone with me, Thomas Hogarth! Not ever! I'm no simpleton! I know what I want and what I don't!"

"You have to marry. So why not me?"

Her eyes met his. He was a handsome-enough man, despite his receding hairline and cleft chin. "I don't love you."

"The love will come," he answered.

"You sound like your father . . . or mine."

"That's because everyone is being sensible about this but you, Deborah." He gazed at her pretty face. "Don't make this difficult. In the end you know you'll go to the altar and marry me as your father's told you. So why not resign yourself to the fact and make the best of it?"

She pulled up on her reins, bringing her horse to an abrupt halt. "Make the best of it! Listen to you! If I marry you, I'll be trapped for the rest of my life."

"And you think marriage isn't a trap for a man as well?"

She laid her leather crop across her knee, pulling off her gloves. "No, not really. I mean, what will change in your life after you marry me? You'll live in the same house, you'll still play cards with your friends on Saturday evenings, your mother will still have roasted chicken for you on Sundays, and your father will still run the plantation while you ride about gossiping with neighbors! The only thing that will be different is that you'll have me to warm your bed at night!"

"Deborah!"

"Now wait a minute. Think of it." She shook her gloves at him. "What's going to happen to me? I have to move into your home with your family. I have to take over part of your mother's work, I have to dress like a matron, I will no longer have the freedom to ride as I wish and come next spring I'll be burdened with the responsibility of a child!"

"It long past time you married," he answered.

James wandered over to them, listening with interest.

"So my life is over at twenty three years old?" Deborah demanded.

"No. You're life is not over," Thomas responded, his ire rising. "But you'll begin to be useful, as a woman should be!"

"Useful!" she spat.

James grinned, enjoying the argument.

"Yes, useful. What do you do now, tell me that? Woman's purpose on earth is to serve man."

Deborah sank her heels into her horse's flanks and pulled forward.

"Deborah, come back here," Thomas ordered. "You can't just keep running away from me! I'm going to marry you!"

She ignored his calls, as well as James's, as she veered right, picking up speed.

"God damn it!" she heard Thomas shout. "Come back here!"

Flattening her body over the gelding's neck, Deborah laid her crop gently on his side. "Come on,

Joshua," she urged. The horse dug his hooves into the soft humus of the earth, stretching to run faster. Leaping a small ditch, the horse and rider sped down an unfamiliar woods path, bent on escape.

Deborah rode and rode, the echo of her horse's hooves pounding in her ears. She wondered what would happen if she just kept riding. She'd been born and raised here on the banks of the Migianac River, but she yearned to see more. She'd often wondered what lay west of the Colonies. Her father told her nothing . . . but how could there be nothing?

Tiring, Deborah slowed the gelding to a trot and then to a walk. She was hot and perspiring as she pulled off her cocked hat and hung it on her saddle horn by the ribbon. A cool breeze drifted through the trees, refreshing her flushed face. Up ahead a tiny stream bubbled, pouring over a bed of bright-colored gravel.

"Thirsty, boy?" Deborah crooned. "How about a drink?" The bay gelding whinnied his approval and she urged him forward, lowering the reins so that he might drink.

Mesmerized, Tshingee sat perfectly still, perched in the oak tree above the tiny stream. He listened as Deborah spoke softly to her horse. Her voice carried on the wind until it was but a breathless caress to his ears. Her dark hair fell from its pins in a halo of shimmering color, framing her oval face. Could this woman with a voice as gentle as the wind of the gods be the same woman who had shouted at him and spit fire only a week before?

Tshingee smiled. He didn't know what it was about this white woman that intrigued him so. He tried to push her from his mind, to escape from her image that lurked behind his eyelids, but he couldn't. He wanted her and that want left an ache deep within him. But he also knew she could never be his, and that he must resign himself to that fact.

Hearing a twig snap, Deborah looked up. A gasp escaped her lips as she spotted Tshingee high in a tree above her. "What the hell do you think you're doing?" she blurted.

Feeling foolish at being caught, Tshingee dropped down two branches and swung gracefully to the ground. He was dressed in a pair of tight breeches with his long raven hair pulled in a single braid down his back. Once again his feet and chest were bare. "I'm sorry. I didn't mean to frighten you."

"You didn't scare me." She looked high into the trees. "What were you doing up there?"

A smile played on his lips. "Watching you, I think."

"Watching me?" His smile was contagious. "Whatever for?"

He took her hand and brushed his lips against it. He didn't know what possessed him to do it.

Deborah blinked in surprise. His mouth was hot and damp against the back of her hand. His touch was exquisite. She didn't know what to say. All she knew was that she didn't want to withdraw her hand from his grasp.

"You haunt me, woman," Tshingee whispered.

"I do?" She couldn't take her eyes from his.

"Come down where I can see you." He settled his hands on her waist and her limbs obeyed of their own volition.

Deborah's riding boots touched the ground softly. "I can't be here with you," she breathed. It was as if

41

she were in a trance. She knew she should turn and run, but she couldn't. She was drawn to him like flint to steel.

"That's all right," he answered. "Because I cannot be with you."

Deborah knew that her Indian was going to kiss her, but instead of pulling back, she leaned into him. Shamelessly she raised her arms to rest her hands on his back. Her fingers spanned the breadth of his bare back as his lips touched hers ever so gently.

Tshingee brushed his lips against Deborah's soft, silky mouth, in awe of the fire that danced between them. *This cannot be!* his inner self warned, and yet he was powerless to stop it. He delved his tongue deep into the recesses of her mouth, exploring the moist lining within.

Deborah's head spun. No man had ever kissed her like this before. No man had ever ignited a heat so deep within her. Breathless, she pulled back. Her eyes met his. Tshingee's eyes were dark pools of ebony, reflecting a strange light. "I have to go," she whispered.

Tshingee stroked her back. "So soon, Red Bird? Must you fly so soon? I would never hurt you."

"I . . . I know," she stumbled. "But my brother, my fiancé. They can't find you here with me."

Tshingee caught a long lock of her dark hair and twisted it in his fingers. The girl was right. He should run, and run far from here. He should never come back. This woman was nothing but trouble and he knew it. So why didn't he go? It was her dark eyes, her quivering mouth. She told him to go, but she beckoned him to stay.

"Oh, Red Bird. A different time, a different place,

and I would carry you away with me."

Deborah wondered if she was dreaming. Could this redman really be holding her? Could she truly be staring up at him with such abandon in her eyes? She took a shaky step backward. "Please . . ."

"Tshingee," he offered.

"Tshingee."

"Deborah!" Thomas's voice called from the trees. "Deborah, by God, where are you?"

"Go!" Deborah murmured urgently.

"Tell me you'll meet me again."

"I can't. Please go before they find you here."

Tshingee shook his head, smiling. Both could hear Thomas growing closer. James's voice had been added to the din. "I won't go unless you tell me you'll come again." He lifted a bronze palm. "I swear to you I won't hurt you."

Deborah caught her horse's reins. "You know I can't come to you. Now go! Hurry!"

Tshingee stood his ground, his arms crossed over his bare chest.

An instant later Thomas came crashing through the trees on foot. "Deborah!"

"Tom." She turned to him. Her heart beat rapidly beneath her breast as she took a step toward him. She wished desperately that she could hide Tshingee from her betrothed's view.

"Deborah, are you all right?" He took her by the arm. "What is this man doing here? Has he hurt you?"

"No. Certainly not!" She looked at Tshingee. He still stood in the same place, her legs spread slightly in an imposing stance. He was shorter than Tom, but his shoulders were so broad, his biceps so well defined, that he seemed a monstrous man in comparison to her gangly fiancé.

Thomas stepped in front of Deborah, coming between the red man and her. "What are you doing here?" he demanded in his manliest voice.

Deborah laid her hand on Tom's shoulder. "Tom, please . . ."

"Just step back, Lady Deborah, and I'll take care of this."

"Tom, there's nothing to take care of."

"I asked you a question, half-breed," Thomas demanded.

Silence stretched in the peaceful forest for a full minute before Tshingee replied. "I was speaking with the lady," he answered with an air of sarcasm.

"Tom! Tom, where are you?" called James from the dense foliage beyond the stream. "Tom, I can't find you!" Twigs snapped and branches swayed in the distance.

"Here I am, James. I've found her!" answered Thomas.

James entered the clearing leading his mount and Thomas's. "You shouldn't have left me behind like that. My father doesn't want me left alone," he whined.

Thomas nodded in Tshingee's direction. "Do you know this man? I found him here with Deborah."

James dropped the horses' reins and sauntered forward. "That's John Wolf's brother, of course." He mopped his brow with a handkerchief from his coat. "Both are half-breeds. One fancies himself a white man, but this one" — he waved the bit of lace — "is all redskin."

"Let's go, James," Deborah insisted. "I wasn't sup-

44

posed to be out long."

James ignored his sister, coming closer to Tshingee. The Lenni Lenape brave eyed the boy calmly. "I understand your brother is being difficult," James said.

Tshingee lifted a dark eyebrow. "Oh?"

"My father needs that land to build a new dock and a prize house. Mr. Hogarth, here"—he nodded toward Thomas—"needs it as well."

"The land belongs to my brother. He even has one of your foolish bits of paper saying he owns the land." Tshingee watched Deborah out of the corner of his eye. *By the gods, but she's beautiful,* he thought.

"There's other land," James told the red man haughtily."

"Yes, there is." Tshingee took a step forward, and James a step back. "So I think it would be better for you to find another piece of land for your docks and tobacco houses."

James dropped his hands to his hips. "Are you threatening me, sir?"

Tshingee smiled. "I do not threaten, child."

James took a step forward, raising his fist, but Deborah stepped up, catching his arm before he swung. "James! Stop this! Now get on your horse and let's get of here."

"No one speaks to James Montague like that!" he seethed. "I'm going to be the Earl of Manchester one day!"

"If you don't get on your damned horse," Deborah murmured through clenched teeth, "Earl or no, I'll put you on it myself!"

James jerked his arm from his sister's grasp.

45

"Don't you come near my sister again, do you hear me, red man?" he shouted shaking his finger.

Deborah waited until James was mounted before she allowed Thomas to give her a hand up onto her horse. Without another word the three rode from the clearing, but as they disappeared into the thick of the forest, Deborah turned in her saddle and glanced back. She lifted her fingers to touch her lips, still warm and tingling from her redman's kiss.

Tshingee stood in the same broad, threatening stance, his arms crossed over his chest. But his face was calm, his ebony eyes fixed on hers. With the smallest gesture of his hand, he beckoned her back.

"Brother, you're not being sensible," Tshingee told John in his native tongue. "These men want this land and they will stop at nothing to get it. Is your life and your family's the price you will pay for your stubbornness?"

John fed his cow handfuls of grass from a basket. A lantern hung from a rafter of the lean-to barn, illuminating his face. "You don't understand, Tshingee," he replied in English. "This is my home, just as that is their home. In these Colonies any man has a right to own land."

"Any white man!" Tshingee replied bitterly, still speaking in Lenni Lenape. It was a game he and his brother played. John always spoke English in his brother's presence and Tshingee insisted on speaking his mother's language. "John . . . this land was once all ours to come and go as we pleased on it. We needed no pieces of paper with wax seals to fish the river or hoe our garden!"

46

"Things change and we must change with them." John brushed past his brother and retrieved a bucket of water from near the doorway. "I am a farmer now and I will learn to live among my white brothers. It is God's way."

Tshingee jerked the bucket of water from his brother's hand and the cool liquid splashed down his bare legs. "Is it God's way that you are threatened, that they try to run you off your land because you will not sell it to them?"

"This is just one of our Lord's trials. I will not go." He took back the bucket and poured it into a hollowed-out log trough for the cow. "I pray for those men's souls each day. They do not know they wrong their brother."

Tshingee groaned. He had had this conversation with John many times in the last two weeks and he was getting nowhere. Men from one plantation or both came each day asking that John sell his land, and each day that he refused them, they became more threatening.

Tshingee divided his time these days worrying over John and his safety and thinking of Deborah. Each day at the same time he walked to the clearing near the stream and waited, knowing she couldn't come but wishing she would. He was obsessed by the sable-haired white woman. It was time he got back to his mother's village; he hadn't intended to stay with John this long. But he just couldn't release Deborah's spirit from his mind, or his heart. He told himself he stayed because of his brother, but he knew that was not the only reason. *She* kept him here on this hostile ground.

"Please think of coming back to the village with

me, John," Tshingee urged, trying a different approach. "Bring your wife and daughter and leave this unhappiness behind. We'll go west, you and I. I'm told there is more land west of the great Chesapeake than a man can imagine. There are no white men there to poison our waters or give us their filthy diseases."

John lifted a wooden pitchfork and began to move piles of bedding. He smiled in the semidarkness. "You forget, Wildcat of the Wolf Clan, that *you* are half whiteman. Your father was a tobacco planter just as these men are."

"And what did my father give me or my mother?" Tshingee leaned against the cow's stall, folding his arms over his chest.

"He fed us, he clothed us. He taught us to speak his tongue and to read the Good Book." John leaned on the pitchfork. "He married our mother beneath the stars. He gave us his love."

"Then he took another wife!" Tshingee scoffed.

"Snow Blanket never cared. You see only what you wish to see, big brother. She gave her blessing to our father's union with the white woman. In times of trouble the Lenni Lenape take on more than one wife. Our mother did not want to live in his brick house with his slaves. She wanted only his love."

"There is no use talking to you," Tshingee said angrily. "I cannot make you understand the danger of staying here. These men do not want us here. They do not wish to live beside us as our brothers. Can't you understand that?"

"The Lord is my shepherd, I shall not want . . ."

A feminine scream pierced the night air and John froze, the pitchfork still clutched in his hand.

Tshingee sprinted from the barn, nearly running headlong into little Mary. "What is it, Mary, tell your uncle." He caught the little girl and swung her into his arms.

"Mama!" she cried out. "There are men in our house. They have mama."

On the edge of John's yard torches burned illuminating the shadows of men on horseback . . . men carrying muskets.

"What is it?" John hollered, running from the barn.

"Mary says men have your wife." Tshingee's dark eyes met his brother's. "Have you a musket?"

John shook his head. "I do not like their firing-guns. I will settle this without weapons." He started across the yard, leaving Tshingee and Mary behind.

Tshingee turned and ran back into the barn. "Listen to me, Mary," he said, setting her on the ground. "I want you to run into the woods and hide. There at our secret place near the old hollow tree." He lifted a cloth feed sack that covered his belongings. He always slept here in the barn when he visited his brother. "Can you find it in the dark?"

"Yes." The little girl nodded.

"Good." Tshingee lifted a wheel-lock musket from the straw and fumbled for his powder and lead shots. "Now go and I will come for you." He brushed past her. "Run, my dove."

Stepping out of the barn and into the darkness, Tshingee loaded his musket.

Chapter Four

John pushed through the cabin door into the brightly lit room. "Let my wife go . . . please!"

Two men held tightly to Bridget's arms. "John," she moaned, tears streaming down her face. "Help me."

A gun fired outside and John flinched. "I said release her!" he repeated.

Lester Morgan, the overseer of Host's Wealth, leaned against the fireplace, casually knocking an earthen crock off the mantel. The pottery hit the plank floor and shattered, spilling precious sugar. "It seems we got a problem here, Mr. Wolf."

John eyed the musket slung over the overseer's shoulder. "You cannot come into my home like this. I want nothing from you or Lord Manchester, but to be left alone."

"Yeah, well, the Earl wants somethin' from you, Injun boy." He extracted a gold toothpick from inside his long waistcoat and began to pick at his teeth. "He says you wouldn't take his money."

"I don't want to sell my land." John's heart went out to his wife, who stood, petrified, between the overseer's henchmen. "I told Lord Manchester that the last time he was here."

Lester ground his boot into the sugar on the floor and Bridget whimpered. "That's why he sent me, Injun boy." He grinned, taking a take step forward. "To see if I could change your mind."

John ducked the instant he saw the overseer's meaty fist in the air, but it was too late. The man caught him square in the nose, sending him reeling backward into blackness.

Tshingee pressed his back to the cabin's rear wall, his musket held tightly in his hands. From the shadows, he watched cautiously.

The men on horses just outside the cabin were becoming loud and unruly as they passed around a bottle of whiskey and took shots at several rabbit carcasses John had left hanging high in a tree near the door. One man with a red beard swung his firearm, knocking another man from his horse, and the two were soon wrestling in the grass as the others surrounded them to cheer them on.

Tshingee held his musket to his chest, his breathing even and rhythmic. He would let John try to handle the matter his own way first, but if he didn't succeed, Tshingee would be there for his brother.

Two more of the men dismounted and Tshingee pulled deeper into the shadows. Then he heard the cabin door swing open and someone step out. He couldn't see who it was but the sound of the footsteps told him it was a man . . . and not his brother. The heavy footsteps were followed by the sound of two more men and Bridget, who cried pitifully, begging the men to release her.

Tshingee pulled back the hammer on his weapon. *Where was John? Why was he not with his wife?* Tshingee moved along the wall of the cabin, inching forward toward the men who stood with Bridget. Out of the corner of his eye he saw two men headed for the barn, but he ignored them. A loose cow could be caught later; chickens could be replaced. Right now all that mattered was John and Bridget's safety.

"So Bridget," came a man's harsh voice. "Got your freedom then sold yourself to a redman, did you?"

"Please, Ethan, let me go," Bridget begged. "Just leave us in peace. All John wants is peace."

"Yea, well, all Lord Manchester wants is this here land," came the male voice again. "Think you could do some convincing on that man of yours?"

The three men and Bridget walked into a puddle of light that poured from the cabin door and Tshingee watched. If these men were just here to scare his brother, then Tshingee would fire no shots. John wanted no violence on his account. But if anyone harmed John or Bridget . . . the man would die.

The big burly man Tshingee recognized from Host's Wealth left the two men with Bridget and approached the six or seven men still on horseback. "Where the hell's Beatty and Jim?" he shouted.

The red-bearded man who had been in the fight stood slowly, nursing his jaw. "Went to the barn, Mr. Morgan."

"I thought I told you sorry sons of bitches to stay on your horses!" He cuffed the bearded man in the side of the head. "Now get up on your horse and stay put!"

Bridget cried out and Tshingee glanced back at her. The man she called Ethan had pulled off her apron and was running his finger along the neckline of her bodice. The other man held her arms pinned behind her back. *Where's John?* Tshingee wondered desperately. If Bridget had been his woman, he would never have let things get this far, but out of respect he knew he had to try and follow his brother's wishes.

Ethan grasped Bridget's bodice and gave a yank, exposing her breasts to the night air. She screamed, struggling to get loose, and he struck her hard across the mouth.

Without hesitation, Tshingee lifted his musket and fired over the men's heads.

"What the hell!" Ethan shouted, throwing himself to the ground. "Where'd that come from?"

Tshingee shrank against the cabin's wall as several gunshots echoed his in the night. Men ran to get astride their horses and two men came running from the barn with a chicken in each hand. The chickens squawked and beat their wings, nearly drowning out the shouts of the men.

Ethan and the other man holding Bridget released her and she fell. More shots were fired at random. The men rode in circles loading and refiring into the darkness. The fact that they had no target nor even knew where the gunshot had come from seemed to make no difference. The overseer had mounted his horse and was riding among the men, trying to gain some semblance of order, but the group was out of control.

Tshingee reloaded his musket in several swift, easy movements. Just then, John appeared in the stream of light outside the cabin. His face was bloodied but he seemed to be unharmed. He took his wife by the arms and lifted her out of the dirt.

"John!" Tshingee called from the shadows. "John! Here!"

John caught sight of Tshingee's movement and directed Bridget to his brother. The Irish girl came running toward "Where's my baby?" she cried out. "Where is my Mary?"

Tshingee took her hand and pulled her against the cabin's wall. "She is safe in the forest. Just stand here with me and be silent."

Another burst of gunshots filled the air and Tshingee looked up to see a man fall from his horse. The overseer leaped to the ground and raced to the man's side. It was the red-bearded one. "Cease fire!" Lester Morgan shouted. "Cease fire, you stupid bastards, you've shot him!"

John ran forward and knelt beside the overseer.

"Keep your filthy hands off him!" Morgan shouted.

John touched his fingers to the man's throat. "He's dead," he declared.

"Yea, and it looks like you're the man who kilt him!"

"Me?" John stood. "How could I have killed him? There's a bullethole through his chest." He spread his arms in demonstration. "I have no weapon."

"All I know, you red-skinned bastard, is one of my men is dead and—"

Bridget screamed, drowning out the overseer's words, and Tshingee turned in the direction she pointed. Long fingers of orange and red flames shot out from the door of the barn and thick clouds of smoke poured from within.

"My barn!" Bridget shouted, running forward.

Tshingee caught her arm, pulling her back. "We can build a new barn!" he insisted, craning his neck to see what was passing between John and the Earl's men.

The overseer held John's arms pinned behind his back and two men were tying them. Tshingee could barely hear their voices for the roar of the fire's devastating flames.

"Stay here, Tshingee commanded. "Do you hear me, Bridget? Stand right here."

The woman nodded, pulling up the torn shreds of the her bodice.

With his musket in his hand, Tshingee walked out into the light. "Where are you taking my brother" he barked.

Morgan looked up. "So that's where the shot came from. Any more you hidin' in the bushes?"

Tshingee raised his loaded wheellock menacingly. "I asked where you take my brother."

"Looks like your brother went and killed one of my men, Injun. We got laws here against murder, you know."

"That is impossible," Tshingee scoffed. "John Wolf has no weapon. I am the only one holding a gun besides your men!"

"Well, ain't that a pity." Morgan tugged on the rope that tied John's hands and began to lead him across the yard. 'Cause he's going to pay."

Tshingee followed them. "If you must take someone take me!"

"John!" Bridget screamed, running toward the knot of men. "John! Our baby! Mary is in the barn!"

For an instant, Tshingee hesitated. Bridget's high-pitched voice pierced the night air. The men were lifting John onto a horse to take him away . . . but Mary . . .

Tshingee spun on his heels, throwing the musket to

the ground. He sprinted across the yard toward the barn and ducked through the door.

Thick black smoke filled Tshingee's lungs and stung his eyes as he made his way deeper into the burning structure. "Mary!" he shouted. "Mary, where are you?"

"Here!" came a tiny voice.

"Mary! It is Tshingee. Speak to me! I must hear your voice!"

"Here, Uncle. I'm here," the little girl answered, her voice becoming louder.

Nearly blinded by smoke, Tshingee stumbled in the direction of the voice. "Mary?"

"Here, Uncle."

In relief, Tshingee swept the child into his arms. He brushed his lips against her forehead as he turned and headed for the door. The heat from the fire was so intense that both of them kept their eyes nearly shut. Bright embers filtered through the air, stinging Tshingee's back and legs. Behind him timbers crashed as the roof began to cave in. Leaping over a pile of burning rubble, Tshingee ducked out of the barn's door and into the night air. Running into the yard, he sucked in great breaths of clean, fresh air.

"My baby!" Bridget shouted, taking Mary from Tshingee's arms. "Are you all right?"

Mary bobbed her head. "My uncle. He came for me. I knew he would. I'm so sorry, Uncle. I was going to our secret place, but my kitty, she was lost in the hay."

Bridget ran a hand over Tshingee's arm. "God bless you, Brother."

He leaned forward, resting his hands on his knees as he tried to clear his lungs of the black filth.

"Where is John?" he wheezed, knowing what Bridget's reply would be.

"Gone," Bridget answered. "They took him away." She smoothed her daughter's hair, brushing at the singed wisps around her face. "But they cannot keep him. He has done nothing. They shot their own man. There are laws in these Colonies."

Tshingee groaned aloud, shaking his head. "Yes, there are laws, Bridget, but those laws are not meant for my brother and me! Don't you see, they have taken him off his land! The land is what they want, not him."

"But I'm here. It's mine too. John says the Lord protects us, and he will." She walked to the well, with Mary perched on her hip, and drew up a bucket of water. Dipping the hem of her petticoat into the bucket, she dabbed at the child's blackened face.

Tshingee remained where he stood, watching the barn groan and crumble to the ground as flames shot high into the trees. He would stand here until it was out, to be sure none of the surrounding forest caught fire.

Sighing, he brushed his hair back off his shoulders. He knew he had done the right thing in rescuing Mary while the men carried John off, but how would he get his brother released? Mary came running to him with a cup of cold water and he drank most of it, sloshing the remainder in his face. Tonight he would stay here and guard his brother's family in case the white men came back. But tomorrow . . . tomorrow he would see to John's release.

"What do you mean he's been arrested?" Deborah

57

cornered James in the horse barn between the wall and a stack of fresh-smelling hay.

"You'd best leave me alone, or I'll tell Father and he'll lock you in your room again," James whined.

"Just tell me what happened to John Wolf." She dropped her hands to her hips.

"Lester Morton says the redskin killed one of our bondmen."

"That's ridiculous! John would never harm anyone!"

James shrugged his scrawny shoulders. "There's a hole clean through him; I saw it myself." He tried to duck past his sister, but she caught him by the tails of his waistcoat.

"Not so fast. Where is he? What have they done with him?"

"They're going to transport him to Annapolis, I suppose, but for now they've got him locked in Marshal MacCloud's corn crib. Father says he'll be tried for murder, so it looks like you're going to have a dowry after all." He looked up at Deborah. "You better let me go or I'm going to be late for my music lesson."

Deborah scowled, releasing him. "Go on with you, then." She watched as he scurried off. *John Wolf charged with murder,* she thought. *How absurd! That man wouldn't harm a kitten! Now Tshingee, that was a different matter.* A tingle ran down Deborah's spine at the mere thought of the man. If James had said it was Tshingee who had been arrested for murder, she had no doubt it could have been true. But John . . . something wasn't right.

"Gaddy!" Deborah shouted.

A young mulatto boy came down a ladder from

the hayloft above the barn. It was rumored that he was one of the Earl's several illegitimate children on the plantation. "Ma'am?"

"Gaddy, could you saddle Joshua for me?"

Gaddy shuffled his bare feet back and forth in the clean bedding, making no move toward the tack room.

"Gaddy," Deborah repeated. "I asked you to saddle my horse."

The boy lifted his head slowly. "The Earl said he'd whip my tail if I saddled up for you, 'lessen someone was ridin' with you."

She sighed, tugging at the neat braid of hair she wore to one side. "All right, Gaddy. I won't have you whipped on my account. Are you studying?"

The boy grinned. "Yes, ma'am. The fig-ures are confusin', but I think I understand."

"Well, you just go up to the loft and get back to the work I gave you yesterday. I won't have a chance to help with your reading today, but I promise I'll help tomorrow. All right?"

Gaddy beamed. "Yes, ma'am."

Deborah waited until the servant had disappeared up the ladder and then she set herself to the task of saddling up Joshua. She wasn't dressed properly to be riding. She hadn't even worn a hat out to the barn. But she didn't dare risk going back into the house to change, so her morning gown would have to do.

After saddling Joshua and managing to mount him by means of an old stool, Deborah rode out of the barn. Just as she went out the door, she caught one of the three-cornered hats worn by the stable boys and stuffed it on her head. Determined, she rode behind the barn and headed south toward the

MacCloud plantation.

Half an hour later, Deborah skirted the barnyard at the MacCloud plantation, keeping in the shadows of the woods. A cool breeze off the bay whipped at her hair and she pushed the loose strands beneath the old leather hat she wore. Pulling up on Joshua's reins, she came to a halt. From here she could see the corn crib where John was supposedly being held. A man stood outside the door with a musket in his hand.

"So, we meet again," came a deep voice.

Deborah didn't even flinch as Tshingee leaped from a tree branch above, his moccasins hitting the ground with a soft thud.

"So we meet again," she answered quietly. "I'm sorry it had to be this way."

Tshingee's dark gaze settled on her face. "Are you?"

"I know John didn't kill that man."

Tshingee smoothed Joshua's rump. "Tell your father that, then. Make him release my brother."

Deborah laughed bitterly. "It would do no good. My opinions mean nothing to the Earl." Unafraid, she watched him. "If I had known they were coming, I'd have warned you."

"Why?"

His harsh voice was unsettling. He was blaming her again for what she had no control over. "I don't know," she answered.

There was silence and then he looked up at her. "So why are you here?"

"I came to see if John needed anything. To be sure they were feeding him and giving him water." She watched with fascination as the muscles of Tshingee's

60

back rippled beneath his sleeveless tunic.

He nodded. "I came to see my brother as well."

"They won't let you."

His eyes narrowed. "They cannot keep me from my brother. The men lied, they shot the red-bearded one themselves."

"I thought it must have been something like that."

Tshingee brushed a speck of mud from her boot. "And that does not surprise you?"

"My half-brother, James, said my father sent our overseer. Lester Morgan is a dangerous, brutal man. He could very well have shot the bondmen himself. John is lucky he wasn't shot."

"I would not think John feels *lucky*."

Deborah sighed, looking through the tree limbs at the corn crib. "I . . . I could help you, if you want."

"I want no help from you, Red Bird. It is your family that harms mine."

"I am not responsible for my father," she answered hotly. "Now don't be stupid. I know these people and I'm telling you that they're not going to let you saunter up and talk with your brother." She shifted her weight in the sidesaddle. "So let me help you. If you truly want to see your brother, it's the only way."

Tshingee was silent in thought for a moment. He hated to admit it, but Deborah was right. "How can you help me?" he asked her softly.

She smiled. "Simple enough. I'll distract the guard in front of the corn crib, while you stand to the rear and speak with John."

"You are a scheming woman."

"Do you or don't you want to see John?" she snapped. "Because if you don't go. I am."

Tshingee lifted his hand and laid it gently on her

leg. "Yes, I will see my brother."

Deborah's eyes met Tshingee's and for a moment both recalled the kiss they had shared a week ago. He withdrew his hand, taking a step back.

"I'll go now," she whispered, but she made no move to go.

"Yes." Tshingee nodded. "Fly, Red Bird."

She tore her gaze from his, her hands shaky, and urged her mount forward. What was it about this man that made her so uncomfortable? Why did she dream of him at night? Deborah shook her head, clearing the cobwebs. Tossing the servant's hat onto the ground, she rode out into the sunlight.

Skirting the corn crib, Deborah pulled Joshua to a halt twenty feet from the guard. She gave the young man her best smile and he smiled back. "Afternoon," she said sweetly.

The tall, reedy blond nodded, his cheeks brightening. He seemed to be about the same age as Deborah. "G—good a—afternoon," the servant murmured, tipping his hat.

She moistened her lips with the tip of her tongue. "Might you help me, sir?"

"H—help y—you?" he stuttered.

"Mmm-hmm." She lifted her dark eyelashes. "Down from the saddle."

The young man took a deep breath, then another. "Y—yeah. S—sure." He slung his rifle over his shoulder and hurried across the grass. "Y—you here t—to see M—Mister MacCloud?"

Deborah settled her hands on the man's shoulders and allowed him to ease her to the ground. "I might be. Is Charlie here?"

The blond gulped. "D—don't know, m—ma'am.

62

B—been here since d—dawn watchin' the In—Injun."

Deborah brushed at an imaginary speck of dust on her bodice, calling attention to her full bosom. As the man gulped, moving his musket from one shoulder to the other, she glanced up at the corn crib. Through the wooden slats she could see John on the far side, speaking to Tshingee. "They let you guard him? You must be very brave. What's your name?"

His cheeks turned redder. "P—Paulie." He grinned.

"I'm Deborah, Deborah Montague."

"I kn—know," he conceded.

"Not bonded, are you, Paulie?" She toyed with a strand of her hair and he watched, mesmerized.

"N—no. F—free man. M—my papa, h—he's a f—fisherman." Paulie dropped his musket butt to the ground. Sweat beaded on his forehead. "M—Mister MacCloud, h—he hired me t—to work here," he finished triumphantly.

Deborah peered over Paulie's shoulder. "Well, I'd better go." She flashed him another smile. "I'm not really supposed to be out."

"W—want me t—to s—see if Mister C—Charlie's here?"

She shook her head. "Nah. I was just out for a ride, anyway. I wanted to see if you really had a redskin here like everyone said you did."

"Y—yea, we got O—one." Paulie started to turn in the direction of the corn crib, but Deborah caught his sleeve with her hand.

"Could you give me a boost up? I really do have to be going" she added louder.

"S—sure." Paulie laid his firearm in the grass and

cupped his hands.

Deborah stepped easily into the saddle and reached for the reins he offered. "It was nice talking to you, Paulie." She glanced across the yard at the corn crib, taking notice of the man's shadow that slipped into the woods.

"N — nice talking to you," Paulie answered, beaming. He left his musket behind and followed her to the woods' edge.

"Listen, Paulie, I'd appreciate it if you didn't tell anyone I'd been here. I'm not supposed to be riding unescorted."

He lifted his right hand. "I s — swear it."

She smiled, nodding her head in the direction of the corn crib. "You'd better get back to your Indian."

Paulie glanced at the corn crib, then at Deborah, and took off across the grass.

Deborah entered the forest on horseback. A few hundred feet straight in, Tshingee waited. "Did you get to speak with John?"

His mouth twitched in a humorless scowl. "I did. I must thank you."

"It's the least I can do. If there's anything else . . ."

"This changes nothing," Tshingee interrupted. He refused to listen to her speak. Her voice was too magical, too enticing. He could not allow himself this attraction.

"What do you mean? I don't understand." Deborah's brow creased in confusion.

"You and I, Red Bird, are enemies."

"Why? I don't understand." She studied his finely sculpture facial features. "What have I done to you?"

"I told you, it is your family." He turned his back on her, not wanting to see the pain in her haunting brown eyes.

"Wait. Where are you going?" She sank her heel into Joushua's side and followed Tshingee. "You didn't even tell me what John said. Does he need something?"

Tshingee turned on her angrily. "You mean besides his freedom?"

She refused to turn away. "I would give him his freedom if I could, but since I can't, I will provide anything else he asks."

Tshingee wiped his full mouth as if he could brush the memory of their kiss away. *Why could I not have met this woman in another place, another time?* he wondered. "If you must make such a gesture"—he answered callously, turning and walking away—"my brother asks for a Bible."

Chapter Five

Deborah rolled onto her side in the massive four-poster bed and tugged the light counterpane over her bare shoulders. The linen sheets felt so soft and smooth against her skin that she smiled sleepily.

She had always slept nude, something that shocked Lady Celia beyond words, but no matter what Deborah's step-mother said or did, Deborah refused to conform. Her numerous cotton and flannel sleeping gowns imported from London and Paris had remained in the trunk at the foot of the bed until she had secretly given them to her sister, Mary, as a wedding gift. It was Mary, only a year her senior who she had shared this room with before she'd been married off to her sea captain.

A soft breeze wafted through the open window, carrying on it the first hint of the approaching autumn. Sighing, Deborah plumped her goosetick pillow, her eyes drifting shut. Tomorrow a tea was being held by Thomas's sister in honor of her brother's betrothal to the Earl's daughter. Deborah had prayed desperately that she would come down with some illness or injury to prevent her from attending, but unfortunately she remained healthy. She knew the morning would dawn, and she'd be forced to stand at her betrothed's side accept congratulations, and listen to the titters of the young maidens not yet wed.

Deborah was uncertain how long she'd been asleep when she suddenly found herself awake. Her limbs were tense and dewy with perspiration, the hair on the back of her neck stiff. Something had startled her in her sleep and she didn't know what it was. Opening her eyes, she squinted in the darkness. It was a moonless night and the air hung heavy with an impending rainstorm. In the distance, she could hear the rumble of thunder as it rolled in off the bay.

"Is someone there?" Deborah threw off the counterpane and swung her legs over the side of the bed.

The hand came from nowhere to clamp over her mouth, preventing even a single syllable from escaping her lips.

Deborah clawed at the hand with her blunt fingernails, struggling as another hand caught her bare arm and pushed her onto her back. Her hands touched the broad expanse of a bare chest and she ceased to struggle. It was him . . . her Indian.

Tshingee's heady masculine scent filled her head, sending odd tingling sensations down the length of her spine. He held her down by her bare upper arm — a place no man had ever touched without the material of a sleeve between.

Deborah blinked. "Tshingee?" she murmured beneath the pressure of his palm.

Tshingee slowly lowered his hand. "Silence!"

"What are you doing here? How did you find me?" Deborah was frightened, but the thought of something so utterly forbidden as a man in her bedchamber . . . this man . . . made her bold.

"I said silence, woman!" he repeated. Tshingee took

67

a step back. He could feel his heart pounding beneath his breast. Perhaps this was not such a good idea after all, he thought, wiping his mouth with the back his hand. He hadn't expected his Red Bird to be unclothed. The impact of her bare breasts brushing against his chest had been far greater than he could have imagined. His entire body was hot and pulsing with desire for this woman who could never be his.

Feeling Tshingee's dark eyes on her, Deborah suddenly realized what he was staring at. With a gasp, she yanked up the counterpane to cover a small portion of her nakedness. "You can't come in here like this," she whispered harshly. "The Earl will have you hanged!"

Tshingee crossed his arms over his chest. "He will have my brother hanged if I do not."

"What?" She scooted backward on the bed, out of his reach.

"You will come with me," he replied starkly.

"I think not!"

Tshingee caught her ankle and dragged her toward him. "Get dressed and keep silent or I will tie your mouth."

"I'm not getting dressed! I'm not going anywhere with you!" Suddenly the excitement of the redman's appearance had lost its attraction. This man was trying to kidnap her!

"I said get up and put on clothing!" He grasped her wrist and with one swift movement lifted her off the bed and to her feet.

Deborah stared at his solemn bronze face as her eyes finally adjusted to the darkness. "You can't do this to me! No man can."

Tshingee turned his face to keep his gaze from settling on her rounded breasts, her narrow waist, her

68

long, lithe legs. The coverlet she held clutched in her hands was more an enticement than a deterrent. His voice caught in his throat, making it raspy. "I said, dress." He spotted a heap of wispy material on the floor and tossed it to her. "Put it on!"

"I will not! Now get out of here before I scream." She let the shift fall to the floor.

"You will not scream. You will do as I say so that no one is hurt."

Deborah took a step forward, her face only inches from his. "Are you threatening me?"

Tshingee caught her by the shoulders and spun her around. Before Deborah realized what was happening, he had scooped up the shift and was tying it around her mouth. In the process of struggling, she lost her grip on the counterpane and it fell to the floor. There was no longer a barrier between his bare flesh and hers.

Deborah's breath caught in her throat as her thigh brushed Tshingee's. The gag was tight against her mouth and cheeks; a whimper escaped her lips.

He stared through the darkness at Deborah's wide, startled eyes and for a moment his constitution wavered. She was frightened and he had caused this fear. Without thought he pulled her slim body against his chest his hands falling to caress her back and bare, shapely buttocks.

"*Maata-wischasi,* my Red Bird." he whispered. He pressed his lips to her forehead. She smelled of rain, and soft, sweet. grass. "I will not hurt you. I do this because your people give me no choice. John Wolf is a part of me. I cannot see him wronged."

Deborah trembled in Tshingee's arms. Her head spun in confusion. She was frightened of him and

69

angry that he would do this to her. But within herself she felt a certain betrayal. His hot flesh felt so good pressed to hers. His voice carried on the night air like an ancient ballad of love.

"We must go," he told her, taking a step back. His thoughts came more clearly with the short distance between them. *"Maata-wischasi.* Do not fear. Do as I say and you will come to no harm. Do you understand?"

She nodded slowly.

"Kihalaalit." He removed a scroll of paper from the belt of his loincloth. "I leave this message to the Earl telling him who has taken you and why. When he returns my brother to me, I will return his daughter." He tossed it onto the bed. "I think it is an even exchange, don't you"

Unable to speak, Deborah glared at him.

"Come, we go."

Taking Deborah by the waist, he lifted her over his shoulder. She struggled, but only for a moment before she came to her senses. As Tshingee stepped out of the window, she quickly realized that the only thing she would accomplish by fighting him was a possible fall from the second story.

Squeezing her eyes tightly shut, Deborah held her breath as Tshingee moved along the outer windowsill, only a brick's width wide. He held her flung over his shoulder and bent at the waist, her arms dangling down his back.

Tshingee pushed away from the wall and for a moment they were airborne before his bare feet touched the overhanging roof of the lean-to pantry off the winter kitchen. A moment later, he was shimmying down her father's prized ivy and then they were on the ground.

Tshingee set her down and her feet sank into the damp grass. "Are you all right?"

She glared at him. *Of course I'm not all right.* she wanted to shout. *I'm being kidnapped stark naked by a crazy Indian. How could I possibly be all right?*

"Good. Now listen, we will go through the woods and to the river. There we will take my dugout. The Migianac will protect us and put a great distance between us and the Earl by morning." He tugged on her arm. "Come along."

But Deborah refused to budge. She'd be damned if she was going to make things easy for him!

"You will not walk?" An angry, muffled protest from Deborah made him smile in the darkness. "That's all right," he told her, throwing her over his shoulder like a feed sack. "You are a worthy foe. If I were in your place . . . I would not walk either."

"What do you mean, she's gone, sir?" Thomas stared in disbelief at the Earl of Manchester standing at the front door of Deliverance. It was barely six in the morning.

"I mean she's gone," the Earl answered, his face red and puffy from the exertion of walking up the hill. "He's taken her from me, boy!"

"Who?" Thomas removed his handkerchief from his waistcoat and mopped his brow. "Where did who take her?"

"The Indian's bloody brother! I'm unable to pronounce his name. Are you going to ask me in or must I stand here like some poor relation?"

Thomas stepped back. "My apologies, please do

71

come in, sir. Have you broken the fast?"

The Earl waved a thick, hairy hand, dropping into a chair in the entryway of the front hall. "Nothing for me, I couldn't possibly eat," he panted.

"W—what can we do? How are we going to get her back?"

"I'm organizing a search party. That's why I came— to see how many men you could bring with you. Thomas, I've been saying for years that we had to clean this shore of the vermin. First one of those redskins shoots and kills one of my men and now this." He hung his head.

"Why did he take her?" Thomas stared in utter shock.

"His brother, boy! Damned, but you're slow. He left a note. A redskin that knows his letters! He says he'll release my daughter, unharmed, when we release his brother. The savage is under the notion his brother's been falsely accused!"

Thomas took a chair across from the Earl and lowered his head to cradle it in his hands. "My poor Deborah," he groaned. Suddenly he looked up. "You don't think he'll kill her, do you?"

"No, but I can't promise we'll find her totally un-scathed." He lifted his eyebrows, his tone suggesting her virtue was at risk.

Thomas gulped. "I want you to know, sir, that if she's alive . . . if she's alive and still has her wits about her, I'll still be willing to wed her."

"I was hoping you'd be man enough to say that." Lord Manchester pushed up out of the chair. "Well, there's no time to lose, son, if we're to catch up with them. Get yourself properly clothed. We'll probably have to go on foot part of the way." He went to the door.

Thomas nodded in agreement, still seated in the chair. He just couldn't believe this had happened. "Where are we to meet, sir?"

"The northwest corner of Deliverance. The Mac-Clouds are meeting us there in an hour's time with whoever else they can round up. The whole county's going to want to be in on this."

Thomas wiped his mouth with his handkerchief. His hand shook with rage. All he could think was Deborah. He was not a violent man, but he wanted to murder Deborah's abductor.

"Well, get up, boy," the Earl chided. "Get ahold of yourself." He opened the door. "I'm depending on you, son."

Thomas stood. "Yes, sir. I'll be there. We'll find them and we'll hang the bastard on the spot!"

The Earl smiled with pleasure. "Precisely my thought, Mr. Hogarth."

Deborah lay on the soft ground, her hands tied behind her back and her cheek pressed into a pile of brittle fallen leaves. Tshingee lay on top of her, his sinewy body pressed against hers. All Deborah could think of was thank God he had allowed her to don her shift at daybreak. He had gagged her again, using a bit of material from the hem of the shift, but at least her nude body was partially shielded.

"Shhhh." Tshingee murmured in her ear. The sound of barking, snarling hounds grew closer with each passing minute.

"Let me go," Deborah murmured. Tshingee had loosened the gag so that she could speak, but her voice

73

was muffled. "Please," she begged. The linen of the shift was dry in her mouth and an insect was biting her bare hip.

"We must be silent, Red Bird," he told her, his voice barely audible.

"I don't have to be silent!" she managed through the gag. "I want them to find me!"

Tshingee rolled her over in the soft humus, his dark, disturbing eyes boring into hers. He straddled her body, leaning forward until his breath was warm on her face. "If you cannot be silent, I will knock you in the head. It will not kill you but it will silence you long enough to get you out of here." He lifted a sooty eyebrow. "Do you want me to hit you, my Red Bird?"

Deborah's eyes narrowed as she strained beneath his solid form. Every part of his body seemed to be brushing against hers and his brief leather loincloth left nothing to her imagination. She had never met a man more hauntingly masculine. "No, I don't want you to clunk me in the head! I want you to let me go!"

A smile twitched across his face and he brushed her hair out of her eyes. This woman held no resemblance to the proper lady he had met on horseback only a short time ago. This morning, beneath the first rays of the new day, she appeared to be some captured woods spirit, wild and untamed with her unruly hair and bright, angry eyes.

Tshingee's smile vanished from his face as quickly as it had appeared. *Where is my head?* he chastised himself. *This was the enemy! This woman's father holds my brother unjustly!* Tshingee rolled her roughly onto her side, tightening the gag. "I said silence!"

The sound of the baying hounds echoed high above

the trees. Tshingee knew he was losing precious time. If the men caught him now, all would be lost. Lifting Deborah to her feet, he shoved her forward. *"Buumska, hokkuaa!"* he snapped.

Deborah stumbled, tripping over an exposed tree root. She fell to the ground and refused to get up.

"We must hurry," Tshingee insisted, lifting her to her feet. "They're nearly upon us!"

She set her jaw in determination. He had tightened the gag so that she could no longer speak, but she was certain he understood her. She'd be damned if she was going to walk a foot voluntarily!

Tshingee groaned, shaking his head. *"Hokkuaa! This is why I have no woman of my own!"* Hoisting Deborah into the air, he tossed her over his shoulder and began to run.

Deborah squeezed her eyes shut, holding back the tears that threatened to flow. She could hear the dogs in the distance and the occasional shout of a man. She knew it had to be a search party, so why couldn't they find her? They were so near! How could one man on foot carrying a woman elude a pack of dogs and a group of men on horseback!

Her Indian was clever, that was how. He traveled through the densest part of the forest, through thickets where no horse and rider could go.

The direction of the sounds changed, and Tshingee ran faster. He leaped over fallen saplings and tore through thickets of briar. His feet barely made a sound on the narrow deer path as he grew closer to the edge of the Migianac River.

Deborah groaned, wrapping her arms around Tshingee's waist to prevent swinging behind him like a broken pendulum. The Lenni Lenape brave changed direction, backtracking a short distance. He came to a halt and dumped her onto the ground.

"Get in!" he ordered harshly.

She blinked. He was pointing to a huge fallen log, hollowed through time by tree rot and tiny organisms. He wanted her to get *inside* the tree! When she balked, he pushed her onto her knees. She ducked in time to keep from bumping her head as he propelled her forward against her will.

Climbing into the dark, moist cave, Deborah lay on her side. Tshingee crawled in beside her and moved a tree limb and a vine of green briars to cover the entrance.

He rested his hand possessively on her hip. "Silence," he whispered. "We have almost reached my dugout, but they cannot see us go down the river."

Deborah squeezed her eyes shut as the sounds of man and dog drew closer. She tried to ignore the sensation of Tshingee's body so close to hers.

How can my flesh betray me like this! How, after all that has happened, can I still be attracted to this savage? she wondered.

The dogs and men were so close now that Deborah could make out the sound of her father's voice. The search party passed within a hundred feet of Tshingee's hiding place.

Damn you, Tshingee, Deborah thought as the sound of hoofbeats and hounds began to die away. Why did the Indian have to be so intelligent? Wrapped up in the heady smell of humus like this, the dogs had not caught the scent of human flesh.

For several more minutes Tshingee and Deborah lay in silence, then he backed out of the log and pulled her out behind him. "Not much further," he assured her.

This time, he slung her over his shoulder without attempting to make her walk.

A quarter of a mile through the woods, they reached the bank of the Migianac River and Tshingee set her lightly on the ground. She watched with great surprise as, out of no where, he produced a small boat from the river's bank. It was a hollowed out log, no more than seven feet long. "Get in," Tshingee ordered.

Realizing that if she didn't get in herself, he would put her in, Deborah did as she was told. She didn't want Tshingee touching her—it was too confusing. Her mind told her he was the enemy; *he* had told her he was the enemy. But she didn't feel like he was.

The dugout rocked as she stepped into it, but Tshingee held it steady. He pointed for her to be seated in the bow. Then, he waded chest-deep into the river and leaped in. Resting on his knees, he lifted a single wooden paddle and began to propel the small boat rapidly through the water.

Deborah was surprised at how easily the crude thing moved, parting the water in near silence.

"If you give your word you will be silent, when we are further downriver, I will take the cloth from your mouth," Tshingee told her in his soft, singsong voice.

Deborah glared venomously at him and he stifled the urge to smile. She was so beautiful kneeling in front of him with the breeze off the water blowing her magical hair. He shrugged, looking away. "It matters not to me, Red Bird. My village is many days from here, but I prefer the silence to a woman's chattering anyway."

Chapter Six

Deborah woke gradually to the sound of water lapping at the hull of the dugout and the swoosh of Tshingee's paddle as he maneuvered the boat upstream. She could hear an osprey flying overhead calling shrilly as it soared in the September sky. Once awake, she lay perfectly still in the bottom of the boat, not yet willing to face her captor.

How am I going to get away from this mad man? she wondered feverishly. Any thrill of the adventure that had been there was gone; she was frightened now. *But what am I afraid of?* she wondered. *I don't think he'll hurt me; he said he wouldn't. All he wants is to have his brother returned safely. If I were in his moccasins, wouldn't I do the same thing?* Deborah nearly giggled at the thought of her analogy. *If I were in his moccasins! I'm as daft as he is!*

"Did you have a restful sleep?" Tshingee asked gently.

Deborah bobbed up, turning to face him. "What? How did you know I was awake?"

He pulled the wide hand-hewn paddle easily through the water in deliberate even strokes. "A man breathes differently when he is awake than when he is asleep."

"Oh." She drew her legs up beneath her, trying to cover as much of her limbs as possible in the torn shift she wore.

For several minutes Deborah watched Tshingee paddle the dugout, observing how his biceps bulged with each stroke of the paddle. He sat on his knees, his buttocks barely brushing his calves, his back straight. Every muscle in his body seem to contribute to the motion of the dugout, although nothing actually moved but his arms. Every pull of the paddle seemed effortless, and yet the boat moved at the same rapid pace in precisely the same direction without ever wavering from some invisible path.

Deborah lifted her hand to shade her eyes. It was nearly noon. "It's very hot," she commented.

"I have left supplies a little further up the river. I will give you proper clothing there."

"You mean all of this was planned?" Her brow furrowed.

"One must always have a plan."

She tucked a lock of dark hair behind her ear. The breeze off the water felt wonderful through her thin shift. She hadn't been outside in the sun and breeze unclothed since she was twelve and had gone swimming in her underthings with Charlie MacCloud. "But you didn't even go to my father. You didn't try to have John released."

"Would it have done any good to speak with him?" His ebony eyes met hers.

Deborah looked away. "No," she answered quietly.

"What other choice did I have but to take you?"

She stretched out her legs. *He's already seen all of me,* she thought pragmatically. *I might as well be comfortable.* "Oh, I don't know," she answered, lowering her hand over the side of the dugout to drag her fingers in the water. "You could have kidnapped *John* instead of me. You could have just broken him out of that corn crib and gotten away."

Tshingee lifted his paddle and rested it across the width of the dugout. "No. My brother would want no bloodshed. It is not his way."

She watched him return to his paddling. "But would it be yours?"

He shrugged his sunbaked shoulders. "Does it matter? We talk of John, not of Tshingee."

"Why has your brother an English name and you an Indian name?"

"We are Lenni Lenape. Indians come from a place called India far across the oceans from here."

"Touché," she whispered, smiling. "All right. Why is it you have a *Len-ni Lenap-e* name and your brother does not?"

"He does, but he chooses not to use it, just as I choose not to use my Bible name. A *tshingee* is a wildcat of the forest."

"Wildcat . . ." she mused. "It fits you." Deborah studied Tshingee's handsome face curiously. "But what is your Christian name?"

"Luke. I think it is not a good name for me." Tshingee spoke evenly, but broke rhythm with the paddle.

Deborah giggled. "No. You're right. You don't look much like a Luke. I like Tshingee better, too." She tried not to laugh, but it seemed so preposterous. This man was no more a Luke than she was!

Tshingee glared at her, but then broke into a smile, joining in her amusement. "You would not laugh if you had not been given such a proper name."

"Deborah? You think it fits me?"

He lifted his chin, stroking evenly again with the paddle. His long, ebony hair blew in the breeze, fluttering across his shoulders. *"Deb-or-ah,"* he said softly. "It sounds like a name that rides on the wind. *Deb-or-ah,* the elusive one, who can be heard, can be smelled, can even be seen, but can never be touched."

She crossed her legs, scooting a little closer to him. Her bare feet nearly touched his knees now. "I never liked it before, but when you say it, it does sound beautiful."

Tshingee continued to paddle the dugout along the shore line of the Migianac River and Deborah watched him in silence. He seemed to enjoy the sights and the sounds of the river as much as she did. Tshingee was not afraid of the silence the way Thomas seemed to be.

Still intrigued by Tshingee's past, she spoke again. "You speak very well for an uneducated man."

"That is because I am not uneducated. My father had a tutor for my brother and me when we were children."

"Did he?" She drew up her knees, leaning forward on them. Her shift fell back, revealing much of her shapely thighs. "Your father was a white man?"

"He had a plantation across the Chesapeake where we once lived. Though my brother and I spent most of our time in my mother's village, we sometimes stayed with our father before he married Madam."

"Then your parents were not married," she said, treading lightly.

Tshingee shook his head. "They were married by the shaman of our village. But my mother had no wish to live in the big house, so my father married Madam so that he might have heirs to pass his plantation to when

81

he was gone."

"It must have hurt your mother deeply."

"It did not. She loved him but she wanted no part of his ways. She was content for him to come to our wigwam when it suited her."

Deborah smiled, looking over the glassy blue water. *When it suited her* . . . She liked the sound of that. "How wonderful to have such a love," she said wishfully.

Tshingee lifted his paddle out of the water. "You think so, Red Bird?"

Deborah was mesmerized by his heady gaze. The man was intoxicatingly masculine. "I would give anything to be loved like your mother must have loved your father."

Tshingee reached out and stroked her cheek. "You are like no woman I have ever known, Red Bird. I wish you were not my enemy."

Her cheeks grew warm and rosy. "I do not consider you my enemy."

He pulled back his hand and lifted the paddle, the spell broken. "Then you are mistaken," he said coldly.

Deborah looked away, tears stinging the corners of her eyes. She was so confused. This man had kidnapped her in the middle of the night. He had stolen her from her father's house and now he held her captive. He had declared them enemies. So why did she harbor no hostile feelings toward him? Why did she like the way he spoke? Why did she yearn for another kiss?

Tshingee and Deborah were silent for the next hour and then, he suddenly veered into a small cove on the southern bank. "Here we will leave the dugout," he told her, his voice devoid of any emotion. "From here we go on foot."

"Where are you taking me?"

"You are my prisoner. I do not have to tell you where I take you." He leaped out of the dugout into waist-deep water and pulled the boat up to the bank. "Get out," he commanded.

Deborah crawled over the side then slipped into the water and waded to the shore. There, she climbed the grassy bank and waited for Tshingee.

He hid the dugout along the bank, tying it to several saplings and covering it with brush. Once on the bank, he brushed past her. "Come."

Deborah obeyed. She knew there was no need to run. Where would she run to? She had not idea how far they had come or in what direction. The Migianac River had so many tributaries that it would be nearly impossible for her to find her way home. If she did manage to escape, how would she defend herself against the wolves and wild dog packs that roamed the area? No, for now, the best thing to do was to remain with Tshingee and bide her time. *Something* was bound to happen. Either her father would find them, or the prisoner exchange would take place.

"Ouch!" Deborah stopped and lifted her foot to extract a thorn.

"Come," Tshingee ordered.

She grimaced. "Can't you see, I've hurt my foot?" she asked irritably. "You could go ahead without me and I could catch up later."

"You are a very funny woman," he said, his voice lacking even a hint of humor. He stood with his legs slightly spread, his hands resting on his hips. "Must I carry you?"

She sighed. "No. I'm coming." She hopped a few

feet then lowered her foot gingerly. She'd removed the thorn, but the ball of her foot was still smarting.

Tshingee followed a narrow deer trail west and then south again back toward the river. Deborah remained a few paces behind. When he stopped, she stopped. "Wait here," he ordered. "I will return for you."

Deborah nodded and sat down on a bulging moss-covered tree root. The forest was so dark and cool; she shivered, rubbing her bare arms. *Fall will soon be upon us,* she mused. *How long will Tshingee keep me? How long will it be before my father finds me or gives in and releases John?* It was strange that although she was angry that Tshingee would do this to her, she found no comfort in the thought of returning to Host's Wealth. *Being captured by Indians would certainly be a good excuse to put off my wedding,* she thought, chuckling to herself.

A few minutes later Tshingee appeared and signaled for her to follow. A few hundred yards into the woods, they entered a man-made clearing. A large garden plot was overgrown with weeds, but other than that, there was no evidence of any human beings.

"What's this?" She hurried to catch up with Tshingee.

"My people once lived here before they were driven further north by the white men. My supplies are here." Tshingee stopped, waiting for her.

"Are we staying here? Is this where we're going to wait?"

"We go on to my village. There we wait for your father's message saying he has released my brother."

"But he doesn't know where your village is." She laid her hand on his arm. It just seemed the natural thing to do. "How will he find me?"

"Our village has messengers. They will contact the Earl." He put his hand over hers. "But it will be some time. The Earl must understand that the situation is grave."

Uneasiness swelled in Deborah. "You mean I won't be going home soon," she said softly.

He shook his head. "But I promise no harm will come to you. Do as I say and you will remain safe in my care."

She yanked her hand from his arm and stalked away. "You've taken advantage of the friendship I offered you."

"I have not," he answered hotly. "You are the Earl's daughter and he is the man who had my brother arrested."

"The Earl has a son." She swung around, her face flushed with anger. She was as distraught with herself as she was with Tshingee. Why hadn't she fought him? Why had she just let him carry her away like that? *Because you wanted him to,* her inner voice responded. "You could have kidnapped *James,*" she snapped.

Deborah's words brought Tshingee to a halt. He lifted his ebony eyes to meet hers. "Mayhap you are right," he conceded as much to himself as to her. "A part of me wanted you . . . wants you. I have not been able to forget you, Red Bird, since I first saw you there in my brother's garden. I think maybe this is my way of having you with me, if only for a short time."

Tshingee's honesty shocked Deborah. She had never known a man so forthright with his feelings. "But you've taken me against my will, Tshingee! My entire life has been dictated by men like you. No one ever cares what I think! No one asks what I want! I don't want to be here! I don't want to be a part of this!"

With two long strides, Tshingee closed the distance between them. He drew his face only inches from hers. "I do not mean to hurt you, but John is my brother." He laid his hand on his heart. "He is of my flesh and I must do whatever is necessary to save him. Don't you see that your father gave me no choice?"

Deborah couldn't tear her gaze from his as he took her in his arms and kissed her trembling lips. "Come," he whispered. "Let us get my supplies. We cannot stay long because they will be looking for us, but first we will eat."

Deborah sighed, nodding. She was caught in such a whirlwind of emotion that she felt as if she were drowning. Her desire for this man was suffocating her logic. Her mind was so clouded with his presence that she could feel no true malice toward him. He was right. What choice had the Earl left him but to take this drastic action?

She threw up her hands in resolution. She would make the best of this bad situation. It was the only thing she could do. "All right. Where are these supplies of yours?" She walked away, needing to feel a distance between them. "Let's eat. I'm hungry."

Tshingee retrieved two leather packs from a hollowed-out hole in the ground near the edge of the woods. It had once been a place his people stored food in the winter to keep it from freezing, he had explained. Tshingee then retrieved fresh water from somewhere nearby and Deborah soon found herself sitting cross-legged in the grass eating corn bread and dried berries.

The two ate in silence, both lost in their own thoughts. Finally, Tshingee stood. "Come. We must go now." He held out his hand and she accepted it, allowing him to help her to her feet.

"I thought you said you had something for me to wear."

From a pack he produced a leather tunic. "It is mine," he told her, "but you can wear it over your . . ." he waved, not knowing the correct word.

" . . . My shift," she finished for him.

He smiled. "Your shift. And you can put these on your feet." He offered a pair of beaded moccasins. "They are mine too but I think they will fit."

Deborah accepted his offerings hesitantly. Dropping the moccasins into the grass, she pulled the sleeveless piece of clothing over her head and fastened the ties beneath her arms. The soft leather tunic fell to her hips, fitting perfectly over her shift. The soft animal hide was pliable, giving her unrestricted movement, yet it covered enough of her torso that she no longer felt unclothed.

Tshingee couldn't resist a smile as he watched Deborah settle on the grass to put on the moccasins. She could nearly have passed herself off as a Lenni Lenape maiden in his tunic with her long, dark hair flowing down over her shoulders. Only the silly ruffles of her shift and the pale hue of her skin gave away her true heritage.

"You're right. They fit fine." Deborah looked up at him, wiggling her toes in the moccasins. "Only a little big."

"If you are ready, we must go." He handed her a length of sinew. "To tie back your hair."

She nodded, running her fingers through her straight hair, pulling back to the nape of her neck. She tied the thick mane with the leather thong.

Without a word, Tshingee picked up the packs and started off across the clearing. Deborah followed.

For hours the two walked. Tshingee followed some imaginary path through thickets of briars and groves of monstrous oak trees. He said little to Deborah except to warn her of a poisonous plant or a low-hanging branch, but he remained courteous, seemingly concerned for her welfare.

At first Deborah walked along, enjoying the stroll through the silent forest, but as the afternoon shadows lengthened, she began to tire.

"We cannot stop yet, Deborah," Tshingee called. "We must go further north and to the west before we make camp." He stopped, waiting for her to catch up. "Do you want a drink of water?"

She wiped her damp brow. Though she had thought the forest cool earlier, once she started walking, she began to fervently wish it were later in the season. "How much further?" she asked, stopping to catch her breath. "We've already walked further today than I've walked in my entire life."

"You are strong. We will go further."

"How much further?" She dropped to the ground.

Tshingee glanced at the setting sun. "Dusk."

"Dusk!" she panted. "That's nearly two hours away."

"Yes. I think so." He started through the forest again. "But do not worry. Tomorrow we will walk longer."

Just as the sun was beginning to set, Tshingee finally declared it was time to set up camp. Stopping on the banks of a tributary of some river off the Chesapeake, the Lenni Lenape brave dropped his packs.

"Here is a good place to stop," he declared, stretching his arms.

Deborah collapsed to the ground. "That's good because I can't take another step."

"You did well for your first day, Red Bird." He watched her, his arms crossed over his chest. "I will go find us some fresh game. You swim. It will wash away the dust of the trail and soothe your tired flesh."

Staring out over the blue-green water, Deborah moistened her dry lips. The river *did* look inviting. "You won't go far?" she asked, getting to her feet. The thought of being alone here in the forest after dark was not a pleasant one.

"I thought my Red Bird was fearless." He grinned.

"She is." Deborah pulled Tshingee's tunic over her head and began to unlace his moccasins. "But she isn't stupid. I've no weapon to defend myself from wild animals or heathens such as yourself."

He nearly smiled, then lifted his hand solemnly. "I will not go far, I give you my word as a brother of the Wolf Clan."

Leaving Tshingee where he stood, Deborah raised her arms, pointed her toes, and dove into the water, just as Charlie MacCloud had taught her years ago. She surfaced a few feet from the bank and stood on tiptoe to touch the bottom. "It's wonderful," she called, leaning back to rinse her hair.

Tshingee regarded Deborah through half-closed eyes, enjoying the pleasure of the moment. She was a vision of glorious beauty to behold in the misty aura of the day's twilight. Dusk . . . that magical time between day and night when spirits haunted the souls of men flying on the winds of the night breeze . . . Tshingee sighed aloud. Was he possessed by this white woman? Was that why it seemed to him that she beckoned him with every move she made as she cleansed her body?

Tshingee lowered his bow and quiver to the soft ground and walked down the bank and into the water.

Deborah watched. The sight of Tshingee coming toward her was as exciting as it was frightening. She knew it was wrong, this ache she had for him, but she was helpless to fight it. When he lifted his arms, she came forward, meeting him in the waist-deep water.

"Have you cast some witch's spell on me Red Bird?" he whispered in her ear, his lips touching her lobe in a gentle caress.

Deborah's eyes drifted shut as she lifted her arms to rest them on his broad, bulking shoulders. "I am no witch," she answered huskily. "It is you who tempt me."

He kissed the length of her jaw line, the width of her flushed cheeks. "I know this cannot be and yet . . ."

Her mouth met his hesitantly. "And yet nothing has ever seemed so right . . ." she murmured against his lips.

Tshingee caught her chin with his palm, his tongue darting out to trace the line of her perfect lips. "You taste of new honey," he murmured. "Honey of the fireplant."

Deborah parted her lips, accepting his probing tongue with trepidation. A hot, molten joy spread through her limbs as he delved deep. Of its own accord her hand lifted to stroke his sleek, thick mane of hair. She reveled in the sensations their mouths created, a soft moan catching deep in her throat.

Suddenly and without warning, Tshingee pulled back. His hands slipped down to rest on her hips. His ebony eyes searched hers. His mouth ached to touch the soft points of her breasts that strained against the water-logged linen shift. "We cannot, Red Bird. We are not meant to be. It is wrong for me to do this."

She shook her head. "How can it be wrong? It's just a kiss. No one has ever made me feel like this. No one has ever been so tender." Her hands trembled as she stroked the thick muscles of his shoulders.

"You were right when you said I was taking advantage of the friendship you offered." He lifted his hands from her hips and took a step back. "We must forget this, Red Bird. I have no right to touch you. It is not in the stars for us."

"But how do you know? What if it is?" she asked softly. She didn't know what she was saying. All she knew was that her heart pounded beneath her breast and her limbs ached with want.

"We must tell ourselves it cannot be. My brother will be released and you will be returned to marry your man."

Before Deborah could speak again, he turned and waded away. She watched in bitter confusion as he climbed the bank and picked up his bow and quiver. When he was gone, she shuddered, lowering herself into the river. He's right, she told herself, fighting bitter tears of frustration. *What's wrong with me to behave wantonly? This man is my enemy, he's kidnapped me and holds me as his prisoner!*

Turning those thoughts over and over in her mind, Deborah paid no attention to the silence that settled over the surrounding forest or to the nearly soundless splash down the river. She was aware of nothing but the river's cool water and her own inner turmoil until a hand came from behind, clamping down hard over her mouth.

Deborah swung around angrily, thinking it was

Tshingee. A lump of sheer terror caught in her throat. It was not Tshingee but another red man, his face painted in a mask of hideous shades of blue and black! Without thought, Deborah lifted her knee hard against the man's groin. He groaned, doubling over, his hand falling from her mouth.

Deborah managed to let out one terrified scream before the savage hit her in the ear with his fist and she sank into splintering darkness.

Chapter Seven

Pain seared through Deborah's mind, clouding her thoughts. As she struggled to climb from the depths of unconsciousness, she became aware that she was being carried again, but this time it was not by Tshingee. This man was shorter, with rolls of sour, sweaty flesh at his middle. It took all of her concentration to not struggle as she became fully awake, but Deborah's inherent desire to survive forced her to remain limp.

The man carrying her was so short that her hair swept the ground as he hurried through the forest. Deborah lifted her eyelashes, but it made her so dizzy swinging upside down that she had to squeeze them shut again to ward off the blackness that threatened her. It was nearly dark now. The mournful cry of a woods owl in the distance echoed hauntingly in the dense foliage.

Where is Tshingee? Deborah wondered frantically. Had her situation not been so desperate, she might have laughed at herself. A few hours ago she would never have believed that she could yearn for her captor's presence. But at least Tshingee was an enemy she was familiar with. She knew what he wanted of her . . . and she knew no harm would come to her as long as she obeyed him. But this man—she listened to the footsteps in front and behind her—*these men,* she did not know. Where had they come from? Where were they taking her?

Were they Tshingee's men? Had he sent them to retrieve her because of what had happened in the river? She doubted it. The tongue these redmen spoke did not sound to her like Tshingee's words with their soft inflections. These men barked back and forth in their strange language, their voices harsh and without rhythm.

Time lost all meaning to Deborah as darkness settled upon the forest. Hanging upside down like this made her head spin and her stomach churn. Her ear ached where the Indian had hit her. *Is this God's punishment for my refusal to follow my father's wishes and marry Thomas,* she wondered. *No,* she reasoned, trying to keep her mind sharp. *I don't care what Celia says, our God is not so unjust.*

But how long can they run like this? The savage was still moving so swiftly that if she didn't keep her jaw clenched, her teeth clattered unnaturally.

Well after dark, the man who carried Deborah dropped her without warning. Falling into a pile of prickly pears, she lay still for a minute, waiting for the earth to stop spinning beneath her. She could feel the red man's presence; she could still smell his sour, hanging flesh. A hand reached out and poked her none-to-gently.

Deborah's eyes flew open. An arm's length from her a red man squatted, studying her. It was the man with the mask painted on his face who had hit her, only now, much of the paint had worn off, running in streaks down his face. His face was round, his jowls heavy and sagging. He grinned, baring broken, black

94

teeth.

Deborah's first instinct was to scramble to her feet and run, but the instant she moved, the savage caught her arm in his iron grip.

"*Assieds-toi, putain!*" he barked.

Deborah's temper flared. Her French wasn't good, but what she had picked up from her young tutor was a string of foreign curses. "Call me a whore will you, you stinking son of a bitch!" She raised her fist threateningly and the red man fell back onto the ground, rolling with laughter.

"*Que me voulez-vous?*" she demanded.

"*Que veut* False Face?" He whipped out a hand, catching a hunk of her tangled hair. "He wants the white whore woman to shut her mouth before he shut it for her!"

Deborah grimaced with pain, leaning back to escape his grip. "Let go!" She kicked him with a bare foot and he released her, chuckling when she nearly fell over backwards. "Silence, *putain blanche!*" he threatened, slipping a knife from his belt. "Silence, or this man will cut your *gorge pre'cieuse.*" He pressed the blade to her throat for emphasis and hot tears formed in Deborah's eyes as she nodded in acknowledgment.

She gulped, drawing her legs back under her shift. Her gaze remained locked with his. *I'll keep quiet,* she thought, *but when Tshingee comes and sees what you've done to me, he'll slit your throat!*

Deborah didn't know why she was so certain Tshingee would come for her. But as her captive tugged her hands behind her back and lashed them with a strip of leather, her tears dried. *I have to be strong,* she told herself. *I have to save myself until he comes for me.* Only hours before, Tshingee had been her captor . . .

and now she prayed he would be her savior.

When Tshingee first returned to the camp sight and found Deborah gone, he thought she had fled. But upon investigation of the area, he realized it was not so. Nothing had been touched in the camp since he'd gone. The leather tunic and moccasins he had given her lay in the same place she'd left them. His Deborah would not have been so foolish as to go into the forest without the moccasins and certainly not at sunset.

On the far bank, Tshingee discovered evidence that someone had been dragged from the water . . . someone unconscious. He murmured an English curse beneath his breath. His Deborah had been under his care; she had trusted him. Someone had taken her . . . and it was not the white men who pursued them. A chilling shiver trickled down his spine as he observed the bent branches and soft indentations of moccasins in the humus near the bank.

The day's light was fading fast when Tshingee noticed a strange smudge of color on a sycamore leaf. He knelt, picking the leaf. He smelled the smudge, then tasted it.

Tshingee's blood turned to ice. Mohawks from the north! A Mohawk raiding party had taken his Deborah. Mohawks, the eaters of men . . .

Deborah observed the harsh-tongued redskins through heavy-lidded eyes. She was too frightened to go to sleep, yet she was so weary she could barely think. There were five men in all, counting her captor.

They lit no campfire so it was difficult for her to see

them in the darkness, but still she watched. False Face was involved in an argument with a tall man wearing red breeches and a cocked hat over a head of long black hair. This man seemed to be the leader; he was the one who had sent two men from the camp earlier — to stand guard, she supposed.

The only man left was a solemn redman in a leather loincloth carrying an ancient matchlock musket and a silver-gilded powder horn. Around his middle he wore a leather belt strung with a dozen or so dried disks. Deborah didn't know what they were, but she assumed they were some sort of prized possessions. When he approached, she dropped her eyelids, hoping he would think she was asleep.

"Jolie," he murmured, catching a lock of her hair.

She lifted her dark lashes. "Could I have some water, I'm thirsty. *Eau potable?"*

He crouched in front of her, stroking her cheek with the back of his hand. His thin, solemn face was freshly painted in hues of blue and brown. *"Mon frère,* False Face, say you are his," he said thoughtfully. "But perhaps Laughing Man will challenge him, *non?"*

"Water, please," she repeated.

The Mohawk lifted his water skin that hung around his neck and offered it to her. "And what does the *putain* whore give Laughing Man in return for this gift of *eau potable?"*

She grasped the water skin and brought it to her mouth. "Nothing!" she replied as the water bubbled from the leather neck, moistening her lips.

The Mohawk snatched the water bag from her hands. "Then you will have nothing, *ma chère."*

Deborah trembled, her eyes fixed on the hideously painted face. He was unsmiling. "I suppose I'm not so

97

thirsty, after all," she said quietly.

Laughing Man took a long pull of the water, letting some of it dribble down his chin. Deborah watched, her tongue darting out to moisten her parched lips. Realizing he was just tantalizing her, she squeezed her eyes shut, leaning back against a tree trunk. For several moments he remained crouched there, then he stood and walked away. Like the others, he moved silently. Only the whoosh of air that brushed her cheeks told her he was gone.

Feeling she was safe, at least for the time being, Deborah wriggled, trying to make herself more comfortable. Her hands were tied behind her so tightly at the wrists that her arms tingled from lack of circulation. Forcing herself to relax, a portion of the painful pinpricks subsided.

She was sleepy now . . . and cold. It was the third week in September and her thin embroidered shift did little to ward off the autumn air that crept along the ground. Another week and the chill that had settled on the forest tonight would be prevalent through the day.

Deborah couldn't help wondering if she'd still be alive in a week. She knew the thought was gruesome — certainly unladylike in Celia's opinion — but it was a distinct possibility. She was positive these men were not of Tshingee's tribe. Charlie MacCloud had once told her that there were more Indian tribes in the Colonies and to the west of them than there were countries in the rest of the world. Whoever these redskins were, they were unfriendly.

What purpose did they have in capturing her? They were all under the impression she was a whore. Would they take her back to their home to serve as one, or would they trade her to some other tribe for muskets or trinkets?

Hot tears formed in her eyes again. *Where are you, Tshingee?* she pleaded silently. *Please help, me . . . I'm so frightened.*

Sometime well after midnight, Deborah drifted into a fitful sleep. She was startled awake when someone knocked her in the side with the toe of his moccasin.

Deborah thrashed out at her attacker, and laughter echoed in the camp, followed by a swift cuff to her head.

It was her captor. Her grasped her arm and yanked her to her feet. *"Viens!* We go."

Deborah stumbled. It was barely dawn. The orange and red rays of sunlight were just beginning to peak through the curtain of the forest. *He didn't come for me,* was her first thought as she became fully awake. *Tshingee didn't come for me.*

All five Indian braves were there, talking among themselves and strapping their assorted bags and weapons to their sides and around their necks. Seeing her on her feet, Laughing Man approached her and False Face.

Laughing Man ignored her presence, stepping up to her captor to speak. He spoke in the tongue of his own people, so she couldn't make out what he said.

False Face, his painted mask carefully restored, shook his head emphatically and began to tie her to a short tether.

Laughing Man barked several more sentences, lifting first the musket he carried, then the powder horn. Deborah's lower lip trembled. *My God,* she thought. *They're bartering for me!* She prayed her captor would not give her up. He was frightening, but not as frightening at the man with the solemn face.

99

Laughing Man stomped his foot, pointing first at her and then to himself. Finally, he untied the sinew belt around his waist and raised it high in the air. It was the belt Deborah had noticed the night before. The one with the dried disks.

She blinked, the bile suddenly rising in her throat. Her mouth was so dry that she couldn't swallow. *Ears! They were dried human ears!* She turned her face away in horror and the braves laughed in unison.

"This can't be happening," Deborah murmured. "It just can't be," she repeated beneath her breath. The sound of her own voice was soothing. Slowly she gained control of herself.

The two Mohawk braves argued back and forth for another minute or two, then Laughing Man stomped off, shouting over his shoulder.

Smug, Deborah's captor gave a final tug on her tether line and shoved her forward. *"Presse-toi, putain!* Walk!" he bellowed.

Deborah stumbled forward, obeying. What else could she do? A whimper escaped her lips, betraying her as she stumbled and went down on one knee. How long had it been since she'd had a drink of water or something to eat?

"Walk!" False Face commanded, dragging her to her feet. "Walk or this warrior will slit your whore's throat!"

Tshingee, Deborah cried out silently as she started forward again. *Tshingee, where are you?* Had they gotten him first? Was he dead somewhere on the trail? No, she refused to believe it, because if it was true, there was no hope left.

The sun rose in the September sky and the raiding party moved north at an undying pace. Midmorning

100

the group stopped and the leader instructed a man whose head was shaven to go back the way they had come. The Mohawks spoke in their own tongue, so Deborah didn't understand what they were saying. All she knew was that suddenly they were wary. Something had happened to alarm them.

The brave with the bald head sprinted back down the path and the other men and Deborah moved north. Again, Laughing Man offered her water, but this time False Face knocked the water skin to the ground. Deborah's heart pounded wildly as she watched the precious liquid spill onto the ground and seep into the soil. The braves argued, their voices soft but threatening, but again, Laughing Man backed down. Deborah tried to retrieve the water skin but her captor gave her a vicious kick.

"Presse-toi!" he ordered. "Keep walking or die . . ."

Tshingee moved silently though the forest, his powerful legs pumping, his arms swinging without effort. The skin on his bare chest pricked with sensation as he listened to the sound of his own pounding heart and the sway of the trees in the morning breeze.

He had discovered the Mohawk camp well after midnight. His first impulse was to rush in and rescue his Red Bird. He had seen her through the darkness, her arms tied behind her, her body slumped over in restless sleep. But Tshingee knew that an attack without a plan would be deadly. There were five Mohawk braves, one Lenni Lenape. It if wasn't for Deborah, Tshingee knew he could overpower them by wit and a little good fortune. But Deborah's life was at stake and therefore his brother's. Tshingee would not rely on luck today to best his enemy. Patience followed by the element of surprise was the solution.

At dawn when the camp moved, Tshingee skirted the group, surveying their strengths and weaknesses. He had watched with trepidation as the two braves had fought over Deborah. It had taken all of his willpower to remain silent when her captor struck her, but Tshingee remained in control of his emotions. His Red Bird's eyes still snapped with a fire that could not be extinguished. She had been beaten and bruised, but not defeated.

Tshingee's chest swelled with pride as he slowed to a walk and sipped from his water skin. He had met few women in his life whose spirit was as strong as Deborah's. He could not help wondering if Suuklan could remain so strong under such circumstances. Suuklan was a young Lenni Lenape maiden in his village who he intended to make his wife in the spring. Suuklan was a beautiful woman, but she did not strike the embers of his heart . . . not the way Deborah did.

At the sound of footsteps on the deer trail, Tshingee stiffened, flattening his body against the rough bark of a grandfather pine tree. Sealing the neck of his water bag, he listened. One man approached. Tshingee smiled. So, the Mohawks had finally realized they were being followed.

Breathing easily, Tshingee's eyes drifted shut. He became one with the forest, as his grandfather had taught him. He cleared his mind of all but the sound of the soft, murmuring breeze and the smell of the musty foliage. Tshingee played the game so well that the shaven-haired Mohawk walked past him. With one swift movement Tshingee brought down the dull end of his hand axe against the back of the man's skull.

The Mohawk slid to the ground, never knowing he had been hit.

Slipping his axe back into his belt, Tshingee stepped over the Mohawk raider and raced down the path. One dead marauder, he thought. Four to go . . .

"What is it? Why are we stopping?" Deborah panted.

False Face gripped her arm. "If you are not quiet, *ma chèrie,* I will not have to kill you. My comrades will do it for me."

Deborah looked up at the three other braves. The leader spoke, signaling a second brave. The brave nodded, barked an answer, and sprinted down the path they'd come.

"Where is the other man?" Deborah dared to whisper.

False Face rolled his eyes heavenward. "It is true, white women are as stupid as my brother Laughing Man says. Can you not see, our *ami* has not returned?"

"If Laughing Man is your brother, why does he argue with you over me?"

False Face smiled, his hideously painted face wrinkling in animation. *"Mon frère* likes white women. He owns seven."

"You want to give me up?" she whispered.

"Non—not at least until the price is higher."

The leader started through the woods and False Face pushed Deborah forward, giving her no chance to speak again. She had to muster all of her energy just to keep walking. Slowly the tether rope between her and False Face grew taut and she had to run to keep up with him. Now there was only she, the leader, and the two brothers, False Face and Laughing Man.

Tshingee leaped high from a tree limb, giving a hoot of victory as he came crashing down on the second Mohawk brave. The Mohawk whipped out his knife as he fell beneath his attacker's weight, but Tshingee moved too swiftly. The brave's eyes widened in terror as Tshingee twisted the man's arm and the knife plunged into his chest. A final twist and the Mohawk died, never getting a chance to call out a warning to his companions.

Rolling off the dead man, Tshingee wiped his bloody hand on a mound of moss. He whispered a prayer of thanks, combining it with a prayer that would send the Mohawk's spirit heavenward. He doubted any Mohawk could get as far as the gates of heaven, but he held that decision for the Holy Father.

Running easily along the path, Tshingee dove into the leaves as another Mohawk came racing around the bend in the old deer trail. Just before the brave passed Tshingee he stopped in midstep, his hand sliding to the knife on his belt.

Tshingee breathed deeply, watching the Mohawk. It was the man with the musket and silver power horn, the man who had tried to buy Deborah from her captor.

The moment the Mohawk walked past Tshingee, the Lenni Lenape brave bounded to his feet, his knife drawn.

Laughing Man snarled, his eyes growing wide in anticipation of the fight. The two men circled cautiously. Tshingee let him make the first move and then leaped, kicking his opponent in the mouth. Blood spewed from the Mohawk's nose, and in the confusion, Tshingee sank his knife into the man's chest.

Laughing Man fell forward in utter surprise, clutching the knife in his breast. He rolled onto his back and went limp.

Tshingee rested his foot on the man's chest and extracted his knife, wiping it on the Mohawk's breeches. The musket, the powder horn, and some of the ears on the belt told Tshingee that the raiding party had been busy.

In disgust Tshingee walked away, then on second thought, he returned to the motionless body and cut the belt of ears off the Mohawk's waist. Digging a shallow hole in the soft humus along the path, he buried the human remains. Satisfied, he started down the path again.

When Laughing Man did not return, the Mohawk leader grew nervous. Stopping near a trickling spring, he shouted at False Face and reached for Deborah's tether rope.

Deborah shrank back. "No! Leave me alone! Don't let him take me, False Face!"

The leader lifted his knife from his belt and raised it to False Face's throat. Begrudgingly, her captor handed the leather strap to his leader.

Just as the Mohawk leader gained possession of the white woman, an arrow whizzed through the air. Deborah screamed and the man fell backward, dragging her down on top of him. Screaming, she scrambled to get up, horrified by the lifeless eyes staring up at her. Crawling across the ground, she pushed herself to her feet to run, but False Face had caught the end of her tether strap.

He lifted her with one swift movement, raising his knife to her throat. Terrified, Deborah struggled. What was happening? Who was shooting at them?

Then he appeared and she ceased to struggle. "Tshingee!" Deborah cried out. "Help me!" She didn't know where he had come from or how he had found her but he had come to rescue her.

Tshingee held his bow, the string and arrow resting against his cheek, poised to shoot.

False Face's breath was hot and sour on Deborah's cheek. "Stop!" he shouted. "Or I kill the white whore."

Tshingee lowered the bow in a slow, fluid motion. His ebony eyes were fixed on the Mohawk's.

Deborah trembled. Never had she seen such wicked vengeful eyes. She almost felt sorry for False Face.

"Ne nipauwi," Tshingee warned in Lenni Lenape. "Harm her and you will put a curse upon your family for years to come." He nearly smiled when he saw the Mohawk stiffen. They were a superstitious lot and he intended to play upon that. "Her father is a great chief among his people. He will hunt you down and take your women. He will spill your life's blood in the lap of your children."

"Enough!" False Face shouted. "You do not frighten this man!"

"Tshingee! Look out!" Deborah shouted. "Behind you!"

Tshingee spun around to find the man who had worn the belt of ears preying down upon him with a long, glistening knife. Dropping to the ground. the Lenni Lenape brave rolled, tripping his attacker with his feet. The Mohawk went down on one knee, slashing out at Tshingee. The man's entire chest was soaked with blood.

False Face dropped Deborah's tether and ran to his brother's aid.

"Tshingee!" she warned.

Tshingee looked to see False Face heading straight for him, a knife clutched in his teeth. Grasping the bleeding Mohawk by his hair, the Lenni Lenape brave managed to climb on top of him and plunge his knife into the man's chest. This time Laughing Man fell back, his eyes rolling back in his head in final surrender.

False Face screamed in a high-pitched cry of attack and hit Tshingee, knocking him off his brother. Over and over the two rolled, first one on top, then the other. Tshingee was a superior fighter, but the Mohawk's ability seemed to match the Lenni Lenape's.

The two struggled, first one gaining control, then the other, until Deborah began to doubt the outcome. Then suddenly Tshingee was on top and False Face's knife was in the leaves. False Face closed his eyes, murmuring a prayer.

Tshingee chuckled. "Have I bested you? Has this Lenni Lenape warrior beaten this Mohawk?"

The Mohawk's eyes flew open in surprise. Then he nodded ever so slightly.

"I think it is your lucky day, Man in the Mask." Tshingee loosened his grip on the Mohawk. "Because you fight well and because you did not harm my woman, I will set you free."

False Face stared in confusion at the Lenni Lenape brave. "You will let this man go?"

Tshingee's eyes narrowed. "Only if you swear to leave in peace, to return to your people in the north and tell them what a wise, skillful warrior Tshingee of

107

the Wolf Clan is."

False Face nodded in understanding. "Will you tell your village what a wise and skillful warrior of the Mohawks you met in this forest?"

Tshingee smiled, rising slowly to his feet. "Go, before I change my mind."

False Face leaped to his feet. "Will you let this defeated man take his brother's body with him?" He nodded in the direction of Laughing Man's lifeless form.

Tshingee nodded. "Go."

Deborah watched in amazement as Tshingee allowed his enemy to lift his brother onto his shoulder and go in peace. The short, stocky Mohawk raised a hand in salute to the Lenni Lenape warrior and then turned and ran, disappearing into the forest.

Deborah stood for a moment, stunned, then suddenly she was running . . . running into the arms of her savage.

Chapter Eight

Tshingee met Deborah halfway, his arms outstretched. "Deborah," he groaned, burying his face in the hollow of her shoulder. *"Maata-wischasi,* my Red Bird. Do not be afraid. I am here."

"I knew you would come," she insisted, choking back a sob. "I knew you wouldn't let them take me away!"

Tshingee kissed her tear-stained cheeks, turning her so that he might cut the leather strips that bound her arms behind her back. Letting the sinew fall to the ground he rubbed her wrists, trying to bring back the circulation. "Shhh," he soothed huskily. "Don't weep, my brave *hokkuaa.* You are safe, now. Tshingee of the Wolf Clan will never let anyone take you away from him again."

Deborah looped her arms around Tshingee's neck and he drew her against his hard, sinewy chest. He kissed the lobe of her ear, then her partially exposed shoulder. The shift she wore was torn in shreds, exposing much of her left breast and the entire length of her lithe thighs.

Deborah trembled in his arms, holding him tightly. "I'm . . . I'm so thirsty," she whispered.

Tshingee lifted his water skin to her lips and let her

drink. "Not too much," he warned. "Some now. Some later."

Panting, she let him draw away the skin. "I feel so dirty, so soiled."

"Can you walk?" He stroked her back, easing the stiff muscles of her quivering shoulders. Tshingee had no desire to take advantage of Deborah, but it seemed natural that he should kiss away the tears, that he should stroke away the fear.

"I . . . I think so," she breathed. She looked up at him and their lips met in a soft kiss of reassurance. When the kiss deepened, Deborah gave no resistance. The taste of him was overpowering, intoxicating. In utter abandon, she wove her fingers through his midnight black hair, straining against him.

Tshingee withdrew breathlessly. He had to keep reminding himself that this was a white woman, not some Lenni Lenape maiden that he could make his own. He studied her face with a dark, steady gaze, leaning to plant a final kiss on the tiny birthmark near her mouth. "There is a river nearby; we can go there and wash," he whispered, not trusting his own voice.

The air was so thick with strained desire that it was palpable. Tshingee could feel her need for him . . . he prayed he could resist. "Can you walk?"

"Yes, yes, I can." She took a deep breath and, clutching his arm, started to walk. She took three steps and tripped before he swept her into his arms. Deborah dared a smile. "I said I can walk," she repeated, resting her hands on his broad shoulders. She made no effort to escape his embrace.

"I know. But I want to carry you. I am sorry for what has happened." He started through the woods. "I am responsible. I should not have left you alone. I

110

should have known the raiding party was so near."

Deborah rested her head on Tshingee's shoulder, listening to the comforting sound of his breathing. "How could you have known?" she defended. She stroked his arm, marveling at the feel of his hard, banded muscles beneath her fingertips.

Tshingee shuddered inwardly. Her innocent caress left his flesh tingling and hot. How much more of this sweet torture could he stand? He wanted this woman like no woman before, and yet he knew he could not have her. Not ever. The safe return of this white woman was his only hope for rescuing his brother.

"They took me from the river."

"I know." Tshingee ducked a low-hanging branch. He cradled her in his arms, enjoying the feel of her soft breasts pressed against him.

"But they didn't . . . they didn't touch me. They hit me a few times, but they didn't *hurt* me, not like I thought they were going to."

Tshingee nodded in understanding. "It is a white man's custom to rape women. Even Mohawks have morals. To take a woman against her will is terrible bad medicine."

She smiled, reaching out to stroke his bronzed, chiseled cheek. "And it is *you* we call the savage," she whispered. This time it was Deborah who leaned to kiss Tshingee's mouth.

"Deborah, we cannot do this." The sound of bubbling water filled the air as he stepped through the trees. A narrow branch of some river stretched out before them. "Don't you understand?" He eased her to the ground, but she clung to him.

"All I understand is that no one has ever cared about me like you do. You tell me you are my enemy and yet

111

you have more respect for my well-being than my own father." She lifted her chin to stare into his dark eyes; her hands spanned his bare chest. "All I understand is that no man has ever made me feel like *this*." She took his hand, pressing it to her left breast.

Tshingee paused, feeling the pounding of her heart beneath his palm. Taking her hand, he laid it over his own heart. "Like this?" he asked.

Deborah's chest rose and fell rapidly. "Kiss me again. I ask for no promises. I know what can and cannot be, but just once in my life I want someone to truly care about me." Tears of sadness and longing welled up in her dark eyes. "I want you to make love to me as Thomas Hogarth, my betrothed, will never be able to."

Deborah's words tore at Tshingee's heart. "You don't know what you offer."

"I offer the only thing that is mine to give."

"But the man you will marry, it is his . . ."

"I was sold to Tom just as surely as False Face would have sold me to his brother when the price was high enough," she interrupted, frowning. "Don't you see, Tshingee? I have never had any control over my own life until now." She glanced toward the river, too unsure of herself to meet his gaze. "I'm afraid I'm in love with you . . ."

Tshingee pulled her hard against him. He ached for her so badly that it was a physical hurt. He could not tell her that he was in love with her; he had to be strong for the both of them. "We've been through much today, Red Bird. Let us bathe."

Deborah looked up at Tshingee with open surprise. Then she looked away. She felt as if someone had thrown a bucket of icy water on her. How could she have been so foolish as to say such a thing? She pulled away from him and walked toward the river. He didn't care for her. What had ever given her the impression that he did? Tshingee was just like all the other men in her life. She was here because he was using her to get his brother back. Nothing more. It was as he had said—she was the enemy.

Lifting her soiled shift over her head, Deborah let it drift to the ground. She didn't care that Tshingee saw her naked. He had turned down her brazen offering; it was obvious he was uninterested in her. She pointed her toes and dove into the cold water.

Tshingee took a deep breath. It was all he could do to force himself to stand still as Deborah removed her clothing. He knew he had hurt her and he was sorry, but he was at a loss as to what to say, what to do. Her words echoed in his mind . . . *I'm afraid I'm in love with you.* Under any other circumstances her words would have sent his soul soaring. No one had ever touched his heart like his little Red Bird. But he had to be strong, for her, for himself, and for John. It was the only way.

Well after dark Deborah lay stretched out on a hide mat, another pulled on top of her. A campfire crackled and spit emitting a bright orange-red flame. On the other side of the fire sat Tshingee, his legs crossed beneath him, his face solemn. He had said little since the afternoon, and then he had spoken only in short sentences. "We will sleep here. Eat this. Cover yourself with this."

Deborah's head spun in confusion. Now that a little time had passed, she knew Tshingee was right. It was better that they not become emotionally involved. If he made love to her now, she would spend the rest of

113

her life comparing Tom with him. She would spend the rest of her life knowing what true love felt like, but never being able to grasp it again.

A chilling southeasterly breeze blew in off the river and Deborah snuggled deeper beneath the warm hide blanket. An autumn storm seemed to be brewing far in the distance. The forest quivered with the sounds of the night, the rustling of leaves, the call of a distant owl, the creeping footsteps of unidentified nocturnal animals in the underbrush.

"I'm sorry," Deborah suddenly said. "You were right, Tshingee. It was wrong of me to put you in such a position. You've been honest with me since the first day we met."

Tshingee lifted his head and stared at her through the iridescent flames. "No one has offered me a greater gift." There was a husky catch in his voice. "I am only sorry I could not accept."

Deborah sighed. "I wish I hadn't been born Deborah Montague. I wished I'd been born Red Bird, of the Lenni Lenape. Then it would be all right, wouldn't it? If I wasn't English? If I wasn't white?"

A sad smile rose on his face. "You forget that I am part Englishman." He shook his head, poking a stick into the flames of the fire. "It just is not in the stars, Red Bird. We are all here for a purpose. We are not expected to understand God's ways, only accept them."

Deborah rose up off the ground, hugging the hide blanket to her breasts. "God? I thought you were a heathen."

He chuckled. "No more than you. It was my mother's wish as well as my father's that my brother and I be brought up as Christians."

114

"I knew John believed in Christ but—"

"But because I wear a loinskin and carry a bow and quiver you thought—"

She chuckled, cutting off his words. "It sounds so silly when you say it. It's just that I was always told—"

"You were always told the red man was a filthy, heathen savage," he finished for her.

She laughed aloud, her voice echoing in the trees. A startled bird took flight above her head and fluttered off, its wings beating rhythmically in the air. Once again Deborah was reminded that she had never known a man like Tshingee. He was such a puzzlement! Every hour they were together, another layer of his true self was revealed. She smiled at him through the darkness. "Good night, Tshingee of the Wolf Clan." She lay down and pulled the hide blanket up over her shoulders.

"Good night, my Red Bird," he answered softly.

"Wake up, Deborah." Tshingee shook her gently. "Deborah, you must wake up."

Deborah snuggled deeper beneath the warm pelt, vaguely aware of the tender voice calling her name.

"Red Bird!" He shook her harder.

"Yes." She sighed sleepily.

"You must get up. We have to hurry. A storm . . ."

Deborah blinked, suddenly becoming aware of the howling wind and the rustle of tree limbs above. The morning air was cold on her face. "A storm?" She looked up at Tshingee kneeling over her. The sky was dark and ominous.

"We have to find shelter."

She sat up, rubbing her eyes. "Shelter? Where?"

Now fully awake, she could feel the change in the pressure in the air. The wind was coming from the southeast, strong and blustering. The smell of rain was thick and cloying.

"An abandoned Shawnee village, but we must hurry." He handed her the moccasins and tunic he had picked up off the riverbank the evening the Mohawks had taken her. "It is many miles to the village."

Pushing aside the pelt, Deborah shivered. She quickly donned the leather tunic over her tattered shift. She hopped on one foot and then the other to put on the moccasins. Her teethed chattered and she rubbed her bare arms briskly. "It's c-cold out here."

"Wrap the hide around your shoulders." He looked up from where he knelt packing his bag of cooking utensils. "One corner will have a tie. Slip it through the hole in the opposite corner."

"That's better," Deborah answered, tying the hide tightly around her shoulders. "What can I do to help?'

"Take the water skins and fill them both." He began to roll up his sleeping hide.

Picking up Tshingee's water bag and one that had belonged to one of the dead Mohawks, she ran down to the river. Getting her footing on a flat rock, she filled the skins quickly. The river was already beginning to run faster, churning white and frothy as it gained momentum. Deborah raced back to Tshingee. "I'm ready," she declared, slipping the Mohawk's water bag over her shoulder.

"Let's go." Tshingee led the way and Deborah followed.

The two headed northwest, leaving the river behind. The wind beat at their backs, blowing brush and loose branches in their path. When the rain finally came, it

116

was hard and pelting, stinging Deborah's face. The trees bent and swayed beneath the southeasterly gusts, and leaves were stripped from their branches and sent sailing into the air.

Tshingee caught Deborah's arm and walked beside her when the gusts became stronger. They had been walking nearly an hour.

"How far?" Deborah shouted above the howl of the wind. "It's gaining on us!"

She didn't use the word *hurricane*. She saw no need. It was obvious to her that Tshingee already knew what they were up against. If they didn't get to shelter before the eye of the storm reached them, they didn't stand a chance of surviving. She had seen too many hurricanes on the Chesepeake. She knew what they could do. Livestock was carried off, roofs from barns and homes were lifted and hurled into the air to splinter into a million shards of flying debris.

"It's been many years since I've been here. Not since I was a young buck."

She leaned to speak into his ear. "You mean you don't know?"

"Not far," he shouted with confidence.

"But if I can't see anything, you can't see anything!"

"My moccasins will lead the way!"

Deborah lowered her head, stiffening her back to remain upright as the wind pushed her from behind. She was so cold and wet that her teeth chattered and her hands shook. A fallen branch sailed over her head, nearly striking them both before it hit a tree and fell to the ground.

Tshingee wrapped an arm around her shoulders. "Keep walking," he shouted as more objects hurled through the air. "I recognize that tree."

117

Deborah was skeptical, but she kept moving, the warmth of Tshingee's arm around her giving her the strength. The minutes turned to hours as they plodded forward. The rain was coming down so heavily that she could barely see a step ahead of her. She relied on Tshingee to guide her.

"There!" he shouted, pointing into the darkness.

Deborah squinted. She still couldn't see anything, then suddenly a dome-shaped structure loomed ahead of them.

"Hurry!" Tshingee shouted. "Step down inside!"

Running beside him, Deborah held tightly to his waist. When he lifted a door flap, she ducked in, stepping down a good foot and a half. She fell to the hard dirt floor, panting. Tshingee came in behind her, slamming the door flap behind him.

"The tie from your cloak! Give it to me!"

She fumbled in the darkness with the sinew tie. "Here!

Taking it, Tshingee tied the door tightly to the frame. "There." He slid to the ground, out of breath. "We will be safe here," he panted.

"Are you sure?" She looked at the wooden structure above her head doubtfully. The house had been built of saplings bent and tied to make a dome frame with bark attached in shingle style.

"This wigwam has withstood many a September storm. It will stand many more." He brushed at a lock of wet hair plastered to her cheek. "You are cold. I will build a fire."

"H — how?" she chattered.

He crawled past her to the far wall. "When we leave a village, we always leave our homes stocked for travelers' use." He picked up a bundle of dry kindling.

"When we leave, we will replenish."

Deborah squinted in the darkness, watching Tshingee as he took his tinderbox from his bag and began to layer the faggots carefully. From his pack he brought out a lump of dry moss. In seconds he had a small flame flickering in the pit in the center of the wigwam. He added several more sticks, carefully nurturing the fire until it blazed.

Deborah smiled, looking up at him. The gold and yellow flames cast shadows across his handsome face, illuminating the curve of his lips and the lines of his cheekbones and forehead.

"Take off the cloak," he told her. "It is wet and will only make you colder." Deborah fumbled with the wet hide, but he came to her, lifting the burden from her shoulders. He hung it high on a peg in the ceiling. "Your tunic. Give that to me too. Then roll out the dry hide in my pack."

Without hesitation, Deborah got to her knees and removed the garment. She rolled out the deer hide from Tshingee's pack and sat down on it. Her torn shift was damp too, but it was thin enough that it was already drying from the heat of the campfire in the firepit.

Deborah watched with fascination as Tshingee removed his leather leggings, his tunic, and knee-high moccasins. He sat down beside her wearing nothing but a leather loincloth. "Your moccasins, take them off too," he told her, reaching down to untie the laces.

When he removed the sodden foot coverings, she wiggled her toes, enjoying the heat of the fire. The wind howled in full force outside the small wigwam, but here she was safe and warm.

Deborah leaned forward, her toes pointed as she

119

stretched to warm her hands. She watched as Tshingee added a small log to the fire and then sat down beside her again. The smoke rose up in a straight line and escaped from the dome-shaped house by way of a hole in the center of the roof.

"Thank you," she murmured, staring into the flames.

"There is no need to thank me." His bare arm brushed hers. "I told you, as long as you are with me, you are my responsibility. No harm will come to you again if it is in my power to stop it."

Deborah leaned back, enjoying the feel of his sinewy arm brushing hers. Seated so close like this, she could feel the heat his body radiated. She could smell that odd, woodsy scent that clung to him, making her senses reel.

Deborah could feel Tshingee watching her. Slowly she turned to face him. Her hand found his. It was obvious to Deborah that he wanted her . . . as much as she wanted him. With slow deliberateness she leaned to kiss his mouth.

Tshingee was suddenly powerless, his self-control gone. He accepted her advance hungrily, sampling the sweet honey of her lips. The pounding of the rain outside blended with the pounding of his own heart. John was forgotten for the moment. All that mattered was the two of them here in this dark, warm wigwam. All that was important was that he was in love with this white woman and he wanted to show her what it was to love.

Deborah settled her hands on his bare shoulders. "You're not going to tell me no this time, are you?" she asked, planting innocent kisses down the length of his neck.

He groaned aloud. "I know no good can—"

"Shhhh," she hushed, pressing her finger to his lips. "Don't be so gallant, Tshingee. Just love me . . ."

Gently, he lowered her onto her back. "You are so beautiful, *ki-ti-hi*," he murmured, his breath hot in her ear. "You are the light in this man's darkness."

Deborah smiled, peering up at him, her fingers laced through his ebony hair. "Are you to woo me, too?" she whispered.

His reply was a deep, satisfying, lingering kiss.

A heavy-limbed aching filled Deborah's being as Tshingee's hot, probing tongue invaded the cavern of her mouth. He stroked her pale shoulders, ripping the remains of her shift until he freed her of the constricting garment. She gasped in surprise when his fingertips first met the hard, erect peaks of her breasts. Moaning softly, she caressed the breadth of his back and shoulders as he brought his mouth down to the arched fullness of her breast.

A surge of molten throbbing joy raced through Deborah's limbs and she arched her back in encouragement. "Mmmm, that's wonderful," she breathed, lifting her dark lashes to watch Tshingee suckle her breast.

Rolling onto his side, Tshingee buried his face in the valley between her breasts, his hands spanning the width of her flat stomach. He played her with his fingertips, caressing her hipbones and inner thighs with a touch so feather-light that Deborah wondered if she was imagining the subtle waves of desire that gave way to a burning deep within her.

Her breath coming ragged, she reached out to stroke the bulge beneath his loinskin, but he caught her hand, kissing her palm. "Lie back," he whispered. He kissed her cheekbones, her eyelids, the soft curve of her lips. "Lie back and enjoy my gift, *ki-ti-hi*. The first time must always be special."

Relaxing on the mat, Deborah's eyes drifted shut. Her entire body quaked with a consuming fire as he kissed her deeply, stroking the mounds of her breasts. Leaving a trail of smoldering want, Tshingee kissed his way down the length of her neck, nibbling at her collar bone. He stroked her arms, massaging her fingertips. "Relax," he murmured in her ear. "Relax and enjoy. This is a time of rejoicing."

With a tantalizing exactness Tshingee made his way down the length of her body, caressing every inch of her pale, quivering flesh. He stroked her thighs, her knees, the tips of her toes.

Then, slipping off his loinskin, Tshingee lowered his body over Deborah's. Her eyes drifted open, a languid smile on her lips. She lowered her hands to his hard, muscular buttocks, massaging them with a steady hand as she moved beneath him, guided by some unknown rhythm.

"I've never felt so . . . I . . . I don't know."

Tshingee kissed her damp brow. "Shhh, no talking, just ride the sea of pleasure," he whispered hoarsely.

Closing her eyes, Deborah continued to lift her hips, enjoying the unfamiliar feel of his hard maleness nestled between her thighs. She was warm and wet, caught in a tide of intense, undeniable sensation. Moving faster, she moaned softly, wanting, needing . . . something mysteriously unknown.

Gently, Tshingee parted her thighs with his knee. Catching her mouth with his, he delved deep within her in one long thrust. Deborah rose up in shock, in relief, taking time only to catch her breath before she began to move beneath him.

Laughing with relief, she hugged him tightly, letting him carry her over one rise then the next. Higher and higher they climbed, her body flaming with an all-encompassing passion. Then suddenly, her breath caught in her throat and she cried wildly in utter surprise. Gripping Tshingee's shoulders, spasm after spasm of sweet ecstasy consumed her. She was so alive with startling sensation that she was barely aware as Tshingee drove home with one final thrust and collapsed in fulfillment.

Gasping for breath, Deborah caught his head between her palms, lifting his face to peer into his dark eyes. "That," she panted, "is the most wonderful thing I've ever felt in my life!"

Tshingee laughed, his voice still husky and strained. *"You* are the most wonderful thing this man has ever felt in his life." He kissed her mouth, rolling off her to rest at her side. He flung his arm over her bare breasts, brushing his lips against her dewy shoulder. "It's not supposed to be that good the first time, my Red Bird."

Deborah laughed, flinging herself back onto the pelt. *"You mean it gets better?"*

Chapter Nine

"I can't believe *that's* what women don't like about marriage." Deborah attacked her handful of dried berries greedily.

The hurricane still raged, but inside the wigwam time had lost all meaning. To Deborah and Tshingee no one existed in the world but the two of them. Nothing else mattered.

Tshingee looked up from where he tended the fire. "It is not the same for everyone, my Red Bird. We fit together as one." He demonstrated with his hands, intertwining his fingers. "Matches are made in the heavens between two souls."

Deborah's dark eyes narrowed thoughtfully. "Have you made love to many women?" When he didn't answer immediately, she prodded him with her bare foot.

"A few." He sat down beside her on the hide mat, taking some of the berries from her palm.

"And was it the same with them? Did you make them all feel the way you made me feel?"

Tshingee nibbled on a berry, a sparkle of amusement in his ebony eyes. "You ask too many questions, woman." He reached out to toy with the tip of her rosy nipple. Both had remained unclothed after they made love.

Deborah giggled. "And why not? I'm just trying to understand. My sister Martha says it disgusts her when her husband demands his rights."

"His rights?" Tshingee scoffed. "No man or woman has a right to anyone. We give of our bodies freely."

"So tell that to Lord Danforth." She finished her berries and brushed her palms together. "No sooner does my sister give birth to one child, then he gets her with another."

"That is not good for a woman's body. The white man does not treasure his mothers as he should."

"But what's there to do to prevent it except abstinence?" She stroked the length of his sinewy arm. "Were you my husband," she said boldly, "I don't know that I could refrain."

"You are such an innocent, my Red Bird." Tshingee caught a lock of her dark hair and wrapped it around and around his finger. "There are ways to prevent birth. Our people have only two children. Our method has worked for centuries."

"Method?" Deborah's brow creased. "You don't —"

"There is a plant, an herb that our women take each month. It prevents unwanted children."

"What . . . what if I were to get with child now?" Her gaze met his.

"When was your last woman's time?"

Deborah blushed. "Th . . . three weeks ago."

He shook his head. "There will be no child."

"But . . . but what if there was?"

"There won't be." He kissed her soundly. He didn't want to talk of such things. He didn't even want to think about them. All he wanted was to be with Deborah here and now, the rest of the world be damned. "I told you, you ask too many questions."

"And I asked why."

"Because . . ." He pushed her back onto the mat, straddling her waist and pinning her arms down. "You are my prisoner and prisoners do not ask questions."

She sniggered. "Oh, they don't, don't they?"

He shook his head, his midnight black hair falling in a curtain around his face.

"Then what do they do?"

"They kiss their captors," he answered, swooping down to take her mouth with his.

"How much further?" Deborah picked up a stick and hurled it into the air.

The forest was littered with branches and fallen limbs as a result of the previous day's hurricane. The leafy ground was soggy and a cold wind chilled the air, but little else remained of the furious storm. Nature was forgiving. The sun had risen bright and bold in the sky, and now it was setting again.

"Tshingee," Deborah repeated, tugging playfully at his tunic. "How much further."

He looked at her, seemingly startled by her voice. Deborah sighed. He had been like this since they'd risen at dawn. Not a trace of the loving, playful man of yesterday remained. This man was dark and moody, a shadow of the man Deborah had made love with.

"Not far," Tshingee answered. "Tonight you will sleep in my mother's wigwam."

Not in yours? Deborah thought. But she didn't dare voice her fears. "Not far? Not far," she teased. "You've been saying that for hours."

He refused to take the bait and was silent again.

126

Undaunted, Deborah walked past him, humming to herself. She felt so free, so happy. She had left her shift behind in the wigwam—the only evidence of her life on her father's plantation. Instead she wore Tshingee's moccasins and tunic and the doeskin robe over her shoulders to ward off the September chill. Today she was Red Bird of the Lenni Lenape, traveling with her lover, Tshingee.

Tshingee walked lightly, his stride long and purposeful, but his heart was heavy. *What have I done?* he mused. Yesterday it had seemed so right, loving this woman. But today, in the sunlight of reality, he realized his grave error.

"What's that I hear?" Deborah asked, breaking his thoughts. "Children?"

The sound of laughter filtered through the trees. The half light of approaching dark fell upon Tshingee and Deborah like a mother's blanket.

"I told you we were not far."

Deborah slowed down, waiting for him. Suddenly she was wary. What would these people think of her? Would they blame her for John's capture? She was thankful Tshingee did not know that John's land was to be her dowry. What would *he* say then?

"Do not worry," Tshingee said, as if reading her thoughts. "My people will treat you honorably. I will explain that it is your father who has taken John and that you had nothing to do with it."

"A pawn," Deborah replied sarcastically.

Tshingee glanced at her, but said nothing. Cupping his hands around his mouth, he made a strange birdsound. A duplicate cry answered from somewhere in the distant trees.

"What was that?"

He led her over a stream and through a grove of black walnut trees, the sounds of a camp closing in around them. "The sentry. I warned him of our approach."

Deborah nodded, taking Tshingee's hand. They were almost upon the village now.

Barking dogs mingled with adult conversation and an occasional cry of a baby. Coming through the trees, Deborah's mouth gaped in wonderment. So many people! The village was alive with activity. Women cooked over fires outside their hutlike houses and children ran in circles laughing and chasing one another.

When Tshingee and Deborah were spotted, children and adults alike ran to greet them. Deborah clung to Tshingee as the villagers circled her curiously, reaching out to tug at her hair and stroke her pale flesh. Tshingee spoke quietly in his own tongue and the group took a step back.

Deborah studied the sea of red faces and dark eyes. Their skin was a deep, suntanned bronze, like Tshingee's, and they were dressed much like she was in soft leather tunics and low moccasins.

"Tshingee giis!"

Deborah looked up to see a plump Indian woman come running across the compound, her ample breasts bouncing.

"Tshingee, giis!" She pushed her way through the crowd, throwing her arms around Tshingee. She kissed him soundly on the lips, making a loud smacking noise.

Deborah took a step back, watching as Tshingee took the woman in his arms and hugged her, laughing. Deborah could feel a heat rising up her neck to color her face. *Who is this woman?* she wondered possessively. The two of them were still laughing and chattering in their native tongue. Though the Lenni Lenape woman was plump, she was heartbreakingly beautiful with a round face and stunning dark eyes. When she smiled, her features lit up with a joy few possessed. *Is all of this happiness due to Tshingee's safe return?* Deborah mused.

Finally, the woman turned and the circle of villagers parted to let her through. Tshingee grasped Deborah's forearm. "Come, Red Bird. We will wash and have our evening meal." He walked through the crowd and she followed. Some of the villagers had dispersed, but others followed in a clump just behind the new arrivals.

"That woman . . ." Deborah swallowed against her jealousy. "Is she your betrothed?" She knew she shouldn't ask. She really didn't want to know, but the words just slipped out.

Tshingee shook his head. "No." he chuckled. "That is my mother, Co-o-nah Aquewa, Snow Blanket."

Deborah's face lit up. "But she looks so young." She caught Tshingee's hand, overjoyed that he was not spoken for here in the village.

"No, she is my mother, but there is my betrothed." He lifted his hand in salute to someone ahead of them.

Deborah paled. "You . . . you didn't tell me there was someone else." On the path ahead a petite young Lenni Lenape woman waited. On a pole across her shoulders she balanced two buckets of water. She was younger than Deborah . . . not more than seventeen or eighteen.

"You didn't ask," Tshingee replied.

The young maiden set down her buckets and came

129

to Tshingee, throwing her arms around his massive shoulders. She was so tiny! She stood on her tip toes to kiss him; her lips lingered over his.

"Welcome, love," Suuklan murmured in Tshingee's ear, and ran her hand over his cheek. She spoke to him in Algonquian, the language used by the Lenni Lenape. "You bring a guest?"

"The story is long and complicated. Let us eat and drink first and then we will talk," he answered carefully.

"I've missed you."

Tshingee tugged at one of her long ebony braids. "You mean you've not been busy fending off Sikihiila's attentions?" he teased.

Deborah looked away, brushing at an imaginary speck of dirt in her eye. She was hurt and she was embarrassed. Though she couldn't understand a word the two said, it was obvious she was listening in on an intimate conversation . . . one between lovers.

Tshingee spoke a few more moments and then signaled to Deborah to come along. She followed him like a wounded hound pup. Suddenly she wanted to go home, not so much that she wanted to be there, but that she wanted to be anywhere else but here . . . with *him*.

"We'll get clean clothes, bathe at the stream, and then we will eat in my mother's wigwam." Tshingee's voice was matter-of-fact; his mind was elsewhere.

Deborah's pain turned to anger as Tshingee gathered clean clothes from his mother's wigwam and led her across the compound. By the time they reached the privacy of the running stream among the walnut trees, she was seething.

"You can put these on after you've bathed," Tshin-

130

gee told her.

Deborah snatched the soft hide dress from his hand. "You didn't tell me there was someone here you intended to marry."

Tshingee's eyes narrowed, his steady gaze turning dark with anger. "Did you ever think to ask me?"

She threw the dress to the ground and tugged her own tunic over her head, throwing it at him. One by one she plucked her moccasins off her feet and tossed them, hitting Tshingee in the chest. "If I'd known, I wouldn't have—"

"If you had known, you would have done precisely the same." He crossed his arms over his chest. "You seem to forget that *you* my chattering Red Bird, are a woman already spoken for."

"But you knew about Tom," she flung over her shoulder as she waded into the stream. "You knew the circumstances." The water was so cold that her teeth chattered as she cupped the water and let it flow over her breasts.

He laughed without amusement. "So that makes it all right?"

Deborah rubbed her skin briskly, as if she could wash away the mark the Lenni Lenape warrior had branded on her "Damn it! No, it doesn't make it right but I thought . . . You know why I did it! I thought you cared about me, you red son of a bitch!"

"My father once told me a tale of a two-headed green monster—jealousy I believe is the white man's word."

Deborah came up out of the water livid. "Jealous!" she raged. "How could I be jealous of that child? Over you?" She snatched the doeskin dress off the grass and pulled it over her head. "You kidnapped me! You came into my bedchamber and you carried me off. I was chased by dogs, kidnapped by savages that eat people, caught in a hurricane, and then raped by a heathen!"

Tshingee caught her wrists, his face equally livid. He spoke with his teeth clenched, his voice barely a whisper. *"Never*, never speak those words again. You came to me of your own free will and you know that to be true." He gripped her so tightly that his fingers bruised her flesh.

Deborah's eyes met his for a brief instant. What was that she saw there beneath his anger? Insult? Pain? No, it couldn't be. She yanked free from his grasp and swept her moccasins from the ground. Thrusting her feet into them, she stomped off.

He stood stoic for a moment, trying to gain control. He hadn't meant to fling such careless words. He hadn't meant to hurt her. It was just that now that he was back in the village, everything was tumbling down upon him again. John was still being held, Rain was begging Tshingee's attention . . . And then there was Deborah. He had made a grave error in making love to her and now he saw no way to right it. The only thing he could do was try to spare her feeling any more. At least if she was angry with him, it would help break the bond between them that he felt growing with each hour.

Suddenly it dawned on Tshingee that she was walking off. "Where are you going?" he demanded.

"Home!" she shouted, crashing through the trees.

"You can't go home! You are my prisoner, Deborah Montague!"

"Well, I don't want to be your prisoner anymore!"

Tshingee shook his head. "It is not your choice!"

132

"That's just it. Nothing is ever my choice, is it, you stupid bastard."

Realizing she was serious, Tshingee sprinted after her. "Come back before you're hurt," he barked.

"What, before wild Indians carry me off?"

Catching sight of her, Tshingee dodged a spruce tree and stepped into her path. "You are not free to go." He dropped his hands to his hips.

"I don't care about your brother! I don't care about you! All I want to do is go home!"

Tshingee didn't flinch, though her words sank to his core. "You want to home, Red Bird? Home to be sold on the auction block like a horse? You want to be a brood mare until it kills you? Who will care then? Your *husband* will have a new wife by the next planting!"

Everything he said was true. Tears flooded Deborah's eyes. "I hate you," she whispered.

"You don't hate me. You hate the reality of this life."

She pushed him so hard with her palms that he stumbled, falling backwards. "I hate you for making me see it!" Circling him, she ran off into the woods.

For an instant, Tshingee sat in the dry leaves. Had he not been so angry with her, he might have laughed. Pushing up off the ground, he ran after her, catching up with her swiftly.

"Deborah Montague, you are my prisoner." She swung her balled fist at him, but he ducked. "You are my prisoner," he stated flatly, "and you will be my prisoner until I set you free." Taking her by the waist, he lifted her and flung her over his shoulder.

Deborah kicked and screamed, pounding his back with her fists. Tears clouded her eyes and ran down her cheeks until she could no longer see. Then, in defeat, she hung limp over his shoulder.

Tshingee dumped Deborah on the dirt floor of his mother's wigwam. "Sit there, or I'll tie you up," he snapped angrily.

Snow Blanket glanced up at her son, lifting a feathery eyebrow, but said nothing, brushing past him. A moment later she returned with two wooden platters of steaming stew. She knelt in front of Deborah, pushing it into her hands. She felt compassion for the white woman with the tearstained cheeks. "Eat," she urged softly.

Deborah accepted the plate hesitantly. "Thank you," she answered, sniffing.

Tshingee stood in the entranceway of the wigwam, his arms crossed over his chest. "You serve my prisoner before you serve your own son?" he asked dryly.

"I don't like that tone of voice," Snow Blanket reprimanded in Lenni Lenape. "You are still my son. Sit down and stop trying to frighten her." She pushed his platter into his hand. "Eat before it gets cold."

Tshingee accepted the dish and sat cross-legged across from Deborah on the far side of the wigwam.

Snow Blanket fetched herself a plate and sat down next to her son. "What have you done here, my son?" she asked, glancing up at Deborah. She shook her head. It was obvious there was much between her son and the dark-haired white girl "What of John? The messenger you sent was brief."

Tshingee spooned the steamy venison into his mouth hungrily. "He is still being held for a murder he did not commit."

"And this girl? How is she tied to the thread of things?"

Tshingee studied his mother's enchanting round face. "It is Deborah's father who wanted John's land. He is the accuser."

"You ask for an exchange of prisoners then?"

He nodded. "I could think of no better way. You know John's feelings on bloodshed."

Snow Blanket licked her fingers. "And what of John's wife Bridget and my grandchild? Why did you not bring them? Surely they are no longer safe among the white men."

Tshingee scraped his platter with a pewter fork, a gift to his mother from his father many years ago. "I tried, but she refused. She insisted that she be there in case John was released. I could not even convince her to let me bring Mary back."

Snow Blanket sighed. "Bridget is a good woman but she is not bright. She doesn't understand the danger she places herself and her child in. These are funny times. It is not like when your father was alive. Our people are no longer accepted among the greedy white men."

"I did not wish to involve Deborah, but I did what I had to, Mother. You know that if there had been another path, I would have taken it."

"I know, my son." Snow Blanket brushed his cheek with her palm, her eyes shining with love as well as pride. "More stew?"

He nodded.

"Good." She smiled, pushing her plate into his hand. "You can get me some more when you are up."

Tshingee chuckled, getting to his feet. It was an old joke between Snow Blanket and her sons. "I am not

135

your white servant," she had always told them.

Deborah watched Tshingee rise and leave the wigwam, the two platters in his hands. She had understood nothing he and his mother had said, but she had heard her name spoken. What had Tshingee told his mother? Had he told her how Deborah had thrown herself into his arms, behaving like some dockside whore? Her cheeks colored at the thought.

Why has this happened to me? Deborah wondered miserably. She kept her gaze fixed on the floor, nibbling at the stew. It was hot and spicy. In other circumstances she would have enjoyed it thoroughly, but today she had no appetite. She set down the plate, the stew only half eaten.

"Eat, Deb-o-rah," Snow Blanket said softly in English. Her voice had the same fascinating lilt as Tshingee's did. "What is a woman without her strength?"

Deborah looked up. "It . . . it's very good. I just . . . I'm not hungry."

"I am sorry that this has happened to you." Snow Blanket studied Deborah with penetrating dark eyes. "But you are safe here. Do not worry. No harm will come to you. My son, Tshingee, is a man of his word. You will soon be home with your family."

A lump rose in Deborah's throat and she looked away. Baskets and bundles of dried vegetables hung from the rafters above. One section of the wigwam was heaped with folded furs and wool blankets. It was a cozy home, warm and richly scented with pungent herbs.

Tshingee stuck his head inside the door. "I've been called to the counsel," he said in English. "I must go, but look what I've found."

To Deborah's surprise a young black boy of five or

136

six came bounding in. He handed Snow Blanket her platter of stew saying, *"N'gattopui, Onna."*

Snow Blanket laughed. "Find your platter and eat then," she answered in English.

Deborah watched in astonishment as the boy ducked out of the wigwam. She looked at Snow Blanket, but said nothing.

The Lenni Lenape woman chuckled. "Bee, is my son. You think I am too old a woman to be a mother?"

"N—no." Deborah's forehead crinkled in confusion. The boy had short, crisp black hair and ebony skin. "But how can he be? He's . . . he's a negro!" she blurted.

Snow Blanket make a clucking sound between her teeth. "He is a child who needed love. I'll never understand why the color of a man's skin is so important to you Englishmen."

"Where did he come from?"

Snow Blanket started in on her second helping of venison stew. "I stole him."

"Ma'am?"

The Indian woman chuckled. "We are not stealers of children." She took a deep breath. "But when I was visiting with my sister in Penn's Colony, she told me of the boy. He was a slave child on a small farm near their village. He was beaten and nearly starved." She shrugged. "So I took him."

"But what of his mother?"

"His parents had been sold to another man. Bee was never to see them again. He would not have lived out the winter if he had stayed with the cruel farmer."

Deborah nodded in fascination.

Just then the boy ducked in.

"Greet our guest," Snow Blanket said, nodding in

Deborah's direction.

The child grinned. "Good evening, guest," he said in perfect, singsong English. He had none of the accent that Deborah's father's slaves had.

"Good evening," Deborah replied.

The boy giggled and ran to sit beside his mother. "Do you think she would play stick and ball after the meal, Onna?"

Snow Blanket shrugged, licking her spoon. "You will have to ask, son of mine."

Chapter Ten

"It was good of you to come, Lady Elizabeth." Thomas pressed his lips to the back of her pale hand. "Come in and sit for a moment."

Elizabeth blushed delicately. "My brother, James, escorted me. The Earl won't allow us to travel alone, not even to neighboring plantations, not since . . ." She lowered her gaze, bringing an embroidered handkerchief to her trembling lips.

"Oh, dear, I've upset you, Lady Elizabeth. Come in and do sit." Thomas stuck his head out the front door. "Lord Loglyn." He waved his hand. "Do come in and share in a refreshment."

James lowered himself from his mount with the aid of a black servant. "Have you chocolate, like last time?" The boy swept past Thomas, and into the front hall. He turned to allow a young housemaid to take his cloak. "It's grown chilly outside. I'd not have ventured out on a day like this, but Elizabeth insisted she bring the news to you herself."

"Come in and warm yourself by the fire." Thomas led the Montagues into the parlor. "So you have news, have you, Elizabeth." He frowned. "Might I call you Elizabeth? After all our families have been through, I think the social rules might be bent a bit, don't you?"

139

Elizabeth smoothed the ruffle of the modesty piece tucked in her décolletage. She had dressed carefully this afternoon in a low-waisted woolen gown the color of harvested corn. It was obvious by the way Thomas looked at her that he had noticed. "I think that would be reasonable, Thomas . . . don't you, James?"

James gave no reply, plopping himself down in the chair closest to the fireplace. He leaned to scratch the head of an old hound bitch resting on the brick hearth. Content to be warm, he paid no attention to his sister and neighbor.

Thomas led Elizabeth to a chair beneath a window and sat down beside her. "So tell the news. It's been nearly three weeks since Deborah was taken."

Elizabeth dabbed at her pale lips with her handkerchief. *Poor Thomas,* she thought, taking notice of his ashen complexion and the dark circles beneath his eyes. *He's worried himself sick over her, and to think she never gave a wink for him.* "A message finally came to my father late last night."

"A message? From the savage?"

Elizabeth nodded, her voice grave. "There was a written note and, and" — she took a deep breath — "and a lock of Deborah's hair!"

Thomas gasped. "No!"

She clutched her handkerchief in her fist. "The man who took my sister is quite serious. He says she will not be returned until my father agrees to release the other red man. He's hidden her too well. No matter how far the search parties go, they can find no trace of my sister."

"What is the Earl going to do?" A maid brought in a tray of hot chocolate in tiny porcelain cups and a plate of small iced cakes. "Something warm to drink?"

Thomas asked Elizabeth.

Elizabeth shook her head. "No, but James, you know how he loves sweets."

"Peggy, please serve Lord Loglyn. There'll be nothing for us right now."

When the maid walked away, Elizabeth leaned forward, lowering her voice. "I don't know what the Earl's going to do,. Thomas," she said desperately. "He's in contact with the authorities, but what can they do? Father says the redskins need to be taught a lesson. They just can't take innocent women from their homes and . . ." She choked on her final words.

"There, there." Thomas took Elizabeth's hand, patting it soothingly. "Don't upset yourself." He studied her plain little face. "Your sister is alive, I'm sure of it. The Earl will get her back, you'll see."

Elizabeth was caught between her genuine concern for her sister and her excitement over the attention Thomas Hogarth was giving her. "I don't doubt Father will bring her home, but . . ." She looked away, staring out the window. "Will she ever recover? "Will . . . will she be able to fulfill her duties as wife to you?" She glanced meaningfully at him, feeling quite bold.

He smiled. "Elizabeth, how good of you to be so concerned for my welfare. You understand how important it is that I have a wife who can be there at my side."

"It's just that after living among those savages for so long, how can she possibly return unscathed?"

Thomas squeezed her hand. "Don't worry your pretty little head anymore. It will all turn out for the best. You'll see."

She blushed, withdrawing her hand for fear of appearing too improper. "I do hope you're right,

Thomas."

"I am. Now please, have some refreshment before you return home to Host's Wealth. A little claret perhaps to take away the chill."

Elizabeth smiled, bringing her thumb and finger together. "Just a drop."

James stood up, crumbs clinging to his chin. "Could I have another cup, Tom? It was quite good." He licked his fingers noisily.

"Certainly, Lord Loglyn." He stood, smiling down at Elizabeth. "Peggy!"

An hour later Elizabeth stood in the front hall tying her cloak. "I must be going. James hates the cold." She lifted her hood.

"Do come again if you've any news, Elizabeth. And even if you don't . . ." He shrugged. "I've enjoyed your company. You've been such a comfort in this trying time."

"Elizabeth! Come along or I'll leave you behind!" James shouted from astride his horse.

"Coming, James!" She gave Thomas a quick smile. "And do come by Host's Wealth. We've missed you."

"I'll do that." He nodded, holding the door for her. "Good- bye, Elizabeth."

She blushed, running down the brick steps. "Good-bye!

Deborah tapped her moccasin to the rhythm of the shaman's gourd rattle, watching him beat out an intricate series of steps in a harvest dance. The light of the great fire burned brilliantly, warming the October night air. The shaman's long white braids swung at the side of his face, whipping to and fro as the beat picked up pace, hollow drums echoing in the background.

Bee sat on one side of Deborah, Snow Blanket on the other. Across the community campfire, Tshingee squatted, speaking to one of the elders. When Tshingee looked up, Deborah smiled, but he glanced back at the elder, not seeming to notice her.

Deborah cursed the Lenni Lenape brave beneath her breath. It had been over two weeks since she'd arrived in the village and for two weeks Tshingee had avoided her. He had left her in the care of his mother, warning her that if she tried to escape, he would only capture her again and then she would be forced to remain tied up until she was returned to her father . . . no matter how long that took.

So, she was under a house arrest of sorts. She lived in Snow Blanket's wigwam, she went to the stream, she wandered about the camp, but she remained within its boundaries. Where was she going to go? She was smart enough to know to travel east until she hit the Chesapeake, but how could she travel alone and without provisions? And what of the Mohawks? Tshingee said their raids went well into the fall. This time of year the Lenni Lenape stood watch over their camp twenty-four hours a day.

Deborah watched as Tshingee stood and walked out of the light of the fire. His broad-shouldered shadow was joined by that of a petite feminine one. Even over the din of the drums, rattles, and voices, she could hear Suuklan's bell-like voice.

Anger and resentment rose anew within Deborah. No matter how much she tried to reason with herself, no matter how many times she reminded herself that Tshingee was her enemy, she still cared for him. Deeply. All reason told her she should just stay away from him. In a few weeks John would be set free and she would be returned to her father. Tshingee had been right; she was not with child, her woman's time had come on schedule. She could go back to Host's Wealth, marry Thomas, and fake her virginity on their wedding night. No one need ever know she had made love with the savage.

But *she* would know. No matter how hard she tried to forget, she could not. Her body betrayed her each time she caught sight of Tshingee's chiseled, masculine features. Her mind betrayed her as she watched him from afar. She found herself searching for Tshingee in the crowd. She watched him swing an axe, cutting firewood across the compound. She watched him squat and demonstrate to Bee how an arrowhead was attached to the shaft. And she watched him laugh and talk with Suuklan. . . .

Suddenly Deborah stood and walked away. She skirted the campfire, her stride long and determined. Ahead she could make out Tshingee's shadow and that of his betrothed.

"I want to speak to you, Tshingee," she said, coming to stand in front of him, her hands resting on her hips.

"Good ev-en-ing," Rain greeted sweetly. "Do you enjoy the dance of the corn?"

Deborah glanced at the young maiden. *"Now,* Tshingee. *Alone."*

"I . . . I go." Suuklan took an apologetic step back. *N'dellemuske."*

"No, you don't have to go, Suuklan. She doesn't mean to be rude."

The young maiden shook her head. "I go." She smiled. "Tomorrow we speak." Taking another step back, she nodded to Deborah and hurried away.

Tshingee's lips curled in fury. "You should have stayed seated with Co-o-nah and Bee. There is no excuse for rudeness. Suuklan has done nothing to harm you."

"I'm sorry if I was rude," Deborah snapped. "I apologize for my crude social graces."

"You are forgiven." He glanced up at the campfire. Other villagers were now rising and joining the shaman in the harvest dance. "Go back and sit."

"What is wrong with you? What have I done?" She caught his hand and his dark eyes met hers. "Tshingee?"

He could barely stand the pain in her voice. The urge to take her in his arms was so great that he had to tense the muscles of his arms to keep them at his sides. "You have done nothing," he responded without emotion.

Feeling him stiffen, she pulled her hand back. "God's teeth! What do you mean I've done nothing? *Obviously,* it was *something* or you wouldn't be treating me like I carry the pox!"

"Lower your voice. It is impolite to share disagreements with others."

"Disagreements.! What disagreement?" Her voice grew louder with each word. "I just want to know what the hell—"

Tshingee took her around the waist, propelling her forward out of earshot of the villagers.

"I want to know what has happened between us!" she finished. "You can't deny that you didn't feel something for me back there on the trail. You can't deny that it's been there since we met that day in John's garden." Her voice had reached a desperate peak. "Tshingee, I don't understand!"

145

He sighed, gazing up at the dark heavens that stretched over them in a canopy of stars. A crisp, northwesterly breeze made his ebony hair flutter on his shoulder. "I have committed a grave error, Red Bird," he said, his voice barely above a whisper. "No, I cannot deny my feeling for you, but don't you see . . ." He bore down on her with a dark penetrating gaze. "Don't you see I'm protecting you."

"I don't understand. What have you done?" She rested her hands on his shoulders.

Tshingee couldn't resist encircling her waist with his hands. It felt so good to hold her again. Suuklan felt comfortable in his arms, but this white woman, she made him tremble. She made his heart pound. He cupped her Deborah's chin. "I had no right to take you. You were in my care, you were my responsibility. I have stolen what belongs to another man."

"My virginity?" She chuckled. "I have no regrets. I told you, I came to you freely. And I told you why. I never felt anything so wonderful." She stroked the line of his jaw. "I don't think I ever will again."

"It makes no difference. I had no right. Among my people" — He looked away — "I would be expected to marry you."

"Marry?" She pressed her lips to his in a gentle, soothing kiss. "Is that what you're so angry with me about? You think I expect you to marry me?" She couldn't help laughing. "Tshingee, you could no more marry me than I could marry you. I'm not *that* naive."

Deborah's words eased his mind, but they disturbed his heart. Somewhere in the back of his mind he had hoped she expected him to marry her. The fact that he couldn't didn't seem to matter.

Their eyes met and he reached out to tug at a thick

lock of her hair. It was the lock he had cut at chin level to send to her father. "I regret I did this."

"It will grow back." Her soft voice beckoned him; her lips trembled. "Kiss me."

"I should not. You belong to the man Thomas. I will wed Suuklan in the spring."

"Do you love her?"

He shook his head mutely.

"Will you ever?"

"Perhaps," he answered, mesmerized by her steady gaze.

"Could you love me? A different time? A different place?"

"I could love you."

She smiled sadly. "Then that's all that matters. We both know that John will be released and I will return to the Tidewater to be Thomas's wife. But couldn't we . . . could we just pretend for a little while that we belong to each other?"

"It would not be fair to Suuklan."

"But you said you don't love her. You shouldn't be marrying someone you don't want to."

"Are you in love with your Thomas?"

"Of course not!"

"Then you should not be marrying him."

"It's not the same thing and you know it." She spanned his chest with her palm, relishing the feel of the soft hide beneath her fingertips. "You have a choice. I have none."

"We always have choices, Red Bird." He traced the outline of her lips with his finger and she touched its tip with her tongue.

"Not so. Don't speak of what you don't know." She bit his finger lightly. "Just kiss me. No one can see us. I

147

won't tell," she teased.

Tshingee took her mouth forcefully, his fingers threading through her long, thick hair. His kiss was rough and demanding, full of unfulfilled dreams.

When he finally withdrew, they were both breathless, their hearts pounding. Her groin was pressed against his so that she could feel the hardness beneath his tunic.

"By the heavens, I want you," he murmured in her ear. He held her against his chest, his face buried in her sweet-smelling hair. "I lie awake in my wigwam thinking of you asleep on your mat." He clenched her tightly. "Why must it be this way?"

"It doesn't have to be," she whispered. "Can't we be together, just until John is released?"

He kissed her brow. "You would hate me when it was time that you go."

"I wouldn't."

He smiled in the darkness. "You are young, Red Bird. Trust me."

"Don't do this to me. Please? I need you."

"In time you will forget." He kissed her eyelids, the tip of her nose, the birthmark at the corner of her mouth.

"I won't."

He took her arms from around his shoulders and lowered them to her sides. The light of the half moon shone down in a bright white stream, illuminating her face. Moisture gathered in the corners of her eyes.

"Don't deny me, don't deny yourself," she begged.

He kissed the tip of his finger and brushed it against her trembling lips. "It is the honorable thing to do." Then he walked away.

Deborah stood alone for a moment in the darkness,

a sob rising in her throat. Choking it back, she ran into the darkness, around the campfire and toward Snow Blanket's wigwam.

Snow Blanket watched Deborah's retreat and then spotted her son standing on the far side of the circle of villagers. His arms were crossed over his chest, his eyes fixed on the burning fire. A single tear trickled down his sun-bronzed cheek.

Slowly Snow Blanket made her way around the circle until she was standing beside her son, watching the dancers. For a long time the two were silent. The dampness dried on his cheek and the pain in his heart became more bearable.

"You are troubled, my son," Snow Blanket said when an appropriate amount of time had passed. She hated to see him in such emotional turmoil. Though she loved her son John fiercely, it was this child who was her heart of hearts. It was *Tshingee* who had filled in the gaps of time when she could not be with his father. It was *he* who had lifted her from the depths of despair when her white man had taken sick and died.

"When John is set free, all will be well again," Tshingee answered, lapsing into Algonquian. He did not dare meet his mother's gaze.

She chuckled. "I think not. It will never be the same, nothing ever is."

"You speak in riddles." He continued to stare at the blazing fire. Having Deborah in his arms again brought back the flood of emotions he had been trying so hard to stifle these last two weeks. He loved her so much—how could he give her up?

"I speak of you and the white girl, my son. I speak of Suuklan, of John, of all of us . . . but mostly I speak of you."

149

"I don't understand."

She removed a clay pipe from a bag around her waist and began to fill it with tobacco. "You are in love with this Deb-or- ah."

Snow Blanket's words echoed in his mind. "What causes you to say that?" he asked carefully.

"The pain in your eyes. The pain in hers."

"After John is released, I will return Deborah to her father. I am a man of honor. My word is my life. She must go."

"All that you say is true. But the fact remains that you love her." She walked into the circle of the camp and lit her pipe, returning to her son's side.

Tshingee turned to Snow Blanket. "Our love cannot be, my *onna*," he said with tragic defeat.

"No, it cannot."

"So what is the point of your words?"

"I am concerned for you and for Suuklan. *She* is in love with you." She exhaled, the sweet smell of tobacco filling the night air.

He sighed. "I still intend to marry her when it is time to plant again. I think it is best."

"But you are not in love with her?"

It was his turn to chuckle. "You are the second person to ask tonight, and she was not one of them." He paused. "But no. I do not love her."

Snow Blanket puffed on her pipe thoughtfully. "I told you when you agreed to the match that she was not for you, Tshingee."

"She is bright; she will make a good wife and mother."

"This is true. But her flame does not burn bright enough for you, my son. Her place is here among her people. But for you, this old woman sees more. You will not always remain at my side."

"I think you have sat too long in the sun, my mother." He drew a pattern in the soft dirt with the toe of his moccasin. "You know I have no desire to live as a poor white farmer like my brother. I am content here."

"You have never been content, my Wildcat of the forest. Not since you were a babe suckling at my breast. You always wanted what you could not have and most often you got it."

"I am no longer a child and you do not have the gift of foretelling what's to come to pass."

"No, I do not claim to know what the gods have in store, but I know you will never be a dirt farmer. I just remind you that there are other possibilities. As many possibilities as there are stars in the heavens."

"I think I will go to my mat. I have the dawn watch." He looked up at the stars and then back at his mother. "These words were between you and I. What is in my heart is mine to guard as I please."

"You mean your Deb-or-ah does not know what is in your heart?" She tapped his chest lightly with the stem of her clay pipe.

"There is no need to tell her. It will only make it harder to part. This way, I spare us both." He nodded slightly. "Good night, mother."

Snow Blanket chuckled, watching her son walk away. It was true, she did not know what the Gods had in store for her younger son, but whatever it was, she was anxious to see it.

Chapter Eleven

"Come along, Deb-or-ah!" Bee tugged at her arm. "It will be fun!"

Deborah shook her head dismally. "No, really Bee, I'd rather not."

The little boy got down on his hands and knees in front of her and stared at her face. "I'm sorry that you are unhappy here. I was unhappy too when first I came, but only because I was afraid. Happiness will soon come to you here."

"I'm not staying, Bee. I must go home to my family." She tossed a stick into the fire burning in the center of Snow Blanket's wigwam.

"Then I am sorry for you, because . . ." He slipped his hand into hers. "But if you will not go harvest nuts, then I will not go. I will stay here and be your *nitis*."

Deborah studied the small dark hand in hers. "Your *nit-is*? What's that?"

"I am Tshingee's *nitis*. He taught me the word. It means friend. But you can be my friend, too. Tshingee says a man counts his happinesses by the number of friends he has."

Deborah laughed. "I could use a *nitis*."

"Will you come then?" His face was bright with hope.

She nodded, smiling. "All right, my *nitis*. I will go nut gathering with you, but only for a while."

The little boy leaped to his feet. *"Onna* says we can take these baskets." He hurried to retrieve two bark containers from the far side of the wigwam. "You just put them over your head like this." He demonstrated, putting his head through the soft leather strap attached to the basket. "Then you can pick with your hands!" He waved his little hands, bouncing up and down.

Deborah took the basket and placed it around her neck. "I'm ready."

"We'll have to hurry." He ran out of the wigwam. "The others have already left."

Deborah followed Bee through the center of the village, listening to his chatter. He spoke half in English and half in Lenni Lenape so sometimes it was difficult to understand what he was saying.

The little boy led her through the walnut grove and over the stream. "These have already been picked," he told her, motioning to the trees that stretched high above their heads. "But I know where there's more!"

"Don't you get me lost," Deborah threatened.

Bee laughed. "I would never do that." He hit his chest with his fist. "I am a brave Lenni Lenape warrior. I will protect my woman!"

Deborah couldn't help laughing at the boy's antics as they moved deeper into the forest. It felt good to be outside in the fresh crisp air. Another week had passed and still there had been no word from Host's Wealth. Since that night at the harvest celebration Deborah had not seen Tshingee. He had gone on a hunting trip, leaving the following morning, and had not yet returned.

153

"Just a little further," Bee hollered over his shoulder.

Deborah ducked and dodged branches, stepping over a fallen log. "Wait for me, Bee! You're going too fast." She followed him into an area where there was no underbrush.

"See, I told you! He spread his arms.

Deborah looked up, smiling. They stood in a small glove of ancient black walnut trees. The trees were massive with twisted limbs and huge blackened trunks towering high above the surrounding trees. The ground was littered with thousands of nuts in their black casings.

"Look at them all! You certainly did know where to find the nuts, didn't you!" Deborah crouched and began to pick up walnuts. Then she tossed one, smacking Bee in the arm with it.

The boy laughed, bombarding her with a nut. Soon the two were laughing and dodging trees in earnest battle.

"Ouch!" came a feminine voice from the brush.

Deborah and Bee turned to see Suuklan coming through a thicket, massaging her forehead. "If you did not wish to share your nuts, Bee, words would have been kinder," she told him in Lenni Lenape. The girl stopped short when she spotted Deborah.

Deborah forced a smile. "Sorry. We didn't hear you coming."

The young woman nodded. "I can go." She walked away.

Deborah stood for a moment in indecision and then ran after her. "Don't be a goose. There are more nuts here than Bee and I could possibly carry back to the village. Pick with us."

Suuklan smiled hesitantly. "The other women are

further west, but the nuts are not so many," she said in English. "I remembered this grove that Tshingee . . ." She dropped to her knees and began to retrieve walnuts.

Deborah sighed. Suuklan reminded her of her own sister Elizabeth. Afraid of her own shadow. She knelt beside the girl, wondering what Tshingee saw in the little mouse.

The two women gathered nuts in silence while Bee continued to chatter. Soon he grew tired of the harvesting and abandoned his basket to chase a squirrel.

"Don't go too far!" Deborah warned. "Our baskets are nearly full. It's going to be getting dark soon."

Bee disappeared into the brush and for a few minutes the women worked side by side filling their baskets in silence. Suddenly there was a rumbling, snarling sound and the crash of brush.

"Deb-or-ah!" Bee shouted. "Deb-or-ah! Suuklan! *Uishameheela!* Run!"

Startled, Deborah stood. "Bee! What is it?"

The boy came running into the clearing. "Bear! Run!" Behind him there was a loud splintering of wood as something large pursued him.

"Into the tree," Deborah shouted. "You can't outrun it." She caught the frightened little boy around the waist and heaved him over her head. Bee grasped a branch and swung up.

"Into the tree, Suuklan!" Deborah shouted over her shoulder, scrambling to climb up behind Bee.

Suuklan screamed in terror, running for the nearest black walnut tree, her basket clutched in her hands. She stretched, but could not reach the lowest limb. Sobbing she ran to the next tree, clawing at the bark of the trunk. The basket tipped over her head and showered her with the pelting walnuts.

A huge black bear burst through the tangled brush howling and throwing itself onto its hind legs. Its mouth gaped open and it gnashed its great white teeth in fury.

"Jump!" Deborah shouted. "Let go of the damned basket and jump, Suuklan!"

The tiny Lenni Lenape woman leaped again and again but to no avail. In utter fright she crumbled to the ground. "I cannot! I cannot!" she shrieked as the bear grew closer.

Deborah hesitated for only an instant and then swung down out of the safety of her tree. "Stay there, Bee. No matter what happens, you stay there!" she ordered over her shoulder.

"No!" the little boy shouted. "It will kill you both!"

But Deborah was already racing across the grove to the tree where Suuklan lay. She darted into the bear's path and the she-bear growled, howling horrendously.

"Get up! Get up!" Deborah demanded.

Suuklan stumbled to her feet, clutching the tree trunk.

Deborah cupped her hands. "Step up. Now, damn it!"

Shaking with fear, Suuklan stepped into the white woman's hand and Deborah boosted her up. "Climb higher," Deborah shouted. "Make room for me, I'm coming up!"

Deborah heard the bear's angry growl and the swoosh her massive paw made in the air as she struck out at the human. Suuklan's scream echoed through the forest. Deborah was in midair as the bear struck with its front paw slicing through her leather tunic and into the soft flesh of her buttocks.

Deborah grimaced, swinging onto the lowest branch and scurrying for the next. She could still feel the bear's hot breath on her legs and smell its heavy, clinging odor. Higher and higher she climbed, shoving Suuklan ahead of her until she was positive they were out of reach of the frenzied animal.

Suuklan sobbed, holding tightly to a branch. "You bleed! You bleed!"

There was a numbness across Deborah's backside that made her brush her hand over it. It was a moment before she realized that the sticky warm stuff was blood. She lifted her hand and looked at the red staining.

"You're hurt." Suuklan wailed. "You bleed. You bleed."

"Oh, for Christ's sake, shut up!" Deborah snapped. "I'm all right." But the moment she tried to sit on a tree limb, she realized she wasn't. Pain shot through her backside and into her back and she winced, bouncing to her feet.

Suuklan continued to sob, tremors wracking her body.

"Deb-or-ah," came Bee's timid voice from a far tree. "Are you hurt badly?"

"No, Bee. Just scratched." The she-bear circled the tree she and Suuklan had taken refuge in. Growling and swinging onto her hind legs. "We're all right Bee," Deborah repeated.

"I'm sorry," the little boy called, trying desperately not to cry. "I knew not to play with the baby bear but he was fluffy. I just wanted to touch him."

Deborah sighed, balancing on a branch while she held on to the one Suuklan was perched on. Through the brush she could see a young black bear cub running for its mother. "Don't cry, Bee. We're safe. It's a lesson you'll not forget, that's all." Through the tree limbs she could see Bee sitting dejectedly on a branch.

"Now what do we do?" the boy asked, plucking a walnut and tossing it to the ground. The mother bear had dropped onto all fours, but still circled the tree the women were in. Occasionally she snapped her massive jaws, growling angrily.

"We wait," Deborah responded, grimacing. There was now a burning heat rising from the pain in her buttocks.

"How long?"

"Until the bear's gone, Bee."

"Oh. How long will that be, Deb-or-ah?"

"I don't know, so just be sure you're well seated. I don't want you falling out of that tree. You'd make too tasty a supper."

Bee laughed in response. "I don't want to be anyone's supper!"

Laughing with him, Deborah glanced up at Suuklan above her. The young woman was now crying silently; fat wet tears rolled down her pretty cheeks. "Stop crying, Suuklan," Deborah said impatiently. "You're safe. Now we just wait."

But an hour passed and the mother-bear remained in the walnut grove, pacing, its cub at its side. They tried smacking the sow with walnuts to chase her away, but that seemed only to aggravate her. Darkness began to settle in and the pain of Deborah's injury began to worry her. The bleeding had slowed to an oozing, but she was beginning to feel dizzy. The backs of her legs were warm and sticky and pieces of her shredded hide tunic stuck to her bare skin. Because she couldn't sit, she stood, leaning in the crook of two branches.

"Bee?" Deborah called across the walnut grove.

"Yes, Deb-or-ah."

"Bee, I think maybe you need to go get help. Could you find your way back in the dark if you could get out of the tree."

The little boy bobbed up. "Of course. This Lenni Lenape warrior is not afraid of the dark."

"All right, listen carefully." Deborah gazed down at the mother bear resting beneath the tree. She seemed to be content to lick at her cub for the present. "I want you to climb out on the limb above you and swing into the next tree," Deborah continued. "Do you understand?"

"Yes!"

"Good. Then I want you to climb through the next tree and find a branch close enough to another. I want you to stay up in the trees until you can't see the bears anymore."

"Just jump from tree to tree?" He nodded vigorously. "I can do that. Can't you, too?"

Deborah glanced up at Suuklan sitting perfectly still on her branch. Her knuckles were ghostly white, she was hanging on so hard. "I don't think so, Bee. You go get someone from the village and bring them back. Can you do that?"

"I can do it!" He scrambled across a tree limb.

"Careful! I don't want you falling! What use is a warrior with a broken leg?" Deborah watched through the fading light of early evening as the boy moved from tree to tree until he disappeared from sight.

"I'm going, now," Bee called from the distance.

"Hurry, Bee. Hurry!"

The mother bear lifted her head in the direction the boy had gone, but she didn't move and Deborah heaved a sigh of relief.

Time passed and Deborah began to grow sleepy. She rested her head on a branch, wrapping her arms around a limb to keep from falling. A warmth was beginning to creep up from her toes despite the chilly air that settled in as darkness fell upon them. Suuklan sat in mute silence above her, hanging on for dear life to the thick trunk of the tree.

Deborah must have dozed off because the next thing she knew, she was falling. She stiffened, crying out, but a soft voice soothed her. "It's all right, *Ki-ti-hi,*" the voice assured her. *"Maata-wischasi.* You are safe."

Deborah's eyes flew open and in the darkness she could see Tshingee's face bent over hers. He was holding her safely in his arms. She smiled sleepily. She wanted to speak, but the words just wouldn't form on her lips.

Pushing out of the tree, Tshingee landed safely on the ground with Deborah still cradled in his arms. "Can you hear me, Red Bird?"

"Yes," she forced herself to say. She didn't know why she was so sleepy. The pain in her buttocks was dull and throbbing, but it seemed to be someone else's pain rather than her own. "Bee? Suuklan?" she whispered, resting her head on Tshingee's shoulder.

"They are well. Bee says you were injured. You must tell me where you are hurt, Red Bird."

Deborah giggled. "In a very unladylike place, I fear," she slurred.

Tshingee brushed his lips against her perspiration-soaked brow. She was burning with fever. The arm he held beneath her was growing warm and sticky with oozing blood. "I'm going to take you back to the village now, so just hold on to me."

Deborah nodded, linking her fingers behind his neck. She snuggled against him, inhaling his familiar masculine scent. "To your wigwam?" she managed.

"Yes." He kissed her flushed cheeks. "Sleep now Red Bird and Tshingee will care for his woman."

The night was a blur of warmth and muddled confusion for Deborah. She drifted in and out of sleep, barely aware of the teas that were poured between her lips and the cool water that was used to cleanse her wounds. At one point there was a hot searing pain across her buttocks as if she was being poked with a branding iron but the pain was gone as quickly as it had come, mixed with the soothing hum of Tshingee's voice. Sometime in the night she grew very cold, but suddenly Tshingee was there beside her, wrapping her in the folds of a warm blanket and tucking her safely in his arms.

When Deborah woke, the sunlight was bright and startling. She was resting on her side, her head cradled in her arm. Immediately she realized that she wasn't in Snow Blanket's wigwam. Where then? She smiled. *Tshingee's* of course.

"So you are finally awake, lazy *esquawa*."

Deborah blinked and Tshingee was there, crouched beside her. He laid his hand on her forehead. The fever is nearly gone."

"I was sick? She started to roll over, but the pain that streaked up her backside made her groan. "Ouch!" She rolled back onto her side, brushing her bare backside with her hand. The tender flesh had been cleaned and covered with a soothing ointment, but here was a line of wiry threads protruding from a cut on her left buttock.

"Bear scratches always give a man illness, no matter

161

how small they are. But my mother's herbs have brought healing. You will be fine in a couple of days."

Deborah touched her buttocks again lightly. "What are these?"

He chuckled. "There was one deep cut. It had to be sewn with porcupine needles."

"Snow Blanket stitched my bottom?" she asked, mortified.

A smile broke the smooth lines of his face. "No, I did. My hand is better than hers."

Deborah laughed, then winced, and then laughed again. She knew she should be embarrassed, but all she could do was laugh. "Ouch, that hurts."

Tshingee laughed with her, relieved that she was all right. "This will teach you not to play with a mother bear and her cub."

"Bee told you what happened?" She held her sides to keep from laughing anymore.

"He did. He told me that you risked your life for Suuklan." Tshingee's eyes were warm and bright with pride.

Deborah frowned, propping herself up on her elbow. "I was tempted to let the bear eat her."

Tshingee chuckled, stretching out beside her so that his face was only inches from hers. He toyed with her shorn lock of hair. "I have never had two maidens to fight over me before. I think perhaps I like it."

"What fighting? You said you're going to marry her. You and Suuklan are going to have little wildcats. I'm going back to Thomas Hogarth."

Tshingee traced her chin with the tip of his finger. "I am considering telling Suuklan's father that I cannot marry her."

"Why? You cannot have me. John's life depends

upon my safe return." Her voice was barely a whisper. "We both know that."

"I know. But my . . . my feelings for you have made me realize that it would be unfair to take Suuklan as my wife. Ours souls are not matched. If we marry, I will be unhappy; she will be unhappy. My *onna* has been against the match since the beginning."

"Will her father be angry?" Deborah studied his bronzed sculptured face, mesmerized by the way the sunlight played off his suntanned skin.

"Not angry. Only disappointed. Our families have been joining for many generations."

Deborah laid her hand on his shoulder, massaging it lightly through the muslin shirt he wore. "What of Suuklan?"

"She will be hurt, but she will understand. I think she already knows. Last night when I came for you, I brought Sikihiila with me among my men. It was *he* that she went to, not me. She is not in love with me."

"I think she is."

He shook his head. "She thinks she wants me but love is not what is in her heart. Suuklan is young. It is easy to confuse a body's wants with love when you are young."

Deborah wondered if he was referring to her as well, but she didn't ask. "I cannot lie." She smiled, brushing the seam of his leather breeches with her fingertips. "I am glad you aren't going to marry her." She giggled. "She's too tiny. You'd squash her here on your sleeping mat."

Tshingee growled, low and animal-like. "You are supposed to be ill." He slipped his hand beneath the hide blanket caressing her flat stomach and the curve of her hips.

163

"And you are not supposed to be taking advantage of your prisoner." She continued to caress the apex of his breeches, noting the rising bulge beneath the soft leather.

"I know," he answered honestly. "The fight within me is strong. I have never wanted a woman more than I want you Red Bird, but—"

She pressed her fingers to his lips. "No buts. I know this cannot be, but can't we pretend for a short time? Can't you give me something to carry within me the rest of days? Can't you let me give you something? Something meant for no other?"

"K'daholel," he whispered.

"What does it mean?" A heat was rising from her middle to radiate to her limbs.

"It means . . ." He took her hand, pressing a kiss to each knuckle. "It means that I love you. Deborah."

She smiled sadly. "No one has ever said that to me." She guided his hand to her breast. "So love me, just for a little while. Let me love you."

His mouth met hers in a searing kiss and the pain of Deborah's injury was forgotten. She clung to him in wanton need, flinging back her head to let him kiss the pulse of her throat.

He suckled her breast, his tongue darting out to tease her nipple into a hard, ripened peak. Deborah laughed huskily, lowering her hand until it touched his hard, throbbing shaft.

A groan rose in Tshingee's throat, but she stifled it with her mouth, kissing him deeply. With his aid she tugged off his breeches and lifted her blanket so that he could snuggle in beside her. Her hand grazed the thick muscles of his thighs as she stroked him, in awe of the power of her own touch. The rhythm of their breathing grew faster in unison as they writhed in glorious pleasure.

Tshingee brushed his fingers against the tight web of curls between Deborah's thighs and she moaned, lifting her hips to meet his gentle probing.

Come to me," Tshingee murmured in her ear. "Come to me, *Ki-ti-hi*."

To her surprise, he caught her around the waist and lifted her gently.

"I do not want to hurt you," he whispered.

She shook her head, flattening her body over his. "The pain is gone." She kissed him, moving carefully as she experimented with this new sensation.

The force of his hard, bulging loins pressed against her woman's mound brought a new wave of pulsating desire. Parting her legs, Tshingee guided her as she slid onto his tumescent member.

Consumed by fire, the two moved as one until the stars of the heavens burst above them, showering them in ecstasy. Kissing her damp cheeks, Tshingee lowered Deborah onto her side and wrapped her tightly in his arms. Bringing the hide blanket over his shoulders, they slept in peace.

Chapter Twelve

Deborah and Tshingee walked arm and arm through the forest in silence, listening to the rustle of autumn leaves and the chirping of night insects. The sun was setting over the western horizon, coloring the dense woods in a glorious array of orange and golds.

Deborah smiled, resting her cheek against Tshingee's arm. Though her buttocks was still sore, she was nearly healed, after a week's time. Yesterday, Tshingee had removed the porcupine stitches and Deborah had turned his surgical efforts into a ribald wrestling match. For a week they had eaten together, slept together, and made love whenever they chose. It had been an enchanting week that left her heart overflowing with joyous contentment.

But as the days passed, Deborah began to grow concerned. The more time she spent with Tshingee, the more she realized she could never leave him.

How could she return to life on the Tidewater after experiencing life as it could be? Here in the village she was treated as a respected member of the community, as a heroine of sorts since she had rescued Suuklan. She chatted with the women at the stream as they bathed their children; she laughed with the elders as they sat smoking their pipes and telling tales of days'

166

past. Here among the Lenni Lenape Deborah witnessed an independence among women that was unheard of in English society.

Among the Lenni Lenape she discovered that women played an important part in the decisions of their own life. Though a father normally made suggestions as to a mate for his daughter, it was the women who made the final choice. And once she was married, husband and wife made decisions together that affected them both. Children were planned and conceived out of want, not as a result of passion. Like many of the other women in the village, Deborah drank an herbal mixture each day to prevent becoming pregnant.

For a brief few days Deborah pretended to be married to Tshingee, and she imagined what it would be like to remain here in the village as one of the tribe. Other white women had stayed among the Lenni Lenape after being in the village for one reason or another. Why couldn't she?

The obvious reason was John. How could Tshingee's brother be released if she stayed with the Indians? For two days Deborah had concentrated on that problem and still she had come up with no solution. She said nothing to Tshingee, wanting to surprise him when she finally solved the puzzle.

"You are as quiet as a woods mouse tonight, Red Bird," Tshingee said, breaking her from her thoughts. "What do you think of?"

She sighed. "I was just thinking of how happy you've made me, of how I wish it could go on forever."

He released her hand and wrapped his arm around her shoulder, kissing her brow. "Nothing stands forever, not even the grandfather oak. We accept the gifts

167

our Heavenly Father grants us, and when those gifts are gone, we treasure the memories in our heart."

"So it's that easy?" She stopped in mid-step. "I leave and that's the end of it? You just pretend I was never here? You pretend this love between us never existed?"

"I could never do that, Red Bird. You are as much a part of me as this." He lifted his palm. "But I accept what cannot be," he went on softly, cupping her chin with his hand. "I did not say it would be easy."

She pulled away from him, walking ahead. "How can you be so damned calm about all of this?"

"Because it is the way of my people. I cannot let the pain I feel in my heart keep me from doing what I must. I cannot forfeit my brother's life for a matter of the heart."

"I can't believe after all we've shared that you can just let me go."

"Don't you hear the pain in my voice, Deborah. It's not that I want you to go. It's just that I have no choice."

Deborah stopped, lowering her head as a rush of tears pooled in her eyes. "Isn't there any other way to save John?"

Tshingee came up behind her, pressing his lips to the back of her dark head. "I don't think so." He encircled her in his arms, forcing her to turn and face him. "I lie awake at night trying to find a way to keep you with me, but there is no answer. It is my own fault. I should never have offered such a bargain to your father. I should never given him my word for now"—his voice caught in his throat—"I am bound to it."

Deborah clung to Tshingee. "You didn't know, Tshingee," she comforted. "You didn't know we'd fall in love."

"No," he whispered. kissing her tearstained cheek. "I didn't know . . ."

A few days later Deborah knelt on the bank of the stream rinsing an earthen pot and several pewter and wooden cooking utensils. Beside her sat Bee, collecting stones to add to the pouch tied to a belt on his waist. The morning air was crisp and refreshing, carrying the scent of the first snow.

Deborah's hands were numb with cold as she hurried to wash the pile of cooking items, placing each clean piece in a bark basket as she finished with it. Bee chattered at her side explaining how he had nearly killed a squirrel this morning with the slingshot Tshingee had made for him.

"If you hit one, you be sure you kill it," Deborah warned. Tshingee will not be pleased if you wound an animal and leave it to die in the forest."

The child shook his head. "This brave hunter would never commit such a sin." He pulled out his slingshot and took aim. A pebble whizzed through the air and hit a tree limb with a satisfying crack.

Deborah laughed. "Do you think you could show me how to use that thing?"

"Would you like me to?" Bee pushed up onto his knees. "I could—"

"Deborah . . ." Tshingee's voice came from behind. Deborah turned to see him standing behind her, his face twisted with emotion. "Yes?"

"Bee, leave us." Tshingee said quietly.

The little boy leaped to his feet and ran off in the direction of the village.

Deborah dumped the remaining utensils in the basket. Tears formed in her eyes. Somehow she knew what Tshingee was about to say. She couldn't bear to look up at him. "What . . . what is it?" She could hear the crackle of paper as he unrolled something.

"It has come, Red Bird."

"What?" she asked foolishly. A numbness was creeping up her arms to spread through her limbs, a numbness that did not come from the cold water.

"Your father has agreed to set my brother free."

"No," she moaned softly.

"The time and place has been set for the exchange."

Deborah stumbled to her feet. "I kept hoping somehow . . ." She fell silent, raising her hands to rest on his chest. When she felt Tshingee stiffen, she looked into his eyes, her own brimming with tears. His lips were tightly compressed, his face etched with pain . . . and anger. "What? What is it?" she asked in bewilderment. "Why are you angry?"

His voice was stark. "Tell me my brother's land was not to be part of your dowry."

"I can't believe you're saying this." She shook her head. "I have to leave you and you're worried about the damned land!"

"Your father says in this letter that it is to be a gift from you to your Thomas."

"Not from me! Never from me!" she flung. "My father was going to give Thomas that land as payment for taking me off his hands!"

"You should have told me. I thought you were not involved. I thought you innocent of the white man's greed."

"Tshingee. I am not your enemy! I love you, remember?" When she tried to touch him, he flinched and she drew back her hand in horror. Tshingee," she whis-

170

pered.

"Prepare yourself. We leave when the sun rises again."

Deborah watched, dazed, as he turned and walked away. Then, in sudden fury she grabbed a pewter spoon from her basket and hurled it at his head. The utensil missed it's mark and aimlessly smacked a tree before tumbling to the ground.

Tshingee never broke stride.

Tshingee stuffed Deborah's extra doeskin tunic into his leather traveling bag. "You are going," he said tersely.

She pulled the tunic out of the bag. "I'm not going."

"Do not do this to me, Deborah." He continued to pack the necessary items. "Do not make this more difficult than it must be."

"Difficult? Difficult for whom?" She threw her tunic at his moccasined feet. "If I go back to my father, I'll be sold to Thomas. If he won't have me, it will be someone worse, while you get to stay here and roll beneath the bearskin rugs with Suuklan."

"I told you. Her father and I have agreed I am not the man for her. Sikihilla has already asked that she be *his* wife."

"So if not her, then someone else!"

Tshingee crouched by the fire in the center of his wigwam and added a few sticks to the blaze. Tonight the wind blew hard out of the north and with it the first flakes of snow. "Yes! he shouted harshly. "Someday I will find a Lenni Lenape woman and we will marry. I have a duty to carry the name of my mother's people!"

"Damn you, Tshingee, do you always have to be so

noble?" She stared at him from across the wigwam, her eyes riveted to his bronze face. "Can't you and your men just ride in there with your bows and arrows and free John?"

"I gave my word, Deborah." He took a deep breath, attempting to control his anger. "I explained that to you before. Among my people a man's word is sacred. I could not go back on my agreement with your father, no matter what the price."

"Doesn't our love mean anything to you?"

"You deceived me. You should have told me John's land was meant to be yours."

"It wasn't! Can't you get that through your thick red-skinned head?" She shook her fist in fury. "I would do anything to change what happened but I can't! What am I supposed to do now?"

"You return to your people and John returns to his. You marry your Thomas as your father wishes. Our paths have met and now they separate."

"Can't those paths ever be altered?"

He stood, returning to his packing. "No. Not this time. There is too much bad blood between the white man and I."

"But *you* are half white man . . ."

He shrugged. "We all carry burdens on our shoulders."

Stunned, Deborah stood in silence, then grabbing her hide cloak, she ran out of the wigwam and into the night air. She went straight to Snow Blanket's wigwam. "Snow Blanket, may I come in?" She shivered, drawing the warm skins closer.

The flap of the wigwam lifted and a beaming Bee looked out. "Come. *Onna* say you are always welcome, Deb-or-ah."

Deborah ducked in, rubbing her hands briskly. "It's gotten so cold," she muttered.

Snow Blanket nodded, patting a hide mat beside her. "Sit and warm yourself, *daanus*.

Deborah sat cross-legged on the mat, leaning forward, her hands outstretched to warm them with the center fire. "That son of yours, Snow Blanket! Talking to him is like talking to a fence post!"

Snow Blanket chuckled. "He has always been my difficult child. She puffed contentedly on her pipe, staring into the flames of the fire.

"I don't want to go back," Deborah confided passionately. "There is nothing there for me but unhappiness."

"This old woman is sorry that you have been caught in the tide."

"I could never be responsible for anything happening to John. He was very kind to me. But isn't there another way, Snow Blanket? Can't John and I both be rescued from my father?"

"These things, they are so hard for the young to understand. My son gave his word when he took you from your father's home that you would be returned safely when my John was set free. A brave of the Wolf Clan cannot go back on his word. It would mean a shame not only upon his face but upon our entire family's."

Deborah sighed, shrugging off her fur cloak as she grew warmer. "I love Tshingee. He loves me. He's mad because John's land is meant to be my dowry, but he'll get over it. Snow Blanket, no one ever told me he loved me, not before your son. How can I possibly leave him? No one understands."

Snow Blanket patted the white girl's hand. "Oh, but

173

I do understand. Tshingee's father, John Logan, was the most handsome man I had ever laid eyes on. He made me laugh. He made the stars shine brighter in the heavens." She shook her head. "Do not tell me that *I* do not understand of a love that cannot be."

"But you managed! You found a way!"

"And the sacrifices were many." The Lenni Lenape woman tapped the bowl of her clay pipe in her hand, emptying the ashes. "It was not easy for either of us. John stayed on his plantation while I lived in the village. There was never enough time to be together."

"But at least you were together sometimes! Tshingee says I will never see him again. He says it's better that way!"

"Maybe he is right."

Deborah shook her head, her long dark braids swinging violently. "He isn't. I know it. He will never be happy without me."

Snow Blanket took out a pouch of fresh tobacco and began to refill her pipe. "No, he will not."

"Then talk to him, please, Snow Blanket. Don't let him take me back."

The Lenni Lenape woman smiled sadly. "John is my son. I cannot ask one son to sacrifice the life of the other."

Deborah was quiet for a long moment. "No. I don't imagine you can." She drew up her knees, hugging them tightly. "I just feel like someone's blowing out the candle. There's no hope left. I know what you and Tshingee say is right, but that leaves me with nothing."

A column of smoke rose and encircled Snow Blanket's dark head. "Never lose hope, Deb-or-ah. It is the stuff that makes our dreams come true."

Tshingee ducked into the wigwam. *"Onna."* He nodded his head. "I come to say good night. It is time I retired to the mat. I will take the prisoner and go in the morning. I will bring your son John home to you."

Deborah rose and pulled on her cloak, ignoring Tshingee. She offered her hand to Snow Blanket. "Thank you for being so kind to me."

Snow Blanket got up and retrieved a small pouch from a basket along the wall. "This is for you," she said, smiling.

Deborah fingered the soft leather pouch, taking notice of the intricate porcupine quilling along the flap. "Thank you, Snow Blanket. I'll treasure it always. I only wish I had something to give to you."

The woman smiled. "But you have. You made my son's heart sing."

Bee ran to Deborah and threw his arms around her. "Don't leave, Deb-or-ah. Don't go back!"

She smoothed his tight cap of dark curls. "You behave yourself, Bee, and stay away from bear cubs. All right?

Tears ran down his cheeks as he backed away, nodding.

Without another word, Deborah brushed by Tshingee and out into the cold. Tshingee turned to follow her but Snow Blanket caught his arm.

"I wish I could heal your pains as I did when you were a child, my *giis*," she said softly. "Take care. The love I see between you is fierce."

"I gave my word, *Onna*. I said I would return her to her father safely and I intend to do it."

"I know what you sacrifice. You have this woman's respect." She stood on her tiptoes and kissed his cheek. "Go in safety and in peace, my son."

When Tshingee entered his wigwam, Deborah had

already made a bed on the floor and was lying still beside the fire, her eyes closed. Lashing the door flap, he removed his fur cloak and stoked the fire. His heart was a hard lump beneath his breast. A part of him was furious with his Red Bird. She had deceived him and that hurt. But a part of him still wanted desperately to hold her . . . to make love to her one last time.

Quietly, he made his bed on the opposite side of the fire and lay down, pulling a heavy woolen blanket over him. Resting his head in his arms, he gazed through the wall of flames at Deborah's sleeping face. Somehow the anger he felt for her betrayal made the pain duller. He hoped it was the same for her. For a long time he lay awake watching her sleep before he finally drifted off.

The first rays of morning light brought Tshingee awake. Anxious to return to the Tidewater and have his brother set free, he moved about the wigwam, packing a last few necessary items. "Deborah," he said firmly. "Deborah. wake up."

She blinked, rolling onto her back. The lazy smile fell from her face the moment she remembered what today was. "You're not really going to force me to go back, are you?" She stood and pulled her deerskin dress over her goose-pimpled flesh.

Tshingee kept his eyes averted to prevent his body from betraying his mind. "I told your father I would trade you for my brother. The time has come to make the trade."

"I'm not going. You find another way to get him back," she answered stubbornly as she stuffed her feet into a pair of knee-high moccasins. "I'm staying here. I'll live with Snow Blanket. You're so clever. *You* find a way to get your brother back safely *without* involving me."

Tshingee ground his teeth. This white woman made the anger rise so easily within him. "You are going if I have to bind you and carry you every foot of the way, now let us go. We've already wasted precious daylight."

Deborah sat down cross-legged in front of the tiny fire. "I'm telling you. I won't walk a step."

Deborah had never been so humiliated in her entire life. Instead of walking out of the village with her head held high, she rode out . . . tied to a short-legged pony.

She had refused to walk and Tshingee had refused to reason with her. Before she knew what was happening, he had bound her hands and feet and thrown her over the little brown pony like a slain deer.

"You could at least tie me on sitting up," she argued, mortified. She hung upside down on her stomach so that the only thing she could see was the pony's underside and her own feet.

Tshingee was unsympathetic. "If I had treated you like a true prisoner from the start," he snapped, "I would not have had these troubles to begin with. You cannot act honorable, then you will not be treated so." Adding a few more bags to the pony's back, he lifted the animal's lead line and started out of the camp.

Deborah was thankful that most of the villagers were still in their wigwams as she rode through the camp. From the way she lay on the pony, she could see nothing. The camp was silent save for the occasional bark of a dog. The sun was just beginning to light the sky.

"Tshingee!" Deborah heard Snow Blanket's voice. "Are you crazed, my son? What are you doing?"

Tshingee brought the pony to a halt. "I am returning the prisoner."

"Is this any way to treat the woman who saved your betrothed from death?"

"Suuklan and I are no longer to wed."

"It makes no difference," Snow Blanket insisted. "There is no reason to treat the girl like this."

"The prisoner refuses to do as she is told," he said coldly. "I have no time to waste coddling her."

Deborah heard Snow Blanket take a step back. "Go, then, son," she said quietly. "May the Gods be with you and may you return with your senses as well as your brother."

Tshingee gave a grunt, tugging on the pony's lead line and started for the forest.

Chapter Thirteen

The sun rose high in the sky and then began to make its descent. Sometime after noon Tshingee stopped for water and untied Deborah, allowing her to sit up before he tied her to the short-legged pony again. Then they moved on; neither Deborah nor Tshingee had uttered a single word since they'd left the Lenni Lenape village at dawn.

For hours Deborah rode in stubborn silence. She was furious with Tshingee; she was furious with herself. How had their love for each other come to this? How could she be so selfish as to ask Tshingee to risk his own brother's life and allow her to stay? But how could Tshingee send her back to Host's Wealth, knowing the woman he loved was to become another man's wife? Nothing made any sense anymore, and the longer Deborah wrestled with her thoughts, the more confused she became.

Finally Tshingee stopped and began to set up camp for the night. Deborah watched him as he gathered wood and disappeared into the forest, returning a few minutes later with a hide bucket filled with fresh water.

"Are you going to untie me now, or do I sleep here

179

too?" she asked sarcastically.

He didn't look up from where he knelt preparing a bed for the campfire. "Depends . . ."

She lifted a sooty eyebrow. "On what?"

"On whether or not you will cooperate. I will not chase you through the forest. I have no time to waste. My brother waits."

"Run?" She laughed harshly. "Where am I going to run *to?* It's obvious I'm not welcome in your village. You think I'm going to run home? They'll not be any more pleased to have me than you were."

Tshingee winced inwardly. Returning Deborah to the Tidewater was the most difficult thing he had ever had to do—couldn't she see that? Didn't his Red Bird know how much this pained him? He removed his tinderbox from a bag around his waist and started the fire. "Do you swear you will not run?"

She rolled her eyes. "I swear. Now please let me down!"

He took his time, feeding the infant flames chunks of dried moss, then small sticks. Finally he added three branches and then came to her. He pulled a long-bladed knife from his belt and cut the leather thongs. Deborah swung her legs over the pony, but when her feet hit the ground, they refused to hold her. Her knees buckled and she swayed. Instinctively, Tshingee put out his arms to steady her.

Deborah lifted her lashes to meet his molten gaze. For a long moment a taut silence stretched between them. She moistened her dry lips with the tip of her tongue, unable to tear her gaze from his. Her hands rested on the broad expanse of his chest. Without thinking she smoothed the linen of the shirt he wore beneath his fur cloak. "You know" she whispered,

180

"your taking me back, it changes nothing between us."

Tshingee could feel his resolve wavering. He had sworn he would never touch her again. He had sworn to separate his emotions from his logic. Still, his hands ached to caress her. He could see her lips trembling in anticipation. . .

"I know." He released her, turning his back on her to add more sticks to the growing campfire.

Deborah sighed. "How long until we reach Host's Wealth?"

"A day on foot, another day and a half by dugout if the weather is good."

"Then what?" She cupped her hands and drank from the hide water bucket.

"Then we wait. Four nights from tonight the exchange will take place."

"Will John go back with you or will he remain at the cabin?" She hugged her cloak, turning her back to the biting wind.

"I do not know what my brother will do." He handed her a hunk of venison jerky, avoiding eye contact. "Eat. We will move at dawn."

The following day passed much like the last, only now Deborah walked beside the pony rather than being tied to it. Hour after hour passed as they traveled east and Tshingee said nothing save to give brief commands. By noon, Deborah had given up trying to talk to him, and suffered the remainder of the day in bitter silence. At dusk the two reached a river and Tshingee began to set up camp. After unloading the packs from the pony, he gave the animal a pat on the backside and it took off in the direction they'd come.

"Where's he going?"

"Home." Tshingee was gathering firewood.

"Home? But how does he know where home is?"

"Bee could find his way home from here. It's a simple line west, around the briar patch and another quarter of a day north."

Deborah nodded, watching the pony wishfully as he disappeared from sight. "Wish I was going with him," she murmured.

The following morning Tshingee woke Deborah. The dew on the grass glimmered with frost and the wind carried the scent of a winter storm. "Put out the fire and make ready to go," he told her, tightening the tie on his cloak.

"Where are you going?"

"There's a dugout within a mile of here. We will take it up the Migianac."

"This is the Migianac?" She stared at the running river, disturbed that she was so close to home and hadn't known it.

Not bothering to reply, Tshingee set off down river, following the bank. An hour later he returned, bringing the wooden dugout to a halt. He treaded water with the single paddle, trying to keep the vessel from moving backward. "The river is swift," he called. "Throw the bags and then I will come for you. Hurry."

Running down the bank, Deborah flung a hide knapsack and then another. Wrapping her water bag and several other leather bags of assorted sizes around her neck, she waved. "I'm ready."

"I cannot get that close to the shore," he called above the sound of the churning white water. "Ahead there is a tree trunk hanging out over the water." He pointed. "Walk out on it and drop into the dugout as I come under it."

"Drop into it?" she asked incredulously.

"That or swim out."

She groaned aloud. "If I drown, it's your fault." She threw up her hands, tromping along the bank. "There's a storm coming. We don't belong out on that river riding on that log," she complained. Reaching the fallen tree, she mounted it and walked out along the trunk, her arms spread for balance.

Tshingee leaned forward, kneeling in the bottom of the boat and paddled, directing the dugout squarely beneath the tree. Deborah gave a little yelp as she leaped, but she landed safely in the bow. The dugout rocked violently in the water, but Tshingee steadied it and began to paddle.

Once in the dugout, the water seemed even rougher to Deborah than it had from the shore. "Are you certain we ought to be doing this?" she asked. "The sky looks awfully dark." The wind howled, whipping her hair in her face.

"I told you. We have no time to waste. We will ride the Migianac until she becomes too angry and then we will go ashore."

Deborah held on to the sides of the dugout as it rocked and swayed violently. She watched Tshingee as he fought to keep the boat on course. He shrugged his cloak from his shoulders and rolled up his sleeves, baring his uncovered arms to the frigid air. He paddled so hard that the veins stood out on his biceps. "How much time are we saving when you have to paddle that hard? We should go ashore and wait out the storm."

"Silence," he muttered. "Perhaps the storm will pass over us."

But it didn't. The wind began to blow harder, the trees along the shoreline bending in submission. The dugout made less and less progress as Tshingee paddled harder. Branches littered the water which churned and splashed, threatening to sink the dugout.

"You don't have to impress me, Tshingee. Enough is enough." Deborah shouted. Water came in over the sides, soaking them both. "We're going to drown."

"I have been in the great ocean in a dugout," Tshingee replied. Sleet pelted his face, soaking his ebony hair so that it hung in a shimmering curtain about his face.

At that moment a large tree stump bobbed up in front of them. Deborah shouted a warning and Tshingee leaned hard to the left, paddling desperately to avoid it. The dugout hit the trunk with a loud crash and splintering of wood and suddenly Deborah found herself in the frigid, churning water.

She bobbed up, catching the corner of the turned-over dugout. "Tshingee!" she shouted. Clutching the bark dugout, she kicked, turning this way and that. For a moment she saw a glimpse of his cloak, but then through the sleet she lost sight of him.

Holding tightly to the log, she kicked to stay free of the floating debris that littered the surface. She was so cold that her hands were blue and her teeth chattered, but she hung on. The water washed her a quarter of a mile farther down the river before the dugout miraculously became caught in a tangle of briars hanging from the bank.

Gasping for breath, Deborah pulled herself onto the bank, wiping the water from her eyes. Which way? she thought desperately. Upstream or down? Which way is he? Down, instinct told her. She would have traveled more slowly hanging on to the dugout.

Racing down the bank, Deborah shouted Tshingee's name over and over again, praying there would be a reply. She was finally rewarded with a hoarse "Here."

Scrambling down the bank, she caught sight of Tshingee's dark head. He hung on to a long branch, caught along the side of the bank. "Deborah . . ." He held his hand out to her.

Deborah dropped her hands to her hips. Her teeth were chattering so hard that she could barely speak. "St . . . stupid, hardheaded redskin!"

"Deborah. Help me!"

"Oh, don't worry, he says! I've been in the great ocean in my dugout log! I'm a great Lenni Lenape warrior. I can ride this out."

Tshingee's hand slipped on the wet bark and he struggled desperately to catch a hold of something more stable. "Deborah! I can't hold on much longer and my legs are tangled beneath the water. Help me!"

"I don't know why I should!" She picked up a long branch from the bank. "Why should I?" she shouted, spitting a lock of wet hair out her mouth. She held the branch over his head, just out of his reach. "Tell me one good reason why I shouldn't let you drown!"

He shook his head in disbelief. If he hadn't been in such dire straits, he thought he would have laughed. This white woman was mad! "Because I love you," he shouted.

Sighing, she lowered the branch until he caught it Then, she held on with all her might, using a sapling to get better leverage as he crawled out of the water and up the bank. Finally the pull on the branch went slack and Tshingee crumpled on the ground facedown. Shaking violently with cold, Deborah kneeled beside him, suddenly frightened.

"Tshingee, are you all right?" She rolled him over. His eyes were shut, his face pale, his breathing shallow.

185

"My God, Tshingee, I didn't mean—"

His eyes flew open and his arms went around her as he pulled her down on top of him, laughing.

"Oh! You!" She slapped him hard in the chest with both hands. "I thought you'd nearly drowned. I ought to roll you down the bank and—" Her eyes met his and suddenly she was pressing her cold, trembling lips to his.

Tshingee hesitated for only a moment before he was threading his hands through her wet hair, accepting her lips greedily. He delved deep into her mouth with his tongue, reveling in the warmth of her desire. Deborah clung to him, her heart pounding.

When their lips parted, Deborah brushed the wet hair from his face. "I . . . I'm freezing," she chattered. "How are we ever going to get warm?"

Tshingee rolled from beneath her and stood, offering his hand to help her up. "An abandoned cabin, northwest of here. We can start a fire and get in out of the cold." Sleet was falling heavily now, pelting them and forming a slick frozen crust over their clothing.

"We didn't lose too much." She grimaced, patting the bags still strung around her neck. "No thanks to you of course."

Tshingee hurried her along, headed inland from the river. "Where's the dugout?"

"Gone. D—didn't you see it pass you? I hung on to it until I got to shore but then it floated away—pieces of it anyway." She hung on tightly to his hand, suppressing a smile. It had been worth nearly drowning to have Tshingee touch her like this again, to feel his lips on hers.

"I am sorry that my foolishness cost us this time and the dugout. You were right, I should have waited for

186

the storm to pass before starting upriver." He shook his head. "I don't know what you've done to me, Red Bird. I was never so unthinking before you came into my life."

Deborah let the comment pass. "You know where a cabin is, and this is the second boat you've had hidden along the river. What else have you hiding in wait at your disposal?"

He chuckled. "A man should always be aware of the dangers along the path; he must be prepared. The first dugout belongs to my brother and I. We use it for duck hunting. The second was very old, belonging to a Shawnee cousin of mine who has gone west. The cabin I knew of because my grandfather once had a friend who lived there." He ducked a low-hanging branch and lifted it to let Deborah through.

"How far? It's so cold." The wind whipped and howled through the trees, blowing their cloaks open with each gust. The wet clothing she wore was so heavy with water that she could barely walk.

"A mile perhaps. Just keep walking." Tshingee slipped his arm beneath her cloak. "Think of the warm fire. Hot tea."

She shook her head. "One of the food bags went down with the boat. The tea probably went with it."

"Then I will find something to make you tea with." He brushed his lips against her forehead.

Just when Deborah thought she couldn't walk another step, a cabin appeared in a small clearing deep in a pine grove. The structure was a tiny, log lean-to with part of one wall missing. The wood was charred black from a fire long ago. "That's going to be warm?" Deborah asked doubtfully.

"Do you prefer a hollowed log? I know of one a few

miles — "

"All right! All right!" Deborah laughed at herself. "Please, just start a fire so I can get these wet things off."

Together the two entered the cabin through the hole in the wall. The whole structure was no more than ten by ten feet, including a crumbling brick hearth and chimney. It was dark and musty-smelling inside, but it was dry save for a small area where the rain and sleet had come in through the hole.

Tshingee busied himself making a fire with the flint and steel he still carried in a bag on his waist. Using pieces of bark he chipped from an inside wall for kindling, the tiny spark of a fire glowed in a matter of minutes.

"Not much to burn in h — here," Deborah pointed out, standing as close to the fire as possible.

"Keep feeding it with the bark. I will find wood." He started back through the hole in the wall.

"Outside in this?"

He didn't reply but ten minutes later he returned with an armful of relatively dry wood. He smiled. "One just has to know where to look."

Deborah watched proudly as he added a thick log to the fire on the tiny brick hearth. Then he removed his cloak and began tacking it over the hole in the wall. "Give me your cloak. The inside will dry while the fur side keeps the rain out."

Deborah handed him her cloak in amazement. He was so clever! "Now what?" She rubbed her bare arms briskly. Already the warmth of the fire was heating the tiny room.

"Take off your clothes."

"I was hoping you'd say that," she said huskily. She

grinned when he turned to look at her.

Both knew that today they would not be able to resist each other. Today their differences would be pushed aside, forgotten for a few brief fleeting moments of pleasure.

Deborah trembled inwardly in anticipation as she stripped off her wet moccasins and sleeveless winter dress. Laying out her clothes so that they would dry, she came up behind Tshingee, wrapping her arms around his waist. "You're shivering," she whispered. "Take off your wet things."

Slowly he turned to her. "I shiver for want of you, Red Bird. I tell myself again and again the reasons why I must keep my distance from you . . ." His hands fell to his sides as she tugged his linen shirt over his head and began to unlace the ties of his leather leggings. "But I long for you. I long to hold you. I long to touch you."

She smiled up at him, letting the legging fall from her fingers to the floor. "Touch me, Tshingee."

"It is not right. You belong to another man."

She dropped to her knees and began to unlace his wet moccasins. "Soon I'll belong to another man. Today I belong to you." She removed the second moccasin.

Tshingee could not stifle a groan as she moved her hands over his knees and up the length of his corded thighs. His eyes drifted shut. "Would that I could change what has happened. What must. But I see no way to keep you and my family safe. If I come back for you once John is released, the whites will hunt us down. I have seen the slaughter of entire villages . . ." His voice caught in his throat.

"Shhhh," Deborah soothed, pressing feathery kisses

189

to his burgeoning flesh. "I know, Tshingee. Don't think about it. I know that if it were in your power, if it were in mine, we would be together, but it's like Snow Blanket told me. It's just not in the stars."

Tshingee looked down at Deborah. He offered his hands to her, intertwining their fingers. His ebony eyes shone bright with a mixture of pride and regret. "I love you, my Red Bird. You must remember that always. No matter what I say, what I do." Slowly he dropped to his knees before her. "No matter what, you must remember that that is what is in my heart." He pressed her hand to his chest.

"I'll remember." She kissed him, wrapping her arms tightly around his neck. Then she smoothed his cheek with her palm.

Tshingee lowered his head, catching the tip of her rounded breast with his mouth. Deborah laughed deep in her throat, throwing her head back. "I'll never forget you, Tshingee. I'll never forget what you do to me," she murmured, caressing the breadth of his back.

Cradling her in his arms, Tshingee lowered her to the floor, stretching the length of his body over hers.

"Love, me," Deborah whispered, threading his long midnight tresses through her fingers. Keep the world at bay just a little longer."

Tshingee lowered his mouth to hers and for a brief time they were lost in the bittersweet flame of ecstasy.

Hand in hand Deborah and Tshingee walked the last mile to the place where the exchange would take place. Deborah said nothing, not trusting herself. She just held on to Tshingee, her cheek resting against his arm.

A chilling breeze whipped off the Migianac River,

blowing Tshingee's ebony hair off his shoulders to tangle in Deborah's. His heart was heavy but he walked with a determined stride of resolution.

"When will they be there?" Deborah asked quietly.

"Dusk."

"They will bring John?"

"I told your father he must if you are to be returned."

Deborah's lower lip trembled. Ahead she could hear the sound of low male voices and the occasional snort of a horse. The sun was just beginning to set over the western horizon. Deborah pulled her cloak tighter around her shoulders as if she could ward off the men's presence as well as the cold. "They're early," she whispered.

Tshingee stopped, taking Deborah in his arms. He knew her father was just around the next bend in the river. "I say good- bye now to you, Red Bird, and I warn you. Do not tell anyone of the two of us."

Deborah stared up into his dark eyes, trying to memorize the curve of his high bronze cheekbones, the line of his long majestic nose. She laughed nervously. "You think me a fool? There will be talk enough without my adding fuel to the fire."

He kissed her lips tenderly. "We must go."

Deborah slid her hand beneath his cloak, touching his neck as she kissed him again. "What's this?" She pulled back his cloak to study a strange braided cord around his neck. It was thin and shiny.

He lifted his hand to his neck. "I must confess, Red Bird. When I cut your hair — " he tugged on her shorn front lock — "I did not send it all to your father. I kept of piece of you for myself."

Smiling, Deborah drew his cloak back and tied the

thong tightly. "Another kiss," she whispered, "and then let's go, before I lose my nerve.

"I love you, Deborah."

"I love you, Tshingee."

Sealing their fate with a final kiss, Tshingee started for the bend in the river and Deborah fell in step behind him.

"Here they come!" came a harsh male voice through the trees.

"Where?" another shouted.

"There, can't you see I'm. The redskin!"

"What of Lady Deborah? She there?"

"Don't know. There's a female but she looks like another red bastard to me!"

Deborah kept her head lowered, following in Tshingee's footsteps. When she heard him stop, she stopped. She could not lift her gaze from her moccasins for fear of losing control.

"So, finally we meet, redskin," came the Earl of Manchester's voice. "Slick devil, aren't you? We combed these woods for a hundred miles looking for you and your filth."

Tshingee breathed evenly, studying the group of men out of the corner of his eye. Deborah's father was a rotund man with hanging jowls and slick dark hair. Behind him were a circle of men on horseback that surrounded John who was on foot. Behind that clump, in the rear, was the boy James and another man holding the reins of Deborah's horse. "Send my brother forward. I will return your daughter and we will all go in peace," Tshingee stated evenly.

The Earl leaned forward on his horse. "What if you mean to trick me, redskin? Doesn't look like much is left of my daughter standing there in those filthy rags.

What other tricks have you got up your sleeve?"

"Tricks? I am an unarmed man, as I'm sure you are." The agreement had been no weapons, but Tshingee was certain he saw the butt of a musket protruding from beneath the Earl's cloak. "*You* bring an army of men. Who is the trickster?"

"Can we get on with this?" Deborah suddenly demanded, stepping forward.

Tshingee reached out with an iron grasp. "First, untie John and send him forward. Then I release your daughter."

The Earl sighed, nodding to one of his bondmen. "Let him go, Lester."

Deborah watched as her father's overseer cut the binding at John's hands. John flinched. Out of the corner of her eye, Deborah saw Thomas move forward on his mount, leading her horse, Joshua.

"So he's loose now, redskin. Send my daughter forward."

Tshingee took a deep breath. John was still surrounded by half a dozen men. Slowly Tshingee let go of Deborah's arm. As he released his grasp on her, he felt his heart slipping. In a moment his brother would be safe, but a blackness settled over his spirit as Deborah walked forward.

The man who was to marry Deborah helped her mount and then began to lead her away. Time stood still as Tshingee watched Thomas lead Deborah around the group of men and into the woods. Her brother trailed behind them.

Deborah kept her back ramrod straight as Thomas led her out of the clearing. She could feel Tshingee's eyes on her and her heart swelled with pride. *I love you,* her heart sang out.

James chuckled, riding up behind her. "Got his red ass, don't we, Thomas?" He waved a musket.

Deborah spun around in horror. The instant her eyes met her brother's, she knew what he meant. "No!" she screamed. Leaning forward she yanked Joshua's reins out of Thomas's hand. Sinking her heels into her horse's flanks, she wheeled him around and headed back through the trees toward her father and his men. As she passed James, her hand shot out and she grabbed his musket from his hand.

Holding the musket over her head, she pulled the trigger, riding into the clearing. The air filled with the booming sound of black powder and the shrill resonance of her voice. "It's a trap! Run, Tshingee! Run!"

Chapter Fourteen

The instant Tshingee heard Deborah's voice, he dove for the cover of a pine tree. Horses reared and men shouted, drawing weapons.

"John!" Tshingee cried out.

John raced forward, dodging horses' hooves as he made his way toward his brother.

"Get them, damn it!" the Earl bellowed, wheeling his steed around.

Deborah rode through the center of the mounted men, shouting and waving James's musket. "Run, Tshingee," she shouted. "Run, for God's sake!"

Spotting a bondman riding straight for John, Deborah sank her knees into her horse's side. "Look out, John," she warned. But it was too late. The bondservant swung the butt of his musket, cracking John in the head.

"Noo!" Deborah urged her horse forward as John crumpled to the ground, his head smeared with blood.

"Deborah, come back here!" the Earl demanded. Deborah ignored her father, heading straight for the clump of pines she had seen Tshingee disappear into.

The Earl shook his fist in anger. "Stop her, Lester!"

Lester rode up beside Deborah and she swung the unloaded musket at his head. The overseer ducked, cursing as he reached out and yanked her out of the sidesaddle.

"Let go of me!" Deborah screamed, flailing her arms wildly. The musket fell from her grip. "Let me go, you son of a bitch! Tshingee!" She pummeled her father's henchman with her fists, causing him to lose his balance, and both of them tumbled from their horses to the ground.

Deborah looked up from the bed of fallen leaves to see Tshingee running toward the river. Instinctively she reached out to him with her hands.

A shot was fired, followed by two more and Tshingee's body jerked unnaturally. Deborah watched in mute horror as he went down on one knee only to struggle to his feet again, his back crimson with blood. The air echoed with a barrage of gunshots and Tshingee was hit again as he dove off the bank and into the river.

"Don't let him get away!" the Earl shouted.

"Kill the red bastard!" James echoed, riding behind his father.

Sinking her face into her hands, hot tears ran down Deborah's cheeks. Lester rolled off her but she just lay there sobbing as the men on horseback raced for the river bank.

"Shoot the red bastard when he comes up," a man shouted from the group.

"We caught him two or three times! How far can he get?" added another.

Wiping her eyes with the back of her hand, Deborah forced herself to her feet and headed for the river. Lester reached out to take her arm but she jerked away. "You touch me again," she threatened viciously, "and I'll kick you in the teeth!"

Lester's eyes narrowed with hostility. "Someone's going to teach you a lesson one of these days," he called after her, wiping his bloody mouth.

Running toward the river, Deborah circled the knot of men still on horseback. They all stood at the bank, staring at the rushing water.

"Drowned, eh, Father?" James asked.

"Had to. No man could survive that and still get away. Not even one of those red devils."

Deborah looked from her father to the water again, staring in mute shock. *He has to be alive!* she thought numbly. *He can't be dead, not after all he's been through.*

"Walk along the river, Stuart, and look for the body," the Earl ordered impatiently. "I want that body!" He wheeled his horse around, perusing the group of men. "Thomas!"

"Yes, sir?" Thomas came riding toward the river-bank.

"Get Deborah on her horse and get her the hell out of here. Take her back to Host's Wealth and James with you."

"Yes, sir." Thomas dismounted, leading his horse to where Deborah stood staring into the icy water. "Deborah." He touched her arm lightly when she didn't respond, but she jerked away.

"Don't touch me," she whispered, drawing her hide cloak closer.

"Deborah. It's nearly dark. Let me help you onto your horse and take you home," he said compassionately. A bondman led Joshua over and Thomas accepted the reins. "Deborah, please."

Suddenly, she was so tired that she thought she would faint. Her mind was numb. "All right," she

197

whispered.

Thomas brought her horse around and put out his hand to help her up. "Up you go."

Mechanically, Deborah obeyed.

Without another word, Thomas mounted and led her through the clearing past John's prone body.

"Is he dead?" she managed weakly.

"No." Thomas righted his cocked hat. "He'll have his trial as set down by English law . . . then he'll die."

"Dear heavenly father," Elizabeth groaned, shaking her head. She crossed the bedchamber to her sister, taking her hands and pressing them to her lips. "If Thomas hadn't told me it was you, I'd never have recognized you. You look like some half-crazed redskin!"

Deborah stared, her eyes dull and lifeless.

"What have they done to you, dear sister?" Elizabeth pulled the cloak off Deborah's shoulders and let it fall to the floor. "Deborah, it's Elizabeth, can you hear me?" She took her sister's cheeks in her palms, peering into her face with fright.

Deborah sighed. She knew she had to get control of herself. Tshingee would have wanted her to remain brave. "Yes, I can hear you, twit." She pushed Elizabeth's hands aside.

Elizabeth took a step back, her eyes wide with surprise. "Are . . . are you all right? What a silly question. Of course you aren't! I can't believe you're back. I thought surely after all this time you were dead, praise the good Lord!"

Deborah studied her bedchamber, ignoring her sister. The room she had loved once upon a time seemed

198

so foreign now, so confining after Tshingee's wigwam and the open forest. "Could you call me a bath?"

"Done." Elizabeth nodded. "Supper too. Cook made apple pie. I told her to send up a big piece."

"I'm not hungry." Deborah walked to the window and pushed it open, letting in the frigid night air.

"What are you doing?" Elizabeth hurried across the room, her heeled slippers tapping on the hardwood floor. "You'll catch your death."

"I can't breath in here. It stinks." Deborah opened the window a second time.

Just then a knock came at the door. "Come in." Elizabeth called.

A strapping young man came in carrying a brass bathtub, followed by two negro boys bearing buckets of steamy water. The women stood in silence until the tub had been filled and the servants departed.

Deborah stripped off her clothes without hesitation and Elizabeth gave a gasp, turning away. "Dear sister! Where's your modesty?"

"And where's my tongue-tied sister? You've said more to me in the last half an hour than you have in the past year. What's gotten into you since I've been gone? Found a man, have you?" She dropped her deerskin dress to the floor and slipped into the tub.

"Don't be ridiculous!" Elizabeth hurried across the room to where Deborah's cloak lay on the floor. "What have those heathens done to you, dressing you in this thing?" she asked, trying to cover her embarrassment. "It's probably crawling with vermin." She picked up the cloak and tossed it out into the hall in disgust.

Deborah sat in the tub, running the water-logged sponge over her breasts. "Done to me? They did nothing but treat me with kindness."

Elizabeth kept her back to her sister for decency's sake. "Father said you might be like this when you came home, but I had no idea!" She busied herself arranging a sleeping gown on the bed.

"Like this? Like what?" Deborah leaned back in the tub in exhaustion. She couldn't allow herself to think of Tshingee, not now.

"Father said that when captives are returned, they . . . they have a tendency to feel some alliance with their captors. It's happened with the redskins before. Father said there are even extreme cases where women have tried to return to the savages!" Elizabeth shuddered.

"Extreme cases, hmmm?" Deborah got out of the tub and reached for a linen towel.

Elizabeth brought her the sleeping gown. "Here, put this on. I can stay if you want, until you're asleep." She kept her eyes discreetly averted as Deborah dropped the towel and walked to her bed stark naked.

"I don't want the sleeping gown and I don't want anyone sleeping with me," she answered in a tired voice. "I just want to be left alone."

Elizabeth nodded. "I understand. You've been so brave. But don't worry, you're safe now." She waited until Deborah had climbed beneath the sheets and then laid the sleeping gown out on the end of the bed. "The Earl has a man outside guarding your windows and Lester will be sleeping in the hall. No one can harm you now.

Deborah squeezed her eyes shut, trying to block out the smell of the room, the feel of the mattress beneath her. All she wanted was Tshingee and he was gone. She felt so empty, so alone. "Elizabeth."

"Yes?"

Deborah choked back her tears. "Could you blow

200

out the candle and go?"

"Of course." She blew out the candle and tiptoed out of the room, leaving Deborah in darkness.

Tshingee's breath came in shallow gasps; his heartbeat was rapid. Under the cloak of darkness he lay on the river's edge battling the unconsciousness that had taken him again and again in the last few hours. It was so cold. Tshingee lifted his head from the frozen bank of the Migianac, trying to get his bearings. How far downriver had he come? He dropped his head to the ground in utter exhaustion.

I must find shelter, he told himself. *Find shelter, Wildcat of the Wolf clan, or your spirit will walk the heavens by dawn's light.* The thought of death was strangely appealing to Tshingee. Without Deborah, what was life? But there were still his responsibilities. There was John. He had sworn to John that he would do everything in his power to rescue him. It was an obligation he could not release himself from.

Rising up on his elbows, Tshingee fought a wave of nausea. When the dizziness passed, he pushed with his knees, crawling up the bank to higher ground. A hot, molten pain seared in his chest, radiating through his limbs. He didn't know how many times he had been hit by the white men's musket balls, but he knew his situation was grave. Slowly he made his way along the river, not knowing where he was headed, only knowing that it was not safe here. If the white men came looking for him, he would be unable to escape. Spasms of searing pain mingled with the cold that seeped through his being and Tshingee began to shiver violently.

Twice he tried to stand, but he could not. His legs refused to hold his weight. Gasping for breath, he rolled onto his back, staring up at the full moon that hung overhead. Impulsively his hand went to his neck. Beneath his sodden cloak and shirt he found the strand of Deborah's hair he wore braided in a necklace. A near smile rose on his lips and for a moment his heart was filled with joy. "Deborah," he said quietly. "Deborah." He repeated her name again and again, gaining a strength from her that made him roll onto his stomach again and crawl forward.

Inching his way along the forest floor, Tshingee crossed the path of slithering snakes and curious white-tailed deer. Owls hooted high in the tree tops and small nocturnal animals scurried through the brush. Once, when Tshingee was resting near a hickory tree a raccoon wobbled past him, stopping to stare curiously at the human.

Tshingee smiled, making a clicking sound between his teeth. For several minutes the masked creature studied him before finally wandering off. His spirit refreshed, Tshingee moved on.

He didn't know where he was headed, but he knew that if he lay still, he would sleep and deep in slumber he would die. Taking an inch of the frozen ground at a time, he crawled on. Sometime in the night a numbness overtook him and the pain of the gunshot wounds and frigid air dulled. His mind was so hazy that he could not think. Mechanically he pushed forward, navigating blindly through the dark forest. When his head hit a clump of briars, he fell over, rolling into a fetal position. The bleeding had started again. He could feel a warm liquid oozing down his back.

With a final effort, Tshingee lifted his head, taking

in his surroundings. By the light of the moon he could see the bramble patch that loomed above him. By sheer luck, his gaze fell to a small opening. With a last surge of energy he dragged himself through the hole. To his surprise there was enough room inside for a man to sit up on his knees or stretch out. In the center of the hollow in the brambles was an indentation in the leaves made by a large animal. The smell of deer hide rose up from the ground as Tshingee lay wearily in the animal's sleeping hollow. With a sigh, he pulled his wet cloak over his head and fell into an exhausted sleep.

"Deborah, at least talk to him." Elizabeth sat on the bed next to her. "This is the third day in a row he's come to see you. He's deathly worried."

Deborah flung herself back on the bed, staring up at the plastered white ceiling. "I want nothing to do with Thomas Hogarth."

"You can't just lie here in your shift forever." Elizabeth twisted her hands in frustration. "The Earl is losing his patience. He says you have to come down and speak with Thomas today, or he's coming up to get you."

Deborah wrinkled her nose. "That's a sight I'd like to see! The Earl of Manchester managing to get me and himself down the steps without killing the both of us! He hasn't picked up anything heavier than a tea cup in years."

"Please. Just come down for a few minutes. What harm can it do?" She got up off the bed and went to fetch one of Deborah's favorite gowns. "You can't sit here on this bed forever."

Deborah sat back up. As much as she hated to admit

it, her sister was right. She *couldn't* sit here in her bedchamber and rot like an old bit of linen. It just wasn't in her. It wasn't the way she knew Tshingee would have wanted her to behave. He was gone and she had to learn to live with that pain. But so could she live with the pleasure of his memory. Just the thought of the sound of his laughter brought a smile to her lips.

"You'll come down?" Elizabeth held out the emerald green woolen gown hopefully.

"I'll come down," Deborah conceded. "But only to get out of this house and breath some fresh air. If Tom wants to speak with me, it will have to be outside. I think I'll walk down to the river and back."

"Oh, Deborah, that's much too far to go. The Earl will never—"

"The Earl will never know as long as you keep your tongue in your head."

Elizabeth dropped the woolen gown on the bed and ran to retrieve a pair of stockings and a corset for her sister. "Let me help you dress." She tossed the dark wool stockings on the bed and held up the corset.

Deborah laughed. "I'm not putting that thing on."

Elizabeth stared in shock. "Well of course you are. You've been wearing a corset since you were five." Deborah sat on the edge of the bed and began to roll on her stockings. "Yes, and I'd forgotten what it was like to take a deep breath."

"The gown will never fit!" Elizabeth protested.

"Then I'll go down in my shift."

Elizabeth responded with a wordless roll of her eyes.

Ignoring her sister, Deborah pulled the green woolen gown over her head, lifting her breasts up before she tightened the strings of the bodice. Though the gown did not fit quite the way it once had, it fit and she could breathe. "There, you see." She lifted her arms in demonstration. "I'll just tell Thomas I got fat. She dropped to her knees to retrieve her leather boots from beneath the bed. Slipping into them, she started for the door. "Well? Are you coming? Surely you wouldn't want to miss the great reunion."

Elizabeth's cheeks burned with a mixture of anger and jealousy, but she said nothing, following in her sister's footsteps.

Deborah walked through the parlor, passing a seated Thomas. "I'm going out for a walk. You coming?" she asked, not waiting for a reply.

Thomas popped out of his seat, creasing his forehead questioningly in Elizabeth's direction.

Elizabeth shrugged. "She says she's going for a walk. You'd better go with her. The Earl doesn't want her out alone," she said as Deborah disappeared down the hall and out of earshot.

"You come too." Thomas took Elizabeth's elbow. "I'll feel better if you're there. I . . . I'm not sure what to say to her."

Elizabeth's facial features softened. "All right, Tom. If you really want me to."

There was a scurry of activity among the servants and in a few minutes' time Thomas and Elizabeth were out the door, following Deborah's footsteps in the snow. It had snowed last night, leaving a soft glistening blanket of white to cover the ground and laden the trees.

"Deborah, wait for us, Thomas called, hanging on to Elizabeth's elbow to guide her through a snowdrift.

Deborah stopped, waiting impatiently. Cupping a handful of snow in her woolen mitten, she flung it at the side of the smokehouse.

"Deborah." Thomas breathed heavily, clouds of frost rising with each word. "I'm so glad to see you out and about. I've been so worried."

Deborah scooped up another handful of snow and packed it carefully. "That was a dirty thing you did back there, Thomas Hogarth. The agreement was that the red men would go free." It hurt her not to use Tshingee's name, but she knew she had to be careful of what she said. "That's the kind of thing men burn in hell for, Tom."

"I had nothing to do with it. You must believe me. All the Earl said was that I was to get you mounted and out of there as quickly as possible."

Deborah scowled, throwing the second snowball. She knew Thomas was telling the truth — not that it made her feel any better.

"But it's all over now, Deborah," Elizabeth assured soothingly. "You're home safe. Everything's going to be all right, isn't it, Thomas?" She couldn't keep her lower lip from trembling as she spoke.

"Elizabeth is right. Everything is going to be fine." Thomas touched Deborah's arm lightly. "The contract's not been broken if that's what you're concerned about."

"The contract!" Deborah whirled around.

"It's all right, darling. I'm still going to marry you. I know that whatever happened to you among the savages wasn't your fault." Despite the frigid air, his forehead was beaded with perspiration. "You were just an innocent victim of their debauchery."

Deborah's eyes narrowed dangerously. "Just what are you saying, Tom?" She pushed back the hood of her cloak, letting her dark hair whip in the wind. Her smoldering eyes bore down on his nervous, darting

206

blue ones.

"Just . . . just that . . ."

"What Thomas is trying to say in the most delicate way possible is that he doesn't hold you responsible for whatever"—Elizabeth's cheeks colored. —"for whatever they might have done to you or made you do."

"I'm still not following," Deborah said, a silly smile on her face. "Could you be more specific, Tom, as to what you're inferring the savages might have *done* to me?" A warning light went off in her head. She knew she should keep quiet, but the fury that was rising inside her was overpowering.

"You know what I speak of," Thomas said, emphasizing each word. He was growing angrier by the moment. "Must I come out and say it in front of your dear, innocent sister?"

"Why not?" Deborah took a step forward, peering into his face. "I get the idea the two of you have discussed it before!"

"Elizabeth," Thomas snapped. "Please excuse us."

Elizabeth caught Thomas's arm. "Please, Tom," she begged. "Just leave her. She doesn't know what she's saying. You don't know what she's been through!"

Thomas gently removed Elizabeth's arm from his. "Beth! Excuse us."

Tears trickled down Elizabeth's face as she backed off and then turned and ran.

"Coward, Tom! You're a coward! Say what you mean instead of making these inane insinuations!" Deborah dared. "Because I'm sick of it! All of you have been tiptoeing around me like I'm a thread of spun glass. Everyone's been so busy fabricating a good story that no one's bothered to ask me what happened! No one asked how I was treated! No one gives a damn about *me!*"

"What do you mean, no one gives a damn? What about me?" Thomas's face grew hard and craggy. "What other man would take a woman soiled as you are?"

"Soiled? Why, you son of a bitch!" Deborah slapped his face so hard that she left a raised red welt on his cheek.

Elizabeth turned at the sound of the loud crack and came running back toward them.

Thomas's hand immediately went up to strike Deborah back.

"Don't hit her, Tom! Please don't hit her!" Elizabeth cried. "She doesn't know what she's saying!"

"Go ahead," Deborah taunted. "Strike me. It's what all of you white men do when you don't get your way, when people don't say what you want them to."

Thomas lowered his hand. "Shut up," he ordered. "You're making a scene. Someone might hear you!"

"And what, taint the Hogarth name? Well, I'm not going to shut up! You want to hear something," Deborah raged. "You want to really hear something?"

"No, no, Deborah, please!" Elizabeth begged, pulling on her sister's arm. "Just come inside. Please don't say anymore. You'll ruin everything. He's going to marry you, that's all that matters!"

"He's going to marry me?" Deborah scoffed. "I have no intentions of marrying him!" She brought her face only inches from his. "Because I can't bear the thought of having to lie with him! Not after Tshingee! Not after being loved by a real man, a man who cared for me, a man who loves me!"

"Oh! Oh!" Elizabeth cried, throwing back her head.

Thomas stood in shock for a moment, staring at

Deborah. Then his gaze fell on Elizabeth, who swayed precariously on her feet. "Elizabeth! Beth!" He grabbed her arm to support her.

"Oh! Oh, dear." Elizabeth's hand went to her forehead, her eyelashes fluttered and she dropped into Thomas's arms.

"God's teeth!" Deborah muttered, getting a hold of herself. Don't just stand there! Take her to the house, Tom. Someone will know what to do with her there."

For a moment Thomas stood in the snow with Elizabeth draped in his arms, just staring at Deborah. "I . . . I don't know what to say."

Deborah sighed, pushing a stray lock of dark hair off her cheek. "Don't say anything, Tom, just go on up to the house. I need to be alone. Just go."

Chapter Fifteen

"I mean I'll not marry him." Deborah stood before her father's desk, her eyes fixed on his bulbous red nose. "You can't force me to do it."

The Earl slammed down his meaty fist. "This is an important alliance we're forming here between the Hogarths and our family. You know full well what influence they have in London. It's viscount Hogarth's good name that's bringing in our tobacco prices!"

"I don't care." She shrugged. "I don't care about tobacco prices. I don't care about your new prize house. You gave your word you would let those men go. You had no intentions of carrying through your end of the bargain. John Wolf was falsely accused and it will be by your hand that he swings by a noose."

The Earl's eyes narrowed. "So that's it, is it? You're worried about the red man?" He rose up out of his chair. "I don't know what they did to you there"—he held up his hand—"and I don't want to know, but you just forget it. John Wolf is going to pay for the crime he committed and as for the other man . . ." He chuckled.

Deborah's breath caught in her throat. "The other man, yes?"

The Earl pointed his finger accusingly. "No woman

should look at a man the way you looked at that redskin, no woman but a man's whore!" he spat."

"What of him? What of Tshingee?" She leaned forward across the desk, unafraid of her father's seething anger. "What were you going to say?"

He sat back in his chair, tucking his hands behind his head. "I was going to say that there's no sense in you waiting for your red man to come back for you, because he won't. Lester found him up along the river, what was left of him, that is."

Tears rose in Deborah's dark eyes. "I don't believe you. You're just saying that."

"Wild dogs — you know there's been a pack of them running this woods for a couple of years now."

Deborah shook her head in disbelief. "You're lying, I know you are," she breathed.

The Earl smiled wickedly. "You'll marry the Honorable Thomas Hogarth as agreed and let me warn you, I'll have no redskinned bastard for a grandchild. You spawn before your due time and that satan's child will never see the light of day!"

Before the Earl had finished his last sentence, Deborah was running for the door. "You can't do this to me," she shouted over her shoulder. "I won't let you!"

Her father laughed. "Oh, but I can, and I will."

Deborah flung open the door of her father's office and ran into the hall, slamming the door behind her. "I hate you," she murmured beneath her breath. "I hate you all!"

For a long time Deborah lay on her bed, the curtains drawn, her head buried in a goose-tick pillow. Was Tshingee dead? No man could survive those bullet wounds, but Tshingee was no ordinary man. Why had her father made such a point of telling her that Tshingee was dead? Was it because he *hadn't* found the body? A glimmer of hope rose in Deborah's chest. Her heart fluttered.

What if Tshingee is alive, lying out there somewhere in the forest? she thought. Leaping off the bed, Deborah ran to her clothes chest across the room and threw open the lid. Coming up with a pair of high leather boots, she stuffed her feet into them.

The first thing I'll do, she told herself, *is go see Bridget. Maybe she's heard from him! Why didn't I think of that before? What if he's there right now?* For the first time in three days, Deborah's heart lifted with hope.

An hour later Deborah urged her horse into the clearing where John's cabin was. Sliding off her mount she stared at the charred skeletal remains of the barn that had been burned to the ground. Shaking her head, she trudged through the snow to the cabin's door. A thin line of smoke rose from the chimney, filling the air with the rich scent of burning wood.

Taking a deep breath, Deborah knocked hesitantly. When there was no response, she knocked harder. The third time she pounded on the door, the latch lifted and the door swung open a crack. Mary's face appeared.

"Mary!" Deborah smiled. "It's Deborah. Is your mama here? Might I came in?"

Mary held up her finger, then closed the door. It was opened a moment later by Bridget. "What do you want?" She wore a brown woolen shawl over her head.

"Tshingee. Have you seen him? He was hurt. Couldn't I please come in?"

"I have seen no one since the last time your father's men came to pay their respects. They stole my chickens, the vegetables in my root cellar. They took the cow."

"Please let me in." Deborah laid her hand on the rough hewn door. "Please, I want to help."

"How can you help? Has my John been set free?"

"No." Deborah hung her head. "Tshingee tried but my father . . . he played them false. It was a trap. Tshingee was shot, but escaped. John is still in custody."

"If Tshingee could not free my husband: no one can. It's not God's will."

"That's ridiculous. You mustn't give up hope, for Mary's sake. Please let me in."

Begrudgingly, Bridget stepped back, and Deborah came through the door.

Deborah was surprised to find the cabin cold and dark. A tiny pile of smoldering ashes was all that rested on the fireplace's hearth. "It's freezing in here! Why isn't there wood on the fire?"

"There is no more wood. All that John split is gone." Bridget draped her arm protectively around Mary's shoulder.

"No more wood!" Deborah nearly laughed. "The whole forest is full of wood—all you have to do is cut it. Even green wood is better than none."

"I do not know how," was Bridget's reply.

Deborah stared at Mary's pale, hollow cheeks. "Don't you have food either?"

"I told you, they took it all. All I've left is a little flour and cornmeal."

Her own troubles forgotten for the moment, Deborah took charge. "I'll get you food, but the first thing we've got to do is cut wood. You can't live here all winter without wood. You'll freeze to death!"

"Whatever the Lord wills—"

"You think it's the Lord's will that you freeze to death when you're surrounded by firewood?" Deborah interrupted. "Well, you're wrong!" She walked to the far wall and took down an axe. Hanging beside it was a long-handled hammer and a small metal wedge. She took them too.

"Dress warmly and come along with me," Deborah told Bridget, an air of authority in her voice.

"We've been afraid to go out. The men who took John might come back."

"They won't hurt you as long as I'm with you. Besides if they were going to do something to you, don't you think they'd have done it by now?" Deborah knelt in front of Mary. "Would you like to go play in the snow?"

The little girl bobbed her head with enthusiasm.

"Good. First we cut wood, then we'll make angels in the snow. Would you like that?"

"Could we? Mama hasn't let me out to play since those bad men took Papa away."

Deborah smoothed a lock of the child's red hair. "Ask your mama."

"Could we?" Mary begged. "Could we go out and play with Deborah in the snow?" She pulled at her mother's hand, hopping up and down.

Bridget looked from her daughter to Deborah in indecision.

"You'll be safe, I promise you. Now come on, Bridget. What would John think if he knew his daughter was cold at night?" Deborah heaved the axe on to her shoulder.

214

"Maybe you're right," Bridget conceded. Deborah smiled. "Dress warmly and meet me outside."

All through the afternoon Deborah labored, chopping wood. Though she'd never done it before, she'd seen it often enough. Choosing a small fallen tree not far from the cabin, she tackled the chore with optimism. Swinging the axe again and again over her head, she chopped the tree into reasonable-sized chunks and Bridget carried them back to the cabin. Meanwhile, Mary scoured the area, collecting branches for kindling.

As the hours passed, Deborah's hands grew blistered then bled through her woolen mittens. But she didn't care—the physical pain was an escape from the pain she felt in her heart. Where was Tshingee? Was he dead as her father had said, or was he alive somewhere out in the forest, suffering?

"Are you certain you've not heard from Tshingee?" Deborah leaned on the handle of the axe, breathing heavily.

Bridget struggled with a large log. "I told you, he's not been here."

"If . . . if he did come, would you tell me?"

"I don't know," Bridget answered honestly.

Deborah nodded, lifting the heavy axe over her head again and letting it fall on its mark. "I'll cut this last and then we're carrying these logs up to the cabin." Splinters of wood flew through the air as she spoke. "But then I have to go. My family will be looking for me."

"You said you would help make angels in the snow!" Mary protested.

Deborah's face softened. "That we will, and the next time I come we'll make a snowman, all right, prin-

215

cess?"

"You don't have to come again," Bridget said.

"I know. But I want to. I'll bring food. I'll go to John for you if you want."

"They'll let you speak to him?"

"No." Deborah swung the axe a final time and a length of wood separated from the tree. "But I'll find a way."

"I just want to know how he is. I want him to know our prayers are with him."

"I'll go tomorrow before I come here. That way I can bring his message to you."

"Why are you doing this?" the Irish woman asked suspiciously.

"Because your husband was kind to me . . . and because I feel responsible for my father's actions." Deborah lifted a log on to her shoulder. "Now come on, let's get this to the cabin and make snow angels."

"Hurray!" Mary shouted, bounding ahead of Deborah down the snowy path.

"Where have you been?" Lady Celia's mouth twisted in a scowl. "The Earl is furious."

Deborah beat the snow from her cloak, taking her time to reply. "I've been out." She removed her mittens.

"Out where?" It's dark, you've been gone half the day." Lady Celia smoothed her already perfect chignon.

"I wasn't aware that I was to be a prisoner in my own house."

"A prisoner? Don't be ridiculous. The Earl is simply concerned for your well-being. It's not safe for you to be out wandering in the woods."

James poked his head around the corner. In each hand he held a slice of apple pie. "We thought maybe the redskins had carried you off again." He wrinkled his pudgy nose. He'd put on weight while Deborah was in the Lenni Lenape village. He was looking more and more like the Earl every day. "Pity," he added.

"Where's Father?" Deborah shrugged off her cloak and allowed a serving girl to carry it away.

"In his office, but he's busy. Said he's not to be disturbed. He and the Viscount are discussing the new land acquisition."

"Good. I can speak to both of them at the same time."

"Certainly not!" Lady Celia protested in a pitched squeak. "You'll do nothing of the sort. Go to your bedchamber. I'll have your supper sent up."

Deborah brushed past her stepmother. "Not until I've spoken to my father." Lady Celia followed Deborah, waving her hands in protest, but Deborah ignored her. She pushed open the door to her father's study.

The Earl looked up from his behind his desk. "Deborah!"

"Father, good evening." She turned to Thomas's father, nodding. "Good evening, sir."

"I tried to tell her you were occupied," Lady Celia offered weakly from the doorway. "But she'd hear nothing of it."

James wandered in, munching on his second slice of pie. "She's been gone most of the day, Father. Wonder where she's been."

"Father, I need to speak to you about John Wolf."

"Not now, Deborah."

"No, it has to be now. The Viscount has as much to do with it as you do."

"Lower your voice before the entire household hears you!" The Earl waved his hand angrily at Lady Celia, and she backed out the door, closing it quietly behind her.

The instant the door closed, Deborah moved forward to her father's desk. "You've got to let him go. He didn't commit any murder and you know it."

The Earl stiffened. "I know nothing of the sort. John Wolf is a common murderer and I mean to see justice done. We can't have these redskins causing unrest any longer. It's time they were driven from our land once and for all."

"Our land!" Deborah scoffed. "It was theirs first! *We* came and *we* took *their* land!"

"Deborah, I think that's quite enough. You're embarrassing yourself and me in front of our good neighbor." The Earl poured himself a healthy portion of whiskey from a decanter and offered the bottle to the Viscount.

"You say you'll see justice done?" Deborah went on, unwilling to give up. "Then tell me why John Wolf is still locked in MacCloud's barn. Why haven't the authorities come and gotten him after all this time? You've taken the law into your own hands, haven't you?"

"Deborah!" the Earl of Manchester boomed. "That is enough!" He came up out of his chair and around his desk. "Now you go to your bedchamber. I'll have a sleeping draught sent up to you." He clasped her arm with his hand, his fingers biting viciously into her flesh. "You've obviously not recovered from your ordeal," he went on, ushering her to the door.

"Father, you can't do this. Just let John go!" she pleaded. "His wife and daughter are near starvation." She didn't dare openly accuse him of having their foodstuffs stolen.

"Good night, dear. I hope you're feeling better in the morning." The Earl opened the door and pushed her out, closing it behind her.

Deborah stared at the closed door in disbelief as she heard the lock turn. "My apologies, Morris," she heard her father's muffled voice saying. "I'm sorry you had to see that outburst, but I can assure you she'll be fine. The sooner we can see her and Thomas wed, the better."

Dejected, Deborah started up the grand staircase. "Is nothing ever going to be right again?" she whispered.

"John! John!" Deborah called in a hushed tone. Slowly she made her way through the dark barn, trying not to run into anything. The sound of the snoring sentry wafted through the early morning stillness. "John Wolf!"

"Here . . ." a weak voice replied. "Who's there?"

"It's Deborah, Deborah Montague." On the far wall she spotted the slumped figure of a man. As she drew closer, she saw that John was shackled to the barn wall, his arms spread so that he was forced to sleep sitting up. "I brought food and some water."

"Bless you." John managed to smile.

Deborah knelt in front of him. A large gash ran down the side of his head and across his cheek, it had been crudely stitched with horsehair. His once shining cap of ebony hair was dirty and blood-encrusted with bits of straw stuck in it. He smelled of human waste. "Here, drink." She lifted the crock jug to his lips and he drank thirstily.

"What of my brother, does he live?" John asked between gulps.

Deborah hung her head. "I don't know. He was shot several times. My father say's they found his body but I don't believe him. He's a liar."

"Such harsh words from such an angelic face . . ." John shook his head. "I am sorry you've been caught up in this. I see your innocence in your face."

She lifted a piece of bread and cheese to his lips and he bit off a hunk. "I think I would feel it in my heart if Tshingee were truly dead but—"

"Then you must look for him."

"Look for him? Where?" She offered him another bite of the fresh bread. "I rode up and down the riverbank until it was dark last night. I'll look again today, but he could be anywhere," she said passionately. "Maybe he is dead."

"No. You are right. He is not dead. I feel his life's blood still in my heart. Our Lord protects him. He is somewhere out there, injured but alive."

"I thought maybe he would have gone to your cabin. I was there yesterday, but Bridget hadn't seen him."

John's face lit up in the dim light of the rising sun. "You saw my Bridget? Mary? How are they? Do they fare well?"

"Well enough, considering your absence," Deborah lied. "Just yesterday Mary and I made angels in the snow." She reached out and tightened the muslin sack he wore around his shoulders for warmth. "Bridget sends her love and reminds you that you are always in her prayers."

He nodded. "I must thank you for the Bible you left. It has been a great comfort to me in these trying days."

"But how can you read with your arms chained like that?"

He smiled. "I slip off my shoe and turn the pages with my toes."

Deborah reached into her leather sack. "I have whiskey too, would you like some before I go?"

He shook his head. "No, no spirits. Just more water."

"Don't they feed you?"

"Yes, bread left out for the poultry, I think." He gulped the water. "But not every day."

"I have to go now before someone finds me here, but I'll come again tomorrow."

"Do not put yourself at risk for me, Deborah. The Lord provides for me. It is in *His* hands that my life lies, not your father's. Not any mortal man's."

"Just the same, I'll be back." She stuffed the empty water crock into her bag.

The Lenni Lenape man looked up at her solemnly. "The greatest thing you can do for me is find my brother . . . alive."

In the dim light of the barn John looked so much like Tshingee that it made Deborah's heart twist beneath her breast for want of him. "I'll do my best, John," she whispered. "I'll do my best."

The following night a light tapping at the paned window of Deborah's bedchamber wakened her. Confused, she lay still in her bed listening for the sound. Yes, there it was again. Sitting up, she stared through the darkness at the two windows along the front wall.

A shadow lingered just behind the first window. Blinking, she waited for her eyes to adjust. How could there be someone at her window on the second story?

"Tshingee!" she whispered. Leaping out of bed she ran across the hardwood floor and flung open the window. "Tshingee," she cried joyfully.

Instantly, she saw that the figure was too small to be Tshingee. "Mary? Mary what are you doing out there?"

"I'm sorry, Deborah. I didn't know how else to find you." The little girl held her cloak tightly at her neck. She was balanced precariously on the window's brick ledge.

Deborah grabbed Mary and lifted her through the window. The child was trembling with cold. "Come to the fireplace," Deborah insisted, leading her to the hearth. "You're nearly frozen through."

"I wanted to come today, but Mama said no." She looked up at Deborah with her dark eyes. "Please don't tell. I waited until she was asleep."

"How did you know which window was mine?"

"I came last night and saw you in the window, but I was afraid to climb up so high."

Deborah grabbed a dressing gown off the end of the bed and slipped it on. Then she knelt before the little girl and pulled off her cloak. "What is it, Mary? What does your mother not want me to know?" She took the small hands in hers, rubbing them briskly.

"It is my uncle."

Deborah grew light-headed. "Your uncle?"

"I found my father's brother. I found Tshingee in the forest and I took my mother to him." The words tumbled from the Mary's mouth. "Only my uncle is very sick and my mama, she doesn't know how to make him better. I told her she had to come get you, but she said no, so I came alone. I knew that you could make him better." Fat tears ran down her copper-colored cheeks. "I knew if anyone could make Tshingee better, it would be you."

Deborah reached out and pulled Mary against her, holding her tight.

"So will you come?" Mary asked, peering into Deborah's face.

Deborah laughed, kissing the top of her head. "I'll come, Mary. Of course I'll come."

Chapter Sixteen

"Bridget, you have to take me to him." Deborah stood on the steps of John's cabin, her hands resting on her hips.

"Take you to who?"

"Tshingee. I know he's alive and I know you know where he is."

Bridget shifted her weight from one foot to the other in obvious discomfort. "How do you know?" Mary peeked from behind her mother's homespun skirts, but remained silent.

"John told me he knew in his heart that his brother was not dead. He told me I must find him."

"I can't believe John'd want you to have any more to do with his brother or him." Bridget brought her fingers to her pale lips. "Don't you think you've done enough harm?"

"I've done nothing. My father's actions are his own. I love Tshingee. He would come to me if I were hurt. I have to do what I can for him."

Bridget shook her head. "Nothing can be done for him. He's fevered bad. He's dying. He's got musket balls in his back." She brought her worn shawl over her shoulders. "Only the Lord can save him now."

"God's teeth, Bridget." Impatiently, Deborah

pushed her way through the door. "Don't start with that again. I fully believe in the Lord's powers, but he put heads on our shoulders for a purpose. I'll not let Tshingee lie out there in the snow and die as long as there's breath in my body." She pulled Mary's cloak off the cabin wall and tossed it to the little girl. Next she handed Bridget hers. "Now get this on and take me to Tshingee. I've brought medicine, warm blankets, and food. I can't be gone long. My father is already suspicious of my disappearances."

Bridget pushed back a stringy lock of flaming red hair that fell forward over her forehead. "If I take you to him, the Earl's men will follow us. They'll kill my husband's brother."

"If you don't take me to him, he'll die anyway," Deborah countered.

Mary slipped on her cloak and tied the hood tightly around her neck. On the front of the cloak the silver broach Deborah had given her months ago was prominently displayed. "If you want, Mama, I could show Deborah where my uncle is."

"You could never find it," Bridget stated hopefully.

"Oh, but I could, Mama. My uncle taught me to always know where I was going and always know where I'd been." She took her mother's hand. "You could stay here where it's warm and bake our bread while I take Deborah."

"Yes, Bridget, why don't you stay here? Mary and I will be fine."

"I . . . I don't know."

"Bridget." Deborah took her arm "John trusts me. You have to trust me too. I would never let any harm come to your daughter. She can just lead me to Tshingee and then come right back."

225

"No. I don't want her in the woods alone. Wild dogs."

"All right. Then I'll bring her back before I return to Host's Wealth." When Bridget gave no immediate reply, Deborah added, "It's what John would want you to do. I'm sure of it."

"You give your word that if I let her go, you won't let any harm come to her?" Bridget conceded.

"I give my word. I wouldn't take her if I thought she'd be in danger." Deborah rested her hand on Mary's shoulder.

Bridget knelt, brushing her fingers across Mary's cheek. "You go and take Deborah to your uncle, and then you make her bring you right back. You understand?"

Mary nodded solemnly. "We'll hurry, Mama. I promise."

Bridget kissed her daughter on the cheek. "Take care that no one sees you in the woods," she said, tightening the little girl's hood. "If the Earl's men find your uncle, they will kill him."

"We'll take care, I promise you," Deborah said, opening the cabin door.

Bridget rose, nudging Mary gently. "Go then, and God be with you."

"Bye, Mama," Mary called running through the snow to catch up with Deborah. She waved a mittened hand over her head.

Bridget stood in the doorway, twisting her hands in the folds of her apron until the two disappeared into the snowy forest.

Mary pointed and Deborah dropped onto all fours

then crawled through the hole in the brush. "Dear, God," she murmured in disbelief.

Tshingee was curled in a tight ball, a moth-eaten blanket thrown over him. His face was slack and hollow. A jug of water and a slice of bread lay near his head.

"Tshingee! Tshingee," Deborah cried, lifting his head to her lap.

Tshingee moaned, stirring.

Deborah smoothed his haggard bronze cheek, pressing a kiss to his forehead. He was burning with fever.

"Tshingee can you hear me? Can you hear me, love?"

"*N'palsi,*" he murmured weakly. "*K'daholel.*"

"I can't understand you." She pulled up the blanket, covering his shoulders. "I don't know what you're saying."

Mary stuck her head into the brush cavern. "He says he is sick." She giggled. "He says he loves you."

Deborah pressed her lips to his damp hair. "I don't know how he can be so hot with it's so cold outside."

"This is the home the doe makes when she has her little ones." Mary creeped just inside the bramble patch. "Here the deer is safe from the wind and man. She saved my uncle."

"Hand me my pack, Mary. We haven't long. I need to start a fire, but I don't dare. Not today at least." In order to get away from the house she had told her father she was going to see Thomas. It had been all she could do to wait until after they'd eaten their morning meal to go.

"Can't we bring him to our cabin? My uncle would be warm there."

Deborah shook her head, digging through the pack.

227

"No. We can't take the chance that my father's men will find him. They keep too close an eye on you and your mother." She smiled at the little girl. "But good thinking."

Removing a small paper packet from the leather pack, Deborah opened Tshingee's mouth and sprinkled some of the precious white powder on his tongue. He grimaced but was too weak to protest as she brought a water skin to his lips and forced him to drink. Much of the warm tea ran out of the corner of his mouth and onto Deborah's cloak but some of it managed to get down his throat.

"What is that you give my uncle?" Mary asked, wide-eyed.

"A powder for fever. If I leave it here, do you think you could return this afternoon and give it to him again? Just a sprinkle on his tongue."

"I could do it. But Mama . . ."

"I'll speak to her. Maybe both of you can come." She smoothed Tshingee's dark hair. "I will come again late tonight if I can sneak out of the house." Laying his head back on his cloak, Deborah rolled him over carefully so that she could see the extent of his wounds.

"Are they awful bad?" Mary asked.

"Bad." Deborah ran her hand over Tshingee's calf as she mentally counted the wounds. *Two in his right leg, one in his lower left back, one in his left shoulder.* "But if he's lived this long, I think he can make it."

"Will you take out the musket balls?" Mary crawled deeper inside the bramble cave to get a closer look.

"I'll try, but I can't do it now. I don't have the proper instruments." She ran her fingers over the wound in his shoulder. Remarkably, there seemed to be little festering. Slowly, she rolled him back onto his side and covered him with the old blanket. She added a second one she'd taken from Lady Celia's linen closet.

"There," Deborah whispered. "There's little more I can do for him now." She ran her hand over Tshingee's sunken cheek. It was so odd to see him like this, weak and unprotected. She wanted to stay here with him, to hold him, but she knew she couldn't. If her father suspected he was still alive and on his property, he'd not give up until he found him. Then Tshingee *would* be a dead man.

"We'd better go." Little Mary laid her hand on Deborah's arm. "We told Mama we wouldn't be long."

Deborah nodded. Leaning over Tshingee, she kissed his lips. "I'll be back," she told him. "Do you hear me, love? I'll be back." Tucking the blankets tightly around his shoulders, she backed up, crawling out of the hiding place.

Standing, Deborah watched as Mary picked up a branch and began to sweep at the snow near the briar patch. Deborah slung her pack over her shoulder. "What are you doing?" She had to laugh. The branch was bigger than Mary was.

"Covering tracks."

Deborah smiled. "You're a clever little girl. Did your papa teach you that?"

She shook her head. "My uncle. We play secret games. I can snare a rabbit and paddle a dugout. Papa and Mama don't like it. Mama says Tshingee will make me into a heathen." She giggled. "So we don't tell."

Deborah dropped her hand onto the little girl's shoulder and kissed the top of her red head. "Wise beyond your years. Your uncle's taught you well."

"You walk ahead and I'll follow. We have to hurry,

or Mama's going to be mad."

Laughing, Deborah started for the cabin.

Smoothing her wrinkled cloak, Deborah released Joshua's reins, allowing a stable boy to lead him off. Taking a deep breath, she started up the front steps of the house at Deliverance. She had no desire to see Tom; she was too worried about Tshingee to deal with her fiancé's nonsense, but she knew, just as Mary had covered their tracks, that she must cover her own. Deborah had told the Earl she was going to visit Tom, so visit him she must. She rapped on the door, and too soon, it swung open.

"Lady Deborah, what a pleasant surprise." Lady Hogarth smiled, offering her hand. "Do come in." Lattice Hogarth was a petite woman with thinning dark hair. "Thomas will be so pleased you've come. He's in the office doing the accounts. Silly men's work, you know."

"Oh. If he's busy, you needn't disturb him," Deborah said hopefully. She followed Lady Hogarth into the airy front hall. "I was out riding. I just stopped for a moment."

"Don't be ridiculous. Thomas would never forgive me if I didn't call him!"

Deborah brought her hand from beneath her cloak. "I brought you some of Cook's apple butter. I know how much you like it."

The elder woman accepted the small crock. "Thank you so much, what a dear. I can't wait until you and Thomas are married. It will be so nice to have another daughter in the house. Now give me your things and go warm yourself in the parlor. I'll have something warm brought to drink. It's a wonder you're not frozen through!"

Deborah allowed Lady Hogarth to help her remove her cloak and then she went into the parlor. She knelt before the fire, thrusting out her numb hands. All she could think of was how Tshingee was lying there cold and injured in the forest while she warmed herself.

"Deborah!" Thomas came into the parlor, taking her hand and helping her to her feet. He brushed his lips against her cheek. This was the first time they had seen each other since they had had words after Tshingee had brought her home. "You look radiant."

She forced a smile. "I was out riding. I only stopped for a minute."

"Stay for dinner." He held her hand tightly in his. "I've missed your company."

"I can't." She pulled away. Somehow, even standing here beside Tom made her feel as if she was betraying Tshingee. It didn't matter that they had parted; it didn't matter that Tshingee had told her she must go on with her life. All that mattered was the love that burned between them.

At a loss as to what to say, Tom suddenly brightened. "Good news, dear!"

"Oh?" Deborah studied him suspiciously.

"Father and the Earl have been talking. They've decided to move up the wedding date. We're to be married on Christmas day."

"Christmas day?" Deborah felt as if the wind had been knocked out of her. "So soon?"

"They thought it best . . . under the circumstances." He watched her walk to the window.

Deborah sighed, scratching at the frosty windowpane with her finger. "Tom, I can't marry you."

"We've been through this before."

"And all along I've told you I can't marry you. I didn't want to marry you before I was taken and now . . . now I just can't."

"Deborah, I don't care what happened." Thomas took a step forward, then a step back. "I told you that. It's not important. All that matters is that you're safe now. Time will pass, you'll forget it all."

Tears glimmered in her eyes. "But I don't want to."

He groaned. "It's not as if you had a choice with this match . . . as if either of us did."

She turned to face him. "Meaning?"

"Meaning it was a business arrangement, we both knew that. But you and I have always gotten along. It's a good, solid alliance between our families."

"Your father's words," Deborah scoffed. "You're a pawn as much as I am!"

Mustering his courage, Thomas came to her, taking her around the waist. "That's not a true. I was given several choices. *You* are my choice as wife. I'm in love with you. You know I always have been."

She shook her head sadly. "You're not in love with me, Tom. You're attracted to me; you desire me. But that's not love. It's not what's in your heart." She tapped him on the chest.

"You'll make a good Tidewater wife."

"I'll make an awful Tidewater wife. I'll never say or do the right things. I'll not be servile, not to you or anyone. I'm not what you want. Why are you doing this to yourself?"

"I've wanted you since we were thirteen," he declared passionately. "Do you remember when you kissed me behind Charlie's barn?"

She chuckled. "You were the third boy I'd kissed

232

that day. I was only trying to make Charlie jealous."

"Don't say that. I told you I loved you then, and I still do."

"You asked me to marry you. Thirteen years old and your father was already pointing out good choices for good alliances!" Her voice had taken on a sarcastic air. "Just because you don't mind being jerked by your father's strings, doesn't mean I don't."

He dropped his hands. "And what will you do if I don't marry you? Who will have you?" His injured feelings were turning to anger and spite. "Who will have you after your red man, tell me that, *Lady Deborah*."

"I don't care! No one, I hope!"

"Your father won't stand for it. He'll marry you to some ancient relative and ship you off to England to rot in some crumbling estate!"

"I'm leaving. I don't have to listen to this."

"You'll waste away, Deborah. I'm your only chance," he called after her vindictively. "Marry me or your life is over."

Not waiting for her cloak, Deborah threw open the front door and ran out into the snow. "I won't marry you, Tom, I won't do that to you. I won't do it to myself."

He came down the steps after her. "All right! Have your way. You always have. I'll tell my father it's off. There'll be no wedding!"

Deborah stood in knee-deep snow, waiting for the stable boy to bring her Joshua. The wind cut through her wool dress but she took no notice of the biting cold. Her dark hair tumbled from the red ribbon, sending it fluttering over her back.

"This is your last chance, Deborah Montague!"

Thomas hollered. "You can't come back in a month begging me to change my mind!"

Deborah laughed, leaping onto her mount with the aid of the stable boy. She snatched the reins from the boy's hand. "Have no fear of that!" Her voice carried on the wind. "It'll be a cold day in hell before I beg any man to take me as his wife!" She laid her crop to Joshua's flank and the horse leaped forward, galloping down the drive.

Pushing her leather bag and a flour sack through the hole in the bramble patch, Deborah crawled in. Fumbling in the bag, she found a candle, a puff of raw flax, and a tin box containing flint and steel. Igniting the ball of flax, she lit the candle. "Ouch!" She stuck her burnt finger into her mouth.

"Deborah?" Tshingee called weakly.

"Tshingee!" Deborah turned, holding the candle over his head. "You're awake."

He tried to laugh, but his chest hurt so badly that the rapid intake of air nearly stunned him. He lowered his head onto his arm. "I think so," he managed.

"I was beginning to think you were just going to lie like that forever. Two days ago I took the lead shots out of your leg and shoulder. You nearly killed me with your thrashing, then you haven't moved since." She laid her hand on his forehead. "Fever's gone."

He raised his head again to look at her. "Where am I?"

"Inside a briar patch. Mary says it's where the deer hide." She reached into the flour sack and brought out a water bag filled with herbal tea.

"How did I get in here?"

"Walked? Crawled? I don't know. Mary and Bridget found you while they were out gathering kindling." She raised the water bag to his lips, thankful to have something to do.

He lifted his head and sipped from the bag. "John?"

"Careful, it's hot. Still being held. I'm doing all I can, but I'm not exactly on good terms with the Earl. I've demanded the authorities be called. They can't just keep him in MacCloud's barn forever."

"What does the Earl say to that?" Tshingee took another sip and lowered his head to his arm again.

"My father *says* the proper authorities have been notified. They just haven't come for John yet. Of course my father also said that his men found you dead, eaten by wild dogs." She spoke matter-of-factly, keeping her emotions under control.

She reached for the flour sack, but he caught her hand. "I never thought I would see you again." He smiled sadly. "Not at least in this world." He brushed her hand against his cheek lovingly. "You look like some biblical angel, Red Bird, with your hair thrown over your shoulders and the light of the candle around your head."

"I think the fever still burns. You're talking nonsense."

He kissed her hand before releasing it. "How bad are my wounds?"

"Two shots in your calf, one in your shoulder, one that went in your back and came out the front. You'll be a while healing. I want to take you somewhere where you'll be more comfortable, but John's cabin isn't safe."

"You were wise not to take me there. This is fine."

"But it's cold!"

"Not too cold. I'll not freeze. These briars have protected the doe and her young. They will protect me until I'm strong enough to go."

And then what, Deborah wondered. But she didn't voice her thoughts. All that was important now was to get Tshingee well . . . and to have John released. She busied herself tearing off pieces of soft bread to feed Tshingee.

"You look tired," he said softly.

"I am." She lifted his head to cradle it in her lap. "Between coming here to see you and going to John at night, I've not gotten much sleep. My family thinks me depressed, sleeping in half the morning."

"You have seen John?"

"They keep him in MacCloud's barn." She fed Tshingee a piece of bread. "I take him food, water, word from Bridget and Mary."

He chewed slowly, even the movement of his jaws sapping his energy. "How is my little Mary?"

"Fine. They were out of wood, but we took care of that. My father's men stole their food, but I've just been stealing it back." She offered him another bit of bread.

"I cannot thank you enough for all you have done for myself and for those I love."

"I don't want thanks." She lowered her head to kiss his cheek. "All I want is your love."

"You have that, *ki-ti-hi*. Now, always."

A comforting silence stretched between them as Tshingee nibbled at the bread and cheese and drank the herbal tea. When he'd had his fill, she lowered his head back to the hide mat she'd brought for him to sleep on.

"I have to look at the wounds now. Can you roll onto

236

your stomach?"

He rolled over immediately, but couldn't stifle a groan that escaped his lips.

Giving him a moment to catch his breath, Deborah peeled back the leather of his leggings and lifted the candle to take a look at his calf. First she removed the bloody cloth bandage. Then, taking a small lump of paste from a crock, she rubbed the salve into the entry wounds. Tshingee flinched, but said nothing. Covering her handiwork with a clean bandage, she moved on to the next wound.

"The holes are pretty big." She helped him roll back onto his side. "But they're clean now. I had to cut away some dead flesh, but now that the lead ball is gone, you'll heal nicely."

"You would make a good medicine woman. I did not know you knew of herbs."

She shrugged. "I don't. Not much. But no one cares for father's servants. They've always come to me with their aches and pains." She emptied the flour sack and rolled it up, placing it under his head. "I have to go soon. But Bridget and Mary will be by around noon. I'll come again tomorrow night."

He took her hand. "Take care, my Red Bird. Do not put yourself at risk for me."

"There is no risk to me." She gathered the dirty bandages and stuffed them into her leather bag. "But I have to sneak around at night because my father has me under house arrest." She laughed, trying not to make her situation seem too bad.

"And why is that?" Tshingee had lifted his head again and was staring at her intently.

The intensity of his pitch black eyes made Deborah look away. "Thomas has called off the wedding . . .

237

because of some things I said. My father and his father still say it will take place."

"You said this Thomas is a good man," Tshingee said gently. "You should marry him."

Deborah brushed a tear from her cheek with the back of her hand. "Rest and I'll see you tomorrow night." Before Tshingee could speak again, she was gone.

Chapter Seventeen

Deborah studied her reflection in the floor-length mirror she'd borrowed from Lady Celia's bedchamber. Two candles burned on the table next to her bed, casting bright fingers of light across the plastered walls. She brushed her hand over the flat muscles of her bare stomach.

"Funny," she said aloud. "But I don't look pregnant."

The initial shock of the revelation had turned to awe in the last two days. She was amazed that a babe could be growing inside her . . . Tshingee's son or daughter.

Her first impulse, when she had realized she was with child, was to run to Tshingee and tell him her wonderful news. Once his wounds had healed sufficiently for him to ride, Deborah had taken him to a vacant outbuilding on the far side of her father's land. The wooden structure had once been used to store bales of tobacco, but after a fire it had never been repaired. There she knew he would be safe and comfortable until he was strong enough to leave.

He'd been there for nearly two weeks already.

Deborah had gone so far as to sneak out of the house, saddle her horse, and travel to the barn in broad daylight to tell Tshingee about the baby. But when she'd reached him, she couldn't bring herself to tell him. It would only make things more complicated.

Pregnant or not, John's life still depended on Deborah remaining at Host's Wealth. If Tshingee took her with him now, John would most certainly die. Deborah just didn't see any sense in making her inevitable parting with Tshingee more difficult. It would be better for both of them if he never knew of the child she carried.

Throwing herself onto her bed, Deborah buried her face in her hands. "So what am I going to do now?" she asked the empty room. "I can't have a baby here!"

Her father's words came back to haunt her in a rush of frightening reality. "I'll have no redskinned bastard for a grandchild!" he had shouted. "You spawn before your due time and that satan's child will never see the light of day!"

Tears sprang in Deborah's eyes and she wiped at them with the back of her hand. The plan was simple enough. She had to get out of this house and out soon—somewhere safe. Deborah rolled onto her back, staring at the plastered ceiling. *I've got to get out of here before I begin to show.* Calculating on her fingers, she realized she'd gotten pregnant on the trip back to Host's Wealth. Before then she had been taking the Lenni Lenape's birthing powders and her courses had come regularly.

240

She stroked her stomach. The obvious immediate solution was Thomas. The fact that she had refused to marry him and he'd agreed to release her from the contract was only a minor obstacle. If she married him at Christmas — only a week from now — she would be out of her father's house and within the safety of Tom's. If she married him right away, the babe could be passed off as premature. With her own dark hair and suntanned complexion, who would notice if the child's skin was a little dark? The thought of marrying Thomas, of lying with him, made her shudder, but to save her child, she would do anything. It was the only way.

Relief flooded Deborah as she leaned and blew out the candles. She wouldn't allow herself to think of Tshingee or how this would end any possibility of her going with him. It was all too painful. Tonight she would sleep peacefully and tomorrow she would see to Thomas and the wedding.

The following morning Deborah dressed with care in a low-cut woolen gown of forest green with red piping. She brushed her hair until it shone and pulled part of it back off the crown of her head to tie in a ribbon. Adding a string of pearls that had been her mother's and pinching her cheeks, she went downstairs for the morning meal.

"Deborah!" Lady Celia exclaimed, rising out of her chair. "This is certainly a change from the sleeping wrap you've been wearing. You look lovely."

The Earl glanced up from his plate of fried ham and sweet potatoes. "Decided to be sensible, have you?"

Elizabeth and the other younger girls kept their eyes on their plates, remaining silent. James gulped his cider nosily, watching with interest as his sister took her seat near the end of the dining table.

Deborah lowered her gaze subordinately. "If it would please you, sir, I'd like James to escort me to Deliverance this morning." Her heart pounded in her ears.

Betrayal! her mind protested. *You betray the man you love!* "I . . . I have to speak to Tom."

"So you've finally seen the ill of your ways? I told you a few weeks in you chamber would change your outlook on your situation." The Earl stuffed a fork full of dripping ham into his mouth. "Of course you've made such a mess of things, I'm not sure they can be salvaged."

"I can fix them. I'll tell Tom I've changed my mind and that I want to marry him. I'll apologize for my behavior. It was just the strain of it all; I didn't know what I was saying." She repeated the words she'd rehearsed before she came downstairs. "I . . . I want to be Tom's wife."

Elizabeth gave a muffled squeak and pushed out of her chair, running from the room. The Earl glanced at his retreating daughter and back at Lady Celia. "What ails her?"

Lady Celia dabbed her lips with her linen napkin. "I assure you, I don't know, sir. Woman's complaints, I should think."

James giggled, reaching across the table for a muffin. "I don't know how we stand it, Father, living among so many females." He buttered the muffin

242

and crammed it into his mouth. Crumbs fell out of his mouth and onto the linen table cloth as he continued to speak. "I had other plans this morning. I'm not certain I have time to ride about with Deborah."

The Earl scraped his plate with his fork. "I'd like to have this settled, James. As a favor to me, would you take her? I've better things to concern myself with than this matter. The sooner Thomas and Deborah are married, the sooner we can begin work on the prize houses."

"Very well." James pushed back from the table, crumbs falling to the floor and onto the chair. "But she'll have to hurry. The dance master will be here at noon. I'd hate to miss my lesson after he's come all this way."

Deborah hung her head. "I'll be ready in five minutes," she said quietly.

"This is certainly quite the surprise." Thomas leaned against the doorway of his mother's parlor.

Deborah rose from her chair and walked toward him, forcing a smile. "I was afraid I might not still be welcome after the way I behaved."

To his surprise, she kissed his cheek. A genuine smile rose on his face. "You look beautiful today, Deborah. Like your old self." He took her hand, leading her to an upholstered settle.

"Tom." She rested her arm on his coat sleeve, fixing her lips in an enticing pout. "I've come to ask your forgiveness. I've said things I didn't mean, things—"

He shook his head. "Don't," he interrupted. "You don't have to do this."

"But I've treated you terribly and I *want* to say I'm sorry." She looked away. This was harder than she'd thought it was going to be. How had she played all those silly games for so many years?

"You've been through such a abhorrent ordeal. I was wrong to be so harsh. I expected too much of you. I think we all did, the Earl included." The scent of Deborah's soft skin taunted his senses. He leaned closer.

"It's no excuse for speaking to you the way I did. I shouldn't have said those terrible things. You must know I didn't mean it, not any of it!" *Liar!* a voice accused from within herself. *Liar! You meant every word!*

"I know you didn't." Tom draped his arm over her shoulder, and feeling bold, he brushed his lips against her cheek.

The bile rose in Deborah's throat as she allowed him to draw her closer. The sensation of his mouth on the soft flesh of her neck disgusted her, but she didn't push him away. Her child's life was at stake and Thomas was the only person who could save it. "Tom." She brushed a hand through his thinning hair. He smelled of shaving soap and ink, nothing like the clean fresh scent of Tshingee.

"Deborah," Tom murmured. He closed his eyes as he pressed his lips to hers.

She let him linger for just a moment and then pushed her hands on his chest lightly. The air in the parlor was hot and stifling. For a moment Deborah was so dizzy she thought she would faint, but she pressed on. This was only her chance.

"Tom. What I said about your father, about mine . . ."

"You were right, Deborah, my father holds too tight a control over me." He rubbed the bare flesh of her arm, nuzzling her neck.

"No. You were right and I was wrong."

"I was?" His wet, slack lips touched hers.

"It's only because your father cares for you. He . . . he wants you to marry properly so that Deliverance will be well taken care of. So you will be taken care of properly." She leaned back, trying to edge away, but Thomas only pressed her deeper into the settle. "Tom! Are you listening to me?" It was all she could do to keep from wiping her mouth with the back of her hand.

"I'm listening, dearest." He tried to fondle her breast but she pushed his hand aside.

"Tom, what I'm trying to tell you is that I want to marry you," she declared in a rush of words. "I . . . I mean I want you to reconsider."

"Reconsider? Oh, Deborah. I've wanted to touch you like this for so long . . ."

"Tom." She took a deep breath, fighting the nausea he evoked. Her hand slid to her flat stomach and her resolve was strengthened. Tom could be manipulated. She could do it, she'd done it before. "Tom. We mustn't do this. Not here, someone will see us. My brother's just in the kitchen. What if one of the servants were to come by?"

"Oh, God, Deborah, I want you so badly . . ." He ran his fingers along the piping of the bodice of her gown. His breath was becoming ragged; his face was

245

flushed.

"Tom," she whispered in his ear. "If you marry me, I'll be yours."

"Yes," he moaned, pressing his lips to her neck.

Striking at her advantage, she pressed on. "If you marry me, you can take me to your bed as your wife." He buried his face between the mounds of her breasts that peeked from the bodice of her woolen gown. "Yes" . . . His face was damp with perspiration, his breath hot and wet. "Oh my, yes."

"If you marry me, I'll be yours forever." Deborah's own words echoed in her mind like a death sentence.

"Yes. When?" he begged breathlessly. "Just say when."

Unable to stand Thomas's mauling another instant, Deborah leaped up. "Before this gets out of hand."

Suddenly made aware of his inexcusable behavior, he pulled his handkerchief from his coat and wiped his mouth. "Yes, I think that's wise," he said, coming to his feet.

"You have to tell your father and the Earl that you've reconsidered. That we've settled our differences and we want to be married immediately." She took the handkerchief from him and gently wiped his brow.

Thomas's eyes drifted shut. "Immediately."

"On Christmas day as planned."

His eyes flew open. "Why that's only a week away. The bans have to be read, invitations have to be sent . . ."

She folded his handkerchief and tucked it into his coat. "There are ways around the bans," she murmured in his ear.

"I guess there are, aren't there?"

She nodded. "If you truly want me . . ."

"Oh, Deborah, of course I do, it's just . . ."

She kissed his cheek.

"Well, I suppose you are right." He swallowed, his Adam's apple bobbing up and down. "The sooner the better."

"I think so," she whispered. *There, it's done,* she told herself. *Your fate is sealed, but no harm will come to your babe. Tshingee's child will be safe.*

Thomas threw his arms around her, pulling her tightly against him. "I can't believe it, Deborah. You're going to be my wife!"

Deborah squeezed her eyes tight against the tears that threatened her performance and buried her head in his shoulder. "I can't believe it either," she muttered.

Deborah smiled woodenly, accepting words of congratulations as she and Tom moved through a crowd of well-wishers, all Yuletide supper guests of the Earl's. Men pounded Tom on the back and women smiled behind their fans, welcoming Deborah to the life of a Tidewater matron. Again and again Deborah's glass was filled with blood red wine and she drank it mechanically. She didn't care for the heavy taste of the expensive French vintage, but it warmed her insides, dulling her thoughts and somehow making it easier to stand at Tom's side.

"Deborah. Deborah. . . ."

Deborah blinked, looking up at the guest who held

247

her hand. A genuine smile brightened her face. "Martha! When did you get here? I thought you weren't coming for Christmas this year." She threw her arms around her elder sister, lowering her voice. "So old goat Danforth gave in, did he?"

Martha chuckled, tapping her sister playfully with her fan. "Hush your mouth before he hears you and makes a scene. You know how Randolph loves a fuss."

Thomas came up behind Deborah. "Lady Danforth." He took Martha's hand, making an issue of kissing it. "I hope you'll be with us long enough to celebrate with Deborah and I on Christmas day."

"Celebrate?" Martha's face fell for an instant then she smiled politely. "Whatever do you mean? I thought the engagement had been called off due to mutual agreement."

"Pshew! You bunch across the bay, you're always a month behind in the latest gossip." He slid his arm around Deborah's waist, giving her a squeeze. "No, indeed, we'll be in-laws, you and I, within the week."

"I suppose congratulations are in order then, Thomas. And to you too, sister." She brushed her lips across Deborah's pale cheek. "Tell me, Tom, would you mind if I borrowed your intended, just for a few moments?" She linked her arm through Deborah's. "It's been so long since I've seen my dear sister."

"Not at all." Thomas released Deborah. "But don't be long, love. Charlie MacCloud is here somewhere and I want to be sure and show you off on my arm. He's been dying to do it for years."

Deborah stood dutifully while he gave her a peck

on the cheek then she walked away, arm and arm, with her sister.

"I can't believe you gave in," Martha hissed as soon as they were out of earshot.

"Martha, please."

"What did those savages do to you? Everyone said you were fine, but . . ."

"Martha, please," Deborah interrupted. "Not here."

"I always looked up you," Martha went on, weaving through the crowd of guests. "You were the only one of us who could ever stand up against the Earl. I didn't think you'd let him trap you like this. You told me you'd never marry Tom. I thought there was hope for you!"

Deborah released her sister's arm, pushing her way through the crowd. "Not here, I said!" Opening a small door beneath the grand staircase, she stepped into the servant's back hallway.

Martha followed, closing the door behind her. A small lamp on the plastered wall illuminated the narrow passageway. "I can't believe you gave in. You said you were going to marry for love."

Deborah stared at her sister's face. "You don't understand. I had to do it."

"I wanted for you what I'll never have." She reached out and brushed at the shorn lock of Deborah's hair. "I wanted you to be happy."

Deborah was tempted to tell Martha of Tshingee, of the babe. She wanted her sister to know her reasons, but she feared telling her. She couldn't put her baby's life in jeopardy, not to rationalize her decision with herself or Martha. "I'll be happy with

Tom."

"You can lie to him. You can even lie to yourself, but you can't lie to me, Deborah Montague. I know you like the back of my hand. Thomas Hogarth will kill you just as Lord Danforth will kill me. If Randolf doesn't throw me down the stairs and break my neck in a drunken stupor, he'll kill me in the birthing bed." She twisted the lace on her sleeve. "I've another babe on the way."

"Not another?" Deborah shook her head. "Little Henry's but three months old!"

"That's the way it is with a man who has no respect for you. I'm nothing to Randolph. Less worthy than a parcel of land or a slave." She laughed bitterly. "Certainly less worthy than his whore."

Deborah bit down on her lower lip. "Thomas says he loves me. He's not like Randolph. He doesn't drink. He's not a brutal man."

"You think I ever saw Lord Danforth strike anyone before the first time he hit me?"

Deborah shook her head. "You're wrong. Tom is less a threat to me than the Earl is."

"So that's it? This is your way of getting off Host's Wealth?" Martha ran her hand over the plastered wall. "You'd have been better to have bound yourself in the New England Colonies. At least then you'd have been free one day."

Tears sprang in Deborah's. "I have my reasons, Martha. Can't you respect that?"

"I had so much hope for you." Martha shook her head. "Don't do it, Deborah. For God sakes don't do it."

"I have to."

Martha shrugged. "You've sentenced yourself then, girl . . ."

Tears ran down Deborah's cheeks as she watched her sister gather her skirts and leave the servants' hall, closing the door quietly behind her. Sobbing, Deborah sank to the cold hardwood floor. "Tshingee," she cried into her palms, rocking back and forth. "Tshingee, why have you done this to us?"

She was tempted to saddle a horse and ride to him now. She hadn't gone to him since she'd agreed to marry Thomas. If she told Tshingee of the baby, if she begged him to marry her, how could he refuse? Deborah pulled her handkerchief from her bodice and wiped her nose. No, she wouldn't do that to Tshingee. She loved him too much. She respected his responsibility to his brother too much.

A distant high-pitched shriek made Deborah suddenly sit up. Wiping her eyes with the lace handkerchief, she listened. There it was again—a woman's screaming.

Slowly Deborah got to her feet and took the lamp from the wall. She followed the passageway to the end where there was a door leading to the kitchen and one leading down into the cellar. Hesitating, she listened. A feminine sob rose from behind the door leading downstairs. Cautiously, Deborah opened the paneled door.

"Hush your mouth," came the Earl's voice from below. "Hush your mouth before someone hears you."

"Lemme go," the terrified blackamoor sobbed. "Please lemme go, sir."

Deborah left the lantern in the hallway and

stepped down one step. Crouching, she peered over the rail. Below in the faint light of a candle's glow she saw one of the young black kitchen maids lying on the dirt floor. Her legs were spread, her homespun skirts spotted with blood. The girl was new in the house, just purchased in Annapolis. She couldn't have been more than thirteen. Deborah's father was standing over the maid, hiking up his breeches.

"Let's just call this your initiation into the Montague household, shall we?" The Earl chuckled. "Now get up and get back to work! We've got guests to attend to!"

The girl cowered.

"I said get up!" He grabbed her hand and jerked her to her feet. "And you tell anyone about this and you'll be gone from here. You understand me? Because that bay out there, it has a way of eating up little girls that don't do as they're told."

The kitchen maid nodded. "I . . . I understand, sir. I won't say nothing," she sniffed, wiping her nose on her sleeve.

Deborah leaned her head against the rough wooden rail, in shock. She'd always heard rumors that her father bedded the servants, but this was rape. Suddenly the Earl turned and headed for the steps. Soundlessly Deborah slipped into the hall and through the kitchen door, taking the lamp with her. She clicked the latch on the kitchen door just in time to hear her father come up the steps.

Chapter Eighteen

Deborah stood at the window in her bedchamber, letting the frigid night air revive her. The last horse-drawn sleigh filled with neighbors had departed, and the house was finally silent save for the plinking of the harpsichord in the parlor and the occasional sound of male laughter. Snow was falling again and the sled tracks were beginning to disappear beneath the fresh blanket of glimmering white.

Every room in the house was filled with sleeping forms, guests who would be staying at Host's Wealth through the wedding celebration. It was only because Deborah had pleaded with Lady Celia that her room had not been made into a dormitory for young girls. She claimed she needed her privacy before the wedding, and Lady Celia had given in to her. Elizabeth and Anne were now sharing their bedchamber with four fourteen-year-olds.

Deborah sighed, fingering the lace-edged curtains that hung in her window. It had been a long evening and her head was pounding. Seeing the Earl with the young kitchen maid had disturbed her more than she realized. She'd known for years of the rumors that her father dallied with the servants, but up to this point, they had been nothing been rumors. Tonight she had seen the truth and it disgusted her.

Deborah's first impulse had been to confront the Earl with what she'd seen, but then better sense told her to bide her time. First she had to get the young girl out of the house and then she would use the information to her advantage. She had to be careful. The Earl's threat of throwing the servant into the bay was too real not to take seriously.

Movement below caught Deborah's eye and she leaned on the sill, brushing the curtains aside. There had been a shadow . . . a man. There he was again. It took only a moment for her to realize who the shadow must be. The man moved across the yard with an animal-like grace, becoming one with the night shadows as he drew closer to the house. It was Tshingee. . . .

Crossing her bedchamber, Deborah sat on the edge of the bed and waited. He came in through the window almost soundlessly and closed it behind him.

"You knew I was coming."

"I saw you below. You'd better take care, Wildcat of the Wolf Clan, or the Earl will have his dogs on you." She kept her back to him, afraid to turn and face him. Her heart fluttered beneath her breast. She had prayed he would come. She had prayed he would not.

"You have not come to me for three days, *ki-ti-hi*. I was worried." He stood at the window in his long cloak, staring at her slim form perched on the edge of the bed. His arms ached to hold her.

"I . . . I've been busy."

"I told you before that you need not come every day. But when you came every day and then did not come, I feared you were sick or injured, Red Bird." He came around the side of the bed and took her hands, raising her to her feet. "I came to be certain you were safe."

She lifted her lashes to gaze into his ebony eyes. "I'm safe," she whispered.

He brushed his thumb against her cheek and she lowered her lashes. "I also came to tell you I am going."

Deborah's heart skipped a beat. Her eyes flew open. "So soon? Going? Going where? What of John?"

He threaded his fingers through her thick hair. "I go back to my village . . . to get warriors."

"So it's come to that, has it?" she asked sadly. Her gaze rested on his solemn face, the most intriguing face she had ever laid eyes on.

"I fear it has." He touched the dark birthmark at the corner of her mouth with his fingertip. "I know no other way. I think time is running out for John Wolf. The Earl says men of the law have been called but I see no men. I see no trial. All I see is my brother chained to a wall in a barn like some beast," he finished bitterly.

"You've been to MacCloud's? You shouldn't have gone." She lifted her hands to rest them on his broad chest. Even through the thick hide cloak she could feel his heart beating rhythmically.

"I did not speak with John. I went only to see where he was and how many men guarded him. I

255

could cut the throats of the sentries. They would die before they saw the Wildcat's shadow, but John wants no deaths on his soul. If I bring others, it may be that we can free him without violence."

Deborah lowered her head to rest her forehead on his chest. "Oh, Tshingee. Why has all of this happened? Why?"

Gently, he smoothed the hair that fell down her back. "I do not know, my Red Bird. The stars, that is all I can tell you. It was in the stars."

She inhaled the scent of him that lingered on his clothes. "I suppose you're right. It just seems so unfair."

"I wish that I could take you with me, Red Bird."

"I know."

"I wish . . ." His voice had a husky catch to it. "I wish that I could carry you off in my arms and make you my bride here beneath the stars."

"But you can't," she murmured against his chest. He shook his head. "I cannot. Perhaps after this is all over," he said hopefully. "Perhaps . . ."

Deborah pressed a finger to his lips. "Don't say it." *It's too late,* her mind screamed. *Too late to turn back now.* "You're right, my place is here and yours is among your people. I cannot ask you to put everyone in the village at risk for a love that was never meant to be. I understand."

"I pray that you do."

"We all do what we think is best, Tshingee. We all have responsibility for someone besides ourselves." She thought of the tiny baby growing within her and tears sprang in her eyes. *I hope you understand why I must marry Tom,* she thought, *and why*

I do not tell you of the child.

Tshingee pulled her against him, pressing his lips into her soft hair. *"K'daholel*. I love you, Deborah Montague."

"Tshingee." She lifted her head. "I have to tell you something.' "

"You do not."

"But . . ." Her lower lip trembled and he kissed her mouth.

"You want to tell me that you will marry your Thomas."

"How did you know?" The smile on her face was bittersweet.

"I see it in your eyes." He tugged on her shorn lock of hair. "I hear it in your voice."

"And doesn't it hurt you?"

"As much as it hurts you, Red Bird, it hurts me more. But you do the right thing and that makes my chest swell with pride."

"Oh, Tshingee," she sobbed. "I love you."

He held her in his arms, stroking her back and shoulders. Then with his hand, he lifted her chin to stare into her teary eyes. "I must go, Deborah. It is not safe for me to be here."

"No!" She clasped his arms. "Stay with me, just tonight."

"It is not right. You belong to Thomas now." I should take to the shadows honorably."

She pressed her lips to his, her kiss hard and demanding. "Please," she begged. "One last time, I need your love."

"But you have my love, always." He moved his lips over hers, down her jaw, into the soft flesh of her neck.

"No. I need to *feel* your love." She fumbled with the leather ties of his cloak, pushing it down off his shoulders. It fell to the floor in a heap behind him. "Please . . ."

Tshingee rested his hands on her narrow waist. His ebony eyes were fixed on hers.

"Please . . ." She showered his face with a sprinkling of kisses. "Love me, Tshingee, love me tonight," she begged in anguish. "Just one last time, make me feel alive."

With a groan, Tshingee lowered his mouth to hers. Threading his fingers through her thick hair he delved deep into her mouth, their tongues meeting in a dance of desperation. Deborah clung to him, moaning softly as his hand fell to the ties of her dressing gown. He released her breasts from the confines of the silky material and fondled one warm mound, testing its weight with the palm of his hand.

Leaning against Tshingee, she sighed, stroking his broad chest beneath the linen of his shirt. Pulling the shirt from the waistband of his breeches, she slipped her hand beneath the material, her fingertips making contact with the hard bud of his nipple.

Sweeping her into his arms, Tshingee carried Deborah to her bed and laid her gently on the counterpane. Then he stood upright and began to remove his clothing. Deborah followed his movements through half-closed eyelids.

Tshingee of the Wolf Clan was a glorious sight as he pulled his linen shirt over his head to reveal his bronzed, sculptured form. The whipcord muscles of his arms flexed as his hands went to the ties of his breeches. Deborah lowered her gaze to watch the buckskin fall to the floor. His stomach was taut and flat, his manhood hard and bulging, his thighs thick and perfectly formed. Tshingee sat on the corner of the bed to unlace his moccasins and Deborah knelt behind, him pressing her bare breasts to his back. She lifted the heavy curtain of midnight black hair and kissed the nape of his neck.

"I love the way you smell," she whispered. "Like the forest before a rain."

Tshingee's eyes drifted shut and he leaned back, enchanted by the feel of her peaked breasts brushing against him.

Deborah slipped her dressing gown off her shoulders then pulled him backward onto the bed. Leaning over him, she caught his male nipple with her mouth and he groaned, lifting his head to catch the tip of her breast. Deborah stroked the hard flesh of his chest, moving her fingers over his flat stomach and down to the apex of his thighs. Her mouth burned a trail of scalding want over his midriff and along the length of his sinewy thighs.

A raspy groan rose in Tshingee's throat as he stretched out on the four-poster bed, his hands moving over her lithe legs, massaging the flesh of her buttocks. Resting his head on one silken thigh, he caressed the mound of her womanhood, glorying in the sound of the soft moans of contentment that escaped her lips.

Caught in the throes of arousal, Deborah rolled onto her back, stretching out her arms to Tshingee.

He rose over her, and their lips met as he caressed the full peaks of her breasts. She clung to him, her hands resting on his hips, as he slipped his shaft deep within her.

Consumed by fire, Deborah cried out and Tshingee muffled her voice with his mouth. Lifting her dark eyelashes, Deborah smiled languidly. She brushed his cheek with her palm, pushing a lock of ebony hair behind his ear. "I love you," she whispered as she moved her hips rhythmically against his.

"*K'daholel*. I love you as the heavens love the stars," he murmured, gazing rapturously upon her. "I love you as the oceans love the tides. *K'daholel*."

Slowly Tshingee quickened the rhythm of his thrusts and Deborah rose to meet his demands. She caressed the thick muscles of his back and shoulders rising higher and higher on the wings of throbbing ecstasy. Tshingee's breath was hot on her face as she lifted her hips in a final drive for fulfillment. Sobbing in utter, sweet abandon, she clung to Tshingee; her world splintered into a thousand shards of bright light. A split second behind her, Tshingee drove home with a final stroke, his voice echoing hers as they both tensed every muscle in their bodies and then went weak.

Tshingee rolled onto his side, covering Deborah's dewy flesh with feather-light kisses. She lifted her eyelids, smiling, her breath still coming in short gasps.

"It is a wonder your father has not brought his hounds to your chamber, as much noise as you make, my love," Tshingee teased.

She lifted her head, covering her mouth with her palm. "I wasn't too loud was I?"

He laughed, kissing her love-bruised lips. "Your voice was nothing but a sigh carried on the wind beneath my kisses."

She dropped her head back on the bed, stroking his head of shiny hair with her hand. "Thank God one of us has got some sense. At least the door is bolted. Wouldn't that be something, Deborah Montague, Thomas Hogarth's betrothed caught with her lover in her own chamber." She giggled, then yawned. "I'm so tired."

Tshingee laid his head on her breast, wrapping his arm around her waist. "Sleep, then," he whispered.

Her eyes flew open. "You won't go, will you? Not while I'm asleep?"

He pulled the counterpane over them both. "No. I will wake you before I go." He kissed her forehead. "Now sleep, my Red Bird."

Hours later, Tshingee woke her and they made love one final time. Deborah held back tears as she watched him get out of bed and begin to dress. She brought the counterpane over her shoulders, kneeling on the goose tick mattress. "I would give anything to change what's happened . . . what must be."

"I know." He pulled on his buckskin breeches. "But we cannot change the stars, can we?" His voice was almost hopeful, as if he expected Deborah to disagree, but she only shook her head firmly.

"Then marry your Thomas and live a happy life."

He thrust his arms into his muslin shirt. "But remember the gift of love the Heavenly Father gave you and I. Cherish that gift deep within your heart."

She watched as he laced up his moccasins, knowing he was right, wishing desperately he was not. All she could think of was the child that grew within her. The son or daughter Tshingee would never know.

Silently, Tshingee finished dressing. A lump rose in his throat so that he could not speak. Tying the leather thongs of his cloak, he put out his arms and Deborah came to him. For a moment he held her in his embrace, then he kissed her lips ever so gently. *"K'daholel,* Red Bird."

"K'daholel, Tshingee," she answered bravely. Then she stepped back. "Go," she whispered, pointing to the window.

Tshingee stood frozen for a moment, then slowly he turned and made his retreat. When he opened the window snow blew into the room. The breeze tugged at the hem of his cloak and whipped his ebony hair off his shoulders. Hesitantly he looked back, as if to say something, but Deborah brought her finger to her lips. Bowing his head, Tshingee turned away, stepping over the sill, then disappeared into the night.

For a long time Deborah stood in the center of her bedchamber, shivering, staring at the open window.

Deborah crept down the grand staircase, her bare

feet padding lightly on the polished hardwood steps. The case clock at the top of the first landing chimed ominously. Two in the morning. In less than twelve hours she would be Mistress Thomas Hogarth.

Clutching her night robe to ward off the chill, Deborah slipped past the parlor. A rumble of snoring wafted through the darkness. The wedding guests had eaten well this evening and drunk their share of Christmas spirits. It was not often that the Earl of Manchester opened his house to his neighbors, but when he did, the occasion was always celebrated on a grand scale. No one could say the Earl watered his wine. The heavy snoring throughout the house was proof of that.

Making her way to the back of the house, Deborah slipped noiselessly down two steps and into the kitchen. On the far wall a fire burned low in the huge fireplace. The new kitchen maid slept on a pallet on the floor.

"Dory." Deborah knelt, shaking the girl's thin shoulders. Dory, wake up."

The maid jumped at Deborah's touch, leaping from the pallet. She clutched her wool blanket to her chin with trembling fingers, her eyes wide with fright.

"It's all right, Dory," Deborah whispered. "Don't be afraid. I won't hurt you."

The slave took a step back. "You . . . you need somethin', lady?"

"Shhh, we mustn't wake anyone, Dory." Deborah put her finger to her pursed lips. "Speak quietly."

The girl took another step back. "Y—yes,

ma'am."

"Dory, I want you to get dressed, get your cloak and mittens, and come with me to the Earl's office."

"I can't go in there! Ain't no body 'llowed in the Earl's office!"

"Dory, do as I ask, please."

Dory's entire body shook with fear. "If I goes in there and the Earl, he finds me, he'll—"

"He'll do nothing, because he won't find out. Now do as I say and hurry!"

Deborah took a candle from a candlebox on a table and lit it from the coals in the fireplace. "Go ahead, Dory," she whispered, going out the kitchen door. "Get your cloak and mittens and meet me in the office."

Walking quietly down the hall, Deborah opened the door to her father's office and went to his massive desk. Sitting in his chair, she put down the candle. Retrieving a sheet of paper, a goose quill, and a bottle of ink, she began to scribble a message.

A few minutes later, Dory slipped into the room. She was dressed in a worn homespun skirt with a tattered shawl draped over her shoulders. In her arms, she carried a patched woolen cloak.

"Now listen carefully," Deborah instructed, sprinkling a few pinches of sand over the wet ink on the paper. "Do as I say and you'll be perfectly safe. No one is ever going to harm you again, Dory."

"H—harm me? N—nobody ever done harmed me, lady," Dory answered. "N— nobody."

"Dory." Deborah looked up. "I know what my

father did, and I know there's nothing I can do to take away that pain but I can keep it from happening again."

"What—what the Earl did?" Dory shook her head. "The Earl, he—he din't do nothin'."

Deborah blew the sand off the sheet of paper. "I also know what he said, what he threatened to do if you ever told anyone."

Dory gulped. "You did?"

"Mmhmm. That's why I'm sending you away from here."

"Away, ma'am?"

"Far away where the Earl can never hurt you again." Deborah dripped a glob of candle wax on the sheet of paper and stamped it with her father's family-crest seal.

"I . . . I don't understand, Lady Deborah."

Deborah came around her father's desk, the sheet of paper in her hand. "I'm giving you your freedom, Dory. This paper, it says you're a free woman. I've made arrangements for you to go to the Virginia Colony. Tonight you leave here; tomorrow you begin your journey."

Dory stared at the sheet of paper in Deborah's hand. "You lettin' me go?" she asked in disbelief. Tears welled in her eyes.

"I am, Dory. Now take this paper." She folded it and handed to the girl." Anyone who asks you who you belong to, you tell them you're a free woman. This paper is proof. It says the Earl gave you your freedom."

Dory stared at the paper, then at Deborah. "If the Earl finds out what you done . . ."

"He won't find out. By the time the wedding fuss is over, you'll be long gone. Everyone will just think you've run off."

"The sheriff, he'll be lookin' for me."

"No, he won't. He'll be looking for Dory, the Earl's slave, not for Sally Freeman."

The maid smiled, showing off a perfect set of even white teeth. "You'd do this for me, Lady Debbra?"

Deborah pushed the folded sheet of paper into Dory's hand. "Yes. Now put on your cloak and go out through the kitchen. There's a man there who will take you away from Host's Wealth tonight. He'll take you to someone's house and tomorrow you'll be bound for Virginia . . . a free woman."

"W—who is this man?"

"You don't need to know. Just trust me. I've paid him well. He's a man I contacted in Annapolis yesterday. He does this sort of thing all the time." She smiled. "So, go on with you."

Dory threw her cloak over her shoulders. Her fingers trembled as she tried to tie her hood. "I thank you, Lady Debra. Ain't nobody ever done anythin' for Dory like this."

Deborah crossed her arms, hugging her waist. "Just promise me you'll be happy, Dory. Leave your old life behind and forget it. You'll be working for a nice family at a tavern somewhere on the James River. But you'll be working there because you want to. And you'll be paid."

Dory's pitch black eyes shone as she put out her hands, taking Deborah's. "Thank ya."

"Oh, I almost forgot." Deborah slipped a small

leather bag from the ribbon that tied her robe shut. "This is for you."

Dory accepted the leather bag and opened it. She snapped it shut. "Good Lord, lady! That's more coin than this girl's ever seen in her life!"

"Take it. You deserve it. It's the price my father paid to purchase you. He owes it to you."

Dory smiled. "I can never thank ya enough."

"Just go. Knowing you're out there free to come and go as you please is all the thanks I'll ever need."

The black girl nodded, stepped back, then ran out of the office.

Sighing, Deborah blew out the candle and crept back up the steps to her chamber.

Chapter Nineteen

"Its not too late, Martha whispered in Deborah's ear as she tugged on the strings of her sister's boned corset.

"It's too late," Deborah responded numbly. She had laid awake in her bed after seeing Dory off, hoping the sun wouldn't rise. She prayed she would somehow be rescued from her impending marriage to Thomas Hogarth. But Tshingee did not return, she came up with no better solution to save the life of the child that grew within her, and the sun did, indeed rise. With the coming of the first light of dawn, Deborah surrendered to the fact that marrying Thomas was the only way to escape Host's Wealth and her father's hideous threat.

Martha eyed Lady Celia fussing with Deborah's wedding gown near the bed. "I can't understand why you'd give up all you believed in so easily," Martha continued, keeping her voice low. "Be certain you know what you're doing before it's too late. Once you're married, it's until death separates you . . . your death most likely."

Deborah stared at the wall, unable to meet her

sister's gaze. "I know what I'm doing," she answered, her voice devoid of any emotion. She couldn't allow herself to think now; all that was necessary was to go through the motions. In a few hours she'd be married to Tom and it would be all over; she just had to endure until then.

Martha sighed, slipping a silky shift over her sister's head. "You tell me that, but what I see is a woman preparing herself for the hangman. There's no joy in your face, no excitement, not even anticipation."

"Would you be excited if *you* were marrying Tom Hogarth?"

"No. But she would." Martha nodded ever so slightly in the direction of Elizabeth, who stood near the window.

Elizabeth's face was deathly white save for the red circles around her eyes. She sniffed quietly into her handkerchief.

"She fancies herself in love with your Tom, you know," Martha observed.

Deborah smiled sadly, raising her arms so that Martha could tie the strings of her furbelow-trimmed petticoat. "Would that she could have him. I think they'd actually make a good pair. She worships the grass he walks on. Tom's the kind of man who wants to be worshipped."

"So why are you marrying the man meant for your little sister?" Martha led Deborah to a stool, and indicated that she should sit.

Deborah took the seat, hiking up the skirts of her petticoat so that she could roll up her stockings. I told you, I have my reasons. Would you

269

rather see me married to cousin Rufus or whatever his name is, living in Essex?" Her voice was strained, but she remained in control. "Now could we talk about something else? I think you've beaten this subject to death."

Martha began to stroke a brush through Deborah's thick, dark hair. "I just don't want to see you hurt. You've always been so alive and full of life. I don't want to see that dimmed." Pulling a thick mane of hair off her crown, Martha tied it in a twist of blue and rose-colored ribbons that trailed down her back.

Deborah closed her eyes, slumping her shoulders. "I'll be all right. Trust me." She sighed, opening her eyes. "Now, just get me through this, Martha. It's all I ask."

Martha patted Deborah's shoulder soothingly. "All right. If I can live with the Earl of Danforth and his hypocritical ways, I suppose you can live with silly little Tom Hogarth."

"Girls! Girls!" Lady Celia came bustling across the room. "You'll have to hurry. Services will begin precisely at eleven!"

Deborah stood, her face whitely resolute. "So bring me my gown and let's get on with it."

The Christmas Day church service that was to precede the wedding ceremony was long and drawn out. The Reverend Godfrey droned on, lulling his congregation into a pleasant stupor. The doors between the twin parlors at Deliverance had been flung open and wedding guests that had come from miles around were pressed together on narrow benches, straining to catch a peek of the bride-to-be.

Deborah sat stiffly in a high-backed chair, her eyes half closed. She tapped her foot impatiently beneath the skirts of her silk and brocade wedding gown. Occasionally, she inhaled deeply, trying to ease the discomfort of her wedding finery. Her corset was too tight and lace on the sleeves of her new chemise were digging into her skin below her elbow.

Fanning her flushed face with one of Lady Celia's silk fans, Deborah leaned forward to catch a glimpse of the clock on the mantel. It was nearly two o'clock, high time this sham took place. Seeing Tom staring at her, she quickly leaned back in her chair. No matter how hard she tried, she just couldn't imagine what it was going to be like to be married to him. Worse, she couldn't fathom bedding him. After the love she and Tshingee had shared, how could she bring herself to let Tom touch her that way? *It's the price you pay for the safety of your baby,* she reminded herself. *It's the only way!*

The Reverend brought his service to an end and suddenly Deborah found herself being escorted before the crowd to the front and center of the room. A harpsichord played in the background as Thomas stiffly took her arm and led her the few feet to the bulbous-nosed clergyman. The crowd of guests murmured their approval, smiling as Deborah turned to face her betrothed.

Lady Celia had done a superb job overseeing

271

the sewing of Deborah's wedding gown. Only a few months ago Deborah would have been proud to wear it; today it felt like a death shroud. Sewn from panels of pale blue brocade and rose-colored silk, the gown had been styled after a pattern sent from Paris. The décolletage was daringly low, covered by a small modesty piece, the bodice long and pointed. The gathered overskirt of the gown was blue brocade edged with a ruffle the contrasting rose. The new petticoat that peaked fashionably from beneath her skirt was trimmed in a blue furbelow ruffle.

Thomas squeezed Deborah's hand, clearing his throat. Sweat beaded across his forehead.

Deborah looked at the Reverend, who was turning through the pages of a tattered leather-bound book. "Get on with it," she whispered, tapping her foot.

Thomas patted her hand. "It's all right, dear," he soothed. "We're all a bit nervous.

Deborah looked from Thomas to the Reverend and back at Thomas again. Her mouth was dry and she was suddenly short of breath. She was certain everyone in the room could hear her heart pounding. Her lower lip trembled as the Reverend Godfrey lifted his hand and began to read slowly from a page in the book.

Moistening her lips, Deborah snatched her hand from Thomas's. She leaned her head against his shoulder. "I . . . I can't do this," she murmured beneath her breath.

Thomas retrieved her hand; his voice was equally hushed. "Nonsense, it will all be over in a

272

minute."

The Reverend continued his monologue.

"No. I mean it, Tom. I can't do it." Deborah's voice was rising in volume. "I can't marry you. I'm not in love with you."

The Reverend looked up in confusion at the young couple standing before him. He stopped in mid-sentence. Lowering his voice so that only Thomas and Deborah could hear him, he spoke. "Have we trouble, my children?"

"I can't marry him," Deborah whispered.

"She says she can't marry me," Thomas said in disbelief.

The crowd of wedding guests began to cough and move about, craning their necks, straining to hear what was being said.

"My children, this is highly irregular."

"I don't want to marry him. I never did."

The Reverend turned to Thomas. "Mr. Hogarth, is this young lady being forced against her will?"

Thomas's eyes widened in horror. "Certainly not, sir. It was she who proposed to me . . . this time."

The Earl of Manchester pushed his way between Thomas and Deborah. "Reverend Godfrey, I demand to know what the delay is! We have guests!" he whispered harshly.

"It's your daughter, sir. She says she does not wish to wed Mister Hogarth. I will not marry a maiden against her will."

The Earl turned on Deborah, his face swelling with engorged blood. "My daughter doesn't know what she's saying. She's recently been through

273

quite an ordeal. Go on with the ceremony!"

Deborah threw her fan to the wooden floor. "I'll not do it," she said stubbornly. "I'll not repeat the vows."

"Reverend Godfrey, I have brought you here at great expense! Need I remind you that if that church of yours is to be built. you'll need my support?"

The Earl took a step forward and Deborah leaned behind her father. "Sweet Jesus, I'm sorry, Thomas. But I just can't do. I don't love you. I never will. I can't do it to you."

Guests were beginning to chuckle. Benches were scraping the floor and whispers were rising to an audible volume.

Thomas took Deborah's hand, raising his voice to be heard above the Earl's ranting. "For the love of God, Deborah, you can't keep doing this." Thomas squeezed her hand. "I've told I loved you. What more do you want?"

"It's not you." She shook her head, disengaging her hand from his. "It's me." She stumbled backward. "I'm so sorry, Tom . . ." Lifting her skirts, Deborah turned and ran through the parlor and out into the hall.

"Deborah Montague, come here this instant," the Earl bellowed from behind. "Damn it, girl. I've signed half of that land over to Hogarth and now you're going to marry the little son of a bitch!"

Deborah raced toward the back of the house with the Earl in pursuit. Just as she reached the door to the winter kitchen, her father caught a handful of her hair.

"Ouch!" Deborah shrieked. "Let go!"

"What ails you, woman?" The Earl bellowed, twisting her hair in his fist. "I've gone to a lot of trouble and expense to get you out of my house and you're going, by God."

Deborah shook her head, tears streaming down her face. "Just let me go. I just want Tshingee. I just want to go back to . . ."

The Earl struck her in the chin so hard that her head went back, slamming against the paneled door.

"Sir!" Thomas shouted, running down the hallway. "That is uncalled for!"

The Earl balled his fist, hitting Deborah square in the eye. "I should have given you a thrashing a long time ago, you little whore!" He twisted her hair viciously. "I knew that redskinned son of a bitch had something to do with all of this!"

"Sir!" Thomas caught the Earl's hand, wrestling it down. Trembling, he slipped his body between Deborah's and the Earl's. "I will not see any woman treated so! You have no right."

"The h . . . hell I don't!" the Earl panted. "As long as she's my daughter, I've the right. It's my duty to knock a little sense into her as will be your duty when you marry the Indian-loving harlot!" The Earl doubled over, leaning on his knees, trying desperately to catch his breath.

Thomas spun around to face Deborah. "Come back in the parlor and marry me now. It's the only way I can protect you." He pulled his handkerchief from his burgundy wedding coat and

275

lifted it to her swelling eye. "Please," he begged. "For once in your life, do something sensible."

Deborah clutched the handkerchief. "I can't," she sobbed. "I can't do it to you, Thomas. I'll ruin your life."

At that moment Lady Celia pushed her way between Deborah and Thomas. "Thomas, take her to our carriage and have one of your boys drive her back to Host's Wealth before he kills her. I'll send one of her sisters out to ride with her."

"If I could only talk to her, Lady Manchester," Tom pleaded.

"There will be no wedding today. Now hurry." Lady Celia turned away, grasping her husband's heaving shoulders. "Are you ill, sir?" She glanced up at the crowd of wedding guests gathering in the hallway. "Someone! Get a chair!"

Grasping Deborah by the shoulders, Thomas ushered her down the hall, shouting for a doorman.

Martha entered Deborah's bedchamber in a flurry of rustling petticoats, locking the door behind her. "I'm sorry it took me so long but I had to send Gabby to the ice house."

Deborah lay stretched out on her bed, her arm flung over her face. Her wedding dress and petticoats were heaped on the floor. "I'm all right, Martha. If that's the worst I get, I'll consider myself lucky."

"Lucky!" Martha pulled up a chair beside the bed and sat down. "I thought he was going to kill you. I've never seen him so angry!"

"It's John Wolf's land," Deborah answered warily. "He signed it over to Tom yesterday. The poor Earl's lost half of his precious plot and he's still stuck with me."

"How can the Earl sign over the land? Aren't the man's wife and child still living there?"

"Apparently that's just a minor inconvenience. He and Tom's father were hoping Bridget would just give up on her husband and go. Now I suppose they'll burn her out or accuse her of murder as well."

"You sound as if you know the red man didn't kill the Earl's bondman."

"I know John Wolf. He wouldn't kill a rat in his grain barrel."

Martha pushed a lock of damp hair off Deborah's cheek. "So why has Tom gone along with all of this?"

"Because he trusts our father and his own. The truth is, I don't think he wants to know the truth. Tom detests upset."

"Well, I have to tell you, Thomas Hogarth certainly surprised me. Here, put this over your eye." She handed Deborah a chunk of ice wrapped in a linen towel. "Who'd have thought Tom had it in him, defending you from the Earl like that? He really does care for you, doesn't he?"

Deborah lowered the ice pack to her eye, wincing when it made contact. "Gallant to the last, isn't he?"

"That's unfair. He kept Father from really injuring you. Maybe you were right. Maybe you should have married him." Martha smiled. "But I'm glad you didn't."

Deborah sat up, leaning against the headboard. She tossed the ice pack into a bowl on the table next to the bed. "But what am I going to do now?"

The doorknob of her bedchamber door turned. "Deborah! Let me in here," the Earl boomed. "Let me in this minute."

"F—father—" Martha leaped to her feet—"Deborah's resting right now."

The Earl pounded his fist on the door. "Martha? That you? Open this damned door before I have Lester open it for me!"

Martha trembled, looking down at Deborah.

"Let him in," Deborah said quietly. "What can he do to me? He'll not kill me here in my own bedchamber. He's not man enough. It's more likely he'd have me thrown in the bay after dark."

Martha brought her hands to her face. "Deborah! How could you say such a thing?" She grasped her sister's hand. "He wouldn't, would he?"

"Open this God damned door, Martha! I'll have your husband up here!"

"Go on, before he breaks down my door," Deborah urged, sitting up and swinging her legs over the side of the bed.

Hesitantly, Martha slid back the bolt on the door. The Earl swung open the door with such force that it hit the plastered wall behind it. "Get out of here!" He ordered, pointing a thick finger at Martha. "Out of here before I thrash you as well!"

Martha backed up, glancing at Deborah across the room.

"Go on," Deborah said quietly.

The moment Martha stepped into the hallway, the Earl slammed the door shut behind her. He approached Deborah, waving his fist in the air. "How dare you! How dare you embarrass me like that in front of half the county!" His thinning gray hair was disheveled, his coat unbuttoned, his linen shirt tucked only partway into his breeches.

Deborah's face remained impassive. "I apologize, sir."

"You're goddamned right, you apologize! And you'd better keep apologizing." He snatched her wedding gown off the floor and threw it at her. "Now put it on and get your ass downstairs. Thomas and the Reverend Godfrey have agreed to go through the ceremony in our parlor."

Deborah pushed the gown aside, her eyes meeting her father's. "I can't," she said steadily.

"You can't!" the Earl exclaimed in disbelief. "What do you mean you can't!"

"The Reverend said he wouldn't marry us unless I was in agreement. I'm not in agreement. I'm not marrying Tom and that's final."

William Montague balled his meaty fists in rage. "All right, all right, Miss Indian whore. You sit there and refuse, but you'll not leave this chamber until you put on that wedding dress and agree to exchange vows with the Honorable Thomas Hogarth. I don't care if you rot here for fifty years, you do not leave this chamber, do you understand me?"

"Yes, sir."

He swung around in anger, pounding a fist into the palm of his hand. "Celia was right," he muttered as much to himself as to his daughter. "I should have married you off to my cousin Rufus when you were thirteen. You've been nothing but trouble since the day your poor mother died, God rest her soul." He turned back to face her, pointing a finger accusingly. "You think I don't know the things you've done? You cause an uproar among my slaves and bonded servants telling them they ought to know how to read. You steal my money from my cash box, you take food from the larder to give to half the poor no-accounts in the county, and you encourage your sisters to go against my word."

Deborah's gaze remained fixed on her father's red, swollen face. *I'm getting out of here,* she thought. *I don't know how, but I'm going. If Dory can work a tavern, I can do the same. Somehow my baby is going to be safe from this raving lunatic.*

The Earl's pigeyes narrowed as a thought struck him. "And just this morning Cook informs me the new negra kitchen wench is gone. I'd lay a gold piece you had something to do with that as well! You know where she is, don't you?"

Deborah was tempted to leap up and tell her father what she'd seen in the cellar a few nights ago, but she held her tongue for fear of putting Dory at risk. "I know nothing of the sort."

Burying his face in his hands, the Earl was

silent for a moment. "Very well," he said, letting his hands fall to his sides. "I've said what I have to say. You are to remain in this room until you come to your senses and marry Tom Hogarth." He lifted a fat finger. "But I warn you, if you try to run away, I'll hunt you to the ends of the earth!" He laid his hand on the door knob. "I don't like to be bested, Deborah, not by anyone," he said venomously. "And especially not by my daughter. You've had your way too long, but this time you lose. You do as I say." He nodded. "Or you'll die in this room."

Three days later Deborah sat near the fireplace in her room, her feet propped up on the warm brick. In her lap rested an old copy of the Bible. It was not so much that she was interested in reading from the Old Testament, as it was she was bored senseless. After remaining in her chamber a full day, she had asked Lady Celia for something to read from her father's less-than-adequate library. Deborah's step-mother promptly produced a copy of the Bible, suggesting she begin with reading the Ten Commandments. "I would pay particular attention to the fifth, were I you," she had commented.

Deborah sighed, getting to her feet. She paced the room, first from east to west, then north to south. She knew exactly how many steps it took to reach any point in her room, from any point. The game had helped to pass the time as she had mulled over her situation.

Deborah knew she must take her leave of Host's Wealth and soon, but so far, she didn't know where she was going. She had to have a well-thought-out plan, because once she left the house she could never come back. And she could never allow the Earl to find her.

Her first thought was to travel north to the New England Colonies and pass herself off as a maid looking for service, but with the babe growing within her, she knew that was no longer an option. She knew too well that those Colonists who lived to the north were not cut of the same cloth as those of the Tidewater. Religious fervor reigned over the New England Colonies and she would likely be publicly whipped for giving birth out of wedlock. A better choice was to go the Virginia Colony, or perhaps even the Carolinas.

Then, of course, there was the option of returning to the Lenni Lenape village. That was what Deborah longed to do. She missed Snow Blanket and Bee. There among the Wolf clan she had felt so secure . . . loved even. But would Tshingee allow her to join the village or would he demand that she be cast out? And what of the baby? She would have to tell him eventually. Would his opinion of her change then? Would he offer to marry her out of guilt? Or would he pack his bags and ride west as he had told her he yearned to do?

Deborah exhaled in exasperation. Nothing seemed like a good choice. But she knew she had done the right thing in not going through the wedding with Tom. His taking up for her with the Earl had served only to solidify her confidence in her decision. It would have been wrong for her to marry him under such false pretenses. No matter what her opinion of Tom was, he didn't deserve to be deceived. She had no right to go to him carrying another man's child. *She* had fallen in love with Tshingee. *She* had bedded him. She had known what the consequences might be. Her child was *her* responsibility, not Tom's.

A loud commotion outside brought Deborah out of her reverie. Running to the window, she pushed it open. A icy breeze hit her square in the face, blowing her hair back off her shoulders.

"Injuns!" A lone rider declared racing up the snowy drive. "Redskins on the loose!"

The Earl's hounds bounded through the snow, barking and nipping at the horse's heels. "Yo! You in the house!" the man shouted, flailing a musket.

The front door below swung open and James stepped out onto the brick stoop. "What is this?" he demanded. "We're dining!"

The rider leaped off his horse, pulling his hat off his head as he ran toward James. "Burt Lutton, sir. Mr. Hogarth sent me from Deliverance. There's been an attack!"

"Attack? God's teeth, man! Get ahold of yourself! What are you talking about?" James shivered, clutching the silk material of his caftan.

The man panted, leaning forward and clutching his chest to catch his breath. "Injuns, sir. They's on the warpath!"

283

Chapter Twenty

An icy tremor ran down Deborah's back. An attack! After all Tshingee had said about wanting to avoid any violence how could he have attacked Deliverance? John wasn't even being held there!

Deborah pulled her head in the window, pressing her back to the plastered wall. After all of his declarations of being a peaceful man, how could Tshingee have injured innocent people? Was it jealousy over Tom? Had Tshingee come to take her back to the village? Something just didn't seem right. . . . She leaned back out the window.

"Father! Father!" James shouted.

The Earl appeared on the front stoop. "What the hell is going on here? What's all of the shouting?"

"Father. Deliverance is under attack! Redskins!" James exclaimed.

"Redskins?"

"Yes. sir." The rider nodded. "Young Mr. Hogarth says come quick with men and munitions. The Viscount's hurt somethin' fierce, a couple men dead, and the Injuns, they carried off some of the kitchen help!"

284

The Earl wiped his brow. "I knew we should have cleared this county of that red vermin years ago! James have horses saddled." He slapped his son on the back. "And for Christ's sake, boy, get dressed!"

Deborah slammed the window shut and raced to throw a gown over her shift. Rolling on a pair of wool stockings, she dropped to the floor to retrieve her kidskin riding boots. Hopping on one foot as she thrust the other into a boot, she rattled the knob on her bedchamber door.

"Someone! Let me out! Let me out of here!" On the lower floor she could hear the commotion as guests from the Christmas holidays scrambled to take up arms.

Deborah twisted the locked doorknob, giving the door a kick. "Damn it! Someone let me out of here!"

There were footsteps in the hallway and James's bedchamber door opened. "James!" Deborah called. "James! Let me out of here!"

"Let you out!" came James's high-pitched voice "Not bloody likely! Your redskin and his men have attacked Deliverance."

"It can't be, James! Someone's mistaken. Tshingee wouldn't—"

"The hell it's a mistake! You come out of that room"—his voice was fading now—"and father will wring your neck with his own hands!"

"James! James, come back!" She pounded on the door but already she could hear him running down the stairs.

"Damn it!" Deborah shouted. She ran to the

window and threw it open again. The courtyard below was a mass of confusion. Men were shouting as they mounted horses, dogs barked, and women cried, waving their handkerchiefs. In the confusion of passing out weapons, a musket went off and a horse shied, throwing a rider into a snowbank.

Suddenly the Earl came bursting into the group, mounted on his horse. "Let's go, men! he shouted, throwing a hand over his shoulder. "You women stay in the house and lock up. Close the shutters. I'll leave Lester and some of my men to stand guard."

"Take care, William, Lady Celia urged from where she stood on the stoop "Don't get yourself killed!"

Deborah watched as the men rode out.

"Ladies! Ladies! Inside, please." Lady Celia directed below. One by one the women went back inside and the front door slammed shut.

Deborah took a deep breath. She had to get to Deliverance to see what had happened. She would not believe Tshingee had led an attack on the plantation until she saw the evidence herself. And the window was the only way out of her prison. She stared down at the snowy ground two stories below. She knew it was possible. Both Tshingee and Mary had managed, but could she do it?

Deborah swung one leg through the window, straddling the sill. If she was going, it would have to be now, before Lester and his men surrounded the house to guard it. Murmuring a prayer beneath her breath, Deborah swung the other leg over.

Sitting on the sill with the skirt of her gown hiked up around her waist, she reached for the brick ledge below with the toe of her boot. The ledge was less than the width of her foot, nothing more than a row of protruding bricks added for decoration.

The first time Deborah's foot slipped on a patch of ice, she reached for the windowsill. "I can't do this," she muttered. "I'll break my neck." But after a few seconds passed, she turned back and started a long the ledge, her back pressed to the wall. She passed James's windows, refusing to look down. The wind was cold and snow blew off the roof, stinging her eyes, but she pressed on knowing there was no time to spare.

Miraculously she reached the roof of the winter kitchen without slipping. Stepping onto the solid wood of the cedar shingles, she heaved a sigh of relief. Slowly, she made her way down the slope of the lean-to roof. Reaching the lip, she stared down at the ground. Tshingee had climbed down a vine of ivy, but the ivy had died back and there was little foliage left to cling to.

She leaned farther over the overhang, searching for the rain barrel. If she could drop onto that . . . Suddenly Deborah's feet flew out from under her. She stifled a scream as she slipped backward and slid over the edge of the roof. The next thing she knew she was lying in a heap of snow near the back door of the kitchen.

Dazed, Deborah shook her head, blinking. Then she scrambled to her feet, praying no one had seen or heard her fall. Pressing her back to the kitchen wall, she slipped around the back of the house. Just as she caught sight of the barn, Lester came out, a musket propped on each shoulder. Deborah watched until he disappeared around the front of the house, then she made a run for the barn.

Sneaking in a side door, she crept through the semidarkness. It was warm and dry in the barn; the comforting smell of sweet hay and groomed horseflesh tantalized her nose. Reaching Joshua's stall, she stuck out her hand, smoothing his velvety nose. "Now about a ride, boy? Wouldn't that be nice?"

Creeping past his stall, she entered the tack room and reached for her sidesaddle. Then, on second thought, she took hold of the pummel of one of her father's saddles and heaved it over her shoulder. Retrieving a bridle, she slipped into Joshua's stall and saddled him up.

Leading Joshua into the main hall of the barn, she took an old patched wool cloak and a battered leather hat off the wall. Throwing the cloak over her shoulders, she stuffed the hat over her head and turned to face her mount. Deborah stared at the stirrup hanging down from the saddle. It made sense that it would be easier to ride astride, but she'd never tried it.

"Now or never," she murmured beneath her breath. Holding Joshua steady, she pushed her foot into the stirrup and swung up. Deborah hit the top of the saddle, grinning. "That was it?" She lifted the reins, proud of her accomplishment. If she'd have known it was that easy to mount, she'd have given up riding sidesaddle long ago!

Deborah caught her breath and stared in horror at the carnage before her. Her hands shook as she rode through the barnyard at Deliverance, unnoticed by neighbors and friends. Disemboweled animals were strewn everywhere, their entrails still steaming in the frigid air. The snow was stained crimson with blood. The warm nauseating scent of a fresh kill lingered over the yard, mixing with the smell of charred wood. Although a fire in the main house and the barn had been successfully extinguished, smoke still clung in the air and ashes littered the slain horses and cows.

A few men from Host's Wealth were riding in circles on horseback, shouting orders to bondmen, while other men dragged several lifeless bodies up the front steps into the front hall of the manor house.

Deborah rode Joshua up to the entranceway and dismounted, tying him loosely to an iron-ringed hitching post. Slowly she walked up the steps, following a trail of smeared blood.

Thomas's mother sat in a chair in the front hall, her face buried in her hands. Her entire body shook with sobs.

"Lady Hogarth?" Deborah ran to her, kneeling on the floor. She gave no mind to the puddles of melted snow and smears of blood the men had brought in on the soles of their boots. "Lady Hogarth, it's Deborah!"

Lattice Hogarth lifted her head. Her face was

streaked with tears and spattered with droplets of blood. "My poor Morris," she moaned. "My poor Morris is gone!"

Deborah lifted the hem of her gown to wipe Lady Hogarth's face. "Where's Tom?" she asked. "Is Tom all right?"

Lady Hogarth raised a hand, pointing into the parlor. "There, with the bodies," she managed.

Deborah got up. "I'll be right back," she promised, patting the elder woman reassuringly on the shoulder. "Stay right here."

Just then two bondmen from Host's Wealth came up the front steps carrying a lifeless body. The face of the corpse had been covered with an old feedsack.

Deborah swallowed hard, following the men into the parlor.

"Here." Thomas instructed. "Lay the body here." Deborah stared in disbelief at the neat row of bodies lined up on the parlor floor. The men laid the body down gently and left the room.

"Tom."

Tom slowly lifted his head. "Deborah? Jesus! What are you doing in here?" He stepped over a body, grasping her arm. "You shouldn't be here!"

"Tom." She took his hands, tears welling in her eyes. "What happened?"

He stared at her, his face pale, his eyes glazed. "I . . . I don't know exactly. It all happened so quickly. I was doing some figures in the office and suddenly people were screaming. No one ever saw them coming. They were just here."

"Who, Tom?"

"Indians. They were everywhere, some with muskets but most of them with bows and arrows and those war hatchets. They killed livestock, they raped women and carried some of them off."

"Your father?"

He nodded in the direction of a body lying near the fireplace. It was covered entirely by a clean linen sheet. "Dead."

"Oh God, Tom. Why?"

"Why?" Tears rose in his eyes and he wiped at them with the sleeve of his bloodstained shirt. "How the hell should I know why!" he shouted at her. "I guess they wanted the halfbreed."

"John? But why would they come here for him? It's common knowledge he's being held at MacClouds'."

"I don't know. I don't know." He shook his head, walking away. "All I know is that there are four women missing from the kitchen and one from the dairy. So far we've found seven dead men, two children. There're still bodies in the barn but they're burned so badly that I don't know how many there were."

Deborah wiped her mouth with her hand, fighting the nausea that rose in her throat "Tom. This just doesn't make sense. They couldn't have been looking for John Wolf. I know Tshingee wouldn't have done this. Are you sure the Indians were Lenni Lenape?"

"How the hell should I know? They were Indians!" He lowered himself into a chair, his hands falling to his sides in helplessness.

Deborah stared at the line of bodies that

stretched across the room. "Why are all of the faces covered?" She knelt to touch one of the cloth coverings but Tom leaped up, grasping her hand.

"Don't."

"What? Why? I wanted to see who it was." The body she knelt beside was a young man dressed in his Sunday best.

"No need to see. It's Paulie Barker."

"Paulie? The boy that worked for the Mac-Clouds?" Deborah stared at the blood-soaked cloth that covered his face. "The one that stutters?"

"Did stutter." Tom's face was ashen. "He was courting one of the kitchen girls. The redskins carried her off." He grasped Deborah's hands, raising her to her feet. "Could you check on Mama? She's in the hall. She needs to be taken up to her room. No need for her to see any more than she's already seen. You don't belong in here either."

"Tom," she said steadily. "You didn't tell me why their faces are covered."

"Deborah, I'm begging you. Please go."

"Tom! Look at me!" She touched his cheek with her fingertips.

"Because they were mutilated," he shouted, choking back a sob.

"Mutilated?" She looked at Paulie's body at her feet. "Mutilated how?"

"My God, Deborah, have you gone insane?"

With one quick motion she yanked the cotton sack from Paulie's face. Her hand trembled.

The ears had been sliced off his head.

Deborah took a deep breath, dropping the covering back over Paulie's face. "Tom," she said quietly. "The Lenni Lenape didn't do this. It wasn't John's brother. It had to be Mohawks."

"It was Indians!" He shouted. "Now go on, get out of here. If your father finds out you've been here—"

"My father! she interrupted. "Where is he?"

"Gone." Tom leaned on the mantel of the fireplace, reaching for a decanter of brandy.

"Gone where?"

"MacCloud's," he answered quietly.

"MacCloud's? Whatever for?" But before the words were out of her mouth, Deborah knew why they'd gone. "John . . ." she murmured beneath her breath.

"Yea. They've gone to do what they should have done long ago," Tom answered bitterly.

Deborah turned and ran out of the parlor, through the hall, and down the steps. Yanking up Joshua's reins, she swung into the saddle and wheeled the horse around and headed for the MacCloud's.

Before Deborah reached the border of the MacCloud plantation, she could hear a crowd of men hooting and muskets being fired. Riding out of the woods and into the clearing, she galloped full speed toward the barn. The farmyard was filled with neighbors on horseback and on foot. Noble and common man alike stood in clumps shouting and raising their fists in protest as they passed around flasks of whiskey.

"What's happening here?" Deborah demanded of the nearest person.

"They come to get the redskin." A boy of fifteen swept off his hat, pointing in the direction of the barn. "Only Mr. MacCloud, he says it ain't right. He says he ain't releasin' the prisoner 'til the sheriff comes for him."

Deborah leaned in her saddle, scanning the crowd of men. The Earl of Manchester stood at the door of the barn, shouting and waving a fist at Charlie MacCloud. "Step aside, boy!" he ordered.

Charlie stood his ground, his feet spread, a musket cradled in his arms. "I will not, sir."

"I said step aside and let justice be done!"

"Justice, sir, will come from the English court, not from a group of drunken men."

The Earl's face reddened with anger. "If you don't step aside, boy, your father—"

"My father is not here. He's in Annapolis celebrating the Yuletide and while he's gone, *I* am master here."

"Do as the Earl says and step aside, Charlie." a man shouted from the crowd.

"Step aside before you're hurt," another added. "By the King's ass, what's wrong with you, Charlie MacCloud," the Earl demanded. "Didn't I just tell you that this redskin's men massacred innocent women and children at Deliverance? Viscount Hogarth is dead, for God's sake!"

"It doesn't matter." Charlie shook his head.

"The man inside this barn killed no one today. It hasn't even been proven that he killed your bond-servant, sir.

"Are you calling me a liar?" The Earl raised a fist below Charlie's nose.

"No, sir. I am not. I'm simply saying that our English law requires that this man have a fair trial. My father will be bringing someone back with him tomorrow to take the Indian to Annapolois. He's been held unjustly too long. He has a right —"

"And what of Morris Hogarth's right?" demanded a voice from the crowd.

Men cheered in response and someone lifted a musket over his head, firing a shot. "Yeah, what of Hogarth's rights?" came a shout. The crowd of angry men pressed closer to Charlie MacCloud, their voices rising in frenzied unison.

"I'm warning you one last time, boy," the Earl threatened. "We want justice and justice we will have."

Before Charlie could speak again, one of the Earl's men darted forward, striking Charlie in the temple with the butt of his musket. To Deborah's horror, Charlie fell to the snowy ground. The crowd cheered, advancing toward the barn.

Someone dragged Charlie's unconscious body out of the way of the front doors and the main bulk of the crowd stormed the barn.

Deborah stifled a cry of protest as the men opened the barn door and swarmed inside. Sinking her heels into Joshua's sides, she rode forward, dismounting next to Charlie's unconscious body.

"Charlie! Charlie! Are you all right? Wake up! You've got to stop them!" She pulled his cocked hat off his head, running a hand through his fiery red hair. "Charlie?"

Charlie MacCloud came to slowly. "Deborah?" He tried to sit up but then dropped his head back again.

"Charlie, you've got to get up!" She cradled his head in her lap, wiping his bloody temple with the edging of her petticoat. "They're going to kill him!"

A burst of applause brought Deborah's attention to the entrance of the barn. The crowd of men stepped out into the barnyard hollering and shaking their fists in the air. John was being held up between two burly bondman, his face battered and bloody. Someone threw a bucket of water in his face and John's eyes flew open.

"You can't do this!" Deborah shouted, leaping to her feet. "You've no right!"

"What the hell is she doing here?" the Earl shouted, seeing his daughter for the first time. "Someone! James! Get her out of here! This is no place for a damned female!"

Two men grasped Deborah's arms, pulling her backward. She struggled, kicking and screaming. Her hat flew off her head as she ducked, twisting free. "He deserves a fair trial," she shouted at the men, pushing her way among them. "You can't do this!"

"The hell we can't," someone answered.

Just then two riders came up the drive. One held Bridget firmly in front of him, the other struggled to carry Mary and still remain astride. The little girl screamed and kicked fiercely, stretching to scratch the man's eyes.

"Mary! Bridget!" Deborah ran toward them. "Why have you brought them here?" she demanded of the men. "Release them immediately!"

The man carrying Bridget lifted her out of the saddle and pushed her roughly to the ground. Bridget rolled into a ball in the snow, sobbing.

"Get up," Deborah insisted, grasping the Irish woman's arm. Giving no heed to Deborah, Bridget only wailed louder, pulling her shawl up over her head.

As the man carrying Mary rode past Deborah, the little girl sank her teeth into the man's forearm.

"Damnation!" the rider shouted, losing his grip on Mary.

Mary fell from the horse, but hit the ground running. "Deb-or-ah! Deborah!" she shouted.

Deborah closed her arms around the child, hugging her tightly against her. "It's all right," she soothed, smoothing back the child's tangled hair. "It's all right, Mary. I won't let them harm you."

Keeping her arm tightly around Mary, Deborah walked up to the man who had brought Bridget into the compound. "What do you think you're doing?" she demanded. "Why have you brought them here?"

"I don't have to answer to you." the man replied, yanking off his hat. He looked up at the sea of angry male faces. "I say we hang the bunch of them and be through with the red bastard and his whore!"

Deborah recognized the man as a farmer from a plot of land near Deliverance. "You'll do no such thing," she snapped. "Father! Father!" She pushed her way through the crowd, spotting the Earl standing near John. "You're not going to let them do this, are you?" she pleaded.

"I've no control over these men."

"No control!" she scoffed. "How can you say that? You brought them here! It was your idea. It's been you from the start. You were the one who wanted to take John's land! *You* were the one—"

"Enough!" the Earl snarled. "I'll not be spoken to like this by my own daughter! You go too far this time!"

Deborah wheeled around to face the crowd of men. "Don't you see what you're doing by taking the law into your own hands? You're as guilty as he is if you hang him!"

"Are we going to have a hanging here, gentleman?" a man shouted from the crowd. "Or are we going to listen to this babbling female?"

"Hang him!" came angry voices from the crowd. "Hang the red bastard! Hang them all!"

Deborah turned to face John; her eyes met his. He hung limply between his captors, making no effort to fight them. His once thick, shining black hair fell in greasy strings about his face. He had a ragged beard and his nose was permanently bent at a peculiar angle. "Bridget. Mary. Save them," he pleaded quietly. "The good Lord has other plans for me, but save my wife and child."

The men lifted John between the two of them and carried him off, heading toward a great oak tree just beyond the barn.

"You can't let them do this, Father," Deborah cried, following her father with Mary still clinging to her side. "You can't let them hang him! He's had no trial! He's an innocent man!"

"She's supposed to be in her bedchamber," James declared, coming up behind her. "How do you think she got out, Father?"

The Earl glanced over his shoulder. "I'll deal with her later," he barked.

"You want me to have one of the men take her home?" James hurried to catch up with his father.

"No. Let her stand here and watch. Let her see what becomes of murdering filth." The Earl of Manchester's eyes glimmered with a macabre excitement. "I remember my first hanging. He patted his son on the back, moving with the crowd of men toward the tree. "I wasn't more than ten. Damn fine day it was, just outside of London . . ."

Deborah stood for a moment, letting the men brush past her. She squeezed her eyes shut, fighting the tears that threatened to spill as she held Mary close to her. Never in her life had she felt so helpless. For a moment, she stood unmoving, unable to accept that she could do nothing to save John.

"No! No! Not my John!" Bridget shouted, running though the barnyard after the crowd of men. "Heavenly Father, not my John!"

A man caught Bridget by the skirt of her gown

and she screamed. Before Deborah could stop her, Mary was running toward her mother. Deborah cursed under her breath.

Beneath the tree two men were stringing up a hangman's noose. John had already been mounted on a horse, his hands tied behind his back.

"Mary! Come back here! Bridget! Come back before you're killed!" Deborah struggled to reach them but they were being surrounded by the loud, jeering men.

"Not my John! No!" Bridget sobbed. Someone knocked her to the ground with his fist and she began crawling toward John.

Spinning around, Deborah sprinted for her horse. She had to get Mary and Bridget out of here! Mounting Joshua, she tugged on his reins, wheeling him around. John was led to the tree and someone slid the noose over his head. For an instant Deborah froze in horror; she just couldn't believe this was happening.

A musket sounded and the horse John was mounted on shied. Deborah squeezed her eyes shut just as the noose snapped.

Chapter Twenty-one

Bridget's scream pierced the air.

Deborah hung her head, tears streaming down her cheeks. She hadn't thought they'd really hang John! Until the moment his body had fallen from the horse, she had for some reason believed he would be spared. How could she have been so naive?

Deborah took a deep breath, slowly gaining control of herself. Her mouth was dry and she was so dizzy she feared she'd fall from her horse's back, but the moment she heard Bridget's voice, she remembered John's last words. Deborah's eyes flew open. "Bridget. Mary."

Up ahead Bridget was running through the crowd of men toward the hanging tree. John's lifeless body swayed gently from the rope. "No! No!" Bridget wailed, her high-pitched voice tearing at Deborah's heart. "Dear God, no!"

Mary raced to keep up with her mother but someone stuck out their foot and the little girl tripped, falling headlong into the snow.

A man in the crowd picked up a stick and hurled it at Bridget. "Whore!"

301

"Redskin whore!" shouted another.

Deborah stared in horror as the men turned from John's body, settling upon a new target. Another stick flew through the air, hitting Bridget squarely on the back. That was followed by the pelting stones and an occasional chunk of horse dung.

"No!" Deborah screamed, urging Joshua forward. "Run, Bridget! Run!"

Charlie MacCloud was on his feet, struggling to reach Bridget. "Gentlemen! Gentlemen! Enough! You've had your justice! This woman has done nothing!"

"Mama!" Mary cried, scrambling to her feet. "Mama!"

Sinking her heels into Joshua's flanks, Deborah rode into the crowd of angry men. "Mary! No!" she shouted above the men's jeers. "Mary! Come here! Come to me!"

The little girl turned. "My mama!" she screamed.

"Come here!" Deborah held out a hand. Frenzied men were pushing past the child, knocking into her in their attempt to throw rocks and sticks at Bridget. "Hurry, before you're trampled!" Deborah shouted. To her surprise, Mary came to her, pushing her way through the men.

Deborah reached out a hand. "Climb up behind me."

"My mama," Mary protested, standing just out of reach. "We have to help my mama! Those bad men are hurting her!"

Deborah shook her head, keeping one eye on

the crowd of men surrounding Bridget. "Mary! You have to hurry!" Out of the corner of her eye, Deborah saw a small rock hit Bridget in the temple. The Irish woman crumpled to the ground. "Now, Mary!"

Mary lifted her hands and Deborah pulled with all of her might, swinging the little girl up behind her in the saddle. "Hold on tight," Deborah ordered, urging Joshua forward.

Seated astride her horse, Deborah could see Charlie MacCloud kneeling beside Bridget. He rolled her over onto her back. Her eyes stared lifelessly at the clouds above; a trickle of blood dribbled down her temple. Charlie lifted his ashen face to stare at the men. "You've killed her," he said quietly.

Without hesitation, Deborah reined Joshua around, heading out of the barnyard at a full gallop.

"But my mama," Mary protested, looking over her shoulder. "What about my mama?"

"Hang on," Deborah shouted, entering the woods. "Just hang on, Mary."

The child tightened her grip on Deborah's waist, leaning her head against Deborah's back. Although Mary had not seen Bridget fall, or heard Charlie's words, Deborah knew that somehow the child sensed what had happened. The two rode in silence the rest of the way to Host's Wealth.

Dismounting in the woods behind the barns at Host's Wealth, Deborah pressed her finger to her lips. "We must be quiet. Mary," she said, lifting her down from the saddle. "No one must know we're here."

"But this is your home," Mary whispered.

Deborah shook her head sadly. "Not anymore. It hasn't been, not for a long time."

"Where will we go? Those bad men, they burned our cabin."

Deborah squeezed Mary's hand. "Would you like to go to your uncle's village? To Tshingee?"

A smile brightened the little girl's dirty face. "Could we? Will Co-o-nah Aquewa be there?"

"Yes." Deborah tied Joshua's reins to a branch. "Your grandmother will be there too."

"And you? Will you stay with me in the village?"

Deborah glanced at the snowy ground. "Yes," she said quietly. "I think maybe I will."

Mary clutched Deborah's hand. "Do we go now? Do we go to my uncle's village today?" she asked anxiously.

"We do. But first we need supplies." Deborah squatted, speaking to Mary at eye level. "You stay here while I go up to the house and bring back some food."

"Can't I go with you?"

"No. It's not safe. They'll be looking for us. You stay here and wait for me." She forced a smile. "Do you think you can do that?"

Mary nodded, her tiny round face solemn. "I can do it. I will wait here."

Deborah kissed the top of her head. "Good. You're a very brave girl, do you know that?" She brushed a lock of red hair off Mary's cheek. "Now I'll be right back. You guard the horse." She waved, and started out through the snow, running toward the barnyard beyond the trees.

Skirting the outbuildings that were scattered in the farmyard, Deborah kept to the shadows. As she got closer to the house, she wracked her brain, trying to figure out how she could get inside to get some warmer clothes and some food.

The journey to the Lenni Lenape village was chancy but Deborah knew it was her only choice. It was her duty to take Mary back to Snow Blanket and Tshingee. She owed that much to John Wolf. The thought of facing Tshingee and having to tell him that his brother was dead frightened her, but she knew that, too, was her responsibility now.

To her dismay, Deborah spotted Lester Morgan sitting on the front step of the house. Just as she had suspected, she wasn't just going to be able to walk in through the front door. And there was no way she could get back up on the roof and get in through her bedchamber window. And even if she did, she'd just be locked in her room again.

Moving along the side wall of the house, Deborah peered in the parlor window. The room was filled with women talking in loud, shrill tones and drinking from small china cups. She dropped on all fours, moving to the next set of windows.

"Deborah!"

Deborah's froze. "Elizabeth?" She lifted her head to see her sister leaning out the Earl's office window.

"Deborah!" Elizabeth hissed. "I thought that was you! You're supposed to be locked in your chamber!"

"Hush, before someone hears you! Lester and his monkeys are everywhere." Deborah straightened up, brushing the snow from the old cloak.

"How are you going to get back inside without being seen?" Elizabeth whispered harshly. "How'd you get out there in the first place? Don't you know the Indians are on the warpath?"

Deborah leaned in the window. "I've been to Deliverance."

Elizabeth's hand flew to her mouth. "Is Tom all right?"

"Yes, he's unhurt, but his father's been killed."

"You're certain Tom wasn't hurt by the savages?" Deborah couldn't help smiling. "You really are in love with Tom Hogarth, aren't you?"

Elizabeth's dull brown eyes met her sister's. "I fear I am," she murmured.

"So tell Father you want to marry him, you ninny. Better yet, tell Tom."

Elizabeth's eyes widened in shock. "I couldn't possibly do such a thing!"

Deborah glanced over her shoulder, keeping an eye out for movement in the barnyard. "I'm not going to marry him; you might as well."

"Father says you *are* going to marry him," Elizabeth said suspiciously. "First you were, then you weren't, then you were, and now you're not again?"

"Look, I haven't got time to argue with you. I'm going and I need your help."

"Going! Going where?"

"Shhh!" Deborah leaned in the window, clamping her palm over Elizabeth's mouth. "The whole house is going to hear you." Slowly she removed her hand. "I can't tell you where I'm going, but I'll not be back."

Elizabeth clasped her sister's hand, squeezing it. "You wouldn't truly go, would you?"

"I'm going, and I need your help. I have to hurry. I need you to get me some food, my wool cloak and mittens and two blankets. I also want you to go to my chamber and bring me the doll in the chest at the end of the bed. Beneath the mattress is a small leather bag with porcupine quilling. Can you bring me those things?"

Elizabeth's lower lip trembled fearfully. "I . . . I don't know. Father . . ."

"I'm not coming back," Deborah said firmly. "And he'll never suspect you helped me." Her eyes grew moist. "Please, Elizabeth? You're the only one who can help me."

Elizabeth studied her sister's face. "You really aren't coming back, are you?"

Deborah shook her head.

"Is it the redskin, like they've been saying?"

"It's better if you don't know where I'm going. That way, if the Earl asks, you can honestly say you don't know."

"All right," Elizabeth said resolutely. "I'll do it."

Deborah smiled. "Hurry. I haven't much time left. Everyone will soon be looking for me."

"Why? What happened?"

Deborah shook her head. "Never mind. Just go!

307

I'll wait right here." She gave Elizabeth a nudge. "Oh, and Elizabeth."

"Yes."

"A musket."

"W—what?"

"I'll need a musket."

"What are you going to do with a musket?" Elizabeth asked in disbelief.

"Don't look at me as if I've grown horns! I'm not going to shoot the Earl if that's what you're worried about." She gave a dry chuckle. "Not that I wouldn't like to. I'll need it to protect myself."

"I . . . I don't know where to find a musket. The men took the weapons with them."

"Go into the pantry. Cook keeps an old matchlock pistol in a small barrel on the top shelf. Be sure and bring the powder and balls. Oh, and I've got to have a tinder box . . . needles and thread, and a pair of scissors."

"I . . . I don't know about the pistol, Deborah." Elizabeth's mouth twitched in indecision. "I'd never forgive myself if you shot yourself."

"I'm not going to shoot myself! Now go. Please Elizabeth. I've got to hurry."

Elizabeth closed the window and Deborah sat down in the snow to wait. Twenty minutes later, the window opened.

"Did you get everything?"

"Where did you get this?" Elizabeth asked, holding up Mary's doll. "She's beautiful."

Deborah took the doll. "She was a gift from a friend." She ran her fingers over the hide clothing. It seemed like a million years ago that Mary had

308

given her the precious toy. "What about everything else? The pistol. Did you get it?"

Elizabeth handed two neatly folded gray woolen blankets, Deborah's red riding cloak, and two lumpy flour sacks out the window. "I couldn't find anything else to put the food in. It wasn't easy getting it out of the kitchen. Cook's bound to miss the two loaves of bread and the apple tarts." Elizabeth caught her breath. "I put in a knife and a cleaver. You need something to cut the bread."

Deborah opened one flour sack and then the other, checking the precious contents. "This is perfect, Elizabeth. She pulled out the dusty matchlock pistol then dropped it back into the bag. "Perfect." She looked up. "Thank you."

"It doesn't seem like much food. Are you certain it will be enough to get you to wherever you're going?"

"I'll be fine. Really." Deborah smiled up at her sister. "Now give me a hug. I have to go."

Tears trickled down Elizabeth's cheeks. "I never thought I'd say it, but I'm going to miss you. You and I, we never got along, but—"

"We got along as well as any two sisters." Deborah put out her arms and Elizabeth leaned out the window to receive her sister's embrace. "Don't cry," Deborah soothed. "I'm chasing after my dreams. If Thomas is what you want, then go after him. Tell him you're in love with him. With his father gone, he's going to need you."

Elizabeth pulled a handkerchief from her bodice and blew her nose. "N—no one's ever needed me before," she said thoughtfully. "But I just don't know if I could do such a thing. To tell him, I mean. I've never been bold like you."

"If you want him badly enough, you'll say what you never thought you'd say. You'll do what you never thought you'd do." Deborah rolled up her red cloak and stuffed it into one of the bags. "Bye, Elizabeth. Have a good life." She smiled one last time at her sister, then with her head low, she ran across the yard, toward the woods.

"Think there's many wolves out there, Deborah?" Mary murmured, staring into the dark forest.

Deborah sawed at the loaf of bread she held in her lap, thankful Elizabeth had thought to throw in a kitchen knife. "No."

Mary's eyes narrowed. "Tshingee says there are many wolves in the woods at night."

"Maybe a few. But not here. They're afraid of the fire." Cutting off a slice of Cook's bread, Deborah pushed it into Mary's small hands. She couldn't let the child know how frightened *she* was of being in the dark forest. When she'd been with Tshingee, the eerie sounds had never bothered her, but here alone, every scratch of a branch made her jump. Every hoot of an owl sent a shiver down her spine. "Eat. It's well after midnight. You must be starved."

Mary sank her teeth into the soft bread. "I like bread, my mama, she always . . ." Tear sprang in her eyes.

Deborah put out her arms to Mary and the little

girl came to her. "I'm so, so sorry," Deborah murmured into Mary's hair. She fought back her own tears as she held the little quaking body. "It just couldn't be helped, Mary. I don't know what else to say."

Mary sniffed, holding tightly to Deborah. "My uncle, he would say it was in the stars."

"Yes." Deborah stared up at the bright canopy of pinpricks of light. "He's right."

"I'm going to miss them, my mama and papa."

"I know you are. I'm going to miss them too."

Mary climbed out of Deborah's lap and sat down on the stump beside her. She began to nibble at the bread again, her tears spent. "How long before we reach the village where my uncle lives?"

"A few days if the weather holds up." Deborah cut herself a piece of bread and began to eat it. The night air was cold, but the sky was clear and the wind wasn't too bitter.

"Which way?" Mary peered up at Deborah. "Do you know?"

Deborah chuckled. "I told you. I've been to the village—with Tshingee. Yes, I know. We just follow the Migianac to a certain point where there's a tree hanging over the water, then . . . then . . ." She struggled to recall Tshingee's words. *Even Bee could find his way home,* he'd said. Deborah shrugged, trying to sound confident. "Once you reach that point in the river, you go west until you hit the giant briar patch, then you go a quarter of a day north and there it is!"

Mary grinned. "You're as smart as my uncle, I

think."

Deborah laughed, tossing a stick of firewood into the small campfire. "Maybe not that smart. Now eat your bread and then I have something very special to show you."

"What is it?"

Deborah smiled mysteriously. "Eat your bread and then lie down on the blanket." She winked. "Then I'll show you."

Mary stuffed the remaining crust of bread into her mouth and scrambled beneath the wool blanket Deborah had spread out, still dressed in her cloak and boots. "I'm ready!"

Pulling something out of one of the flour sacks, Deborah approached Mary, her hands behind her back. "Close your eyes."

Mary squeezed her eyes shut, giggling.

Deborah knelt, pressing the little girl's doll into her arms.

"Olekee!" Mary cried. "Olekee, my baby!" She hugged the doll to her chest.

"I thought you would want me to bring her along."

"Oh, yes!" Mary beamed. "She will want to be with us at the village."

Deborah brushed Mary's hair back off her forehead. "Now sleep. We've got a long way to go tomorrow. We have to get as far away from Host's Wealth as possible."

Mary's eyes drifted shut. "Thank you," she whispered. "Thank you for bringing Olekee."

"You're welcome," Deborah whispered soothingly. "You're welcome, my brave little girl."

The following morning Deborah was awake with the first streaks of dawn. Slipping from beneath the wool blankets, she tucked them around Mary's sleeping form. Shivering violently, she tied the hood of her cloak beneath her chin and began to pack up their few belongings. By the time she had Joshua saddled and the bags packed, she was warm enough.

"Mary. Mary," Deborah said gently. "Wake up, love. We have to get moving."

The moment Mary's eyes were open, she was scurrying to her feet.

Deborah brushed the sleep from the little girl's eyes and tucked her braids beneath the hood of her "We'll eat once we get moving."

Mary nodded sleepily.

Helping her into the saddle, Deborah wrapped Mary in the wool blanket they'd slept on. "Warm enough?"

"Aren't you going to ride?"

Deborah lifted Joshua's reins and made a clicking sound between her teeth. "I think I'll walk for a while," she answered, leading the horse forward. "Close your eyes and rest if you like. It's going to be a long day."

All through the morning Deborah followed the Migianac River. Although occasionally she rode Joshua, she walked most of the time. The foliage was so dense, even in the winter, that often she had to backtrack to find her way through a thicket or a bramble patch, but she pressed on, her confidence in herself increasing with each hour that passed.

I can do this, she told herself over and over again. *Just follow the river; put one foot in front of the other. If Bee can find his way home, you certainly can. Home.* It was funny how she'd come to think of the Lenni Lenape village as home. The prospect of returning to the village was as exciting as it was frightening. She yearned to see Snow Blanket and Bee again. How many times since she'd returned to Host's Wealth had she dreamed of sleeping in Tshingee's wigwam?

Tshingee. Just the thought of his name made her tremble. How was she going to face him? How was she going to tell him John was dead? What did she expect of him? Did she think she was going to walk into the village and say hullo, your brother's dead, I've brought your niece and now I'm going to stay? Did she expect him to welcome her with open arms?

And what of the baby? Deborah's hand instinctively went to her stomach. Everything was such a mess. How could any of it ever be made right again? She wouldn't blame Tshingee if he wanted to have nothing more to do with her. But she wanted him so badly. She needed so desperately to be held. . . .

A strange sound brought Deborah from her thoughts. She stopped immediately, raising her finger to her lips to tell Mary to be quiet. For a long moment the forest was silent, then she heard it again. The faint wail of a woman.

Or was it some strange bird, or an injured

animal? Deborah was unsure. "Did you hear that?" she whispered to Mary.

Mary nodded solemnly. "We are not alone in the forest."

"How can you tell?"

Mary lifted her delicate chin, inhaling. "The air smells different. My uncle says one must not only use his eyes and ears, but also his nose."

"You can *smell* other people?"

Mary nodded. "I think so."

Deborah's hands trembled as she nervously wrapped Joshua's reins around and around her hand. *Now what?* she wondered. The sound of the human voice had come from ahead of them. It wasn't anyone come in search of her. Another wail filled the air. It was definitely female.

"Can't . . . can't we just go around them?" Mary asked after several minutes had passed and Deborah had said nothing.

"I'm afraid of getting lost," Deborah answered evenly. She was also afraid she knew who was ahead of them.

Deborah's hand shook as she dug into one of the flour sacks tied to the back of Joshua's saddle. Carefully she removed the matchlock pistol Elizabeth had taken from the kitchen pantry. It was already loaded—she'd done that last night after Mary had gone to sleep.

"You gonna shoot someone?" Mary asked, watching Deborah pull the strap of a small leather bag over her head.

Deborah patted the bag of tiny lead balls and black powder. "I hope not, Mary. It's just a precaution. Now listen to me. I'm going to go up ahead and see who it is. You stay here."

"No."

Deborah looked up Mary. "What?"

"I'm going with you. I'm afraid to stay here by myself. What if you don't come back?"

"I'll come back."

Mary hugged her doll close to her chest. "We can leave the horse here. I can be very quiet, quieter than you."

Deborah exhaled slowly. She didn't want to put Mary at any more risk than was necessary. The little girl had already been through so much. But Deborah had to know who it was that camped up ahead of them. "All right, Mary." Deborah put out her arms to help the little girl dismount. "But you must do as I say and be very quiet. There may be bad people on the path ahead us. Bad people who might try to hurt us."

Mary nodded. "I know about bad people."

Deborah dropped her arm over the little girl's shoulder. "I know you do, love. Now tie Joshua up and we'll go have a look."

A few minutes later Deborah and Mary were creeping along the bank of the river, staying just within the woods line. Ahead they could hear male voices, though they still couldn't make out any of the words. There was laughter and an occasional shout. Someone was celebrating something.

"They camp by the river," Mary whispered.

Deborah looked for tracks as they neared the encampment, but she found none. Either the strangers had come from downstream or they'd come by boat.

Coming around a bend in the river, Deborah dropped to her knees, pulling Mary down with her. Deborah clasped the pistol so tightly in her hand that her fingers ached.

"Mohawks," Mary whispered.

Chapter Twenty-two

Deborah crawled forward on her belly, the matchlock pistol held securely in her hand. Mary was right and Deborah's suspicions were confirmed. It was a Mohawk camp, and these were the same Mohawks who had raided Deliverance the day before.

A fire burned near the river's edge and the Mohawk braves danced in a circle around it, passing a small keg from one man to the next. They were dressed in an assortment of men and women's clothing mixed with their own hide and leather tunics and moccasins. A tall Mohawk wearing a cocked hat grabbed the keg and held it high over his head, letting the clear liquid pour into his open mouth. It was rum, stolen from the cellars of Deliverance, no doubt. The other braves laughed, clapping their hand rhythmically as they swayed faster, raising their knees high in a jaunty drunken dance of victory.

Just beyond the campfire three women were tied to a clump of saplings. A young yellow-haired girl lay on the ground, her gray homespun skirts pulled up to her knees, her head thrown back in a state of unconsciousness. The other two women huddled around her, trying to keep her warm by sharing their long cloaks.

One of the Mohawks pulled a small drum from a leather sack and began to pound on it, adding to the rhythm of the other braves' stomping feet. A warrior wearing a woman's shift over his leather tunic danced in frenzied circles laughing and clapping as he drew closer to the women tied to the trees. In one swift movement he yanked a steel-bladed knife from his moccasin; the sunlight reflected off the shiny metal flashing in the air. One of the captured women screamed and he burst into laughter. In another quick movement the Mohawk cut the ties that bound her to the tree and dragged her forward.

The young mulatto girl screamed, flailing her arms in an attempt to ward him off, but her captor only laughed harder. He hurled his knife into the air so that it stuck straight into the tree above the other women's heads. Then he took the mulatto girl's hands and pinned them behind her. Moving his hips suggestively against hers, he forced her to dance in his arms.

"Why are those ladies tied to the tree?" Mary whispered, lying in the snow beside Deborah.

"They were captured from Deliverance. Taken from their home."

Mary nodded. "More bad men. We cannot leave the ladies here. We have to help them."

Deborah looked at the little girl staring intently through the brush. "We can't help them. There are two of us, there are"—she glanced back at the

319

encampment — "one, two, three . . . ten Mohawks. We have one pistol. They've got enough muskets and war hatchets to fight the entire county."

Mary chewed at her bottom lip. "It would not be right to leave those ladies."

"We can go on to the village, get Tshingee, and bring him back to help them."

Mary propped up her chin with her mitten-covered hands. "I think they would be gone . . . or dead. That lady with the gold hair is sick."

Deborah knew the child was right. But there was no way she could possibly rescue three women from ten Mohawks and still manage to get away safely with Mary. "No," Deborah said firmly. "Tshingee will be able to track them. The smartest thing for us to do is to go around the camp and get to the village as quickly as possible. Tshingee will bring back other braves and they will rescue the women."

Deborah glanced back at the Mohawk campfire. The men were dancing faster now, spinning and laughing as they shoved the mulatto girl from one warrior to the next. The girl screamed again and again as they pulled at her hair and clothing, but the men only laughed harder, fueled by her fear.

Deborah clasped Mary's arm. "I think we'd better go," she insisted.

"This brave thinks not . . ."

Deborah rolled onto her back in horror. Standing over her was a Mohawk brave. There were eleven warriors in the war party, not ten. How could she have been so stupid? She kept her hand beneath her cloak, her pistol hidden in the folds of the red wool.

The Mohawk swung his war club lazily. "You like the dance, no?" He chuckled. "My friends would be disappointed if you did not join us."

Deborah stared at the warrior above her. Though he was dressed in hides and wore his hair shaved save for a scalplock, his skin was lighter than the others. The remaining lock of hair that hung down his back was a chestnut brown. A half breed, she surmised. He spoke as well as Tshingee—an educated savage, which was even more dangerous.

"Get up!" the Mohawk ordered, swinging his club past her head. "Get up and come dance with me, white woman. It has been too long since I have held a woman between my legs." He glanced at Mary, who lay in the snow, her eyes wide with fright. "The child is quite pretty. She will bring a good price on the lakes."

"No!" Mary shouted. Before Deborah could stop her, Mary scrambled to her feet and took off running through the woods.

The Mohawk set out after her, cursing foully beneath his breath.

"No, Mary," Deborah shouted. "He'll kill you!"

The half-breed Mohawk swung his club, missing Mary's head by a fraction of an inch. The little girl tripped on a patch of ice and went down on one knee. To the Mohawk's astonishment, she whipped around, wielding a knife in her hands. Caught off guard, the warrior failed to move fast enough and Mary caught his sleeve with the tip of the kitchen knife. Slicing through the hide covering, the knife nicked his skin and blood immediately flowed to stain the leather.

In fury the warrior swung his war axe directly at Mary's head . . . just as Deborah pulled the trigger of the pistol clenched in her hands.

The Mohawk's eyes lit up in utter surprise, the axe falling uselessly to the ground. Mary screamed as the half-breed pitched forward, dead before he hit the snow.

Through the trees, Deborah could see the other Mohawk braves gathering weapons and heading in her direction. "Run!" she screamed, pulling Mary by her arm off the ground. "Run to the horse." She gave the little girl a shove in the right direction and Mary took off through the woods with Deborah following directly behind her.

Through the thick curtain of tree limbs and vines, Deborah could see Joshua standing, his ears pricked at attention. Behind her she could hear the warriors footsteps on the soggy ground. Then suddenly a hand clamped down over her mouth and she bit down on it, trying desperately to scream. The arm wrapped around Deborah's waist and lifted her from the ground. At the same moment a red man caught Mary, lifting her onto his shoulders.

"Tshingee," Deborah breathed.

"I should have known it would be you running through the forest dressed in red," he hissed, racing along the path.

She wrapped her arms tightly around his neck, shaking in fear and shock. Before she could speak, he dropped her on Joshua's back and yanked

Mary out of the arms of another Lenni Lenape brave, throwing her behind Deborah on the saddle. Tshingee gave the horse a slap on the backside and spun around to hurl a knife at a Mohawk brave descending upon them.

"Lachpi!" Tshingee shouted as his knife struck home in the Mohawk's chest. "Ride, Deborah!"

Deborah hung on tightly to Joshua's mane, trapping Mary securely between her arms as the horse shied and swerved right, descending into the woods. Pulling up on Joshua's reins, Deborah slowed him to a walk, turning him right. Behind her she could hear the masculine battle cry of her lover echoed by several other deep voices. A bloodcurdling scream rattled her composure as a warrior on one side or the other lost his life.

Skirting the warring men, Deborah rode toward the Mohawk encampment, set on releasing the captured women. Mary held tightly to Joshua's mane, her jaw set in determination. Cautiously Deborah rode into the camp from downstream. Luck was with her. All the Mohawks had abandoned the women prisoners to fight the Lenni Lenape.

At the sight of Deborah, the mulatto girl thrust out her hands, sobbing, her words nearly incoherent. "Miss Deborah!' she cried. "They got you too, Lord bless."

Deborah reined up on her horse and Mary squirmed from between her arms, slipping to the ground. The child raced across the muddy campsite, the kitchen knife Elizabeth had packed, still in her tiny hands. The mulatto girl thrust out her

323

bound hands and Mary sawed at the sinew ties, releasing her.

Deborah leaped down off Joshua and ran to help Mary. "What's wrong with her?" Deborah asked, indicating the yellow-haired girl with a flip of her chin.

"Frightened near to death, I think," the mulatto answered, rubbing her raw wrists.

Mary sawed at the ties that bound the third woman, a redhead, while Deborah knelt, giving the blonde a harsh shake. "What's her name?"

"Gert," the mulatto answered.

"Gert! Gert!" Deborah shouted. "Wake up!" Grabbing a handful of melting snow, she rubbed it in the woman's face.

Gert choked and sputtered, thrashing to escape the bitter snow.

"Get up, Gert. If you mean to be spared, you've got to get ahold of yourself," Deborah insisted.

Gert's eyes flew open in fright.

"It's all right," Deborah murmured, pulling the woman to her feet. "You've got to stand. I think you're being rescued."

Behind them, in the forest, the women could hear the battle raging as the Lenni Lenape fought the Mohawk war party.

Coming to her feet as Mary cut the last leather strap, the woman threw her arms around Deborah. "Thank the Holy Mother, someone's come, but what are you doing here, Lady Deborah? Where's Master Hogarth?"

"Good God a'mighty!" screamed the mulatto girl. "Here comes more Injuns!"

Deborah turned to see Tshingee and six Lenni Lenape braves coming out of the forest and in their direction. "It's all right," she soothed, her own voice quivering. "They've come to rescue us. They're not the same Indians."

The redhead took a step back. "Redskin's a redskin," she murmured, crossing herself.

"No. I know these men. Don't be afraid. They won't harm you." Deborah turned her back on the women.

Tshingee was walking directly toward her, his stride long and purposefully. He was without a cloak, his bare arms swinging at his sides. He wore his hair free flowing across his shoulders; his bronze face was lined with fury. He had a small cut over one eyebrow, but other than that, he seemed unharmed.

"Tshingee!" Mary shouted, running toward her uncle. "My uncle! I knew you would come! I knew you wouldn't let the bad men hurt us!"

"*Elke,* Mary." Tshingee swung the child into his arms. "What is this?" He pulled the kitchen knife from her hand. "I think my brave little warrior needs a weapon more suited to her size." He dropped the knife to the ground and flung her in the air, catching her over his head.

Mary squealed in delight. "Again! Again!" she shouted, giggling.

Tshingee threw the little girl into the air a second, then a third time, then he placed her feet gently on the ground.

Deborah's eyes locked with his dark gaze as he stared over his niece's head. He squatted, taking

325

Mary by the shoulders. "I am glad to see you, my fierce little kitten. You defended yourself well against the enemy. It is a day to be remembered."

"That bad man, he almost got me," Mary told her uncle. "But Deborah, she shot him and he fell, plunk up!"

Tshingee glanced up at Deborah. "Then our Deborah is a brave warrior too, is she not?"

Deborah took a step forward. "I have to speak to you." Her voice was barely a whisper. "Alone."

"I would say that you do." He gave Mary a pat on her bottom, handing her his water skin. "Could you fill it for me? I am very thirsty."

The child beamed. "Be right back."

Tshingee motioned with his hand, speaking to the other braves in his own tongue. The Lenni Lenape warriors scattered, blending into the trees. "How many Mohawks did you count?" Tshingee asked, keeping his emotions well under control.

"Eleven," Deborah responded evenly.

"There was twelve," the redhead offered cautiously. "But one got drunk this morning and fell in the river. Got washed away, may the devil take him."

"Then they are all dead." Tshingee's arm shot out to catch Deborah's. "I would speak to you. Now."

Deborah glanced back at the women. "It's all right," she assured them. "You must be hungry. Eat whatever you can find." She glanced around at the Mohawk camp. It looks like they stole plenty."

"You sure you're going to be all right, Lady Deborah?" The redhead eyed Tshingee suspiciously.

"I'll be fine," Deborah answered over her shoulder as Tshingee dragged her away by her wrist.

The moment they were out of earshot, Tshingee turned to face her. His face had a taut, wild look.

Deborah struggled to find her voice, dropping her gaze to the muddy ground. Slowly she lifted her lashes to find him staring intently at her. "John is dead," she said simply.

Tshingee stood stock-still, his facial expression unchanged. "I know."

"There was nothing I could do!" she choked. "The . . . the Mohawks, they raided Deliverance. They killed Tom's father, they burned the barns and murdered the servants."

"What had my brother to do with this?"

She hung her head. "Nothing."

"Then how did he die?"

Deborah wiped her eyes with the back of her hand. "The men . . . they, they thought it was you, only I knew it wasn't you, but I couldn't stop them! They were drinking. A whole crowd. They went to MacClouds and they . . ." She squeezed her eyes shut. "They hanged him."

"What of my brother's wife?"

"Dead too." She opened her eyes. The pain on Tshingee's face made her want to put out her arms to him. All she wanted was to touch him, to hold him. But her arms remained at her sides. Tshingee held his body hostilely rigid. It was obvious to her that he wanted no comfort.

"Did they hang her too?" he asked bitterly.

"No." She shook her head. "It was by accident. I don't think they meant to kill her. But they were throwing sticks and things. A rock caught her in the temple. Killed her instantly."

Tshingee lowered his head, covering his eyes with his palm for a moment. "So you have brought my niece to me."

"Yes. I was so afraid they would hurt her."

"I thank you for saving my brother's daughter. It will mean much to Co-o-nah Aquewa."

"Tshingee, I'm so sorry." She stared at his finely sculptured bronze face, but he refused to meet her gaze.

Without another word, he brushed past her. "These women, they came from the plantation?"

"Yes." She ran after him. "We have to get them back home. Their families have probably given them up for dead."

"You can take the women back with you." Deborah grabbed his arm and he stopped in his tracks, but did not turn around. "I'm not going back," she whispered.

"You're going." He snatched his hand from hers.

"But I can't. Not ever. I'm going back to the village with you. All I ever wanted was you, Tshingee," she declared.

He whipped around to face her. "And now that my brother is out of the way, you see no reason why you cannot have what you want, is that it, my Red Bird?"

"No! Of course not! I told you! I had nothing to do with the hanging. There was nothing I could do." She put out her hands, pleading. "Don't you think that if I could have saved him, I would have?"

"Your father, he initiated the action, did he not?"

Deborah's lower lip trembled. She had expected Tshingee to be angry, to take out his pain on her, but she'd never anticipated such hostility. "Yes, yes, he did. But I have no control over my father's actions! I was locked in my chamber when he went to Deliverance. I nearly broke my neck climbing out the second-story window to get there so I could tell them you weren't the one who raided the plantation."

"And what good did that do?" He shook his bronze fist at her. "Did it save my brother's life? Did it save his wife's?"

"No!" Deborah's voice trembled with emotion. "But it saved Mary's. They'd have killed her too!"

Tshingee turned away from her again and started across the Mohawk camp. "I have thanked you for that. Now pack yourself food and go. You found your way this far, you can find your way back."

Deborah stood, watching him walk away from her. A part of her ached to run after him, but a part of her willed her to stand her ground. It was cruel of him to blame her for John's death. And it made her angry. How could he have once proclaimed to love her so deeply and now accuse her of playing a part in his brother's hanging? Wiping her tears with the sleeve of her gown, she turned away, unable to bear watching him. Seeing Joshua grazing on a patch of brown grass, she walked toward him. How could the love she and Tshingee had shared have become tangled into such an ugly web of anger and resentment?

Heavyhearted, Deborah clasped Joshua's reins and led her horse forward. The women prisoners were pulling through the Mohawks' bags.

The red-haired woman took a bite from half a loaf of bread and thrust out her hand to Deborah. "The name's Anne. I didn't thank ye proper for rescuin' us."

"No need to thank me," Deborah responded quietly. "If it hadn't been for him"—she pointed to Tshingee standing near the river's edge—"I would have been tied up beside you . . . that or dead."

"If that doesn't beat all!" Ann shook her head, taking another bite of the bread. "Saved from one bunch of redskins by another bunch. They'll never believe it back at Deliverance."

"No, they'll never believe it, will they?" Deborah echoed.

"Say . . . you all right?" Ann studied Deborah's pale face. "You and that redskin have words?"

"I'm fine. Just tired." She ran a hand through her hair, pushing a lock behind her ears.

"How do ye know that redskin, anyway? He the one that kidnapped ye and brought ye back?"

"He was the one."

"Funny thing. Never heard of one bringing a woman back before. We thought you was long gone, beggin' your pardon."

Deborah glanced at the blond woman who had been unconscious. She was now sitting on the ground near the fire, a chunk of bread in her hand. "Is she going to be all right?" Deborah nodded in the woman's direction.

"Gert?" Anne turned her attention on the woman. "I dunno. She ain't said a word since they took us yesterday. I think the redskins thought she was touched in the head. Probably the only reason she didn't meet her maker the way the other two young ones did."

Deborah's eyes met Anne's. "Dead?"

Anne crossed herself and took another bite of her bread. "God rest their souls. Weren't pretty either."

"Their bodies?" Deborah scratched Joshua behind the ears.

"Gone. Threw 'em in the river."

Deborah sighed. "Well, do you think Gert can travel?"

"Gonna have to, ain't she?" Anne returned the half loaf of bread to the Mohawk bag she wore over her arm. "Who's takin' us back, the redskins?"

"No. I guess it will just be us."

Anne studied Deborah's face. "How'd ye get out in the middle of nowhere like this anyway? Did ye get separated from the menfolk? Where's the rest of the *white* rescue party?"

"It's a long story, Anne." Deborah looked toward the river bank.

Tshingee and his warriors stood in a clump, speaking in hushed tones. Occasionally, one of the braves raised his voice in protest. Mary stood at her uncle's side, brushing the deer hide cloak he wore with the palm of her hand. Some kind of decision was obviously being made.

"Get the other two ready," Deborah told Anne.

She pushed Joshua's reins into the woman's hand. "We'll let Gert ride. We need to get moving upriver if we're to make any time before it gets dark."

"You're comin' with us, ain't ye?"

Deborah glanced at Tshingee, then back at Anne again. "Looks like I am," she answered quietly.

Taking Mary's doll from her pack, Deborah walked toward the Lenni Lenape men. She put out her arms, forcing a smile. "Mary," she called. "I have something for you."

Mary came running toward her immediately. "Eleke?" She took the doll in her arms. "But she's yours, I gave her to you."

"Yes, but I need you to take care of her for me." Deborah crouched on the ground so that she was eye level with the little girl. "Mary, I have to go now."

"Go?" Her face fell. "Go where? My uncle says we leave for the village before the sun begins to set."

"I'm not going to the village." Deborah glanced at the muddy snow at her feet, not wanting Mary to see the tears that welled in her eyes."

"Not going? But you said—"

She cut the child off. "My plans have changed. You have Tshingee now. He will take you to your grandmother."

Mary threw her arms around Deborah. "But I want you, Deborah! You said you would go!"

Deborah kissed Mary's soft cheek, smoothing her mussed hair. "I have to take these women back to their home."

"But then you'll come to the village. Won't you?"

"I don't think so, Mary." She stood, fighting back her tears.

"But I don't understand . . ." Fat tears rolled down Mary's cheeks as she clung to her doll.

"Go to your uncle. He's waiting for you." Deborah pointed to Tshingee, who stood with his hands on his hips, watching the exchange between Deborah and his niece.

"Mary, *n'matunquam. Yuh, shimoitam!*" Tshingee called, putting his hands out to her.

With a sob, Mary ran into her uncle's arms. Tshingee kissed the top of her head. His dark eyes met Deborah's for just an instant then he looked away.

Deborah forced herself to turn and walk back toward the women prisoners. Gert sat astride Joshua while Anne and the mulatto woman stood beside the horse, waiting for Deborah. Both woman carried leather bags that had belonged to the Mohawks.

"Never guess what we found," Gert told Deborah as Deborah picked up Joshua's reins and began to lead the horse out of the camp. "Found a gold watch, a whole bag o'silver, a ladies silver-handled toothbrush, and two gold snuffboxes. I don't think none of it belongs to the folks at Deliverance, so you think we can keep it?"

"I don't see why not," Deborah heard herself answer.

"You shore you know how to get back to Deliverance?" Anne asked, running to keep up with

Deborah.

"Just follow the river."

For the next half an hour the women walked through the forest, always keeping the Migianac River on their left. Anne kept up a running commentary while the other women remained silent.

For the first mile, Deborah felt nothing but an overwhelming numbness. But the farther she walked, the more she began to think. *What is there for me if I go back to Host's Wealth now? I can't marry Tom. There's not time to be shipped to England to be married before it's obvious I'm pregnant. How am I to save my child's life if I return to the Tidewater? Tshingee may not want me, but at least in the village, my baby will be safe. . . .*

Deborah topped dead in her tracks.

"What is it? What's wrong?" Anne stared into the darkening forest. "Good God a'mighty! Don't tell me there's more Injuns!"

Deborah opened Anne's hand and pressed Joshua's reins into it.

"What are you doing?"

"I'm not going back." Deborah pulled the flour sacks off Joshua's saddle and began to empty the contents on the ground. "Trade me, Anne. The Mohawk bag for the sacks. No need for you to carry it; just strap it back on the horse." Before the woman could speak, Deborah was pulling the leather bag off Anne's shoulder and emptying it on the ground.

"What're you doin', Lady Deborah? You ain't makin' sense. What do you mean you ain't goin'

334

back? Where *are* you goin'?"

"With them." Deborah stuffed her own food and assorted items into the leather bag. "I'll take one blanket, but let Gert keep the other." Deborah motioned to the blonde, who was astride the horse and had the blanket wrapped around her shoulders.

"Saints in hell! Ye ain't goin' with the Injuns, are ye?"

"Do me a favor, Anne. All of you. When you get back to Deliverance, don't tell them you've seen me. I don't care what you say, just don't tell them I had anything to do with your rescue. Tshingee, brother of John Wolf, rescued you from the Mohawks. Tell them you found this horse wandering in the woods."

"God sakes," the mulatto woman cried. "Yer not leavin' us, Miss Deborah. How are we gonna get home?"

"I told you. Follow the river. You'll hit the dock at Deliverance by tomorrow noon time if you hurry. When it gets dark, light a fire. It will keep the wolves away."

"Wolves!" Anne rolled her eyes. "Don't tell me there's wolves in this here woods."

Deborah swung her Mohawk pack onto her back, threading both arms through the strap. Tearing a strip of the flour sack, she made a belt around her waist. Tucking the pistol into the crude holster, she raised her hand. "Good luck, ladies. Do as I say and you'll be sleeping on feather ticking by tomorrow night." Giving Joshua a final farewell pat, she turned and walked away, leaving the other women staring with open mouths.

Chapter Twenty-three

Skeletal limbs hung from the bare trees, casting dark fingerlike shadows across Deborah's path. The sun had already begun to set and still she had not caught up with Tshingee and his men. The partially melted ground squished beneath Deborah's feet as she ran along the riverbank, positive that around the next bend, she would find the Lenni Lenape warriors.

Pushing her hood off her head, Deborah brushed back a lock of hair that stuck to her perspiring skin. The thought of spending the night alone in the forest made her continue to run even after her stomach began to ache and her lungs burned. Though she'd spent last night in the forest without the comfort of Tshingee's protection, somehow that seemed different. With Mary to look after, Deborah had wasted no time with concern for herself. But tonight, as twilight settled in, Deborah's own fears began to seep into her logic, clouding her thoughts.

Inhaling deeply, Deborah began to run again. She prayed that with the coming of darkness Tshingee and his men would have set up camp for the night. As long as she kept to the river's bank, she could still travel.

Slowing to a walk, Deborah panted heavily. She didn't know what she was going to say when she met up with Tshingee. All she knew was that she couldn't go back to Host's Wealth, not ever again. Her only hope for her baby was to be accepted among the Wolf Clan of the Lenni Lenape.

It had been done before. Snow Blanket had told Deborah of a white woman who had been rescued by the Lenni Lenape in a fight with the Hurons. When the Lenni Lenape had offered to return her to her home in Penn's Colony, she had chosen instead to remain with them and marry one of the braves. She had lived out the remainder of her life with the Wolf Clan and died at the age of seventy-three only a few years ago.

Deborah heard a twig snap behind her and she spun around. Seeing nothing, she laid her hand on the pistol tucked into her belt. An instant later someone leaped from the tree above, landing just behind her. Deborah whipped around, yanking the pistol free to aim it at the intruder.

"What are you doing?" Tshingee demanded angrily.

Deborah heaved a sigh of relief, lowering the weapon. "You scared the wits out of me." She looked up at the tree above them. "Was that really necessary?"

He rested his hands on his narrow hips. "Have you not had enough of the enemy for one day? Had I been Mohawk, your throat would have been cut, your life's blood flowing onto the ground."

"But you're not Mohawk."

"Why are you here? Where are the other women?"

"I sent them on alone."

"Why?" Tshingee's voice was stark and hostile.

Deborah's resolve wavered. Where was the man she loved? This man couldn't possibly be the father of her child. The father of her child was warm and caring, a shimmer of light in the darkness. This man, standing before her, was darkness itself. "I . . . I'm going back to the village with you and Mary."

"You are not welcome among the Lenni Lenape any longer."

"What happened to John was not my fault. I did everything in my power to save him." Deborah pulled the heavy pack off her back and threw it onto the ground. "I risked my life to save him and his family. Why can't you see that?"

"Your father—"

"My father, my father! Why can't you get this through your thick skull! I had no control over what the Earl did!"

"Among my people what one man does reflects on his name, on the name of his children and grandchildren."

"Well, among my people, a man is responsible for himself!" she spit. "You blame me because you couldn't save John yourself!"

Tshingee turned and walked away.

For a moment Deborah stood watching his silhouette. Then she scooped up her bag and ran after him. "Tshingee, I'm sorry. It's not true. I know it isn't."

Tshingee walked faster.

"Tshingee, please! I have nowhere to go."

"That is not my concern," he called over his shoulder. "What is it you told me, a man is responsible for his own actions? If you have nowhere to go, that is not my responsibility, it is yours."

"I'm not going back!" she hollered. "There's nothing left for me back there."

"There is nothing for you on the path ahead."

Deborah stopped following him. "What about you?" Her voice caught in her throat. "You once said you loved me."

He made no reply, and a moment later, he disappeared into the shadows of the trees.

"You can't do this to me," Deborah murmured beneath her breath. "You can't turn your back on me. You're all I have." Her hand went to her belly. "No, not all I have." With a sigh she lifted her backpack onto her shoulder and started along the riverbank. Ten minutes later she spotted the Lenni Lenape warriors' campfire.

Halting, Deborah stared at the bright flames. With the coming of night, the temperature had dropped. Her breath formed puffy white clouds as she laid her pack on the ground and pulled up the hood on her cloak. "So I'm not welcome, am I?" she said aloud. "I may not be welcome at your campfire, but you can't keep me from building my own!" She picked up several dry twigs and branches and dropped them into a pile. "The forest doesn't belong to you, Tshingee of the Wolf Clan," she went on as she gathered more wood. "A person can camp where they want to for the night."

Kneeling, Deborah crumpled several leaves she'd found clinging to a branch, and with the implements from her tinderbox, she soon had a tiny flame. Adding small sticks and bits of branches. her fire grew larger until it put off a soft, glowing heat. Wrapping herself in the blanket she'd kept, Deborah nibbled on a crust of bread brought from Host's Wealth, watching the Lenni Lenape camp.

Once it became completely dark, she could see nothing but the braves' campfire and the circle of light it cast. Shadows moved in and out of the light, giving Deborah a certain reassurance. Twice she saw Mary's silhouette as the child prepared for sleep. Even if Deborah couldn't spend the night with Mary and the warriors, she could at least see them. Resting her head on her backpack, Deborah pulled her blanket over her head and forced herself to close her eyes and try to sleep. At dawn, when the Lenni Lenape men moved, she would move with them. She didn't care if Tshingee said she was unwelcome in the village. She would see for herself.

The following morning Deborah woke with a start. Cold and shivering, she sat up and looked through the woods to where the Lenni Lenape had camped the night before. It was barely daybreak and they'd already broken camp. Cursing beneath her breath, Deborah struggled to get to her feet. Her limbs were stiff and achy and her head pounded from lack of sleep. Wrapping the blanket around her shoulders for warmth, she went to the river and gathered a skin of water to put out the remainder of her campfire. Then, pulling on her mittens and tightening the string on her hood, she heaved her pack onto her back and started downriver. Tshingee and his men couldn't have gotten too far.

Before noon, Deborah caught up with them. Sitting on the frozen bank, a hundred yards from them, she munched on an apple turnover and drank water from her water skin. Tshingee and his men ignored her presence, and she ignored theirs. Once, Mary lifted her hand in salute, but Tshingee quickly scooped up the little girl and threw her across his shoulders. Mary squealed in delight and the two started downriver with Tshingee imitating a horse while Mary beat him on the back with a wool mitten.

Late in the afternoon the Lenni Lenape turned west. Recognizing the log Deborah had walked out on to jump into the dugout weeks before, she picked up a stick and hurled it into the slow-moving river. "Good-bye, Migianac," she said aloud. "Wish me luck." Turning west, she hurried on.

It was after dark when Tshingee and his men finally set up camp. Exhausted, Deborah gathered an arm full of wood and knelt to start her own fire within view of theirs. The remaining snow had melted completely during the heat of the day but the ground was cold beneath her, the dampness seeping through her skirts. Deborah's fingers were so numb that twice she dropped the flint and steel before she was finally able to strike a spark. Then her kindling refused to light, it smoked and went out. Nearing tears of frustration, Deborah got up and went in search of some dry bark or leaves. Just as she snatched a handful of shriveled moss from the side of a tree, she heard an eerie howl, followed by a second one.

Wolves.

Groaning aloud, Deborah returned to her campsite. "That's all I need," she mumbled as she knelt and diligently began the process of starting a fire again. This time she succeeded and soon had a blaze roaring at her fingertips. Gathering more wood, Deborah wrapped up in her blanket and settled down for the night. Leaning against a tree trunk, she stuck out her hands and feet to warm them. If her calculations were correct, they would reach the Lenni Lenape village by tomorrow night.

Letting her eyes drift shut, Deborah listened to the howl of the wolves in the distance. It wasn't her imagination. They were getting closer. Nervously, she threw another branch onto her fire and laid her pistol next to her on the ground. Through the woods, she could see the Lenni Lenape campfire. "He wouldn't let them eat me," she grumbled, poking at the fire with a stick. "At least I don't think he would."

An hour passed and then another as Deborah struggled to stay awake and keep her vigil over her burning fire. As long as she kept the flames alive, she knew the wolves could do her no harm. The Lenni Lenape braves slept, all save for one who stood guard over the group, pacing in the shadows beyond the fire's light.

Deborah suddenly sat upright, blinking the sleep from her eyes. She hadn't meant to doze off. Her eyes fell to the flames burning at her feet. She couldn't have been asleep long; the campfire still burned brightly. A twig snapped outside the circle of light and Deborah looked up. Her heart rose in her throat. Carefully she lowered her hand to the pistol at her side.

She was surrounded by wolves, their golden eyes piercing the darkness. The huge gray animals sat on their haunches just outside the fire's light, shifting their weight in anxious anticipation.

Deborah stabbed a tree limb into the flames and when it caught, she raised it above her head. "Get back!" she hissed. "Go on, get out of here!"

The closest wolf growled deep in its throat, taking a step back.

"I'll not be your supper," Deborah said shakily. "So just go on and go!" She heard a growl from behind and she leaped up, holding the torch in her hand. The yellow eyes followed her movements in unison.

"I said get back!" Deborah said louder, shoving the torch forward. One of the wolves turned and ran, circling the pack, only to find another position.

"A game is it?" Deborah asked. "Well, I'll not be had."

The wolves regarded her in macabre silence.

"If you want a good meal, why not try my neighbors. Nice young men," she said, adding another stick to her fire.

For several minutes Deborah just stood there listening to the pounding of her own heart and the wolves' heavy panting. She was so close to the flames that she feared she would catch her cloak on fire, but the moment she took a step forward, one of the wolves growled, rising up on all fours. When she stepped back, the animal again sat on its hindlegs.

Deborah glanced at the pistol at her feet. With only one shot, the weapon was nearly useless. There were so many wolves, and shooting one shot at a time, she'd be lucky if she could kill half of them before she ran out of ammunition. Besides, she was afraid of riling them. If the beasts were bold enough to come this close to the fire, it might only be a matter of time before one grew daring enough to try and reach her.

Slowly Deborah lowered herself to the ground. Kneeling, she threw her burning torch into the fire and reached for another branch. Her firewood supply was growing low. She hadn't anticipated needing to keep it blazing all night. Hesitantly she peered over the wolves' heads into the darkness. The Lenni Lenape campfire burned brightly, but there was no movement, no sign of the guard. Surely they knew the wolves had surrounded her!

Suddenly a wolf lifted its head and howled, its low mournful cry raising in pitch as it grew in volume. Another wolf joined in and then a third, rattling Deborah to the bone. A huge male with broken teeth and a torn ear stood only a few feet from her, his golden eyes boring down on her.

"It's only a game," she muttered. "Only a game. If I can just hold off until dawn, if the fire will just keep burning, I'll be all right. I don't need Tshingee, I don't need any of them." But as Deborah's second torch burned down and she tossed it into the fire, she realized she didn't have enough wood to keep it blazing like this until morning. She had barely enough fuel for another hour.

Moistening her dry lips, she glanced at the campfire through the woods. She weighed her odds against making it to the other camp. With so many beasts, she doubted she could make it, even carrying a torch. These animals were hungry and they were impatient. If she fell, running, she'd surely lose her life and that of her child's.

Out of the corner of her eye, Deborah watched the male wolf with the ragged ear shift positions. Slowly, methodically, he was edging his way toward the fire and toward her.

Suddenly there was loud human cry. Deborah looked up to see a lone figure racing toward her, a torch held high above his head. Deborah leaped to her feet, raising her own torch.

The wolves rose, backing away as the human grew closer. Low, guttural growls filled the air and the beasts turned and ran. The man waved his arms, shouting, his voice echoing high above the trees. The frightened animals ran for cover, diving through the brush and racing into the forest.

Deborah trembled with fear as she watched the man sprint past her in pursuit of the wolves.

A minute later Tshingee came walking into the sparse light of her dying campfire. His face was an emotionless mask. Without speaking, he picked up Deborah's backpack and started for the campsite in the distance. Sweeping her pistol off the ground, she grabbed her blanket and followed. Neither said a word as they crossed the distance between the two camps.

Reaching the Lenni Lenape campfire, Tshingee dropped her pack on the ground. Leaning over another warrior, he gently shook the man. The brave woke and scrambled to his feet. Tshingee slid beneath the brave's hide blanket and pulled it over his shoulders, rolling onto his side.

Exhaling in exasperation, Deborah laid her blanket out beside Mary's sleeping form and settled in for the remainder of night.

The following morning Deborah rose with the Lenni Lenape and when they broke camp and started northwest, she followed them. Mary was delighted to have Deborah among them and chattered non-top as they made their way toward the village.

Tshingee and the other braves ignored Deborah, behaving as if she didn't exist. They didn't speak to her; they pretended to see through her when they spoke among themselves. Tshingee led the group through the forest in silence, speaking to no one but Mary. When his niece grew tired, he lifted her onto his shoulders and carried her, never breaking stride. Noon passed and the group stopped for a short time then moved again. Not long after the sun had set, Deborah heard Tshingee sound the warning cry and a sentry answered. They hád arrived.

Nervous with apprehension, Deborah followed the braves into the Lenni Lenape camp. Mary took her hand as the villagers came forward, surrounding them to greet their husbands and sons. Each man, woman, and child seemed to notice immediately that John Wolf was not among them. No one laughed, and voices were kept to hushed tones.

Snow Blanket greeted Tshingee with a hug. Her face was grave. "*Gikiitte, giis.* Tell us what has happened, Wildcat of the Wolf Clan."

Tshingee raised a hand and a stiff silence settled upon the group. He spoke in a hushed tone, his dark eyes moving from one person to the next. Deborah didn't know what he said in his native tongue, but she could tell by the villagers' faces that he was informing them of John's death.

Tears welled in Snow Blanket's eyes as her younger son took his mother's hand, squeezing it tight. He murmured in her ear and Snow Blanket looked up at Deborah through the crowd. "Mary. *N'nitsch undach aal.*"

Mary glanced up at Deborah.

"Go on, go to your grandmother," Deborah whispered. "She needs you."

Hesitantly, the little girl released Deborah's hand and walked toward her grandmother. The crowd began to disperse, leaving the family to deal with their pain undisturbed.

Deborah could not hear what Snow Blanket said to her grandchild, but after several moments the two of them, hand in hand, started for Snow Blanket's wigwam. Tshingee turned his back on Deborah and followed.

For several seconds Deborah stood frozen, watching the threesome cross the camp. Campfires burned, casting bright light to illuminate the center of the camp. Families gathered around their fires, talking quietly and dishing out hot, meaty stews to their newly arrived husbands and sons.

Deborah sniffed, wiping her nose with her sleeve. She hadn't expected Snow Blanket to welcome her with open arms, but she hadn't expected this either. What was she going to do now?

A slim figure came out of the darkness, headed straight for Deborah. When a nearby campfire threw light across the person's face, Deborah smiled. "Suuklan!"

Suuklan smiled. "It is good to see you safe, *n'tchu.* I am sorry we do not meet in better times. You must be cold. Come to my fire and eat."

"Is . . . is it all right?" Deborah looked up at the other villagers mingling with their neighbors. "It seems I've become invisible to everyone else."

Suuklan picked Deborah's pack up off the ground and took her hand. "Come and sit. Eat. I have English tea. A wedding present from Tshingee."

Deborah's heart rose in her throat and she stopped in mid-step. "You're married?"

The Lenni Lenape woman smiled shyly. "To Siki-hiila. Yes."

"Oh." Deborah gave a sigh of relief.

Suuklan giggled, leading Deborah to a nearby campfire. "Tshingee and me . . ." She paused. "I do not know how to say it. We love as brother and sister, but not as man and wife. The Blackbird is my husband." She looked up at Deborah, her cheeks rosy with embarrassment. "He makes me very happy."

"Then I'm happy for you, Suuklan." Deborah sat

down on a hide mat in front of the fire.

Just then the flap of Suuklan's wigwam lifted and her husband, Sikihiila, came out. He passed Deborah and his wife without saying a word.

Deborah watched him cross the compound and enter another wigwam. "Suuklan, I don't want to cause trouble between you and Blackbird." She started to get up. "I'll go."

"Matta. No." Suuklan laid her hand gently on Deborah's shoulder. "There is no trouble. My husband understands my debt to you. If you had not saved me from the *onna*-bear. I would not have lived to be his wife." She took a wooden spoon and began to dish stew from a pot onto a wooden trencher. "Sikihiila understands, just as I understand that he must stay true to Tshingee. Tshingee is his friend. My husband will eat with his mother tonight." She giggled. "Tomorrow night he will enjoy my meal the better."

When Suuklan offered her the steaming plate of venison stew, Deborah accepted. "Thank you, for the meal and for your kindness. I'm so tired. Just worn out." She took a bite of the hearty stew. "And confused. I didn't mean for any of this to happen." She stared at Suuklan across the campfire. "I'd have done anything to save John Wolf if it had been in my power."

Suuklan nodded, drinking from a handleless earthen cup. "I know of your bravery, *n'tchutti.* I believe. Tshingee is a wise man. He needs time for his wounds to heal. Then he will come to know you truly meant his brother no harm."

"I love him so much, Suuklan. I would do any-

350

thing to make everything all right again. We were so happy here in the village before he took me back to my father's home."

Suuklan handed her friend a cup of hot tea. "Do you go tomorrow?" she asked sympathetically.

"Go?" Deborah laughed without humor. "Go where? I have nowhere to go."

"You cannot go back to your people?"

Deborah scraped her plate with her wooden spoon. "No. My father tried to force me into marrying a man I did not love. I refused. Then I said yes, then I refused again. And now . . ." She stared into the firelight. "Now I carry Tshingee's child."

Suuklan rose up on her knees. "You would have the Wildcat's baby?"

Deborah stared at Suuklan with surprise. "I don't know why I told you that. I haven't told anyone."

"Not even Tshingee?" the Lenni Lenape woman asked gently.

"Him least of all." She set down her trencher and drew her red cloak closer around her shoulders. "I wanted him to want me for me. Not out of a sense of responsibility for the child. I ask that you not tell anyone about the baby."

"I would not. But now you carry the Wildcat's child and have nowhere to go."

Deborah nodded. "Really made a mess of things, haven't I? Tshingee told me to marry Tom. I guess I should have done it. At least then I'd have a roof over my head." She picked a twig up off the bare ground and tossed it into the fire. "How am I going to care for a baby when I haven't got a place to live?"

351

"I would ask you to come into my wigwam, but I cannot." Suuklan said sadly. "If you stayed, my husband could not."

Deborah smiled, her dark eyes meeting Suuklan's. "Thank you. It's the thought that's important. I understand. I'll just go into the woods and make a campfire for tonight. Tomorrow . . ."

"You cannot go into the woods. There are wolves in the forest. She stood up. "Sleep by my fire. Snow will not fall tonight. I have plenty of wood. You will be warm enough."

Deborah stared at the campfire wishfully. "It would be nice to at least sleep within the compound. I've had my share of wolves and Mohawks this week."

Suuklan lifted a large log and laid it on the fire. "Then stay here. I will bring a mat and blankets.

Deborah rose to her feet. "What about Sikihiila?"

Suuklan shook her head. "I am free to let you sleep at our fire. That can cast no shadow on my husband's face. This way, he keeps his honor and I keep mine. I only wish I could offer you more."

Deborah put her arms around the slight woman, hugging her. "You weren't the person I would have expected to stand by me, Suuklan. Thank you."

Suuklan returned the embrace. "This grateful woman welcomes you." Smiling, she withdrew. "I will get you a robe and blankets."

A short time later, Deborah snuggled down on a bearskin, pulling several hide blankets up to her nose. With the campfire blazing and the protection of the deerskin covers, she was nearly as warm as she would have been inside the wigwam.

"There. You will be safe and warm." Suuklan tucked a hot brick beneath the blankets, at her feet.

Just then, Sikihiila approached them. Walking past Deborah, without seeming to see her, he laid his hand on his wife's shoulder. Suuklan smiled, accepting the hand he offered her. Together the two ducked into their wigwam and the door flap fell.

Rolling onto her side, Deborah stared out over the Lenni Lenape village. Everyone had retired now and the campfires were beginning to die down. A wolf howled far in the distance and Deborah shivered, snuggling deeper beneath the deer hide pelts. Out of the corner of her eye she saw the shadow of a man across the compound. Squinting, she stared into the darkness.

The lone figure of a man stood in front of Snow Blanket's wigwam. His legs were slightly spread, his arms crossed over his chest, his shoulder-length hair blowing in the slight breeze. For a long time he remained there, staring into the dark, moonless night. Then as quickly as he'd appeared, he was gone.

Chapter Twenty-four

The following morning Deborah woke to find two small faces studying her intently. "Mary. Bee." Deborah smiled sleepily.

"We waited for you to wake up," Mary said. "My *cocumtha* wants you to come to her wigwam."

Deborah sat up. "Snow Blanket?"

"Yes. My *onna* says come now while the tea is still hot," Bee answered. "She knows you like your tea hot."

Deborah stared up at the little dark-haired boy. "Bee! I think you've grown a foot since I last saw you!"

The boy squirmed with glee. "You said you weren't coming back, but I knew it wasn't true. You and I were destined to be friends. My *onna* says it is in the stars." He grinned, holding out his hand. "*Nit-is* always."

Deborah accepted the small black hand, rising to stand up. "Friends always," she echoed.

Fastening the hood of her red wool cloak, Deborah allowed the two children to lead her across the village compound. Villagers were beginning to move about, adding wood to their fires and fetching water for their morning meal. Everyone took care not to make eye contact with Deborah. She remained invisible.

"*Onna*," Bee called, lifting the flap of Snow Blanket's wigwam. "We found her!'

"*Cocumtha*, we didn't wake her, just like you said," Mary told her grandmother, ducking into the wigwam.

Hesitantly, Deborah followed the children inside. The hut was warm and cozy, the aroma of hot cornmeal mush cooked with maple syrup rising from a pot on the fire in the center of the floor.

"Aquewa Co-o-nah." Deborah nodded to the Lenni Lenape woman, smiling slightly. "The children said you wanted to see me."

"Deb-or-ah." Snow Blanket came forward, offering her hands. She took Deborah's, squeezing them. "This old woman says her sorries for not greeting you properly last night. I am glad Suuklan knows her duty, even if I do not. You should not have had to sleep outside."

"It's all right, Snow Blanket. I understand. It was quite a shock for you to learn of your John's death."

Snow Blanket released Deborah's hand and indicated that she should sit on a mat near the fire. "No excuse." She lifted Deborah's cloak from her shoulders and hung it on a hook hanging from the rafters of the wigwam. "You have given me nothing but goodness from your heart. My good sense was clouded by Tshingee's words."

Deborah watched Snow Blanket kneel and begin to dish out a bowl of steaming porridge. Deborah couldn't help smiling in amazement. Snow Blanket was so young-looking with such an utterly beautiful face. She had forgotten just how young Tshingee's mother appeared. "What did he say last night? I couldn't understand."

"It does not matter what my foolish son said. His pain and guilt cloud his thinking. He is not always as wise as he thinks. I know that you were not responsible for my John's death. It was in the stars." She handed Deborah a wooden bowl filled with porridge and a pewter spoon. "My heart aches for the loss of my son and his wife, but they are now with their God."

"Snow Blanket, I did everything I could. But they wouldn't listen. Any of them. The Mohawks raided a neighboring plantation and my father and his men thought it was Tshingee. They took their revenge on John." Her eyes met the Lenni Lenape woman's. "I just couldn't stop them."

Snow Blanket handed Bee and Mary a bowl of cornmeal porridge and the children took a seat on a mat at the far side of the wigwam. "I know in this heart of mine that you would have helped my son if the choice had been in your hands." She served herself a bowl of the porridge and sat down across from Deborah. "You risked your life and your place in the white man's world to bring my granddaughter to me safely and for that I am ever grateful. Mary has told me of what happened. You are a brave woman. I do not know if this woman would have had the courage to go against her people the way you did."

Deborah took a bite of the hot breakfast concoction, savoring its delicious flavor. "They were wrong."

"I know. But it still takes strength to stand as one among many."

"I Just wish I could have done more." Deborah stared at her bowl in her hands. "I just wish Tshingee believed me. He thinks this is all my fault. He won't even listen to me when I try to explain."

"My son, the Wildcat, has much anger within him for the white man. I think, were he not half white, it would not be so hard for him."

"But I thought he loved me." Deborah lifted her head to stare across the fire at Snow Blanket. "How could he think I would be a part of his brother's death?"

"He does not blame you for John's death. He blames you for not being Lenni Lenape."

Deborah sighed in exasperation. "That's ridiculous. How can I be responsible for who I am? I'm no more responsible for being born Deborah Montague, the Earl of Manchester's daughter, than he is being born Tshingee of the Wolf Clan."

"Love is a tangled web. It does not always make sense, my child."

Deborah finished her porridge and set the bowl down on the floor. "I don't know what I'm going to do, Snow Blanket. I can't return to my father's home. Tshingee will have no part of me. Except for you, Suuklan, and the children—" she nodded in Mary and Bee's direction—"everyone here acts as if I don't exist. What am I going to do? Where am I going to go? The snow will fall again before spring. I can't live in the wilderness on my own."

"You will stay here for now," Snow Blanket said, gathering the dirty wooden bowls.

Deborah's face brightened. "I can? Oh, thank you. I've missed you and Bee so much. I dreamed of being here with you the entire time I was in my father's home."

"And you dreamed of being with Tshingee . . ."

"Yes," Deborah admitted. "But now it seems hopeless."

"We are never without hope. Deb-or-ah."

Just then the door flap of Snow Blanket's wigwam lifted and Tshingee stepped in. All eyes turned to him.

Tshingee looked from Deborah to his mother. "Why is she here?" he demanded.

"She is my guest, my son," Snow Blanket answered evenly.

Tshingee lapsed into Lenni Lenape. "She is your eldest son's murderess. She should not be welcome at your hearth, at any hearth in this village!" he insisted between clenched teeth.

Bee and Mary picked up their cloaks and darted behind Tshingee and out of the wigwam.

"She is not responsible for the world's ills, my Wildcat."

"We are all responsible."

"That is it, isn't it? You feel responsible for your brother's death." Snow Blanket approached her son, trying to take his hand, but he jerked it from her reach. "You think you should have prevented John's death. Well, you couldn't have."

"I should not have left him there among them! I

358

should have spilled his captor's blood and rescued him when I had the chance."

She shook her finger at him, raising her voice to match his. "He wanted no deaths. He would never have forgiven you if you had killed for his sake."

"I could have lived better without his forgiveness than without him," Tshingee responded bitterly.

"No. You don't understand, my dear son. His lot was cast from the day he fell from my womb. John lived. John died. He brought light to us in this world and he will bring light to us in the afterworld. It was never up to you, up to any of us. We have so little control over our lives. You think you hold too much responsibility in your palm."

Tshingee clenched his fist, lifting it in the air. "His life was in my palm and I let it slip from my fingers like water from the river."

"Ahh! You are not thinking." Snow Blanket threw up her hands." *You* are not responsible. *She* is not responsible."

Snow Blanket pointed to Deborah and Deborah looked up at Tshingee, wishing desperately that she knew what the two were saying. The pain in Tshingee's eyes was so obvious.

"I do not want her here!" he shouted.

"I did not ask you. She is welcome in my wigwam. She risked her life to bring me my only grandchild. She will always have a mat at my hearth."

"I do not have time to argue with you, Mother." He started for the door. "I must prepare my men."

"Prepare? Prepare for what?"

His dark eyes met his mother's. "Revenge. My brother's murderers cannot go unpunished."

"You cannot lead an attack! Not without the council's permission!" Snow Blanket scoffed.

"I have no time to wait for permission. We must strike and strike quickly. The white man must know the Wolf Clan will not be slaughtered like livestock."

Snow Blanket stepped between her son and the door. "You know the rules, my son," she declared in English. "The council must hear you out. The decision must be made by the people, not by one man."

"I have no time to call a council meeting!" he shouted back at her in English.

"I will call one. Tonight." She grasped her son's shoulders. "Tell me you will wait until tonight. Promise your mother that you will hear your fellow men and women."

He took a deep breath.

"You owe your mother that much."

He nodded. "I will wait."

Deborah watched as Tshingee ducked out of the wigwam. "Call a council meeting for what?" She jumped up. "What's he going to do?"

Snow Blanket's bronze face was grave. "He means to lead an attack on the men who killed his brother."

"No! No! He can't!" She grabbed her cloak from overhead. "He'll be killed as well!"

"Deb-or-ah . . ." Snow Blanket called, but Deborah was already ducking out of the wigwam.

"Tshingee!" Deborah shouted. Spotting him

walking across the compound, she ran after him. "Tshingee! I know you hear me! You can't pretend that you don't!"

Several villagers looked up to see what the commotion was, but turned away when they saw Deborah. Tshingee walked faster, refusing to face her.

"Tshingee!" she shouted. Catching the sleeve of his leather jerkin, she stepped in front of him. "You can't do this. You can't lead an attack!"

His dark eyes narrowed with hostility. "You claim you had no part in my brother's death and yet you defend his killers." He jerked his arm from her grasp.

"I don't defend them! But leading an attack will serve no purpose! How many of *you* will die? How many of them will you kill?"

"As many as is in my power."

"And then what is the difference between you and the Mohawks?"

"The white men have committed a grave sin against me and my people. They have been doing it for years. This will be a fair battle, enemy against enemy. It is what should have happened long ago."

"But you can't win. There're too many of them. The government will send soldiers. They'll find the village! They'll kill us all."

"No. Not all of us." he said venomously. "Not you, because you are one of them."

"No," she moaned. "I'm not, not anymore. I want to make a life here, here with you and Snow Blanket and Bee and Mary. I am no longer welcome among those you call my people. Why can't you see that?"

He took her by the shoulders, shaking her. "Don't you see, Red Bird? You are not welcome here! Go! Go back to your white men and their murdering ways!"

"Please, Tshingee. Don't launch an attack."

"You worry for your Thomas, do you?" he asked bitterly.

"Yes, of course." She lowered her head. "I mean no. I mean of course I don't want him to die. He had nothing to do with any of this either. The Mohawks killed his father. But I don't want you to go because I don't want you to be hurt. You could be killed!"

"To die fighting your enemy is a noble thing."

She groaned aloud. "But you'll still be dead! You spoke of responsibility. What of your responsibility to your mother . . . to your mother's name? What good will it do her to have two sons dead by the hands of the white men? Answer me that." She touched his cheek with her fingertips "Tshingee, look at me."

Tshingee stood with his hands clutched at his sides, refusing to meet her gaze. "You waste my time, woman. Do not come to me again in defense of your people. They have spilled my brother's blood and now I will spill theirs."

Deborah stood and watched Tshingee walk away, his back stiff with resolution. Never in her life had she ever felt so powerless, so hopeless. The one person she loved more than life itself had turned his back on her and she was at loss as to what to do. Slowly she turned and walked through the village, her hand pressed to her stomach beneath

362

her cloak. "For you," she whispered. "For you, little one, I promise I won't give up. Tshingee has not heard the last from me, I promise you."

"Deborah!" Suuklan came running from her wigwam. Did you see Co-o-nah Aquewa?"

Deborah wiped at her eyes with the sleeve of her wool dress. "Yes." She tried to smile. "She's invited me to stay with her in her wigwam."

"I am so glad. But this does not please Tshingee?"

Deborah couldn't help laughing. "That's an understatement."

The Lenni Lenape woman linked her arm through Deborah's. "I am on my way to the river to wash cooking pots and clothing. It is going to be a warm day again. Will you come?"

Deborah shrugged. "Why not?" She shook her head dismally. "I certainly haven't anything else to do."

Hours later Deborah sat before Suuklan's campfire, stirring the contents of a pot with a long wooden stick. The heady aroma of fricasseed rabbit rose to tantalize Deborah's nose.

"Deborah! Deborah!" Mary sobbed, running toward her.

"Mary, what is it?"

Fat, wet tears streamed down the little girl's cheeks. "I think I've done something bad. My *cocumtha* will be so mad at me."

"What? What could you have done to make her angry with you?"

Mary pushed back her hood to reveal her head. One long braid had been snipped off at chin length. The other red braid still hung on the opposite side.

"Oh, Mary." Deborah breathed. "How did you do that?"

From behind her back. Mary produced the scissors Deborah had brought with her from Host's Wealth and the cut braid. Only an hour before, Deborah had sent Mary with her pack of belongings to leave it in Snow Blanket's wigwam.

"Mary." Deborah put out her arms, hugging the little girl against her. "It's all right, don't cry. Just tell me why you did it."

"My papa," she sobbed. "My papa and my mama. I did it for them."

"Mary, I don't understand. Why would you cut off one for your braids for them?" She took the scissors from her hand.

"I didn't want to cut off the whole thing. I just cut off too much," she managed as a fresh flood of tears began.

Suuklan came out of her wigwam. "Is she hurt?"

Deborah handed Suuklan the scissors. "No, but she's cut her hair. Something about her mother and father. Do you know what she's talking about, Suuklan?"

"Among our people, it is our way when someone we love dies. We cut a lock of hair and burn it in a ceremonial fire in honor of their death."

"My *cocumtha* cut hers but she said I couldn't do it," Mary admitted. "She said I was too little, but I'm not. I'm not too little to give them honor!"

364

Deborah kissed the top of Mary's head. "Of course you're not. Now come along and let's see what we can do about this, shall we?"

"My *cocumtha* will be so mad at me." The child stared up at Deborah, tears still falling down her cheeks. "Can you fix it?" She held up the lopped-off braid.

Deborah took the scissors from Suuklan and ushered Mary across the compound toward Snow Blanket's wigwam. "Well, I can't put your braid back, love, but maybe I can fix your hair so it looks a little better. Would that be all right?"

The moment Mary stepped into her grandmother's wigwam, Snow Blanket threw up her hands. "Mary! What has happened to your hair, my child?"

Deborah stood behind Mary, resting her hands on the little girl's shoulders. "It seems she tried to cut a lock of hair from her head with my scissors and she cut off too much." Deborah noticed immediately that two locks of Snow Blanket's hair had been cut off.

Snow Blanket brought her palms to her cheeks. "No! You didn't!"

"I'm sorry, grandmother." Fresh tears ran down Mary's face. "I wanted to do what was honorable. Please don't be mad. I won't do it again."

Snow Blanket knelt, holding out her arms for her granddaughter. "Come here, my sweet child." Taking Mary in her arms, she kissed her damp cheeks. "It is a custom meant only for the old like your grandmother. You did not have to cut your hair to show honor for your *onna* and *nukuaa*.

365

Honor is in your heart. It is a silly old custom anyway."

Deborah held up the scissors. "I thought maybe I could fix it as best I could," she offered.

"That is wise." Snow Blanket nodded. "Now wipe your tears," she told Mary, "and go to Debor-ah. She will make it better."

Seating Mary on a mat in front of the fire, Deborah carefully cut off the remaining red braid and then trimmed the little girl's jagged hair in a neat bob. Handing Snow Blanket the thick red braids. Deborah stood Mary up and walked around her. "There you go." She smiled. "You look like a little princess."

Mary's hands went to her shorn locks. "Bee will tease me." She stuck out her lip in protest. "His hair is longer than mine."

"Bee will not tease you, or he will have to answer to me," Deborah promised, returning her scissors to her pack. "Now go on out and play while it's still nice out. Suuklan says it will snow tonight."

Mary left the wigwam and Deborah sighed. shaking her head. "Little girls," she murmured.

"Here." Snow Blanket pushed something into Deborah's hand.

"What is it?" She opened her palm to find the narrow braid of her own hair she had seen around Tshingee's neck. "Where did you get this?" Deborah whispered.

"I think my son mislaid it. Keep it for him."

Deborah stared at the strand of dark hair, then closed her fingers around it. "Oh, Snow Blanket, it hurts so much."

"The hurt heals, and the sun will shine again." She dismissed the subject with a wave of her hand. Now we must dress for the council meeting. It begins at dusk."

"The council meeting? But I'm not allowed to attend the meeting."

"I have asked the elders and it has been approved. It is your people Tshingee wishes to wage war upon. They will not let you speak, but my son should see your face among the sea of faces." Snow Blanket offered her a soft doeskin dress, leggings, and moccasins. "These are for you. A gift. You must be dressed properly to go to council."

"Thank you," Deborah murmured.

"I go to the sweat house now, then I will be back. Dress quickly." Snow Blanket left the wigwam, leaving Deborah to dress alone.

Deborah stared at the doeskin dress in her arms. She had wanted so desperately to be here among the Lenni Lenape . . . and now, everything was all wrong. If Tshingee waged war against the English on the Migianac, there would be no future for her here either. And then what would she do. . . .

Chapter Twenty-five

The rhythmic beat of a hollow drum filled the crisp night air, calling the members of the Wolf Clan to their tribal meeting. Villagers walked with their hands clasped, their heads bent in respect of the duty that called them. Each adult member of the tribe would be expected to listen carefully to the evidence presented and then cast their vote. A tribal meeting was no place for prejudices or grudges; it was the place where decisions would be made that would affect each and every member of the Wolf Clan for the rest of their days.

Copying Snow Blanket's show of reverence, Deborah lowered her head and followed her out of the wigwam. The eerie cadence of the drum lifted the hair on the back of Deborah's neck as she crossed the compound in Snow Blanket's footsteps. Ducking, the two entered the Big House and Snow Blanket took her appropriate seat. Deborah sat crosslegged beside her.

One by one the villagers entered the Big House and took their positions within a circle according to age and importance within the clan. Suddenly the drum picked up in beat and another higher-pitched drum was added. A hollow gourd rattle filled the crevices in the alternating drum beats, and the sounds joined as one, rising in the air to escape through the hole in the center of the meeting house

The ancient wizened shaman entered the Big House and all eyes turned to him. The old man pounded his feet on the dirt floor, beating out an intricate grapevine-step to the center of the circle. His waist-length white braids swung rhythmically as he waved a small chamber of burning herbs, turning around and around in an established invisible path. The shaman's voice rose clear and true in some primal call to the gods of the heavens and the villagers echoed him.

Behind the shaman came the council members, twelve in all. They walked, just as the villagers had, with their heads bent and their hands clasped in prayer. A few feet behind the men and woman of the council came Tshingee.

Deborah's heart rose in her throat at the sight of the man she loved. He was dressed in otterskin leggings and a long beaded tunic. His hair fell free down his back, but two narrow braids brushed his broad, bronze cheeks. His face and the backs of his hands were painted in blue and red and white in a complex pattern of diagonal slashes and vertical and horizontal lines.

The door to the Big House was closed and lashed shut, and the villagers rose in unison, allowing the council members to take their seats. Swinging his burning pot over the heads of the council members, the shaman changed the rhythm of his chant and the drums followed in pattern.

Snow Blanket leaned to whisper in Deborah's ear. "Our shaman blesses the council members, sending prayers heavenward. He prays the members will guide the clan well. He asks the gods in the Twelve Heavens to help us make the right choice."

Deborah followed Tshingee with her eyes as he paced back and forth behind the seated council members. Suddenly the drumbeats ceased and the silence that followed seemed as unearthly as the music. The tribal chief raised his hand in greeting and the members of the clan responded in the same manner.

"Good evening, children of the Wolf Clan," Gimewane greeted in Algonquian. "Tonight I call you to this special meeting at the request of Co-o-nah Aquewa."

Snow Blanket nodded slightly. "The chief welcomes us and tells us why we are here," she said quietly to Deborah as he went on.

"First our brother Tshingee will speak, then each one of you will have a chance to give your opinions. We will then vote and the council will make the final decision." Gimewane withdrew a clay pipe from beneath his tunic and began to pack it with tobacco from a pouch on his waist. On cue, more than half the tribal members, male and female, withdrew pipes and began to do the same.

"I do not need to instruct you, my children," the chief went on in Algonquian. "Listen with your ears, weigh with your hearts, and speak with your heads." He tapped his temple lightly. "You

370

must not only consider your own personal feeling, but how your decision will affect the other members of our clan."

"Gimewane tells us to weigh our decisions carefully," Snow Blanket whispered, lighting her own clay pipe with a blazing stick that was being passed around. "Our chief reminds us that we must take care to consider how our vote will affect the other members of the clan."

Deborah nodded solemnly. "Now what happens?"

"Tshingee will speak," Snow Blanket replied. "Then others will speak, and then we will vote."

Tshingee walked slowly into the center of the circle, his eyes fixed on the flames of the central fire that burned in the firepit. His hands fell to his narrow hips as he studied the members of the council. "Greetings, members of the council. I thank you for calling this special meeting so that I can make my plea."

Snow Blanket rose, lifting her hand.

"Yes, Co-o-nah Aquewa," the chief said. "Speak."

"This old woman asks the council if those who speak the English tongue will do so . . ."

Tshingee whipped around to face his mother. "We do not speak the white man's tongue within the Big House!"

Snow Blanket lifted an eyebrow and Tshingee lowered his gaze. Silence filled the room for a moment and then she spoke again. "I ask this because the woman, Deborah, is among us and the decision we make here tonight will change her life as well as ours. I remind you all that no matter what you feel for the white woman, you must remember that it is she who saved my son Bee and the woman Suuklan from death only months ago."

"This decision is to be made among us," Tshingee snapped in English.

Gimewane nodded thoughtfully. "This is true, my son. But Co-o-nah does not ask that we give the white woman a vote. Co-o-nah asks only that the woman be able to understand what we say."

Tshingee scowled as all eyes turned to rest on Deborah. Deborah took a deep breath, lifting her chin a notch. For the first time since she'd arrived in the camp, other villagers allowed her to make eye contact with them.

Gimewane took a puff of his pipe, watching the smoke rise above his head. "Yes. I think we will speak the English tongue." He studied his people's faces. "Those who speak the white man tongue, please do."

Snow Blanket lowered her head. "Thank you," great chief. She took her seat, patting Deborah's knee.

Deborah smiled. "Thank you, she whispered.

Heaving a sigh, Tshingee turned his back on Deborah and his mother. With reluctance in his voice, Tshingee lapsed into English. "As you all know, my brother was falsely accused of murder by this white woman's father. My brother, John Wolf, was taken from his home, held prisoner, and hanged for a crime he did not commit. His wife was killed by these white wolves and my brother's daughter barely escaped death."

As Tshingee paused for emphasis, Deborah watched the villagers and their reactions. They all seemed to be concentrating. She saw no ill will on their faces, only concern. Here within the bark walls of the Big House their malice feelings toward her seemed to be nonexistent.

"Brothers, sisters of the Wolf Clan," Tshingee went on. "I ask that we seek revenge on my brother's murderers. I ask that we remind these white men that we will not stand to be slaughtered at their will. They have driven us from our homes on the Chesapeake. Each year they drive us further west, taking the land that our grandmothers once walked on. I ask that we teach these white men a lesson. I ask that we tell them no more." He lifted a bronze fist in the air. "We will stand for their disrespect for us and our ways no more."

A middle-aged man rose from his place and the chief gave a nod. The man cleared his throat. "Elene, too, is tired of the deaths, but he thinks we number too few. The white men carry muskets when many of us still carry the bow. I cannot leave my wife, my children, my grandchildren, to fight. Right or wrong, I am needed here."

Tshingee nodded with reverence to the man. "I do not ask for you to lift your bow, my friend. I already have men who are willing to fight beside me. All I ask is the council's permission to beat the drum of war."

A young woman stood. "It has been a long time since this clan has banded to fight. I think we should take our children and run like our cousins the Shawnee. I want no more deaths."

The moment the woman sat down, a young man jumped up. "The Lenni Lenape do not run at the sight of their enemy. I say we drive the white men off our land. I say we burn their tobacco and send them back across the great waters of the Chesapeake." He hit his bare chest with his fist. "I will fight beside the Wildcat."

An elderly woman stood and the young man immediately took his seat. "Ah, to be young and full of dreams," she said in Algonquian. "This young buck has not tasted the blood of his loved ones as it spills to the ground. To fight is not the answer. I am sorry for John Wolf's death. I feel Co-o-nah's pain as if it were my own, but I want no battle. It is a battle we cannot win."

Snow Blanket repeated to Deborah what the old woman had said.

One after another the members of the village rose and spoke. Deborah was fascinated by how calm and collected the villagers remained when someone stood in complete opposition of what they had just said. She was amazed at how well the council's method seemed to work. Each member of the clan spoke as often as he liked, voicing his concerns. After hearing others speak, men and women sometimes changed their minds; sometimes they did not.

As an hour slipped by and then another, Tshingee paced, listening to the villagers voice their opinions. Sometimes he gave a rebuttal; sometimes he did not.

Finally, Gimewane lifted his hands. "Does anyone else wish to speak before we vote?"

Deborah started to stand, but Snow Blanket caught her hand. "You cannot speak," the Lenni Lenape woman whispered harshly.

Ignoring her, Deborah came to her feet. "I wish to speak."

Tshingee laughed. "She cannot speak within these walls. She is not a member of the clan.!"

Gimewane shook his head. "I am sorry, but the Wildcat speaks the truth. Only a member of the clan may speak in the Big House."

"But I know these white men. I know Tshingee and his men won't have a chance in—"

The chief clapped his hands sharply. "Enough! Gimewane has spoken. Sit."

Realizing the fruitlessness of her attempt, Deborah did as she was told. If she tried to speak again, she was afraid the chief would order her out of the ceremonial wigwam.

"And now a vote," the chief said, slipping back into Algonquian. "Those who wish to give their consent to Tshingee's request, lift your hand."

Hands lifted and a member of the council counted, making marks on the dirt floor.

"Those opposed."

Hands came up again, but this time there were more.

A silence fell over the villagers as the members of the council put their heads together. A moment later, Gimewane stood. "My children. The council has agreed with the voice of the people. We are too few to wage war on an enemy that is too many. We will not fight the white men. There will be no revenge," he finished quietly in English.

A buzz of voices rose in the Big House.

Deborah clasped Snow Blanket's hand. "Oh, thank the Lord, Snow Blanket. He's safe! He can't go! There'll be no more killing."

Snow Blanket stood up, beginning to file out with others. "I hope you are right," she murmured, watching her son strut out of the Big House. "This old woman hopes you are right."

Outside the Big House bright campfires were burning, casting a golden light over the wigwams and mingling villagers. A light snow had begun to fall, filling the air with its powdery white flecks of light.

Around a nearby campfire, Deborah spotted Tshingee standing with a group of other young braves. The men were armed and stood close together, their heads bent in heated conversation.

"What's going on?" Deborah asked Snow Blanket. "Why do they have muskets?" Her breath formed puffy clouds of white as she spoke.

"I think they band to fight," the Lenni Lenape woman answered solemnly.

"Fight? But they can't," Deborah protested, running after Snow Blanket. "The council denied Tshingee's request."

"They gave their disapproval. Tshingee is still a free man as are they all free men."

"You mean they can still go and fight, even though the council has said no? What will happen if they go?"

"There will be a punishment for those who survive," Snow Blanket answered sadly.

"Punishment? What kind of punishment?"

"It will be up to the council. They could be cast out."

"Cast out?" Deborah breathed. "Oh, no!" Turning, she ran toward the clump of men. "Tshingee! Tshingee, please!"

The group separated, stepping back.

"Tshingee, please," Deborah begged. "Don't do this. It's not worth it."

"What is my brother not worth?" he barked.

"No, not John. Revenge."

Tshingee grasped her arm, pulling her out of earshot of the other men. His gaze rested on the curves of her face and for a moment he could not speak. His voice caught in his throat at the sight of the pain in her dark eyes. His anger with her was so strong that it was palpable, but at the same time, his heart ached for her. His arms cried out to hold her. No matter what had happened, he knew in his heart of hearts that he would always love this white woman.

Deborah stroked Tshingee's cheek with her fingertips. "Please. For me. For the love we once shared. Don't go out and die for this. John is dead, and no matter how many men you kill, John will not come back."

Tshingee held her arm so tightly that his fingers bit into her flesh, bruising her. "You do not understand, Red Bird. My brother is gone."

"I understand loss." Their eyes met. "I loved you more than anyone on this earth, and I have lost you."

Releasing her, Tshingee walked away. Calling to

377

his men, he raised his hand over his shoulder and together the young braves set out across the compound.

Those villagers still standing outside their wigwams turned to watch the men go. Men and women ceased to speak and the air was filled with silence save for the bark of a dog in the distance and the sound of the men's feet as they walked over the frozen ground.

Walking to Snow Blanket's wigwam, Deborah stood, watching until the men disappeared from view. One by one the villagers entered their wigwams in strained silence until no one occupied the Lenni Lenape campground but a few ponies, a few dogs. Deborah stood alone, shivering with cold.

"Deborah." Snow Blanket appeared, laying her hand gently on Deborah's shoulder. "Come in. It is cold out here. Come in and sleep."

Deborah shook her head. "No."

With a sigh, Snow Blanket went back inside and closed the door flap.

An eternity seemed to pass as Deborah stood, huddled beneath her red cloak, staring into the forest. A tiny sliver of a moon rose, casting a silver light across the sky. The snow continued to fall in silence. Then, just beyond the circle of firelight, just outside the perimeter of the camp, Deborah saw a shadow.

Tshingee came walking out of the forest, his head held high. Behind him, in single file, followed his men. Without a word, the braves passed her and one by one they took their leave, entering wigwams. Tshingee was the last man to reach his wigwam and before he went inside he turned to look at Deborah. For a moment they stared at each other through the darkness and then he disappeared inside.

The following night Deborah waited until everyone had fallen asleep in Snow Blanket's wigwam, and then she rose. Slipping her soft doeskin dress over her nude body and donning her new moccasins, she crept silently out into the cold crisp air. Hurrying across the compound, Deborah's feet crunched in the fallen snow. An old hound dog keeping vigil over a wigwam lifted his head, then settled again, accepting Deborah as one of the villagers. Smiling to herself, she hurried on by.

All day long no one had said a single word about the departure of the braves following the tribal meeting the night before . . . nor had they said anything about their return. It seemed to have to do with some code of honor. Because Tshingee and the braves had not actually gone against the council's decision, the Lenni Lenape villagers pretended the men had never left the camp. The day's activities had been so normal that Deborah began to wonder if she'd imagined the whole thing.

Only the hard, pained expression on Tshingee's face was evidence of the decision that had been made concerning John's death. Tshingee had not spoken to Deborah all day and she had made no attempt to speak with him. They had simply watched each other from afar, but always turning away before eye contact was made.

Reaching Tshingee's wigwam, Deborah glanced around to be certain no one saw her, then she lifted the flap and slipped inside. A small fire burned in the firepit in the center of the floor, casting a soft glow of shadows across the walls of the dome structure. On the far wall Tshingee lay stretched out on a sleeping platform, his hand flung over his face. Without making a sound, Deborah pulled off her moccasins, then her dress, and slowly walked toward him.

Tshingee lowered his hand and turned his head to watch her.

Without speaking a word, Deborah knelt, wrapping her arms around him and lowering her mouth to his. She kissed him gently, thrusting the tip of her tongue out to tease his lower lip.

Tshingee responded sleepily, hesitantly. "You are a ghost," he murmured.

She shook her head ever so gently, parting her lips to deny it, but he pressed his finger to them, silencing her. "You are a ghost, else this man would not allow you into his wigwam."

Deborah lifted her eyebrows in puzzlement, but then smiled. Slowly, ever so painfully, she was beginning to understand this man and his people. "Yes," she whispered huskily. "I am a ghost." If being a ghost was the only way he would speak to her, and hold her in his arms, then she would be a ghost. "This ghost comes to you on her knees," she continued as she kissed the length of his cheekbone . . . the tip of his nose. "This ghost asks for nothing but that she be permitted to give of herself. This ghost is very proud of the difficult decision Tshingee of the Wolf Clan has made."

Tshingee lifted his bearskin pelt and Deborah slipped beneath it, stretching out over him. At every point that her bare flesh touched his, a spark ignited, spreading rapidly to warm her chilled body. Threading her fingers through his ebony hair, she pressed her mouth to his, her kiss hard and demanding. All the weeks of yearning for Tshingee and his touch rose and bubbled over as Deborah strained against him, glorying in the feel of his touch.

Brushing her hands over his broad chest, she ducked her head beneath the animal pelt and caught one hard male nipple between her teeth. Nibbling gently, she reached down to stroke his belly. Slowly she lowered her hand and he lifted his hips in encouragement.

"This ghost loves this man," she whispered, stroking him. "This ghost is sorry for all that has happened and wishes only to make things right again."

Tshingee rolled her nipple between his thumb and finger and Deborah groaned softly. Sliding her off him and onto her side, he buried his face in the valley between her breasts. Deborah's pulse quickened and her breath became more rapid as he stroked her with his hand, suckling the rising bud. A heavy-limbed aching consumed her as he kissed his way down the length of her torso, his fingertips brushing her flushed skin with a tantalizing deliberateness.

"Tshingee," Deborah moaned softly. "Tshingee." He muffled her soft sighs of contentment with his mouth as he stroked the length of her creamy white thighs. Pushing off the heavy bearskin pelt, Tshingee straddled her, tucking his head in the hollow of her shoulder.

Deborah lifted her eyelids, gazing up at him. She stroked his bronze cheek with the back of her hand. The pain and anger were gone from his face; all she saw now was the heat of his desire for her. "Love me," she whispered, parting her thighs.

Lowering his body over hers, Tshingee took her with a single fluid movement, filling her with a sweet aching. Taking a shuddering breath, she ran her hands over his sculptured shoulders, lifting her head to accept his urgent kiss.

Limbs intertwined, Deborah and Tshingee moved as one, rising and falling in an ancient rhythm known only to them. A sense of urgency coursed through Deborah's veins and she moved faster beneath him, calling his name in utter abandonment. Again and again Tshingee took her to the brink of fulfillment, then slowed his pace until her breath came more evenly. Laughing in frustration, Deborah caressed the hard muscles of his buttocks, her blunt fingernails sinking into his flesh. "Enough," she cried. "Enough!"

Nibbling at her earlobe, Tshingee took Deborah's hands in his. Pressing her palms above her head, he drove home, lifting her over the brink and filling her with the ultimate joy of consummation. Shuddering with pleasure, Deborah held tightly to him, basking in the serenity of his love.

Tshingee kissed Deborah's temples, brushing

back the damp tendrils of hair that clung to her cheeks. He cradled her in his arms, pulling the bear pelt over them. Without a word, he closed his eyes and slept.

Sometime near dawn, Deborah slipped from Tshingee's sleeping platform and dressed. Adding a log to his fire in the center pit, she kissed his cheek and turned to go. If she had to be a ghost, she knew she must not be here when he awakened. Whatever game he was playing, if she wanted him, she would have to play as well.

Then, on second thought, Deborah turned and went back to him. Out of her moccasin, she pulled the braid of dark hair Tshingee had once worn around his neck, and she laid it in his palm, closing his fingers around it. Smiling with satisfaction, she slipped noiselessly out of the wigwam.

Rolling onto his side, Tshingee pulled the bearskin pelt up over his shoulders and sighed contentedly. Bringing the braid of hair to his lips, he kissed it. *"K'daholel, ki-ti-hi,"* he whispered. *"K'daholel*, ghost of mine."

Chapter Twenty-six

Days passed and Deborah slipped into a simple routine in the Lenni Lenape village. Since the night of the tribal council meeting, the villagers had accepted her without question. They no longer seemed to blame her for John Wolf's death and little by little they welcomed her as one of them.

Only Tshingee kept his distance. He gave no acknowledgment of the visit she had made to his wigwam. She had been a ghost the night they had made love and she remained a ghost. Still, Deborah felt a breath of hope deep in her heart. She caught Tshingee following her with his eyes as she crossed the compound carrying water or delivering an herb to an ailing villager. And on more than one occasion he had visited Snow Blanket's wigwam on weak pretenses at suppertime, stalling until he was invited to stay for the evening meal. When he did stay, he spoke only to his mother, his conversation brief and stilted. But his eyes wandered to rest on Deborah's face when her attention was elsewhere.

Snow Blanket accepted her son's odd behavior with a sense of humor and encouraged Deborah to do the same. "He has been hurt by his brother's death, and he is confused by his love for you," the Lenni Lenape woman had said. "Play his buck games. Ignore him and soon he will realize he cannot live without you."

Though it was difficult, Deborah took Snow Blanket's advice and went about her daily business. She had made the first move to settle their differences and it was now Tshingee's turn to do so. In the meantime, Deborah kept herself as occupied as possible.

Nearly two weeks after Deborah had arrived in the Lenni Lenape village, she stopped at Suuklan's wigwam. "Suuklan?"

The young woman came out of the bark hut, her laughter soft and joyous.

"Are you ready? Why are you so happy today? What's happened?" Suuklan's smile was infectious.

The Lenni Lenape woman picked up a bark bucket near the wigwam door and fell into stride beside Deborah. "I have just told my husband that we will have a little one by the time the leaves of summer fall again. He thinks he will begin making a cradleboard today."

"You're going to have a baby?" Deborah laughed. "Congratulations. I'm so happy for you."

"But yours will come first," Suuklan reminded her as they cut off into the woods.

Deborah's hand fell to her slightly rounded stomach as it did often these days when she was in private. She sighed. "Sometimes I wish I weren't — "

"Don't say such words!" Suuklan warned. "You

will tempt the evil spirits to take your child from you!"

"It's not that I don't want the baby, it's just that—"

Suuklan patted her companion's arm soothingly. "I know it is Tshingee. But do not worry. The Wildcat paces. I see him in the village watching you. His love for you has not weakened. One morning the sun will break and your brave will be at your side."

"I hope you're right, Suuklan, because I don't know how much longer I will be able to keep the baby from him, from the rest of the village."

"I will say nothing."

Deborah smiled. "I know you won't. You've become a good *n'tschutti*, Suuklan. You are a friend this woman is proud to call her own."

Coming to a tree with a bucket hanging from a wooden peg in the trunk, Suuklan set down the bucket she carried in her hand. A golden stream dribbled from the hole and into the bucket hanging on the peg. "I have seen Dame Elene watching you as well." She giggled. "I think the Wildcat does not like it."

Deborah removed a bucket hanging from a peg on a tree a few feet away. "The man with the red feather that dangles down the back of his head?" She couldn't help being flattered. Dame Elene was known throughout the camp as an excellent hunter. He was also a skilled carver, spending much of his free time making utensils for the women of the village and toys for the children.

Suuklan nodded. "He came to us only last year.

His mother was Shawnee, his father from Gime-wane's family. It is said he came looking for a wife."

"And you think he's been watching me?"

"I know it to be true. Just two nights ago he came to our wigwam and shared our meal. He was full of many questions."

"About me?" Deborah replaced the bucket of sap with an empty one.

Suuklan giggled, nodding. "My husband, the Blackbird, says he thinks a Red Bird would make a fine wife."

"But I'm white!"

The Lenni Lenape woman shrugged. "He thinks you are smart. He asked my husband if you belonged to the Wildcat."

"And what did Sikihiila say?"

"He told the Corn Man that he did not know and that he should ask you himself." She picked up her bucket of sap from the ground and started back toward the village, taking care not to spill the precious contents.

Deborah grabbed up her bucket and followed after her friend. "He didn't!" She kicked a pine cone along ahead of her.

"It was the truth."

"Yes, I know but . . ." Deborah's voice trailed off, her mouth forming a silly smile. "And you think Tshingee might be jealous of Dame Elene?"

"I do not know your word, *jeal-os*, I only know that the Wildcat paces faster when the Corn Man is near you."

Leaving the woods line the women headed for

Suuklan's wigwam where they would begin boiling down the syrup.

"Red Bird." A Lenni Lenape matron waved a hand in Deborah's direction.

Deborah stopped. "Go ahead, Suuklan. I'll be along."

The elder woman approached Deborah, offering her hands. "I am Kesathwa."

Deborah accepted the woman's hands, bobbing her head in reverence of the older woman. "Good afternoon to you, Kesathwa," Deborah said formally in Algonquian.

"This woman should have come sooner to speak to you," Kesathwa replied in heavily accented English. "She says her sorries."

Deborah smiled. "It's all right, but I'm glad to meet you. Isn't your grandson Il-le-nah-qui? The little boy that plays with Bee?"

"Yes." Kesathwa smiled, baring a row of dark broken teeth. "Il-le-nah-qui is the sunshine in my day since my husband's soul went hunting heavenward two winters past."

"I'm sorry." Deborah set down her bucket of tree sap.

The woman waved a wrinkled hand. "He was old man, sick and tired. Happy to go on and make the way for me."

Deborah nodded, glancing up to see Tshingee in front of his wigwam. He sat cross-legged on a hide mat, fashioning a new bone flute. He had been working on it for days. Deborah forced herself to return her attention to Kesathwa and what the woman was saying.

". . . told this woman you might teach her grandson to speak the white man's tongue."

"You want me to teach your grandson?"

"Snow Blanket tells me you teach Bee to read the white man's letters, to write them in the dirt. I would like for the same for Il-le-nah-qui."

"I would be happy to, Kesathwa. But tell me, why do you want your son to learn the white man's ways?"

"It is better to know the wolf's path than to walk blind through the forest. This old woman will not see the joining of the white man and the red, but my grandson" — she nodded — "he will see the day. The Wolf Clan cannot live as a single star in the heavens forever."

Deborah glanced over Kesathwa's shoulder to see Tshingee watching her. He quickly lowered his head, raising his flute to his lips. A soft string of notes flowed from the instrument. Deborah chuckled to herself, returning her attention to the old woman. "I teach Bee and Mary each morning after they've gathered wood for Aquewa Co-o-nah. Il-le-nah-qui could come then."

The old woman nodded. "This would be good. The grandchild Mary is great comfort to Aquewa Co-o-nah. This woman knows what it is like to hear a child's laughter in the wigwam after many years of silence. You were a brave woman to bring the child to her grandmother. A strong woman to leave her people behind for the child's sake."

Deborah smiled. "Thank you, but I came here for myself too. You and the others of the Wolf Clan have made me feel welcome. I feel safe here, loved even. There was no love in the house I came from."

The old woman patted Deborah lightly on the arm. "You are always welcome at this woman's hearth. Come, eat with this lonely woman. Anytime is a good time."

"Thank you, Kesathwa. I will. Soon. In the meantime, send your grandson after he does his morning duties. He can start tomorrow if you wish."

The elder woman nodded, raising a hand in salute as she started back across the compound.

Taking care not to look at Tshingee still seated in front of his wigwam, Deborah lifted her bucket of sap and started for Suuklan's wigwam. Beneath her breath, she whistled a haunting tune.

A day later Deborah stepped out of Snow Blanket's wigwam and nearly tripped over Bee and Mary. "What are you doing?" Deborah asked, watching the little boy shovel dirt from a hole in the semifrozen ground.

Mary squatted near the hole. "Bee's buildin' an eagle trap!"

"Mary! Shhhh!" Bee scolded. "You said you wouldn't tell anyone."

"Deborah's not anyone, she's my friend!"

"But it's supposed to be surprise!" The dark-skinned boy threw a shovel of dirt on Mary's moccasins. "If you tell everyone, the surprise'll be ruined."

Deborah couldn't help but smiling. "I promise I

won't tell anyone, Bee, but do you really think you ought to be digging a hole in front of your mother's door?"

"It's not a hole, it's a trap."

"An eagle trap," Mary echoed.

Deborah tried to keep a straight face. "Well, I don't know what an eagle trap is, but if Snow Blanket comes out of her wigwam and falls into that hole, I know she's going to be angry."

Bee looked up, leaning on his small wooden shovel. "But I got to have an eagle trap if I'm going to catch an eagle."

Deborah nodded. "Of course you do, but why not build out a little further?" She took several steps forward. "Say . . . out here maybe."

Bee grimaced. "But I already started digging."

"He already started digging," Mary chided.

"You didn't dig too much. Why don't you go ahead and start the new eagle pit out here and I'll fill in the other hole. All right?"

Bee sighed. "All right. But you have to promise you won't tell Onna what we're makin'. It's still a surprise."

Deborah lifted a palm. "I promise," she vowed solemnly.

After filling in the hole the children had dug, Deborah gathered a bucket of dirty cooking utensils and started down toward the stream. Halfway across the compound, Dame Elene, approached her.

"The sun shines bright today," he commented, falling in stride beside her.

"It certainly is warm for February," Deborah

answered. Out of the corner of her eye she saw Tshingee standing near his wigwam, his eyes fixed on her. She glanced up at the handsome brave walking beside her. "If it stays this warm another day or two, the snow will be gone."

He nodded. "You go to the stream?" He spoke English well.

Deborah lifted her bucket with amusement. "Wash."

He took the bucket from her hands. "I go to the stream as well. I will carry it."

Deborah smiled up at him. He was taller than Tshingee. "Thank you, Dame Elene."

"Do you think you will stay here among the Wolf Clan, or will you return to the Tidewater when spring comes?"

"This is my home now," she answered. "Your people have been good to me. There is nothing left for me on the Tidewater. This will be a good life for me."

Entering the woods, Deborah and the Lenni Lenape brave walked through the grove of trees and into the clearing where the stream flowed. Taking her bucket of dirty cookware from him, she knelt on the hem of her red cloak and began to dip the utensils in the icy water. Using a square of soft leather, she scrubbed a wooden spoon.

Dame Elene sat behind her on a tree stump. The two made idle conversation as Deborah washed Snow Blanket's cookware. Several other women came down to the stream to wash and children laughed and played, sliding down a melting snowbank.

Replying to one of the Corn Man's questions, Deborah lifted her head. From somewhere in the distance she could hear the soft harmonious sounds of a flute. It was the same tune she had found herself humming, some strange, haunting, nameless tune. Rinsing a wooden spoon, Deborah stared into the trees across the stream.

On the far bank Tshingee sat cross-legged, partially obscured by an evergreen tree. He held his new bone flute to his lips and played softly. Deborah couldn't help smiling. The Wildcat had followed her here and now watched her. She lowered her gaze, taking care not to look at Tshingee again, and continued her conversation with the Corn Man.

When Deborah had completed her task, she gathered her clean utensils and stood to go.

Dame Elene reached to take the bucket she held in her hand. "I will carry it," he told her.

"You don't have to."

"I want to." He smiled, stepping back to let Deborah go ahead of him back down the path to the village.

Following Deborah back to Snow Blanket's wigwam, Dame Elene handed her the bucket. He nodded in the direction of the hole Bee and Mary had dug. "What is it?" he asked.

Deborah laughed, her voice carrying across the compound. On the outskirts of the camp, she could see Tshingee standing and speaking with another brave. Her eyes met Dame Elene's with amusement. "I'm not quite sure. Bee says it's an eagle trap, but I don't know what an eagle trap is."

Dame Elene broke into an easy smile. "A man digs a hole and lies down inside it, covering it with sticks and brush to conceal himself. Raw bait is tied on a string to the center of the brush. When the eagle swoops to take his meal"—he motioned with his broad hand—"the hunter reaches from below to catch the great bird. It is a great honor to take two eagle feathers and set him free to soar again."

Deborah nodded. "Somehow I don't think Bee will be catching any eagles. I'll be lucky if I don't fall in the thing and break my neck!"

The Lenni Lenape brave laughed with her. "I like the sound of your voice," he said. "It carries gently on the wind."

Deborah blushed, looking up to where Tshingee still stood. Their eyes met for a brief moment and then he turned sharply away, hurling his flute against a tree. Deborah covered her mouth with her fingers to keep from giggling.

Missing the interaction between Tshingee and Deborah, Dame Elene shuffled his feet, glancing at the pot of rabbit stew that simmered over the campfire. "Smells good," he commented. "I am fond of rabbit."

Deborah grinned. "Would you like to come and eat with us tonight?" She toyed with one of her dark braids.

He nodded. "This man would be honored to share your meal."

"We eat at dusk." Still smiling, Deborah disappeared into Snow Blanket's wigwam.

Precisely at dusk Dame Elene arrived at Snow Blanket's wigwam and the older woman welcomed him inside, giving the favored position at the fire-pit.

"I bring this gift to you, Co-o-nah Aquewa," he said, offering her a small leather pouch.

Snow Blanket smiled, opening the pouch to get a whiff of the fragrant tobacco. "Thank you, Dame Elene. You are a good man to bring this old useless woman a gift." She turned away, giving Deborah a wink.

Dame Elene took his appropriate seat on a mat, holding out his hand to Deborah. "For you."

Deborah accepted the present. It was a tiny fat-bellied bird carved from a piece of white wood. She smiled, looking down at him. "Thank you, Dame Elene."

He reached back into his leather tunic and withdrew two more carvings. "For the children."

Bee and Mary bounced up from their places on the mat and thrust out their hands. The brave handed Bee a small wooden bird with its wings spread in flight.

"An eagle!" Bee breathed.

Mary accepted her gift, a tiny cup. "For my doll, Eleke!" she squealed.

"Thank you," the children murmured in unison. Taking their gifts back to their seats, they sat side by side, giggling with glee.

Grinning, Snow Blanket gathered wooden trenchers to serve the meal on, but Deborah took them from her. "You sit, Snow Blanket, and let me bring in the stew."

The Lenni Lenape took her place across from their guest. "She is a big help to me," Snow Blanket told Dame Elene as Deborah slipped outside to fetch supper.

Dame Elene nodded thoughtfully. "She is hard worker, and smart. She is a woman who could care for herself when her man went hunting."

"Our Red Bird knows of healing. She will be good for this clan." Snow Blanket crossed her arms over her chest. "She will make some brave in this camp a very good wife."

Deborah groaned aloud as she entered the wigwam. She offered Snow Blanket the first plate as was customary because the Lenni Lenape woman was the eldest present, but Snow Blanket shook her head. "Serve our guest first, Red Bird. A man needs his meal."

Deborah rolled her eyes. Giving Dame Elene the first plate, she handed Snow Blanket the second. When Deborah went outside to retrieve food for the children and herself, she spotted Tshingee leaning against the entry flap of his wigwam. His handsome bronze face was twisted in a grimace. When Deborah's eyes met his, for the first time in days, he did not look away.

Deborah pressed her lips tightly together to keep from laughing aloud. Her heart swelled with joy as she leaned over the cooking pot to dish out a helping of stew. Tshingee's eyes were filled with jealousy . . . and love. With each passing hour she could feel him growing closer to her, in the spiritual sense if not the physical one. He wanted her, that was obvious. He had only to gain enough courage to come to her and apologize for his accusations. He had only to say he was sorry and they would be united again. Filling another trencher, Deborah went back inside the wigwam. *It's funny,* she thought *but saying I'm sorry must be one of the most difficult phrases to say . . . in any language.*

Snow Blanket and Deborah enjoyed a pleasant meal with their guest. The three laughed and talked, savoring the spicy stew. Dame Elene was a simple man who could be taken at face value. It was obvious he was taken with Deborah, but he directed most of his conversation to Snow Blanket. As the head of the household, it was Snow Blanket that he had to impress as well as Deborah if he was to be granted permission to woo the white woman.

Just after the meal, Alagwa, an elderly widowed friend of Snow Blanket's, came by. Snow Blanket offered her tea and the old white-haired Lenni Lenape woman sat by the fire to talk with them. Surrounded by the warmth of the wigwam and the comfort of a full stomach, Deborah sat cross-legged listening to the after-supper conversation.

The two older women and Dame Elene lit their clay pipes and then Alagwa begin to spin a tale of a Lenni Lenape man caught on the great ocean and rescued by a sea animal. Bee and Mary sat on each side of Deborah, resting their heads against her as they listened in fascination to the old woman's yarn.

Though Alagwa spoke only Algonquian, Deborah found herself able to understand much of the story. Between the old woman's hand motions, and the words Deborah found herself recognizing, the tale held her spellbound. As Deborah listened to the woman's eerie, captivating voice, she became aware of the slow beat of a drum outside. If the others in the group heard, they paid no attention. Alagwa went on with her story and the others listened. Only Dame Elene seemed to notice the drum beats, and they appeared to make him restless and uncomfortable.

Just as Alagwa was bringing the story of the man and the sea monster to an end, the wigwam flap lifted and Tshingee walked in. He nodded slightly to the others in the group and then walked to Deborah,

She gazed up at him, forcing herself to appear impassive.

"Undach aal." Tshingee's dark eyes bore down on her. "Get your belongings."

"What?" Deborah blinked. "What do you mean?" She looked up at Snow Blanket but the woman's face was an emotionless mask. Everyone in the wigwam seemed to know what Tshingee meant except Deborah.

Tshingee took Deborah's hand and raised her to her feet. "I said collect your belongings." He pulled her cloak from its hook in the rafters. "Now."

"I'm not going with you. Not unless you tell me—"

Tshingee dropped her cloak to her shoulders.

"You will see soon enough, Red Bird. Do as I ask." Outside the drumbeats grew louder.

Deborah wondered if he was forcing her to leave the village, but when she glanced back at Snow Blanket, the elder woman was nodding ever so slightly. A hint of a smile played on her face. The old woman Alagra grinned toothlessly. Dame Elene seemed genuinely upset.

Hesitantly, Deborah gathered the leather sack she'd brought with her and retrieved her extra doeskin dress and leggings.

Tshingee lifted the flap of the wigwam and waited for her to exit. Deborah stepped out into the frosty night air and he came up behind her, taking her leather bag from her hand. Looping his arm through hers, he led her across the compound. Behind them, Snow Blanket, Dame Elene, Alagwa, and the children followed.

"Tshingee, what are you doing? Where are you taking me? What's the big mystery?"

"You talk too much, Red Bird." He brought her before Chief Gimewane's wigwam.

"We are ready," Tshingee called in a clear, strong voice.

Gimewane came out of his wigwam, followed by the shaman. The shaman swung a burning pot of herbs and chanted softly to the tune of the drumbeat echoing through the village.

The chief led Tshingee and Deborah to the fire-pit blazing before his wigwam. Entwining his hands he began to speak in Algonquian, offering some prayer to the heavens.

"Tshingee!" Deborah murmured. "What's happening? What are they doing?" She glanced at him in confusion.

Tonight Tshingee wore his hair unbraided to fall in an ebony curtain down his back. He was dressed in a quilled, sleeved tunic and long leggings. Thrown over his shoulders was a short cloak of otter skin, and beneath the folds of the soft otter pelt, Deborah could see her braid of hair tied around his neck.

Tshingee slipped his hand beneath her red cloak, resting it on her hip. He brought his lips close to her ear. "The shaman and our chief make you my *n'dochqueum*."

"Your what? What's that mean?" She glanced around to see the villagers gathering just outside the light of their chief's fire pit. "Tshingee! Answer me!"

"The shaman makes you my wife," he answered above the beat of the drum.

"Your wife!" She dropped her hands to her hips and stared at his bronze face. "You didn't ask me to be your wife!" She lifted her hands and waved them, catching Gimewane's attention.

He stopped in midsentence and lowered his head. "Speak, Red Bird."

She hooked her thumb in Tshingee's direction. "I'm not marrying him."

Chapter Twenty-seven

The Lenni Lenape chief knitted his dark eyebrows. "You do not wish to marry the Wildcat?"

"Deborah!" Tshingee stared at her in disbelief.

She ignored him, keeping her eyes fixed on Gimewane. "He didn't ask me to marry him."

Tshingee groaned aloud. From behind him came several giggles and a chorus of male laughter.

"Tshingee," the chief said gravely. "This woman says you have not asked her to join with you. I cannot join you to a maid who does not wish to marry."

"She wants to join with me."

Another fit of giggles erupted from behind and Tshingee lowered his voice. "She loves me. I love her. We were meant to be one," he explained to the chief.

Deborah shook her head. "The brave, Tshingee, accused me of playing a part in his brother's death. I cannot marry him with such shame on my face."

Gimewane looked up at Tshingee. "She tells the chief—"

"I know what she said!" Tshingee interrupted

sharply. For a moment he stood in silence, listening to the beat of the wedding drum. Then he glanced over his shoulder. Nearly everyone in the village had gathered to witness the marriage of Tshingee and Red Bird.

Taking a deep breath, Tshingee lowered himself down on one knee and took Deborah's hand. He bent his head. "*Gimewane,* tell this woman that this man, Tshingee, says his sorries for the things he has said. He knows she is not responsible for his brother's death."

Gimewane chuckled. "This brave says his sorries, Red Bird."

"This brave," Tshingee went on, "apologizes for the pain he has caused this woman and asks her forgiveness."

"Tshingee of the Wolf Clan asks your forgiveness, Red Bird," Gimewane echoed.

Deborah stared down at Tshingee's lowered head, a bittersweet smile on her lips.

"This brave wishes to tell this woman that he loves her and that he wants to join with her," Tshingee finished quietly.

Before Gimewane could repeat Tshingee's last words Deborah tugged on Tshingee's hands and he stood. Her dark eyes, brimming with tears, met his. "This woman grants her forgiveness," she said in a strong, clear voice. "This woman tells this man she loves him. Yes, she will marry him."

The crowd of villagers broke into laughter, clapping and stomping their feet as Tshingee's and Deborah's lips met.

Brushing the hair back off her face, Tshingee

held Deborah against his chest. He smoothed her dark hair, kissing her forehead, then he turned and faced Gimewane and the shaman.

"Are you ready to begin again?" the chief asked with obvious amusement.

Deborah laughed, wiping her tears with the back of her hand. "This woman is ready," she responded.

Tshingee lifted the flap of his wigwam and Deborah entered. She watched him come inside and lace the door shut. Suddenly she felt apprehensive.

Tshingee lifted his gaze to meet hers. "I'm sorry for the fool I've been," he said simply.

Deborah came to him, pressing a finger to his lips. "Shhh, we have both said things we do not mean. Things we did not truly feel in our heart of hearts." She stroked his cheek, bringing her lips to meet his softly, ever so gently.

Tshingee wrapped his arms around her waist, drawing her against his hard, sinewy chest. "Even when I felt a burning anger with you, I could not deny my love for you, my Red Bird."

She lifted her chin to let him kiss the soft flesh of her neck. "I have loved you since the first day I saw you standing there in John's garden. You were so angry." She laughed. "So arrogant."

He chuckled with her. "Arrogant? You accuse this brave falsely."

She looked up at him, growing more serious. "Tshingee, I want you to know that if I could have prevented John's death, even with my own

403

life I would have done so."

He tugged at her shorn lock of hair. "I know," he whispered. "And now let us speak of it no more. It is your wedding night." Taking her hand, he led her to a mat near the fire and knelt, bring her down with him. From a small pot he poured a cup of simmering herbal tea and offered it to her.

Deborah sipped the tea, glancing over the rim of the cup. Never in her life had she felt so completely fulfilled. She handed the cup to Tshingee and he drank from it. Then setting it down, he took her in his arms.

"I do not have a wedding gift for you, *ki-ti-hi*."

Deborah smoothed his bronze cheek with her hand, drawing an imaginary line down the bridge of his nose with her finger. "That's all right, because I have a gift for both of us." She took his hand and laid it on her stomach. "This is my gift to you, Tshingee of the Wolf Clan."

His eyes narrowed in confusion, then a smile broke out on his face. "A child?" he murmured with surprise.

She nodded. "A child that grows quickly."

He stared at her face for a moment. "Why do I think you have known about this for some time?"

She smirked. "Because I have."

"You should have told me. I had a right to know," he chastised.

Deborah kissed his mouth. "And what, have you accuse me later of forcing you to marry me? I wanted you to want me."

Tshingee touched the birthmark near her lip with the tip of his finger. "This man has always wanted you, Red Bird. He always will."

"Even when I'm old and fat?"

His laughter mingled with hers as their lips met. "Especially when you are old and fat."

Tshingee stroked Deborah's stomach with his broad hand. "I have been thinking, Red Bird," he said hesitantly.

"Yes?" She rested her head in his lap, staring up at him.

"I have been thinking that perhaps you and I . . . we should go west."

"West?"

"This land goes on for many moons. There is talk between some families of crossing the Ohio and walking into the sunset." His hand moved to the neckline of her doeskin dress. "West there are no white men. Plenty of land. Sunshine to raise our children in."

"Yes!"

"If we go west, it will be another hundred years before our children's children see another white man," he warned.

She shook her head, guiding his hand to the curve of her breast. "I don't care. I want our child to be safe. I don't know that I could ever feel safe here, not so close to my father."

Tshingee brought his mouth to the soft doeskin that covered her breasts. "Then it is done. Come spring, this man and this woman will walk west."

Deborah threaded her fingers through his hair, pulling his head down until their lips met. "Enough talk now, husband," she said, a husky catch in her voice. "We've other matters to attend to now."

The peaceful silence of dawn was shattered by the bellow of muskets and the pounding of hoofbeats as the white men rode into the sleeping Lenni Lenape village.

Tshingee leaped to his feet, pushing Deborah out of his arms.

"What's happening?" she cried as he stepped into his leggings and reached for his musket.

Tshingee grasped her by her bare forearms and lifted her to her feet. He pushed her doeskin dress into her arms. "Run, he ordered harshly. "Cross the stream and go to the walnut grove where you saved Suuklan from the bear." He strapped his knife to his waist and his bow and quiver to his back.

Outside the wigwam the sound of musket shots reverberated through the trees. Men shouted and women screamed as the camp leaped into action.

Deborah pulled the doeskin over her head. "I'm not going anywhere without you!"

He took her by the arm, his fingers sinking sharply into her flesh. "For our child, you must. They've come for you."

Tears ran down Deborah's cheeks as she rushed out of the wigwam in Tshingee's footsteps. The orderly Lenni Lenape camp had dissolved into a melee of screaming women and booming firearms. Thick black smoke filled the air, nearly blinding Deborah. "Tshingee," she choked, reaching out to him.

Turning back to her, he pulled against his bare chest and kissed her fiercely. Before she could respond he was racing into the smoke.

"What about Snow Blanket and the children?" she called after him.

"I will get them! Run!" he shouted.

At that moment a man rode through the smoke, lowering a torch to set Tshingee's wigwam on fire. Recognizing the man from Deliverance, Deborah fled. But instead of following the path to the woods, she doubled back, heading for Snow Blanket's wigwam. She had to be certain the elder woman and the children had escaped safely.

Deborah's bare feet pounded on the frozen ground as she raced through the camp, her lungs burning from the acrid smoke. A foot away from her, an arrow sliced through the air. Deborah screamed. Out of the wall of smoke a body pitched forward off a horse, falling lifelessly to the ground. Deborah swung around to see Dame Elene notch another arrow onto his bowstring.

"Uishameheela!" the brave urged. "Run, Red Bird!"

"There she is!" someone shouted in the distance. "There with the Injun!"

Deborah spun around in horror to see Lester Morgan riding straight for her. He lifted his musket and fired. Behind her she heard Dame Elene fall.

"No!" she screamed, covering her ears with her hands.

Lester Morgan rode past her on his horse, catching her by her dress and hauling her off the ground. Deborah struggled, sinking her teeth into his arm. He cursed foully, throwing her roughly over his lap and pinning her down with a massive arm.

"Let me go you son of a bitch!" she screamed. "I'll kill you! I'll kill you," she moaned.

"I got her! I got her!" Lester shouted above the sound of gunshots and bellowing male voices. He pulled up his horse to reload his musket and out of the curtain of smoke stepped Snow Blanket.

"Let her go," the Lenni Lenape woman ordered starkly. In her arms she held a musket, pointed directly at his chest.

Lester threw back his head in laughter. "And if I don't, *squaw*?"

"You will be dead man."

"No, Snow Blanket," Deborah cried, struggling beneath Lester's hold. "Please, take Bee and Mary and run."

"Too late," Lester murmured, lifting his musket. 'Cause she's already—"

Before the final word slipped from his mouth, Snow Blanket's musket belched a cloud of smoke and Lester's body was blown backward off the horse.

Deborah screamed, falling from the animal. By the time she lifted her head from the ground, Snow Blanket was at her side, helping her to her feet. "You must hurry," Snow Blanket insisted. "Tshingee does not want you here. My son cannot stand to lose you to them again."

"But the children!"

"Mary has gone with Suuklan. Bee, I cannot

find him. Can you load this weapon?" Snow Blanket pushed the musket into Deborah's arms.

Deborah took a musket ball and the powder horn from Snow Blanket and began to load the rusty weapon with trembling fingers. "We'll find him together and then we'll go."

Snow Blanket wiped a streak of Lester's blood off Deborah's cheek. "No. I am old. I will face my enemy, but the child you carry is the future of the Wolf Clan."

"How did you know?"

Snow Blanket took the loaded musket from Deborah's hands. "This woman is old, but she is not so old that she does not know the look of a woman who carries a child." Smiling, Snow Blanket pressed her lips to Deborah's cheek and then disappeared into the smoke, shouting a cry of attack.

"Deb-or-ah! Deborah," another voice called from the distance.

"Bee!" Deborah spun around, squinting. The smoke burned her lungs and stung her eyes. "Where are you?"

"Here!" The boy came running in Deborah's direction with a man on horseback in hot pursuit.

It was the Earl.

"Father! No!" Deborah screamed, running toward Bee.

The boy turned and threw a toy war axe at the giant of a man, and the Earl burst into sinister laughter as the miniature weapon bounced harmlessly off his leather coat.

Bee turned to run but he tripped, and the Earl

of Manchester rode his horse over the child as he scrambled to escape the steed's massive hooves. Deborah screamed in terror as the Earl wheeled his mount around to make a second pass over the boy.

Bleeding from the mouth and arms, Bee struggled to his feet.

"Here!" Deborah shouted. "Here, Bee!"

The little boy put out his arms to Deborah, tears running down his face as he raced toward her.

His laughter echoing above the sound of the musket roar, the Earl bore down on the child. Bee made a sharp left turn and suddenly the Earl's horse went down. The animal's front legs buckled as it sank into a hole in the earth, throwing its rider.

Bee gave a squeal of delight as the Earl flew through the air, landing in a motionless heap. "My eagle pit!" the little boy shouted. "My eagle pit!"

Deborah felt not even a stirring of remorse as she seized the little boy's hand and led him to where her father lay. The Earl of Manchester's neck was bent at a peculiar angle, his eyes closed in finality.

The sound of musket fire died away. The horses were suddenly gone and the sound of retreating men could be heard in the distance.

"Did you know him?" Bee asked.

Deborah stared at her father then lowered her eyes to meet the little boy's concerned gaze. Bee's face was battered and bloody and across his bare chest were the purpling bruises of hoofprints.

410

"No," she answered, taking Bee away. "Not really."

Leading Bee through the camp, Deborah stepped over two more bodies, both white men. Although three of the wigwams still burned, it looked as if the attack was over. Lenni Lenape women and children ran through the compound carrying buckets of water. A few older braves stood watch over the villagers, but the young warriors who had survived the attack were pursuing the white men.

Bee released Deborah's hand. "There is Mary and *Onna*!" he called, running across the smoky compound.

Deborah followed in his footsteps. "Mary! Snow Blanket! Thank God you're all right!" She grabbed Mary and lifted her into her arms. "Have you seen Tshingee, Snow Blanket? I can't find him."

Snow Blanket shook her head, snatching two buckets off the ground. "Not yet." She pushed the containers into the children's hands. "We must hurry and put out the fires."

Deborah set Mary on the ground. "If any of you see Tshingee, tell him I'm looking for him."

Snow Blanket squeezed Deborah's shoulder with a sooty hand then took up her own bucket and hurried off.

Wandering through the camp, Deborah called Tshingee's name over and over again. Braves were returning from the woods where they had followed the white men, but he was not among them either. She walked along the row of injured warriors being cared for near the Big House; he was not there. He was not one of the four dead Lenni

411

Lenape.

Becoming frantic, Deborah circled the perimeter of the camp. Everything was in a state of chaos. Dogs barked and villagers ran to and fro, still attempting to extinguish the fires.

Then she saw him . . . just at the edge of the forest. His back was to her, streaked black with smoke.

"Tshingee!" she cried, running toward him. When he didn't turn around, she called his name again, but still there was no response. Breathless, she ran to his side. "Tshingee! Oh, thank God you're all right! Why didn't you—"

She came to an abrupt halt, staring at the face of the prisoner Tshingee held at gunpoint. "Tom," she whispered.

Tshingee's bloodstained face was grim. His finger rested gently on the trigger of his musket. "The others fled," he stated evenly. "But this white man, he chose to forfeit his life."

Deborah stared at Tom, resting on his knees, his head hung in defeat. "Why in the hell are you here?" she demanded. "You're not a fighting man!"

"The Earl, the others, they came to avenge my father's death. I knew you told the truth when you said these weren't the men who killed him, but the others wouldn't listen."

Tears ran down Tom's smoke-blackened face. "The kitchen girls that were captured by the Indians . . . they told me what had happened. They didn't tell me you were here, but I knew you were." He lifted his head, his eyes meeting hers. "I came for you, Deborah . . ."

Scalding tears ran down Deborah's cheeks. "Oh, for Christ's sake, Tom. You should have run while you had the chance! Most of the others got away."

He shook his head. "I couldn't leave you here, not with the Earl dead. It's my responsibility to save you."

Deborah squeezed her eyes shut. "Tom, I didn't want to be rescued. This man, Tshingee, is my husband."

Tom drew a shuddering breath. "Your husband?"

"Tom, I'm in love with him. I carry his child."

Fresh tears ran down Tom's cheeks. "Elizabeth tried to convince me not to come . . ."

Deborah turned her gaze on Tshingee. Their dark eyes met, each one trying to read the other's thoughts.

Slowly, the Lenni Lenape brave lowered his musket. He reached out with one hand to caress Deborah's cheek. "Last night you gave me a wedding gift," he said, his voice barely audible. "Today I give you mine." He pointed at Thomas with the barrel of his musket. "I give you this man."

"You give me Tom?" Deborah whispered. "I don't understand."

"It was to this man that you belonged first. His life is yours. You may go with him if you wish." Tshingee lowered his lips to Deborah's, kissing her ever so gently. Then, he swung his musket onto his shoulder and walked away.

For a moment Deborah stood in shock. Her heart pounded wildly in her chest. She hadn't realized, until this moment, just how deep Tshingee's love for her ran.

Suddenly snapping out of her stupor, Deborah grasped Tom's hand. "For God sakes, get up," she ordered impatiently. "Can't you see he's spared your life? You won't get a second chance!"

"I . . . I can't return without you." Tom stumbled to his feet.

"If you go, you go without me." Her eyes met his. "Tom, if you ever loved me, you'll go home to the Tidewater and marry Elizabeth."

"Elizabeth?"

"She loves you. She'll make the wife I never could have been to you."

"Elizabeth loves me?" he breathed.

"Don't be a goose. Of course she does. Now go on." She nodded in the direction of the forest. "Go home and tell everyone I was killed, but tell Elizabeth that I walk into the sunset of my dreams. She'll know what I mean." Deborah pressed her lips to Tom's quivering ones. "Now go on with you before Tshingee changes his mind and scalps you!"

Tom stood for a moment in indecision, then whirled around and ran.

Deborah watched until he disappeared into the safety of the woods then headed back toward the Lenni Lenape camp.

"Tshingee," she cried. "Tshingee, where are you?" Her bare feet beat across the frozen ground as she raced toward his wigwam.

There, near the smoldering ruins of his home, stood the Wildcat of the Wolf Clan. The sun was just beginning to rise in the eastern sky, and it cast an amber glow of light over his striking bronze face. He stood with his hands at his sides, his ebony hair blowing in the slight breeze.

"Tshingee," she shouted.

He lifted his arms to her and she ran into them, laughing, crying, as he covered her tear-stained face with kisses.

"I love you," she murmured.

"K'daholel," he answered huskily. "I love you, my Red Bird . . ."